SECRET WATER

By the same author

SECRET WATER

ARTHUR RANSOME

Illustrated by the Author

RED FOX

A Red Fox Book

Published by Random House Children's Books
20 Vauxhall Bridge Road, London SW1V 2SA

A division of Random House UK Ltd
London Melbourne Sydney Auckland
Johannesburg and agencies throughout the world

First published by Jonathan Cape 1939
Puffin edition 1970

Red Fox edition 1993

3 5 7 9 10 8 6 4

Set in Linotype Century Schoolbook by
Falcon Graphic Art Ltd, Wallington, Surrey

Printed and bound in Great Britain by
Cox & Wyman Ltd, Reading, Berkshire

RANDOM HOUSE UK Limited Reg. No. 954009

Papers used by Random House UK Limited
are natural, recyclable products made from wood grown in
sustainable forests. The manufacturing processes conform to
the environmental regulations of the country of origin

ISBN 0 09 996360 4

TO
THE BUSK FAMILY

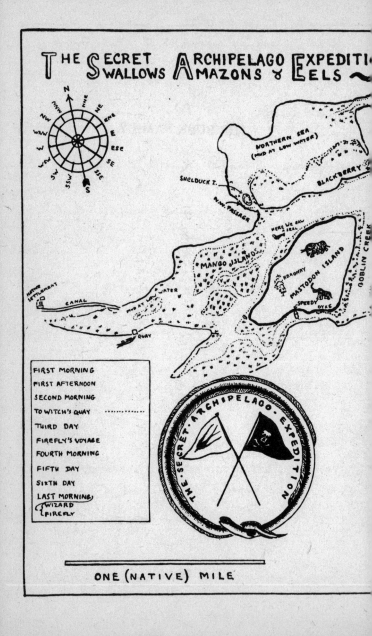

THE SECRET ARCHIPELAGO EXPEDITION
SWALLOWS AMAZONS & EELS ~

FIRST MORNING
FIRST AFTERNOON
SECOND MORNING
TO WITCH'S QUAY ....
THIRD DAY
FIREFLY'S VOYAGE
FOURTH MORNING
FIFTH DAY
SIXTH DAY
LAST MORNING
WIZARD
FIREFLY

NORTHERN SEA
(MUD AT LOW WATER)

SHELDUCK I.

BLACKBERRY

N.W. PASSAGE

HERE WE SAW SEAL

MANGO ISLANDS

KRAKNEY

MASTODON ISLAND

GOBLIN CREEK

NATIVE SETTLEMENT

CANAL

MUD AT LOW WATER

SPEEDY DYKE

QUAY

· THE SECRET · ARCHIPELAGO · EXPEDITION ·

ONE (NATIVE) MILE

CONTENTS

ILLUSTRATIONS

WHAT SUSAN FOUND IN THE CAMP

CHAPTER I

FAREWELL TO ADVENTURE

THE First Lord of the Admiralty was unpopular at Pin Mill.

"I hate him," said Roger, sitting on the foredeck of the *Goblin*, with his legs dangling over the side.

"Who?" said Titty.

"The first of those lords," said Roger.

"We all hate him," said Titty.

John and Susan, perhaps, did not hate the First Lord in particular, but their thoughts about the Admiralty were as bitter as Roger's.

"I don't see the good of Daddy's coming home," said Bridget.

That was it. Daddy had come home and had been looking forward to a week or so of freedom before settling down to work at Shotley. The last thing Jim Brading had done before being whisked off home by an aunt (who had said that a young man with concussion would be better there than in a yacht, even if it had been turned into a hospital ship), had been to lend Daddy the *Goblin*. More: he had given Daddy a chart of a place, quite near by, where there were inland seas and dozens of islands. Everything had been fixed. The whole family of the Walkers were to sail round in the *Goblin*, to land at the place where Jim had marked a cross on the chart. Daddy and Mummy were to sleep afloat in the *Goblin*. The five Swallows and Sinbad the kitten were to camp

ashore. They were going to do real exploring and
make their own maps of those secret waters and
unknown islands. Daddy, who had been looking
forward to exploring as much as if he had not
spent half his life at sea, had made a blank map
on which their discoveries were to be put down. He
had sent to the north for their camping things. He
had got them bamboos for surveying poles. He and
Mother had laid in stores as if they were planning
an expedition into the desert. The little inner room
at Alma Cottage was crammed with tents and
sleeping bags and packages of all sorts. Everything was ready, and then, that morning, the
postman had handed over the letters, and Daddy,
who had been ragging John about taking a
compass bearing of the coffeepot from the cruet,
saw the O.H.M.S. on one of them, tore it open,
and said one "Damn" as if he really meant it.

"What is it?" Mummy had asked.

"We can't go. It's all off. The First Lord's chucked
a spanner in the works."

"Not really?"

He had passed the letter to her.

"There it is. They want this and they want that.
It means going up to London the day after tomorrow. And they want me to start in at Shotley as
soon as I get back. You'll have to come to London
with me, Mary, if you're to get all you want in
time. I'm awfully sorry, you people. It just can't
be helped. Orders is orders. The expedition's off.
No exploring for us till next year."

It was as if the curtain had been rung down
at the very beginning of the first act of the
pantomime.

*

Breakfast was hardly over before a young man in naval uniform had stopped his little car at the foot of the lane, run up the steps to the cottage, saluted, given a message, and taken Daddy and Mummy away. John, Susan, Titty, Roger, Bridget and Sinbad, the kitten, had rowed off to the *Goblin*, to keep their promise to her owner and, even if they were not going to sail in her, keep his little ship clean for him.

*

Titty was sitting on the cabin top.

"The Admiralty just likes spoiling everything," she said. "The lieutenant who came and took them off to Shotley was fairly gloating. I saw his horrid grin."

"And everything planned," said Susan. "And Daddy and Mother were just as keen on it as us."

"By the time they let him go, we'll be getting ready to go back to school," said John. "Well, it's no good sitting about. Let's get to work and tidy her up."

"If it wasn't for that beastly Admiralty we'd be stowing cargo instead," said Roger.

"Keep Sinbad out of the way," said John. "We don't want to sweep him o.b."

Work made everybody feel a little better, though not much. John dipped the big mop over the side and sent the water shooting along the decks and pouring out of the scuppers in the low rail. Susan had found that the *Goblin*'s saucepans, though clean enough inside, had smoky patches

outside that took a lot of rubbing off. Roger and
Titty with a tin of metal polish between them
settled down to smarten up portholes and cleats.
Sinbad walked about on the cabin roof and on the
decks, lifting first one paw and then another and
giving it a shake after treading in the damper
places left by John's sluicing. Bridget told Sinbad
he ought to be wearing sea-boots. There was not
much talking among the others. They all knew
that this tidying up of the *Goblin* instead of being
a beginning was like the words "THE END" on the
last page of a book.

Work went steadily on all morning. Decks grew
spotless. Coils of ropes were re-coiled so beautifully that they looked like carved ornaments. John
and Susan joined the polishers and porthole after
porthole that had been dull with salt and verdigris
glittered in the sun. Even Bridget did her bit and
rubbed at a porthole till she could see her face
in it.

Now and then barges with the tall sails towered
past, going up to Ipswich with the tide. Yachts
came in from the sea, and the workers on the
Goblin watched each in turn round up into the
wind, with someone on the foredeck dropping the
staysail and reaching with a boathook for a moor-
ing buoy.

"Gosh," said Roger at last, "isn't it awful not
to be going anywhere after all."

"Hullo," said Titty. "Look at that little boat,
just like *Swallow* only with a white sail."

"Two of them," said John.

"Three," said Roger. "There's another just leaving the hard. Getting her sail up."

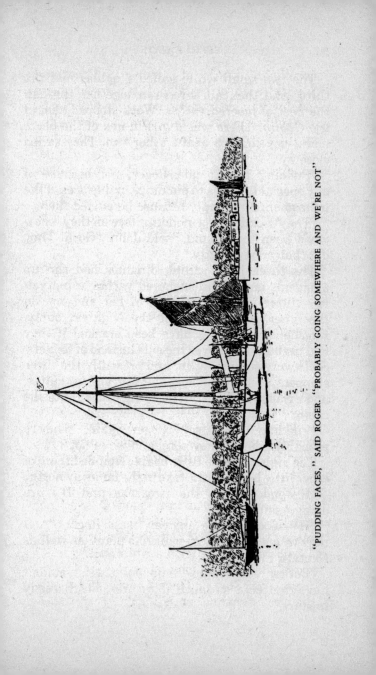

"PUDDING FACES," SAID ROGER. "PROBABLY GOING SOMEWHERE AND WE'RE NOT"

The two small white sailed dinghies met the
third, and then all three ran together through
the fleet of moored yachts. Work stopped aboard
the *Goblin*. There was a girl in one of the boats
and a boy in each of the other two. They sailed
close by.

"Pudding faces," said Roger, not because of
any special likeness to puddings in the faces of the
helmsmen, but simply because he envied them.

"They'd call you a pudding face if they knew
you'd been to Holland," said John. "Gosh! They
did that pretty neatly."

The three little sailing dinghies had run up
alongside one of the anchored yachts, a big yellow cutter, two on one side of her and one on
the other. There was not the slightest bump.
Eggshells would not have been cracked if they
had been hanging over the side instead of fenders.
Sails were coming down, and presently the three
skippers climbed aboard the big yellow cutter,
and disappeared one after another down into the
cabin.

"Pudding faces," said Roger again. "They're
probably going somewhere, and we're not."

The sight of those little boats reminded them of
other little boats on the lake in the far away north.

"I wonder what the Amazons and D's are
doing," said Titty.

"Houseboat battle anyway," said Roger. "And
they've got Timothy to walk the plank as well as
Captain Flint."

"Bother everything," said John. "It wouldn't
have mattered so much if we weren't all ready
to start."

"Hang that first lord," said Roger. "I say, I wish we had him here, with a good springy plank and the water thick with sharks."

"Brrrrrrrrrrrrrrrrrr."

Susan's alarm clock that had been brought aboard the *Goblin* went off down in the cabin.

"Come on," said Susan. "I set it for ten minutes to one. Daddy and Mother'll be back and you know how Miss Powell hates people to let her cooking get cold."

In two minutes they were all in the dinghy and John was pulling for the hard.

Daddy met them at the top of the hard.

"Well, what have you been up to?" he said.

"Cleaning up the *Goblin*," said Roger.

"Polishing," said Bridget.

"I wish I could take her for a sail," said Daddy. "But I can't. I've got to go back to Shotley this afternoon. That lad's coming for me after lunch."

"That beast?" said Titty. "That gloating beast?"

"Oh come, Titty," said Daddy. "He can't help it. Even sub-lieutenants are God's creatures, though it's hard to believe it sometimes."

They were just following Daddy up the steps to Alma Cottage, when Titty saw a woman coming down the lane and waving to them. She stopped.

"Isn't this for your mother?" said the woman, holding out a letter. "Postman left it at mine by mistake."

Titty looked at the envelope. "Yes," she said, and then, seeing the postmark, she ran up to the cottage calling, "Mother, Mother, here's a letter from Beckfoot."

Mother was already at the round table in the parlour, cutting slices of roast mutton. She took the letter and looked at Daddy. "Oh dear," she said, "I do hope it's to say 'No'."

"No to what?" asked Roger.

"Just something I asked her," said Mother. She opened the envelope, took out the letter, read it through, and passed it across to Daddy. "What on earth am I to say?" she asked.

"Is one of them ill?" said Susan, seeing Mother's face.

"Oh no, it's not that," said Mother. "They're all quite well and Mrs Blackett sends her love to you."

"What about the D's?" said Titty.

"They've gone home."

"Oh well," said Titty. "There's still Timothy and Captain Flint."

Daddy finished reading the letter. "Can't be helped," he said. "Impossible. I can't get out of going to London, and it'll take us all our time anyhow, and I shall be up to the ears after I get back. . . . "

"In water?" said Roger.

"In work," said Daddy, and then, seriously, looking at Mother. "You'll just have to tell her the sort of fix we're in."

He folded up the letter and passed it across the table. Mother folded it up and put it in its envelope.

As she did so, she found that it would not slip in comfortably. There was something in the way at the bottom of the envelope. She turned the envelope upside down, and shook out a narrow card with a picture on it. There was no writing, not even an address, only a skull and crossbones in one corner and a picture of dancing savages.

"I expect this is for you people," said Mother, and gave the card to Susan.

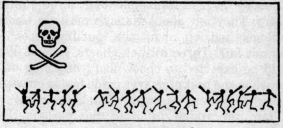

NANCY'S MESSAGE[1]

Susan looked at it. "What's that first one, John?" she said.

"Left arm over his head. Right arm pointing at half-past ten.... That's T.... The next one's H.... Both arms straight out.... That's R.... Half a minute.... "

"Let me see too," said Titty.

John pulled a pencil out of his pocket and scribbled a letter of the alphabet under each of the dancing figures. "T.H.R.E.E ... M.I.L.L.I.O.N ... C.H.E.E.R.S. ... Three million cheers."

Commander Walker burst out laughing. "Right under your very nose," he said. "We ought to have that young woman to teach signalling to naval cadets."

[1]See page 287 for Semaphore Alphabet.

"Three million cheers," said Titty. "What for?
She must have done something and thinks we
know all about it."

"Captured the houseboat I should think," said
Roger. "Or drowned the Great Aunt. She wouldn't
send three million cheers about nothing at all."

Nobody at Pin Mill felt like three million
cheers. They felt about Nancy's message almost
as Roger had felt about the "pudding faces". It
was not fair. Three million cheers, indeed. Who
could be expected to cheer about anything on a
day when the best plan ever made had been wiped
out by stony-hearted Lords of the Admiralty?

From the round table in the parlour they
could see through into that inner room, with
the bamboo poles for surveying leaning up in
a corner, the bundles of blankets, the cases of
provisions, the tent rolls and all the other things
they had got ready for the expedition.

Titty got up from her chair and quietly closed
the door.

Dinner was hardly finished before Daddy was
taken off to Shotley again. And then Mother
said she could not come out with them, because
of letters to write. Bridget and Sinbad played in
the garden. The others had no heart for boats,
and went for a walk along the woods above the
river. But even there, they could not forget what
had happened. Yachts were coming up the river.
Yachts were going down. Each one of them was
going somewhere, or coming back, and Roger,
until the others told him to shut up, kept telling
them he was sure this yacht or that was carrying
an expedition like the one Daddy had planned,

on its way to the very islands they had meant to explore.

And then, when they had come back for high tea at Miss Powell's they learnt that something had happened that had made Daddy at least feel quite different. Tea was over before he came in smiling to himself.

"Get out," he said jovially as if nothing was wrong with the world. "Committee meeting with your Mother."

They went, and as they went, heard just two sentences.

"Been sending a few telegrams," said Daddy. "Must have sent half a dozen I should think. One thing after another."

"Have a look at my letter and see if it'll do," said Mother.

"It won't," said Daddy. "Not after my telegrams."

"Oh Ted," said Mother. "What have you gone and done?"

And then they heard their father's cheerful laughter. Cheerful and rather mischievous.

"Daddy's up to something," said Titty.

"I say," said Roger. "You don't think he's thought of a way of dishing the first of those lords?"

They went back aboard the *Goblin*, watched Roger's pudding faces racing their three dinghies, gave another rub round to the portholes, and finally, though there was really no need, lit the *Goblin*'s riding light before coming ashore. She lay there, with her light twinkling below her forestay, just as it had twinkled in the evening when they had been at anchor with Jim Brading in command.

"Awful to think we shan't sail until next year," said Titty.

"But if Daddy's squashed that lord ... " said Roger.

"He can't have done that," said John.

Daddy was putting away a map as they came in. He and Mother went upstairs together to see Bridget into bed.

"They've got a secret," said Titty.

"They've got lots probably," said Susan.

"Something to do with us," said Titty. "Didn't you hear what he was saying?"

"What did he say?"

"He said, 'Better keep mum about it till the morning'."

CHAPTER II

ADVENTURE AHEAD

"ALL hands!" said Daddy, as they sat down to breakfast.

"Wait till they've had their porridge," said Mother.

Daddy laughed.

"Oh do tell us now," said Titty.

"You heard what your Mother said."

"Oh Mother!"

"You get your porridge down," said Mother. "But don't go and eat it too quickly."

"Or too slowly," said Roger, swallowing fast. "Slop it in, Bridget. Bridget doesn't know how to eat porridge. When you've got a mouthful in, don't just wave the spoon about. Get it filled while you're swallowing."

"Don't you hurry, Bridgie," said Daddy. "News'll keep."

"Anybody want any more porridge?" said Mother presently.

"Nobody does," said Titty.

"What about Roger?"

For a minute or two everybody had been watching Bridget, whose eyes wandered from face to face as she worked steadily on, spoonful by spoonful. Roger looked at the porridge still left on her plate. He could have a little more and yet be done as soon as she was.

"Yes, please," said Roger, and passed his plate.

Bridget eyed him balefully and put on speed. It was a very close thing. Roger was still swallowing his last mouthful while Susan was wiping a stray bit off Bridget's chin.

Daddy looked at Mummy. She nodded.

There was a breathless pause.

"Now look here," said Daddy. "Mummy and I have been talking it over. We can't come. I've got to be in London. Mummy's got to come with me for part of the time anyhow. It all depends on John and Susan. If John and Susan will guarantee to keep the rest of you out of trouble, how would you like to take on that bit of exploration for yourselves?"

"Gosh!" said Roger.

"We won't need to be kept out of trouble," said Titty.

"Well, John?" said Daddy.

"But would Jim Brading let us have the *Goblin* without you?"

"No, he jolly well wouldn't. Not if he could help it. Once was quite enough for him. What I propose to do is to take you round in her, dump the lot of you at the place he told us about, and come back and take you off as soon as my Lords of the Admiralty give me a chance. What about it, Susan?"

"We'll be awfully careful," said Susan.

"You'll have to be," said Daddy. "Tidal water. This won't be like camping in the lakes. Where's that chart? And the blank map?"

Daddy showed them the chart Jim had lent him, with a cross marking the best place for landing. "That's where we'll land," he said putting

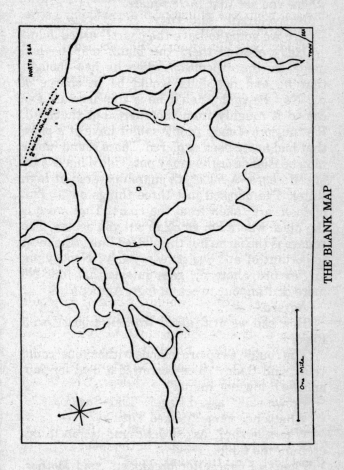

THE BLANK MAP

his finger on the spot. "And there's a farm here, where you see that little square."

"Native kraal," said Titty.

"Are we going to have the chart?" asked John.

Daddy showed them the blank map he had made for the expedition when he had thought that he and not John would be in charge of it. "No," he said. "You'll have this instead. I've copied it roughly from the chart, but that's all. It's the sort of map people might have of a place that had never been explored. Those round lumps may be islands or they may not. Tide'll make a lot of difference. A lot of it's marsh covered at high water. I've marked just three things on it. Two of them are taken from the chart. That cross is the place where I'm going to put you ashore. The square is the farm, but this dotted line is the most important of all. See it, everybody? Nobody, on any excuse whatever, goes outside that line. No more drifting out to sea in fogs. Agreed?"

"Agreed."

"How can we drift at all without a boat?" said Roger.

"You couldn't explore islands without one, could you?" said Daddy. "I've borrowed a boat for you, and we'll tow her round."

"Brown sail?" asked Roger. "Like *Swallow*'s."

"What's her name?" asked Titty.

"Where is she?" asked John and began to get up from the table.

"Plenty of time after breakfast," said Mother. John sat down again and looked out of the window. Close to the boat-builders' shed two men were cleaning a dinghy, and a brown sail, wrapped round its spars, was propped against the wall beside them.

"Is that her?" asked John.

"Maybe."

"But no sailing outside the dotted line," said Mother. "No going out to sea, even without meaning to."

"It won't happen again," said Susan.

"Anyway not in a dinghy," said John.

"Going to let me finish what I was saying?" asked Daddy.

"Do go on," said Titty.

"You'll start with a blank map, that doesn't do more than show roughly what's water and what isn't. You'll have your tents, stores, everything we'd got ready when we thought we were all going together. You'll be just a wee bit better off than Columbus. And with all the practice you've had at exploring, I think you'll do pretty well. But you'll be marooned fair and square. You'll have to depend on yourselves alone. There'll be nobody coming along every day to see that you're all right."

"Marooned?" said Roger.

"What happened to Ben Gunn," said Titty. "They gave him a gun and put him on an island and sailed away and never came back."

"Oh," said Roger.

"We'll come back for you all right some day," said Daddy.

"When?" said Susan.

"Don't say," said Titty. "Much better if we don't know. We'll grow old and grey watching for a distant sail. . . . "

"Not very old," said Daddy. "And you won't have time to get very grey before you have to stop being explorers and go back to school."

"Don't spoil it," said Titty.

"Do you really think you'll be all right there by yourselves?" said Mother.

"We will," said almost everybody at once.

"Hullo, Bridget," said Daddy, "what's the matter?"

"What's going to happen to me?" said Bridget, who had been growing more and more solemn. "You said you were going to take me when we were all going. Don't let them leave me behind again. I'm quite old enough to go."

"Ask Susan if she'll have you," said Daddy. "I'll be glad if she will. May as well maroon the lot while we're about it."

"You'll be a strong expedition," said Mother, half smiling, and half comforting herself. "A captain and a mate and two able-seamen and a ship's baby."

"What about Sinbad?" asked Titty.

"We can't ask Miss Powell to look after him," said Mother. "There'll have to be a ship's kitten as well."

"Then I won't be the youngest," said Bridget.

"Not by several years," said Daddy. "Ah, thank you, Miss Powell. . . . "

Miss Powell had come in and set a huge dish with a cover on it before Commander Walker. She lifted the cover and the little room was full of the smell of fried bacon. There was a busy minute or two while people were burning their fingers passing round hot loaded plates.

"No more talking," said Daddy. "Finish your breakfasts. No seaman lets hot bacon and toast get cold if he can help it. And there's no time to waste. High tide today about a quarter past two. We've got to be at the islands before then. All that stuff to be put aboard and we'll have to be sailing by twelve."

"Gosh!" said Roger. "Today. . . . "

He was too busy to say more, and after that there was silence except for the crunching noise natural to toast when being eaten.

*

Four men were carrying a sailing dinghy down the hard to put her in the water. Four explorers, who only an hour before had thought that for this summer at least their exploring days were over, raced down the hard in pursuit. Daddy followed in less of a hurry. Bridget had stayed behind to help Mother to turn a thick woollen blanket into an explorer's first sleeping bag.

"She's as big as *Swallow*," said John.

"She's called *Wizard*," said Titty, looking at the name on the boat's stern.

"Because she whizzes, I expect," said Roger.

The men slid her into the water. Daddy had a look at her gear and hoisted her brown sail. John and Daddy went off to try her while the others waited. Then John came ashore and Susan took his place. Then Daddy sailed with Roger and Titty together and watched them handle her in turns. Everybody got full marks, including *Wizard*.

"Now then," said Daddy. "We'd better borrow a wheelbarrow. We've got our work cut out to get all that stuff aboard."

The boatbuilder lent them a wheelbarrow and they took it to the steps below Miss Powell's cottage. Mother was sitting on the wooden seat at the top of the steps, sewing away at Bridget's sleeping bag. Bridget was telling Sinbad he was going to sea. Miss Powell was cutting an enormous pile of sandwiches to be eaten on their way down the river. Daddy had hurried up the hill to buy all the chops in the village so that they could take them ready-cooked to make things easier for their first meals on the island.

"I don't believe you'll ever get all that stuff into the *Goblin*," said Mother.

"There's a lot of room in her," said John, but that inner room at Miss Powell's looked pretty full.

"Come on," said Titty. "Let's everybody carry something."

Journey after journey was made from Alma Cottage to the dinghy floating by the hard. John, or Daddy after he had come back with the chops, pushed the wheelbarrow at the run, while others ran alongside keeping things from falling off. Voyage after voyage was made from the hard to the *Goblin*. Bit by bit that inner room began to look more like a room in somebody's house and less like a general store. It was extraordinary how different everybody felt. Yesterday it had seemed that adventure was over at least for these holidays. Today, adventure was ahead . . . just round the corner. Real exploration . . .

Islands, and islands of a kind they had never seen . . . an empty map to be filled with the discoveries they would make themselves. A little way upstream among the other yachts they saw the big yellow cutter with the three sailing dinghies clustered round her, and a boat from the shipwright's lying astern of her. Men were working aboard her. That girl and the two boys dropped into the dinghies and went off for a sail up the river. But today it never occurred even to Roger to call them pudding faces. There was no need to envy them. *They* were not going to sleep that night on an unknown island. *They* were not going to be marooned. *They* would not watch a ship sail away into the distance leaving them to pitch their camp and face the world alone. Roger looked at them with pity. "Those children again," he said.

"I do believe that's all," said Susan, back at the cottage looking round the room. The table had been cleared. Chairs that had been piled high were fit to sit upon once more. Everything left in the room belonged to it and not to an exploring expedition. Susan looked carefully round, straightened the tablecloth, and put a chair (that had somehow strayed) neatly in its place against the wall. "I don't believe we've forgotten anything."

"*Swallow*'s flag," said Titty, and darted upstairs to fetch it.

"Will it be all right to fly it on *Wizard*?" asked Roger, as she came down with it.

"We must fly it over the camp," said Titty.

Mother's voice came from outside. "A glass of milk for everybody," she said. "You've earned it after all that racing up and down."

"Pretty good work," said Captain Walker, pulling at his pipe. "Well done the Able-seamen."

"How soon will I be counted Able-seaman?" asked Bridget.

"Not till you can swim," said John.

"And she mustn't try swimming this time," said Mother, "because of the tides."

"And the mud," said Daddy.

"And the sharks," said Roger.

And then Daddy asked how many of the others had got their life-saving certificates, and handed out half a crown to each of them, on hearing that Roger and Titty had got theirs in the summer term at school, and that John and Susan had got theirs the year before.

"Penny for your thoughts, John," said Mother, after John had been silent for a minute or two.

"No good offering him a penny when I've just made him a rich man," said Daddy. "Out with it John, all the same."

"I was only thinking what a pity it is that Nancy and Peggy can't come too."

Daddy and Mother looked at each other but said nothing.

"Captain Nancy'd just love being marooned," said Titty. "But I expect they're doing something too. Sure to be. They'll probably write and tell us about it. She wouldn't have sent three million cheers unless they were up to something pretty larky."

"They won't be doing anything as good as this," said Roger.

Captain Walker looked at his watch.

"NO NEED TO ENVY THEM NOW"

"Are you ready, Mary?" he said. "All aboard. Hurry up and say goodbye to Miss Powell. We'll have to start at once to make sure of having the tide with us going in."

PIN MILL

CHAPTER III

INTO THE UNKNOWN

THE *Goblin* was floating well below her usual water line as she left Pin Mill to sail down the river into the unknown. She had never been so laden before. Inside her there was hardly room to move. Stuffed knapsacks, cases of ginger beer, tin boxes and bundles were piled on the cabin floor and in the bunks. Huge rolls of oilskins and ground sheets had been lashed down on the cabin top. A bundle of long bamboos for surveying was made fast on one of the side decks. And beside their gear there were all the members of the expedition. John, Susan, Bridget (on her first sea voyage) and the kitten, Sinbad, were in the cockpit. Titty and Roger were on the foredeck. Down below in the saloon, Commander Walker was ticking things off on a list and telling Mother that everything was really quite all right and that there was nothing about which to worry.

"It isn't as if there wasn't Susan," he said, "and it isn't as if John had no sense. I say, John. You keep straight down the middle of the river. I'm going to turn the engine on to get us quickly down over the tide."

"Aye, aye, sir," said John seriously. He, like Susan, had heard that their father was depending on them.

The engine started chug, chugging beneath them. Roger scrambled aft in a hurry, to be

25

allowed to push the lever forward and put it into gear. The *Goblin*'s wake lengthened, and the water creamed under the bows of *Wizard*, the sailing dinghy, towing astern.

In the cockpit, they had to shout to each other to make themselves heard over the noise of the engine, and could no longer hear what was being said by the friendly natives in the cabin. But there was little need for talk while everybody, even John the steersman, was busy with sandwiches and ginger beer.

They passed boats not in a hurry going slowly down under sail alone. They met boats coming up fast with the tide. They were interested in all of them, but the *Goblin*, they knew, was the only boat that was on her way to maroon a party of explorers on an island. The wooded banks slipped by and were left behind. The river opened into the wide harbour. They looked up the Stour and pointed out to Bridget where they had spent their first night in the *Goblin* anchored off Shotley pier. They drove down past the dock where (how long ago it seemed!) they had seen Jim Brading row in for petrol before the fog had come down on them like a blanket. Ahead of them once more was the Beach End buoy.

"Listen!" said Titty at the top of her voice.

"I can hear it," shouted Roger.

"Clang! . . . Clang! . . . Clang. . . ."

It was very different, hearing the bell buoy now with Mother and Daddy aboard, and bright sunshine everywhere, from what it had been, hearing that "Clang . . . Clang . . . " coming blindly nearer in the fog.

"We're nearly out at sea," said John.

"John says we're nearly out," Bridget called down into the cabin.

Commander Walker put his head out, looked round and went down again. The chug, chug of the engine came to an end.

"We shan't want that now," said Daddy, coming on deck again and talking quietly in the sudden silence made by the stopping of the engine.

They made as much room for him as they could and he sat on the after deck looking at Jim's chart.

"I'll take over now," he said. "John, you've got the best eyes. Get forward by the mast and keep them skinned. Look out for a small black buoy with a square topmark." He changed the *Goblin*'s course, and looked at the compass. "We ought to be heading for it now."

John scrambled forward. The sea was smooth, the wind light, but the *Goblin* seemed to be moving faster than when she had been coming down the harbour with her engine going. The tide was with her now instead of against her and they could see by the buildings ashore how fast they were moving. Nobody even felt like being seasick.

Away to the south was a bit of a hill with a tall narrow tower. Ahead of them was a wide deep bay with a low straight coastline far away in the distance. John, standing by the mast searched for the buoy. Suddenly he saw a black speck dancing on the water.

"Small black buoy almost dead ahead," called John.

"Piccaninny," said Roger.

"It's got something on the top of it," said Titty, who, looking where John was looking, had managed to bring her telescope to bear.

"That's the fellow," said Daddy. "See any others?"

"There's another beyond it."

"Good."

Soon they were sailing close past it, a black tarred barrel, with a stick and a sort of squarish box on the top of it. Ahead of them was another black barrel, and far ahead of that was a red one with a pointed top.

"In the channel now," said Daddy, and Mother came up the companion ladder and put her head out and looked away over the water which seemed to stretch for miles on either side of them.

"Pretty narrow just here," said Daddy.

"It doesn't look it," said Mother.

"It is, all the same. There's hard sand just below water on that side, and rocky flats on the other. At low tide we wouldn't be able to get in."

"What would happen if we went over there?" said Roger, "so that we could have a better look at that tower."

"A good old bump," said Daddy, "and no more *Goblin* if we weren't lucky. Lots of boats have been smashed up on that."

"Are you sure it's deep enough for us here?" asked Susan.

"Plenty," said Daddy.

"I don't see any islands," said Bridget.

"Right ahead of us," said Daddy.

ON THE WAY TO THE ISLANDS

Ahead of them the land seemed hardly above the level of the sea, just a long low line above the water, with higher ground away behind it. But that low line of coast seemed to have no gaps in it. It looked as if it stretched the whole way round across the head of the bay. Even John began to doubt if there could be islands ahead. But Daddy was ticking off one buoy after another on Jim's chart and seemed quite sure of his way. A couple of men were hauling a trawl net in a small boat and a cloud of gulls hovered above them. A motor boat appeared ahead, came to meet them and passed them in a flurry of foam.

"She must have come out from somewhere," said Titty, but still could see no gap in the coast line.

"We're nearly there," said Daddy at last. "Look out for a round buoy with a cross on a stick above it."

"There it is," called John. "Close to the shore."

Almost at the same moment, everybody saw a break in the line of sand away to the south, and a thread of water going in there, and one or two tall masts showing above sand dunes. And, as they came nearer to that round buoy with the cross they saw that a much wider channel was opening before them with smooth shining water stretching to the west and low banks on either side.

"There you are," said Daddy. "That buoy marks the cross roads. Turn left, follow that creek in there, past those masts, and you'll come to a town."

"I can see houses now," said Roger, "and lots more boats."

"You can get right up to the town at high water in a dinghy. But if you go, don't wait there too long, or there won't be water to take you back."

"But we're going to an island aren't we?" said Titty. "Not a town."

"We are," said Daddy. "We leave that buoy to port and carry straight on."

"Crossroads buoy," said Roger as they passed it.

A minute or two later they had left the open bay and the *Goblin* was slipping easily along in the quiet water of an inland sea. A low spit of land with a dyke along it already hid the creek that led to the town, though they could still see the tops of distant masts. Far away, on the opposite side, was another low dyke. Standing on the deck and in the cockpit they could see bushes here and there. Ahead of them the inland sea seemed to stretch on for ever.

"What's it called?" asked Titty, from the fore-deck.

Daddy smiled. "Do you want the name on Jim's chart? I thought you'd give it a name yourselves."

"It's a very secret place," said Roger. "You don't see it until you're almost inside."

"Secret Water," said Titty. "Let's call it that."

"Why not?" said Daddy and Titty scrambled into the cockpit and pencilled in the first name on Daddy's blank map.

"How far does it go?" asked John.

"Good long way at high tide," said Daddy.

"It's like a lake with no mountains," said Titty.

"But where are the islands?" asked Roger.

"All round us," said Daddy. He looked at his

chart. "That's one, right ahead. And that's another, over there. And this is the island you're going to be marooned on." He pointed to port. "At high water you'll be able to sail right round it through an inland sea wider than this, and get into the creek going to the town. At low water that's probably all mud. Jim's chart shows a track across it . . . My blank map'll give you a general idea, but you'll find it all out for yourselves."

"Unexplored," said Titty, "until we've explored it."

"Just so," said Daddy.

"Gosh!" said Roger. "This is the real thing. Hullo! There's another creek over on that side. And another on this. . . . "

"That's ours, I think," said Daddy.

The *Goblin* slipped on. A wide creek opened to starboard. But Daddy was taking no notice of it. He was watching a smaller creek that was gradually opening on the other side, and glancing now and then at Jim's chart.

"That must be the place," he said. "I think we can run in now. Roll that jib up, John."

"Aye, aye, sir."

"Ready? Haul away. Make fast. Now come aft and take her."

John hauled on the line that made the jib roll neatly up on itself, made fast so that it should not unroll again, and clambered back into the crowded cockpit. Already the *Goblin* had left the Secret Water and was in the creek, moving more slowly now, under mainsail only, between green shores.

"Keep her as she's going," said Daddy, and

went forward to deal with the anchor. There was the grumble and rattle of chain being hauled up and ranged on deck. Then Daddy was busy at the mast. The green banks slipped by. A heron got up and flapped slowly across the creek. A curlew cried. Daddy stood up on the foredeck watching the eastern bank, looking for something. Suddenly he flung out his right arm.

"Starboard," he said quietly, and John steered towards the western bank.

"Now. Right round into the wind. Helm hard over." John swung her round and the sail spilt the wind and flapped heavily as the *Goblin* headed back across the creek.

Splash!

The anchor was down, and Daddy was paying out chain. He was at the mast again. The boom lifted over their heads in the cockpit, and the sail came down with a run.

"Two tiers," said Daddy. "We shan't need more."

In a minute or two, he had bundled the sail along the boom and put a couple of tiers to hold it there.

"We'll call this Goblin Creek," said Titty, pencil in one hand and the blank map in the other.

"Good name," said Daddy. "Now then, John, haul in that dinghy. Will you put your Mother and me ashore?"

"What about us?" said Roger.

"Your turn'll come," said Daddy. "We've got to visit that kraal and make sure the natives won't want to tell you to clear out after we've sailed away."

CHAPTER IV

THE EXPEDITION GOES ASHORE

"You can see it's an island now," said Titty. "Look at all that water behind it. And, I say, Daddy's blank map's wrong. That lump isn't a peninsula. It's another little island."

"Rum islands, aren't they?" said Roger. "No rocks."

"They're landing," cried Bridget.

John was rowing Daddy and Mummy ashore. They were close to a sort of gap in the green bank, where the tops of some piles showed above the water. Daddy was pointing. John looking over his shoulder and took a stroke or two. The *Wizard* grounded. Daddy had taken an oar from John and was prodding over the side. He was feeling for foothold. He was stepping out into the water.

"Daddy's landed," said Bridget.

They saw him pull the boat a little further up. Mother was getting out, then John, carrying the anchor. They saw all three, splashing a little, lifting their feet high and putting them down carefully, walking one behind the other, as if in a narrow path, towards the dyke. They were on the dyke, clear against the sky. They had stopped by a row of bushes and small trees. Daddy was pointing this way and that. John was stamping about, as if trying the hardness of the ground.

"Come on, the Able-seamen," said Susan. "All hands to untying those knots. They'll be wanting those groundsheets off the cabin roof first of all."

"Daddy and Mother have gone," said Bridget. "John's coming back. No he isn't. He's taking the mast and sail out of the *Wizard*. He's carrying them ashore. He nearly fell down. He's going to fall down. No he isn't . . . I say, can't I go ashore and help?"

"You can't till he comes back," said Susan.

"Why's he taking the mast and sail out?" said Roger.

"To make room for the stores, of course," said Susan.

Presently they saw John back at the *Wizard*, sitting on the gunwale and washing his boots in the water. Then he came rowing off to the *Goblin*.

"Groundsheets first," he said as he came near. "You'll have to get them unlashed."

"They're all ready," said Susan.

"Well done. Can you heave them down?"

"Have you got a good place for the camp?" asked Titty.

"Gorgeous," said John. "But it's going to be an awful job getting the things ashore without covering them with mud."

"Hadn't you better wash your hands?" said Susan.

"I've done it once already," said John, but glancing down at his hands he dipped them again over the side of the dinghy.

"He can do his face afterwards," said Roger.

"You shut up," said John. "Just wait till you've tried it. It's all right once you're on the dyke, but getting across the saltings the mud splashes up over everything."

"What are saltings?" asked Titty.

"That's what Daddy called it . . . sort of marshy ground between the creek and the dyke. He says it goes under water at very high tides. Good, Susan. Hang on just a moment. Now let it come. . . . "

The first bundle of groundsheets was lowered into the dinghy. It was followed by another and yet another.

"Can't we come ashore too?" said Bridget.

"Susan had better," said John. "To help carry the things up. You can come too."

"And Sinbad?"

"All right. The Able-seamen had better stay in the *Goblin* to pass the things down. We don't want to bring more mud aboard than we can help. Come on. Room for a couple of tent-rolls. . . . Now Susan."

Susan slipped down into the dinghy.

"Bridget next. . . . "

"Give me Sinbad," said Susan. "You'll want both hands."

"I'll never manage," said Bridget looking down from *Goblin*'s deck into the loaded dinghy.

"You will," said John. "Sit on the edge . . . right at the edge. Now let yourself go."

Bridget found herself in a heap on the groundsheets.

"I did it all right," she said and her face which had for a moment been serious broke into a pleased smile.

"Fend off, Susan," said John, and the *Wizard* started on her second voyage to the shore.

There was not far to go, but the loaded boat

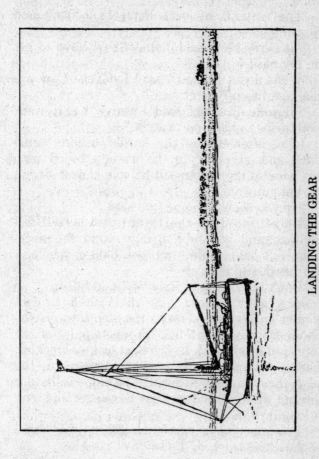

LANDING THE GEAR

grounded a little further out than she had last time.

"The water'll be over Bridget's boots," said Susan.

"I'll carry her," said John. "She'll have to get on my back."

"What about Sinbad?" said Bridget. "Can you manage two people at once?"

"I'll take Sinbad," said Susan. "You'll want both arms to hang on to John."

John, after taking the anchor ashore, came back and, standing in the water stooped with his back to the dinghy till he was almost sitting on the gunwale.

"Up you come, Bridgie," he said.

Bridget stood on the thwart, let herself fall forward and got John firmly round the neck. John felt behind him and took hold of her legs. He lifted, and choked.

"Don't throttle him, Bridget," said Susan.

John gave a good jerk that jolted Bridget higher on his back, and took a step towards the shore. Down went his foot through a patch of soft mud and he all but fell. The next foot was luckier, finding a stone. Step by step he staggered up the path through the saltings till he came to harder ground where he dumped his passenger and took a long breath.

"You must have eaten ten times your share of those sandwiches," he said.

Susan, taking now a long stride, now a short, now sliding back, now slipping forward, came after them with Sinbad. Then, while Susan and John went back to bring the things up from the boat,

Bridget and Sinbad climbed up the dyke, and were presently standing guard over a growing pile, as the Captain and the Mate staggered to and fro across the saltings as fast as the mud and their loads would let them.

Meanwhile, aboard the *Goblin*, the Able-seamen were busy lugging things up from below and stacking them on the decks and on the cabin roof ready for the ferrying ashore. Presently John came back for another cargo, and then again for another.

"I do believe that's the lot," said Titty at last.

"Nothing left down below," said Roger.

"Hop in then," said John. "But jolly well sit steady, or we'll have the water over the gunwales."

The *Goblin* lay deserted and the last of the explorers landed on the island. The last boatload, with four porters instead of only two, did not take long to carry up across the saltings to the dyke.

The dyke for the most part was narrow, just wide enough for a path along the top of it, but at the place where the explorers had dumped their stores it widened, giving plenty of room for a camp well above the level of the marshes. On the inner side it sloped steeply down to meadowland, with a drain running along the foot of it, and close to the camp there was a small pond. Just here there was a row of little stunted trees and bushes, and beyond them they could see cattle grazing in the distance, and the roof and chimneys of a farmhouse. Looking northward they could see where Goblin Creek opened into the Secret Water, and to the south they could see the creek again, curving round and opening into another inland sea.

"It's a lovely place for a base camp," said Titty. "And luckily the native kraal's a good long way off."

"What's in this box?" said Roger. "Can I start unpacking?"

"Not yet," said John. "All hands to pitching tents. Let's have it looking like a camp before Daddy and Mother come back."

"Lay the groundsheet first to see how they go," said Susan. "We can have the little ones facing the creek, but the big one'll have to go between these two trees. Let's get that one done first, so that in case Mother comes back too soon she'll be able to see where Bridget's going to sleep."

The big tent was one of the two they had used on their first visit to Wild Cat Island. It had to be slung on a rope between trees, not like the little tents, which had their own poles, and could be pitched anywhere. It was always rather a job to get it up, because of the difficulty of getting the rope high enough and taut enough. With these little trees it was worse than usual, but John and Susan managed it at last, and Bridget found her way inside it even before its walls were properly pegged down. They looked round to see that Roger's and Titty's tents were already pitched. Titty was unrolling Susan's own tent, which, as she was not going to sleep in it, was to be used for a storehouse.

"Where's Roger?" said Susan.

But just then Roger came running along the dyke.

"I've been to the corner to look at the other

island," he said. "Daddy and Mother are in sight, coming from the kraal. They'll be here in a minute."

There was frenzied work in the camp. Boxes and knapsacks were bundled out of sight. The last two tents went up in record time. Titty had pulled one of the surveying poles from among the others and was hurriedly fastening *Swallow*'s flag to it. The moment it was done John drove it into the ground, and Daddy and Mother came back to find all five tents up, and the *Swallow* flag on a bamboo flagstaff fluttering in the breeze.

"Good work," said Daddy.

"Everything's ashore," said John.

"Not properly stowed," said Susan. "We've pushed things in anyhow, just so that you could see the camp."

"Good camp, too," said Daddy. "Well, you're lucky, there's a very decent chap at the farm and he says any friend of Jim Brading's a friend of his, so that's all right. But he says you mustn't drink from the pond. Salt water got into it and spoilt it. All right for washing but keep it out of your mouths. I'll put ashore two full water carriers from the *Goblin*, and when you want more you'll have to get it from the well at the farm. I'll bring them ashore now, and then we'll have to be starting. The tide's going down fast."

"What about your fireplace, Susan?" said Mother, as Daddy hurried down to the landing place.

"There's a good place on dry ground just below the tents," said Susan.

"No stones here to build it with," said Mother.

"Plenty of earth," said Susan, "and we've got a spade."

"There's no post on the island," said Mother, "but you can send messages through the man at the farm. He goes to the mainland nearly every day. And you've got Miss Powell's telephone number."

"But is there a telephone?" said Roger.

"No there isn't. Not on the island. But the farmer'll telephone for you if you want anything, or you can if you go to the mainland yourselves. And we've got the number of his dairy in the town, so that we can get a message to you through him. What's become of Bridget?"

Susan pointed quietly to the big tent. Mother looked into it. Susan had already made up her bed and Bridget's with rugs and sleeping bags. From the smaller of the sleeping bags came a loud snore.

"Sure you wouldn't rather sleep comfortably in a bed at Miss Powell's?" said Mother.

Bridget sat up suddenly. "Oh, Mummy!" she said.

"Oh well," said Mother. "I suppose you have to grow up some time."

"Sinbad's the youngest now," said Bridget.

Aboard the *Goblin*, Daddy had already lowered the two big galvanized water carriers into *Wizard* lying alongside. He was busy at the foot of the mast.

"Look," said Titty. "He's hoisting a flag."

A blue flag with a white square in the middle of it fluttered up to the *Goblin*'s crosstrees.

"It's the Blue Peter," said Mother. "He's ready to sail."

BLUE PETER AT THE CROSSTREES

In another few minutes Daddy had rowed ashore and brought the water carriers up to the camp.

"Here you are," he said. "And a good weight too, as you'll find when you take them to be refilled. You'll be treating water like liquid gold when you have to carry every drop of it."

"That's what Jim said, when we were with him in the *Goblin*," laughed Roger.

"Sensible chap," said Daddy. "Now then, Mary, we've got to be off. The heartless skipper and his cruel mate will now sail away leaving their victims on the unknown shore. Come along, Mary. You're the cruel mate. Goodbye all of you. Use sense. Watch the tides. John and Susan in charge."

"You will be careful, won't you?" said Mother, kissing the explorers goodbye.

"You aren't going away altogether," said Bridget.

"Sure you wouldn't like to come too?" said Mother.

Bridget wavered for a moment.

"No thank you," she said.

Daddy laughed. "Well done, Biddy," he said.

Mother got very muddy kissing John, who had forgotten to rub the splashes off his face.

"John," she said, "you look like Ben Gunn already."

"He'll have a matted beard by the time we come back," said Daddy. "Come on John and get some more mud on you putting us aboard."

John rowed Daddy and Mother back to the ship. For a moment or two he waited, watching Daddy hoist the mainsail. Then, remembering that he was in charge of the expedition, he rowed back and joined the others who were watching by the camp.

Already Mother was at the tiller of the *Goblin* and Daddy was hauling up the anchor hand over hand. The jib unrolled and filled with wind. Daddy was getting the anchor over the bows and sloshing the mud off with a mop. The *Goblin* swung round and headed out of the creek.

"Goodbye ... Goodbye...." The marooned explorers shouted from the camp.

"Goodbye and good luck," an answering call came from the *Goblin*. The Blue Peter fluttered down. Daddy went aft and took the tiller. Mother waved a handkerchief. The *Goblin*, leaving the shelter of the creek, heeled over and moved faster. She was gone. Only her red sails showed above the long line of the dyke as with the ebb to help her she hurried to the sea.

Everybody felt a sudden emptiness.

"We're in for it now," said John.

"Come on," said Susan. "We've got an awful lot to do."

"What about unpacking those boxes?" said Roger.

Bridget had taken Sinbad from Titty. For a few minutes she watched the red triangle of *Goblin*'s mainsail moving above the dyke.

"It's all right, Sinbad," she said. "They'll come back for you."

CHAPTER V

MAROONED

UNPACKING had begun in earnest. The explorers were taking stock. Susan with pencil and paper was making a list as they dug into the three boxes that Daddy had sent down to Pin Mill from the Army and Navy Stores. Bridget and Roger were trying to count the apples and oranges they could see through the open slats of a crate. Titty and John were going through the contents of a large parcel with all the things Daddy had put together for map-making, a drawing board, lots of paper, pencils, a bottle of Indian ink, parallel rulers, drawing compasses, a protractor, a box of drawing pins.

"Daddy was going to do it really properly," said Titty.

"So are we," said John. "He'd be awfully pleased if we manage to go everywhere and get the whole thing mapped."

"Secret Archipelago Expedition," said Titty.

"What's Archipelago?" said Bridget.

"Lots of islands," said Roger. "Look here, Bridgie, you haven't counted that apple showing through the paper."

"Two dozen tins of milk," said Susan. "Eleven . . . No . . . twelve tins of soup."

"Monsters," said Roger.

"Three big tins of steak and kidney pie. . . . Three tongues."

"Oh good!"

"Three tins of pemmican.... Six tins of sar-
dines.... One tin of golden syrup.... One stone
jar of marmalade.... Six boxes of eggs.... One
dozen in each box."

"Why such a lot of eggs?" said Roger.

"You and John always have two for breakfast
and one each for the rest of us.... That's seven at
a single meal.... And what about scrambled egg
suppers? Come on ... Roger, it's no good counting
apples in their crate. You can't see through them.
You be putting the tins in the store tent. Four
packets of cornflakes. Six loaves of bread. The
bread and the cornflakes'll have to be kept in
one of the boxes. One tin of ginger nuts.... One
tin of biscuits.... "

"Can I tear the paper off?" said Roger. "Good.
Garibaldi. That's squashed flies. What about opening this box? We're bound to want to.... "

"Shut up just a minute. One bag of potatoes....
What's that other bag?"

"Beans," said Bridget.

"Three slabs of sticky cake.... "

"A whole box of chocolate," said Roger. "Nut
and raisin kind, in slabs. Let's ... "

"Leave them alone," said Susan. "Six pounds
of butter.... Two boxes of lump sugar. Two of
soft. One tin of salt.... One bar of cheese....
Good.... That's the crustless kind in silver
paper."

"First rate for marching rations," said John.

"I say," cried Bridget suddenly. "This box has
got Sinbad on it."

It was a cardboard box, and in it was a packet

of cat's biscuits, a small bottle of Bovril and half
a dozen very small tins of salmon.

"He'll love the salmon," said Roger. "But what's
the Bovril for?"

"It's to put with the hot water you have to
pour over the biscuits," said Susan. "What's the
label on that basket?"

"Tonight's supper," read Titty. "And there's
a parcel labelled 'Tomorrow's Dinner'."

"We won't open that till we want it," said
Susan. "Look here, Roger. Fishing lines and fish
hooks. You'd better look after them."

"Shall I take the spade, too? For digging worms."

"No need to put the spade in your tent. But
do put those fish hooks where Sinbad won't
tread on them. I'll want the spade in a minute
to make a fireplace. I'll tell you one thing we
are going to be hard up for and that's firewood.
It's not like Wild Cat, with dead branches everywhere. . . . "

"Come on," said John. "Let's see who gets
most. High-water-mark's the likeliest place."

Exploration in a small way began at once.
While Susan was busy making a fireplace exactly as she wanted it, cutting slabs of earth and
arranging them in a circle, the others soon found
out that every bit of burnable wood took some
finding. They worked along the side of the dyke
nearest to the creek, picking up here and there
small pieces of driftwood. All along the foot of the
dyke, marking the highest tides was a wide belt of
old weed-stalks like reeds that had been washed
up there and left.

"I expect they'll burn all right," said Titty.

"Too fast, probably," said John. "We want every scrap of real wood we can get."

"What about the dead crabs?" said Roger. "There are hundreds of them in among the reeds."

"They won't be much good," said John. "I say, we'll have to make a rule that nobody leaves the camp without bringing back a bit of wood."

Gleaning carefully along the dyke, John and Titty got together two bundles of scraps of wood and a few bigger bits that looked as if they might have come from an old railing.

"Enough to boil a kettle anyway," said John. "Let's take it along and something to carry reeds in. Where's Roger?"

"Somewhere round the corner," said Titty.

They found Susan sharpening the ends of two forked sticks she had cut from a willow. A long piece to carry the kettle was already lying on the ground beside her round fireplace.

"Is that all you've got?" said Susan. "I thought it was going to be difficult. There's hardly any dead wood under these bushes. I've got a little, but not much."

"There's lots of that reed rubbish. We'll take a basket ... No ... oilskins'll be better. Lay them flat and pile the reeds on them, and bundle them up for carrying. Hullo! What's the matter?"

Roger, who had not, like Titty and John, been able to put wood-gathering before everything else, came running into the camp.

"I say, John," he cried. "I've been down to the landing. The island's growing like anything. *Wizard*'s high and dry."

"Tide's going down," said John. "I'll come and have a look. Haven't you got any wood?"

"One bit," said Roger. "There simply wasn't any where I was looking."

"One bit," said Susan. "Oh Roger."

"Well it's a jolly good one," said Roger.

"You take your oilskin and fill it with as much of that reed stuff as you can carry," said John.

"All right," said Roger. "Dead crabs and all."

John and Titty took their oilskins too and went down over the saltings to look at *Wizard*. A few hours had made an enormous difference. They had brought the things ashore from the *Goblin* almost to the edge of the saltings. Now the saltings were far above the water level. There was a widening strip of mud beneath them. The narrow pathway between the heads of old rotting piles stretched down over the mud, and into the water.

"Good," said John at the sight of it. "Jim said it was a proper hard. We'll be able to get afloat even at low tide. But we won't shift *Wizard* now. We'll be able to slide her down over the mud if we want her."

"What's happening to Bridget Island?" said Roger. "The little one . . . It's almost not an island any more."

They went floundering along the saltings to look at it. That little island that had been divided from the big one by a wide channel was an island no longer. The channel had narrowed and broken up, into little streams trickling down both sides of a mudbank. Roger tried to get across, but soon stuck and struggled back to firmer ground.

"Gosh!" he said. "It'll be easier to get to it

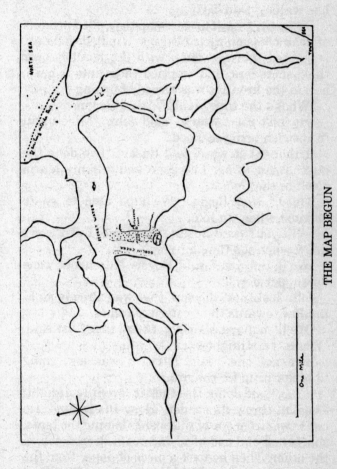

THE MAP BEGUN

when it's cut off at high water than when it's part of our island. This is a rum place."

"We'll have to mark that channel, 'Mud at low water'," said Titty.

On the way back to the camp they piled armfuls of dead reeds on their oilskins, bundled them up, staggered into the camp with the bundles over their shoulders, and emptied them into a heap, beside the fire that was already burning.

"What's the time, John?" asked Susan.

"Haven't got a watch," said John. "Mine's still in Ipswich being mended."

"I thought it was," said Susan. "I've done the most awful thing. I've gone and left my alarm clock in the *Goblin*."

"Good," said Roger. "We'll be able to go to bed just when we like."

"Will you?" said Susan. "We'll see. But I won't know when it's time for meals. . . . "

"We'll tell you," said Roger. "It's about time for supper now."

John looked at the sun, that was already sinking low towards the western marshes.

"We'll manage all right about time," he said. "Where's a straight stick?"

"I've got one," said Titty. "I was just going to break it up for the fire."

"Fine," said John. He stuck it carefully upright. The sun threw its shadow along the ground. He cut a twig from one of the bushes behind the tents, sharpened one end of it and cut a deep notch in the other. Then he took a piece of paper from the pad on which Susan had been writing her list of stores, folded it, wrote "SUPPER" on it in large

letters, fixed it in the notch, and then pushed the
pointed end of the twig into the ground exactly
in the thin line of shadow cast by the upright
stick.

"Gosh!" said Roger. "A meal-dial."

"It'll have to do," said John. "We can't be far
wrong now. It must be about supper time. We'll
have supper each day when the shadow falls on
the supper stick. We'll watch for midday tomorrow
when the sun's highest and the shadow's shortest,
and we'll shove in a dinner stick too."

"Regular meals is what matters most," said
Susan.

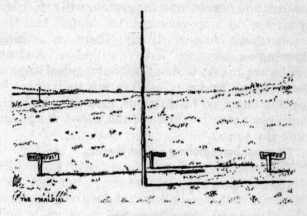

THE MEAL-DIAL

"Well, the sun's regular enough," said John.

"What if it's cloudy?" said Roger. "And it might
rain. Don't we get anything to eat unless the sun's
shining?"

"We'll just have to guess," said John. "But tides

are going to be a bother. Daddy gave me a tide-table, but it won't be much good if we don't know the time. The tides keep shifting round. We can't keep track of them without a clock."

"I say," said Titty. "We ought to count days, like Robinson Crusoe."

John bent down and cut a notch in the flagstaff. "That's for today," he said. "Every day we'll cut another notch until the *Goblin* comes back. . . . "

"And then when we lie exhausted on the sand . . . " said Titty.

"Jolly wet mud," said Roger.

"We'll see a sail far away. And it'll come nearer and nearer. And the captain will say, 'Clap your eye to a spyglass, Mister Mate.' And the mate (that's Mother) will say, 'There's something moving on the shore. They're still alive.' And we will wave and try to shout, but our parched throats won't let us. And they'll sail in, and we'll hear the anchor chain go rattling out. And then we'll all sail away together and see the island disappear into the sunset."

"It may be morning," said Roger.

"The tops of the palm trees will show like feathers above the sea, and then even they will be gone, and we shall be telling the people on the ship about the discoveries we've made and the long years we've spent here."

"Not years," said Bridget.

"Ages anyhow," said Titty.

"We'll have to get the palm trees from somewhere and plant them," said Roger. "Susan. Do look at the meal-dial."

"Well," said Susan.

"The shadow's left the supper stick already."

"Supper's ready," said Susan.

"But where?" said Roger.

"Mother's done the whole thing," said Susan. She went to the store tent and came back with the basket with a label on it, "Tonight's supper". Out of it came a parcel of chops, ready-cooked, a bag of tomatoes, two lettuces with a bit of paper on which was written "The lettuces have been washed", and a bag of rock buns. At the bottom of the basket was another bit of paper with a message. "Fill up with bananas."

"There's nothing to do but to make the tea," said Susan, "and the kettle'll be boiling in a minute."

"What about Sinbad?" said Bridget.

"He shall have cold salmon and a drink of milk," said Susan.

"Jolly good supper," said Roger.

It lasted a long time, and when it was finished, there were only five mugs, five plates and one saucer to wash up. Then the explorers made ready for bed, after planning to begin work in earnest first thing in the morning. The sun had set and the wind had dropped. John, Titty and Roger brought into the camp fresh armfuls of the dead weed-stalks, which smoked for a moment and then blazed up on the fire. Bridget, already in her pyjamas, crouched at the door of the big tent looking out at her first camp-fire and at the figures of her elders moving in the dusk.

"Off you go, Roger," said Susan.

"I'm going to bed now," said Titty. "Wake me in the morning, whoever wakes first."

"Everybody got their own torches?" asked John.

"Have you filled the hurricane lantern?" asked Susan.

"Just doing it," said John. "We'll have it burning in the camp all night."

"Like a riding light," said Roger.

"To frighten away wild beasts," said Titty. "But we've got one tiger of our own. Come on Sinbad. You're going to sleep in my tent. Bridget's got Susan."

The stars came out all over the enormous sky that came right down to the flat marshes and the open sea, a sky much bigger than the sky of the mountain country of the north. John lit the hurricane lantern and stood it on the ground outside the big tent.

"No good trying to bank up a reed fire," he said. "Not even charcoal burners could do it. . . ."

"Damp reeds would keep it going," said Susan.

"They'd only get dry and then blaze," said John. "Better not. We'll look for more driftwood in the morning."

"You get quickly into bed while you're still warm," said Susan to Bridget.

"I'm in," said Roger.

"So am I," said Titty . . . "Hullo. Sinbad's out. No, pussy. Oh all right. He's trying to curl up on my bed like he did in the boat."

"Why don't the curlews go to bed too?" said Roger. "And the gulls."

"Duck, too," said John.

"I say, was that splash a fish?"

"Aren't you going to bed, John?" said Susan.

"In a minute."

Roger, in the middle of asking questions about the noises of the birds, chattering along the edge of the mud, had fallen suddenly asleep. Bridget thought of last night. She had been in bed long before this, in a real bed, in a room with dark curtains. For the first time in her life she was sleeping, just like the others, in a tent. She wriggled a little. It was not so comfortable as a bed, but the others had always seemed to like it. So would she. She wriggled again. That must be a crease in the rug with the hard groundsheet and the ground underneath. That was better. A faint whiff of burnt reeds drifted in through the open mouth of the tent. A curlew called. Again there was a sudden chatteration of gulls. Yes. They were alone, on an island. And she was old enough to be with them at last. She put out a hand to feel for Susan.

"That you, Bridget?" said Susan. "Are you all right?"

"Very all right," said Bridget. "I was only making sure you were there."

John was last into his tent. Standing outside he listened. Dimly, far away, he could hear the slow murmur of the sea on the sands on the other side of the island. . . . No. . . . that must be farther still, where the open sea came in beyond that other creek. He listened to the birds. Far away, as the dark closed down, he saw a bright line of lights on the mainland to the north. He half thought he ought to keep awake this first night. Just in case. But, after all, there was nothing against getting into his sleeping bag. He could lie awake in it, ready to jump up. Tomorrow they must explore the island. . . . Hullo. That was Titty whispering.

"John."

"Yes."

"It's about Nancy's message. We never answered it."

"We couldn't," said John. "It'd be rather beastly to tell them we've started another adventure already, when they're all by themselves without even the D's."

"Whatever Nancy's doing can't be as good as this," said Titty. "I wish they were here."

"So do I," said John. "But we can't help it. Good night."

"Good night."

An hour later John woke. The fire had gone out. The hurricane lantern was burning. He could see the light of it through the thin canvas of his tent. He remembered that he was in charge, in charge of a party of explorers marooned on a strange and desert island. He wriggled out of his sleeping bag, crept out and stood up outside, in the cool night. The camp was silent. The birds had quietened down. He heard an owl somewhere on the mainland. . . . If that *was* the mainland over there. He crawled back into his tent, wriggled into his sleeping bag, and, with the torch, looked at the blank map Daddy had made. There seemed to be water almost everywhere. He found his eyes closed and the torch still lit. How long had he been using the battery all for nothing? He put it out and was asleep once more.

CHAPTER VI

FIRST HINT OF SAVAGES

BRIDGET stirred in her sleeping bag.

"Mummy," she began, and suddenly remembered that Mummy was far away, and that she was really ship's baby for the first time, sharing adventure with the others. She rolled over, sleeping bag and all. One side of the tent was pale with sunlight. She looked out through the open door. Wisps of white smoke were drifting past and there was a sharp smell of burning reeds. She wriggled out of her bag and crawled to the door. Smoke was pouring from the fire. A kettle hung in the smoke, and Susan was stooping beside the fire, poking sticks under the kettle. Flames licked up round the kettle and the smoke blew away. Titty and John were not to be seen, but Roger was hopping about at the edge of the little pond, first on one leg and then on the other, scrubbing himself with a towel and saying "Grrrrrr. Grrrrrr. . . . Jolly co . . . old."

"Well, you needn't have gone right in," she heard Susan say. "I only told you to get washed. There's boiled water for your teeth in that mug."

"They're chattering too fast to be brushed," said Roger.

"If they're chattering as fast as that you won't be able to eat any breakfast."

"Where's John, and Titty?" asked Bridget.

"Hullo, Bridgie. They've been up ages. They've

gone off to get more wood. Hurry up now and get dressed. Breakfast's nearly ready. Water in that bucket. And soap."

"Don't forget to wash behind your ears," said Roger.

"Used they to say that to you?" said Bridget earnestly, and wondered why Roger grinned a little sheepishly and Susan laughed.

Five minutes later Bridget, more or less washed and fully dressed, was explaining to Sinbad that he would have to wait till his soaked biscuits had cooled. Roger was watching the shadow of the meal-dial, with one eye on Susan, and a cleft stick with a "BREAKFAST" label all ready. Susan had opened a tin of condensed milk and mixed it with the right amount of water in a jug. Five plates heaped with cornflakes lay in a row. She had filled up the kettle with water and had begun to scramble seven eggs in the frying pan. She put the pan down for a moment.

"Hold tight, Bridgie," she said. "I'm just going to blow it."

She blew a piercing blast on her mate's whistle, and Roger drove the "BREAKFAST" twig into the ground exactly in the shadow of the upright stick. "That's two meals marked on the dial anyway," he said.

"Coming, coming," sounded in the distance, and presently John and Titty, each with an armful of sticks, came into the camp.

"I've put the breakfast peg in," said Roger.

"Good," said John, and cut a notch in the flag-staff to mark the expedition's second day.

"The inland sea's nearly dry," said Titty. "We

saw someone coming across in a horse and cart."

"The tide's right out," said John. "We've found why Daddy's map makes Bridget Island look as if it was part of this. The line he's drawn goes round outside the saltings. So it makes everything that's joined at low water look like one."

"Our map's going to show them separately," said Titty. "We're going to put in all the channels we can sail through when the tide's up."

"We're going to survey the dyke first," said John. "Everything inside that's always dry. And we're going to make a good lot of copies of Daddy's map, so that it won't matter if we make a mess of them. We'll keep Daddy's own map in the camp, and mark in each bit as we do it. Titty's going to do the explored bits in ink. Daddy's done his blank map in pencil so that we can rub the lines out and our map'll spread day by day till there are no unexplored parts left."

"Where do we begin?" asked Roger.

"With breakfast," said Susan.

*

"Morning!"

Everybody jumped. The mixture of breakfast and plans had made them deaf and blind to everything else, and here, standing close above them, smiling down at them, was a tall man in corduroy breeches, muddy sea-boots and a rough tweed coat.

"Good morning."

"Hostile or friendly?" whispered Roger, hoping Titty would hear him.

The man held out a large bottle.

"When your dad and mam were over to mine," he said, "I tell 'em there's be milk to spare some days. This any good to you?"

"Thank you very much," said Susan. "We didn't mean to bother you. We've brought lots of milk in tins. But this'll be ever so much nicer. Would you like a cup of tea?"

"I won't say 'No'," said the man. "Up early this morning and over to the town. Just come back across the Wade."

"We saw your cart in the distance," said Titty.

"But isn't it an island?" said Roger.

"Not at low water it isn't."

Susan had filled a mug and handed it up to him. She offered him the tin of lump sugar and his own bottle of milk. "You won't like ours after the real milk," she said.

"Do you mean it's really just part of the mainland?" said Roger. What was the good of an island, he was thinking, if people could get to it in carts?

"Oh no. It's an island all right. But when the tide's out, there's just one way you can get across if you follow the track over the mud. When the tide's in you can't get nowhere without no boat."

"That's all right," said Roger.

The man emptied the mug down his throat. "If you keep to the dyke you'll be all right," he said. "But the saltings is treacherous. You might easy get in soft and not get out in a hurry. I've lost more'n one pair of boots myself. Friends of young Brading's aren't you? Well, if there's anything I can do for you, let me know. But you'll find it a dull place, I reckon. No life, if you know what I mean. Nobody about. Only you and them savages. And as for them savages . . . "

"What savages?" asked Titty and Roger together.

"Savages?" said Bridget.

Susan stared. John opened his mouth to speak but said nothing.

"I tell your dad about 'em, and he say you'd deal with 'em all right."

"But what savages?" said Roger. "Where are they?"

"Ain't seen 'em for a few days," said the man chuckling. "Not more'n one of 'em. But they might be back any day now. You'll know 'em when you meet 'em. Well, so long." He turned to go, and then, over his shoulder, he asked, "You ain't got no dog? I meant to ask your dad."

"We've got a kitten," said Bridget.

"That's all right," said the man. "He won't take to chasing buffaloes. . . . That's what they called it. We had to make 'em send their dog away." He waved his hand in a friendly manner and was gone, striding along the top of the dyke.

"Gosh!" said Roger.

"Savages!" said Titty.

Bridget moved a little closer to Susan.

"Well that settles it," said John.

"Settles what?" said Roger.

"What we do this morning. You heard what he said about savages. The first thing we've got to do is to make sure the island's clear of them. We'll do the survey at the same time."

"Let's start," said Roger.

But there was a good deal to be done first,

while Susan was washing up and Titty and Roger
were doing the wiping and Bridget was keeping
Sinbad from licking the cleaned plates. "He's trying to help, really," she said, but Susan thought
he'd be more use if he didn't. John, putting a piece
of paper on the top of Daddy's blank map and then
holding it up to the light was making a careful
tracing. "We want about a dozen of them," he
said. "We're sure to spoil a good many. And we
ought each to have one to put down anything we
discover." Then, for the purpose of the survey, he
made on a larger scale a copy of the big blob that
on Daddy's map showed the island on which they
had landed. In the corner of it he made a copy of
the compass rose that Daddy had drawn, using
the parallel rulers to make sure it was pointing
in the same direction. North, South, East and
West were easy to mark, and then with a pair
of dividers, he cut each half circle in half, and
marked North-East, South-East, North-West and
South-West. There really was some use in some of
the things they taught at school. Then the quarter
circles had to be cut in half in the same way, to get
North-North-East, East-North-East and the rest
of them.

Then, when the washing up was finished, Roger
was sent off to plant one of the bamboo surveying
poles at the corner of the dyke to the south of the
camp, while John and Titty went off with the map,
the compass, a note-book and another bamboo to
the corner north of the camp, where the dyke
turned sharply eastwards near the mouth of Goblin Creek. Titty planted the post, and John took
a bearing from one post to the other, which was

easily seen with Roger standing beside it.

"This bit of dyke's about north by east. It'll do for a base line. Now for the kraal." He turned and faced inland towards the clump of small trees and the farm chimneys. "South-east. Got the parallel rulers."

Kneeling on the ground, he ruled a line between the two posts, and then ruled another across the middle of the island from the dot on the map that marked the northern post.

"It's somewhere on that line," he said. "Come on. Now we'll take a bearing of it from the other post."

The two surveyors hurried along the dyke to join Roger, who was getting a little tired of holding up his post, because he had not been able to drive it far enough in to make it stand by itself.

John jammed it in, and then, compass in hand, looked across at the distant chimney of the farm-house. "Bit south of east," he said.

"Let me try," said Roger, put the compass on the ground for steadiness and straddled above it. "Jolly nearly east-south-east."

Titty tried. "It looks to me just between the two."

John looked carefully across the compass at the farm, agreed.

"All right," he said. "We'll call it east by south. Now let's try." He made a mark on the compass rose halfway between east and east-south-east, and putting one edge of the rulers on the centre of the rose and on this mark, he used the other edge to draw a line east by south through the dot that marked the position of the southern post.

"It's all right,", he said. "Look."

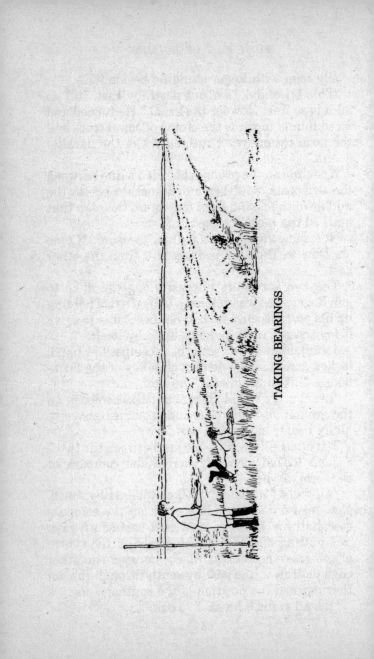

TAKING BEARINGS

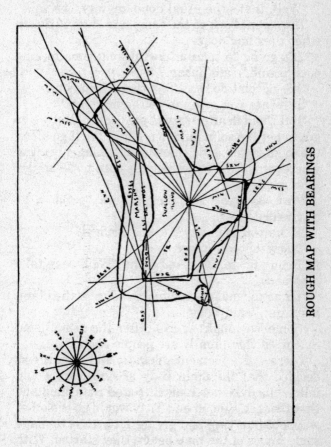

ROUGH MAP WITH BEARINGS

The two lines crossed each other just about in the middle of the blob where Daddy had put a little square to make the farm.

"Well, that's the kraal done anyway," he said.

They went back to the camp and showed Susan what they had done.

"It's going to take an awful long time to map each island," said Susan.

"We needn't do it all like that," said John.

"How are you going to do the marshes?"

"Put them in afterwards," said John. "But we've got to get the solid land done first. We'll go along the dyke right round the island, taking a bearing wherever it turns a corner. It's sure to be all dry land inside it."

"Any savages," said Roger, "are bound to be on the dry."

"Have you seen any?" asked Bridget.

"Not yet," said Roger.

"Ready to start?" asked John. "We'll each take a bamboo."

"I'd better make some more copies of the blank map first," said Titty.

"Somebody ought to look after the camp," said Susan, "if there really are people about."

There was a moment's debate, and then it was decided that the main body of surveyors would follow the dyke north-about round the island and that Bridget, Sinbad and Titty would go the other way, not hurrying and giving Titty time to make some copies of the map before they started. With the whole island flat and open between the two parties, it was felt that prowling savages, if there were any, would stand a poor chance of not being seen.

"If we see any savages near the camp," said Bridget, "we'll . . . "

"Blow the mate's whistle for us," said Roger.

"We won't," said Bridget. "We'll send Sinbad at them like a tiger."

"His claws are pretty sharp," said Roger. "But he'll probably only purr at them."

"There won't be anybody," said Bridget. "Or will there?"

"There can't be anyone at this end of the island," said John, "or we'd have seen them already. Do let's get started."

The surveying party, with bamboo poles, compass, drawing board and instruments, was on its way.

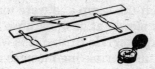

CHAPTER VII

HOOFMARKS IN THE MUD

Titty forgot about savages while, one after another, she made a dozen copies of the blank map. It was not difficult, but it needed careful doing, and she enjoyed doing it, and, as usual when she had a pencil in her hand, could think of nothing else. But when eleven of those copies were piled in John's tent, with his barometer for a paperweight, and she had taken the twelfth and had set out with Bridget and Sinbad to follow the dyke along the southern side of the island, she remembered the savages once more. Bridget, who had been keeping a look out, had not forgotten them for a moment.

They had left the camp and were moving along the dyke very slowly at first, because Sinbad was not a quick explorer. He trotted this way and that in the short grass, wrinkling his nose and sniffing at things, and then going back and sniffing again. The only way to get him to come on was to walk backwards in front of him. "We'll have to carry him if we're going to get anywhere," Titty said at last and hove him up in her arms.

That was better. The Able-seaman and the ship's baby were able to get going at human instead of kitten speed. They stopped now and then, and Bridget took the kitten for a minute or two while Titty, who found she could do quite well without surveying poles or the compass, dotted in the line of the dyke on the blank map, and with little scrabblings of her pencil showed the marshy saltings between the dyke and the channel that joined Goblin Creek to the inland sea. The tide was still too low to let her see the water in the channel, but she could see where it was and dotted it in, to be marked properly when they were able to sail through it in the *Wizard*.

"No savages yet?" said Bridget, when they had moved on and Titty, with the kitten on her shoulder, was looking across the island through the telescope.

"No," said Titty.

"Where have the others got to by now?"

"There's somebody. Right away on the other side. They've got on jolly fast."

"May I look?"

Titty handed over the telescope. It had not been easy to use it with the ship's kitten thinking he would like to get down and do some more exploring on his own. Bridget put the telescope to her eye, and pushed it in and pulled it out.

"It's all blurry," she said. "I can see better without it."

Far away on the skyline on the other side of the island small figures were moving, figures so small that it was hard to tell who was who.

"If we wanted help, they're too far to come," said Bridget, looking at Titty's face to see how she took this bit of news.

"We shan't want help," said Titty. "Not three of us." But she lowered her voice a little and looked warily round. Not a savage was in sight.

They went on. Below the dyke the saltings were narrowing. Wide mudflats stretched beyond them, divided by a ribbon of water. On the landward side they could see the farm, sheltering among its trees, green meadowland and grazing cattle.

"Well, there are plenty of buffaloes," said Titty.

"But no savages," said Bridget. "Couldn't we let Sinbad explore for a bit?"

For some time now Sinbad had been more difficult to hold. He was down in a moment, crawling through the grass, pretending to pounce on a dry bit of reed that was lifted by the wind, and then shaking a paw almost angrily after stepping in the damp mud of the footpath.

"Come along," said Bridget. "Puss, puss, puss!" And Sinbad, in his own good time, moved slowly after her.

"Try with a bit of string," said Titty, and took a coiled up bit from her pocket, tied a small handful of dry grass at one end of it and gave it to Bridget. Bridget walked backwards, jerking the little bundle of grass along the ground. Sinbad crouched, leapt after it, rolled over, crouched and leapt again. "He likes that kind of exploring," said Bridget.

"Good," said Titty. "Keep him going."

She walked slowly on. The saltings below the dyke grew narrower, and were now no more than a fringe to the wide expanse of mud that stretched across from the island to the mainland instead of the bright, shimmering sea that they had seen from the deck of the *Goblin* when they had sailed into the Creek. A ribbon of water was spreading in the middle of the mud. Tide was coming up. Soon the mud would be a sea once more.

In the saltings, close below the dyke, was a

narrow ditch, leading out towards the mud. At the side of the ditch was a landing stage made of a few planks, and a big heavy rowing boat lay beside it. Titty carefully marked it on her map and wrote "Native Harbour". That, she decided, must be the boat the native from the kraal used when he could not use his cart.

She was walking on, looking far out over the mud. Suddenly she stopped. On the edge of the ribbon of water out there were wading birds. But the water, slowly rising, was lapping at something that no birds could have made. If it had been sand, she might have thought that someone had been playing there with a spade and bucket. But no one builds castles in the mud.

She pulled out the telescope. Yes. She could see that the mud had been freshly turned, as if with a spade. Savages after all? It was not piled high enough for even the smallest savage to hide behind it. But someone had certainly been digging. With the telescope she followed a long line of diggings, here quite a big heap of mud, there only a few spadefuls turned over. There were marks in the mud going from one digging to the next. The line of marks curved in over the mud towards the island. It looked as if it ended by a sort of promontory, where there were no saltings, and the mud came close to the foot of the dyke. Whoever had done that digging might have come ashore there. He might be behind the promontory. Or he might have crossed the dyke and be on the island itself, hiding, perhaps, on the landward side of the dyke.

Titty looked back. Bridget, stooping down, was

coming slowly along, enticing Sinbad as she went.
There was no sign of anybody moving on the
meadows. John, Susan and Roger were not in
sight. By now, she thought they must be at the
other end of the island, somewhere beyond the
part she had already called the "prairie", where
a large herd of cows were calmly grazing, not
suspecting for a moment that they had been promoted to be buffaloes. The other party of explorers
would be coming round behind them. Whoever
had done those diggings might be between the
two parties, or somewhere in the middle of the
island. She turned her telescope on the buffaloes.
Yes, some of them had stopped grazing, but they
were looking all in the same direction, not towards
the middle of the island but the other way. They
must have sighted the surveying party. Not a
single buffalo seemed to be interested in anything between them and herself. It was safe to
go forward.

"Bridget," she called, not very loud. "Pick up
Sinbad and come along."

"Wait for us," called Bridget.

"Hurry up."

Titty looked first one way and then the other
along the green dyke. She looked across the wide
flat meadowland. There was not a moving thing to
be seen. No. Yes. Those were rabbits close to the
railing that enclosed the native kraal. But the rabbits were peaceably feeding. And the birds, too, all
seemed busy about their own affairs. Those must
be pigeons near the kraal. Those were peewits
on the meadows. Well, there are no fussier birds
than peewits when human beings are about, but

these seemed not to have a care in the world. No. They were quite safe in moving on. There was no danger of any savages cutting them off from the camp. And John, Susan and Roger must be much more than half-way round by now. It ought to be safe to go as far as the promontory.

"Come on, Bridget. . . . There's something we've got to go and look at."

"Where?" asked Bridget. "Those birds?" She looked out over the mud, following Titty's pointing finger.

"Don't hold your arm out," said Titty. "Just in case somebody might be watching us. Point like this, if you have to." She crooked her wrist, and pointed with a finger, her hand held close in against her body. "Not the birds. Someone's been out there on the mud."

Already she was moving on, along the top of the grass dyke, that divided the meadowland from the reedy saltings and the shining mud beyond them. She could see that line of diggings leading over the mud towards the point. From there she would be able to see just what those marks were like, that made a trail from digging to digging. Would they be the prints of naked feet? Or did these savages wear boots?

As she came nearer to the point, she noticed something else. At long intervals a withy, a thin, leafless sapling, was stuck upright in the mud. There was one, and then another beyond that, a long line of them leading away over the mud towards the mainland. As she came nearer she saw that they marked a cart track.

"That's how the native from the farm gets to the

town to do his shopping," she said to Bridget. "He
gets across at low water, when the tide's out like
this. And then when the tide comes up if it isn't
too deep he comes splashing across in his horse
and cart, and those little trees show him where
the road is. That's what he meant when he said
he'd come across the Wade."

"Oh," said Bridget. "Was it him that was digging
in the mud?"

"We'll soon know," said Titty. "We'll look at
those footmarks. The native was wearing seaboots, just like ours. But ... I say ... Giminy
... The native never made tracks like those."

She waited for Bridget no longer, but ran forward. There was something very funny about
those footmarks. They seemed ... She hardly
knew what they seemed. The boots of the native
had certainly been big, but she did not think a boot
had ever been made to make prints as big as these.

Bridget, clutching the unwilling Sinbad, panted
up to find Titty staring at huge round marks in
the mud. Yes. They were a track all right, but
what native could leave huge round footprints
nearly two feet wide? Two lines of these enormous
prints, two double lines, lay on the mud stretching
far away till they disappeared at the edge of the
incoming tide.

"Giminy," said Titty. "They aren't human footprints at all. They're the hoofmarks of a mastodon." She looked across towards the mainland.
Those marshes might stretch for miles. Anything
might live in them and nobody would know.

"What's a mastodon?" said Bridget. "A sort
of savage?"

"THE NATIVE NEVER MADE TRACKS LIKE THOSE..."

"No. A sort of elephant."

"With a trunk?"

"Yes. Hairy all over."

"Horrible?" Bridget looked at the huge prints on the mud and then anxiously over her shoulder.

"No. Gorgeous," said Titty, hurriedly.

"Oh. Then it's all right," said Bridget.

"Quite all right," said Titty, though she did not think so.

"Hullo!"

They had gone down to the edge of the mud to have a closer look at the hoofmarks, but at that shout Titty ran up again to the top of the dyke. Yes. There they were, John, Susan and Roger, coming along on the other side of the point. She beckoned eagerly.

In another two minutes they joined her. Roger was telling her their news long before they arrived. "We've been all round," he shouted. "We've been to the kraal. We've been to the edge of the sea. We've seen those anchored dhows. And there are islands. Lots of them. Some all sand. Some just marshy, with bushes on them. And there's a huge lot of blackberries close to our camp. What's the matter?"

John as he came was looking at his map. "We've got all the bearings clear," he called out. "We've just got to work them out with the rulers. I say, what is it?"

"Come and look," said Titty.

John and Roger dumped surveying instruments and bamboo poles on the top of the dyke, and ran down to the edge of the mud. The others followed.

"What on earth are they?" said John.

"It's a sort of elephant," said Bridget. "Titty says it's quite all right."

"The hoofmarks of a mastodon," said Titty. "At first I thought they were the footprints of a savage, but they can't be."

"Too big," said John, peering about on the ground. "It's by itself, whatever it is. There's no sign of a human being."

"Perhaps there was a human being on its back," said Roger.

He ran out on the mud to have a nearer look, and instantly sank to the top of his boots. He floundered, trying to pull out first one foot and then the other. He fell forward on his hands and lifted them, black to the elbow, dripping and shiny.

"Oh, Roger!" cried Susan.

"Black gloves," said Bridget.

"Come out, Roger!" said Susan.

"I'm coming," said Roger. He tugged mightily, left one boot in the mud, then the other, sank to his knees, lost both socks, and staggered ashore. He put up a dripping black hand to brush the hair out of his eyes, and grinned at them, a sort of piebald negro.

John, stepping with great care, sinking deep but keeping his balance, rescued Roger's boots and threw them to the foot of the sea wall. It was no use even trying to rescue the socks. John, balancing himself with his arms, had a good look at those enormous prints. Then, slowly, using his hands to keep his boots on, he rejoined the others.

"It's very rum," he said. "The thing can't be

a mastodon or any kind of elephant, or it would have sunk in deeper than Roger or me. Those hoofmarks hardly go in at all."

"Whatever it is, it's alive," said Titty.

"I've got most of the mud out of the inside," said Roger, who had been wiping out his boots with a handful of grass.

"We'll never get them properly dry," said Susan. "Come along. Let's get back to the camp."

"It must be nearly time to put another mealstick in the dial," said Roger.

"And Sinbad's thinking about that milk," said Bridget.

Titty felt a little disappointed. Nobody seemed to take those hoofmarks seriously.

She showed John her map.

"Jolly good," said John. "We can check it by taking bearings from that place where the dyke turns round at right angles. Half a minute. We want a bearing to see how that road to the mainland lies over the mud."

"I'm going to put in the buffaloes," said Titty. "And we'll have to call all this the Red Sea." She waved her hand towards the muddy plain with the cart road across it with withies sticking up. Already the water was creeping over the mud towards the road, a tongue of water from the east moving slowly on to meet another tongue of water from the west.

"Why?" said Roger.

"Pharaoh and the Israelites," said Titty. "Just the place for them. The waters divide when the tide goes down and they can rush across where those sticks mark the road, and then the water comes back from both ends and joins and sweeps them away, chariots and all."

"Right you are," said John. "Red Sea. I've put down the ford. That's what he means by the Wade. At high water we'll take *Wizard* and sail across it."

"If it's safe to leave the island," said Titty. "We haven't seen any savages yet. But what about those mastodon marks? They must have been made by something."

"Not a mastodon anyway," said John.

"Well, if it isn't a mastodon, what is it?"

"We'll keep a look-out," said John, "and see if we can find any more. But I think the native was just rotting. I don't believe there's a single savage about. I say, come on. Susan and Bridget are miles ahead."

Susan, thinking more of the explorers' dinner than of strange hoofprints, had picked up Sinbad and was hurrying back to the camp with Bridget close behind her, keeping up with two steps and a run. The others followed.

"Don't go so fast," said Roger. "It's awful with bare feet."

Ten minutes later he had forgotten they were bare. Susan had hardly reached the camp before they heard the frantic blast of the mate's whistle, and saw her beckoning, looking first one way and then the other and then waving again. She was not making proper signals. But anybody could see that what she meant was "Come as quick as you jolly well can." Something serious had happened. John, Titty and even Roger, covered with mud and carrying boots as well as a bamboo pole, broke into a run.

Susan was standing by the fireplace, pointing. Bridget was close to her, as close as she could get.

Susan had a finger to her lips. "Sorry," she whispered. "I oughtn't to have whistled. Someone's been in the camp. Look at that!"

A stick, painted red and green and blue, and carved so that it looked like a snake, with a long narrow head, was stuck upright in the ground. Round the neck of the snake were hung four small yellow shells.

"Gosh!" said John. "What about our boat?"

He put down compass and drawing board and bamboo poles, and raced down to the edge of the saltings, Titty, Roger, and Susan close behind.

"I'm coming too," shouted Bridget, and Susan waited for her.

The tide was rising in Goblin Creek. The *Wizard* was as they had left her, with her anchor well up on the saltings. There was still a strip of mud between her and the water.

"The mastodon," cried Titty. "It's been here too."

From the edge of the saltings, close by the *Wizard*, a double line of those same enormous prints crossed the mud.

"Look, look," shouted Roger. "Too late. . . . "

"What? Where?"

Roger was pointing. "A boat. I saw it. It was just going behind the other island."

The others looked up the Creek where Roger was pointing.

"We can't see it now," said Roger. "It simply disappeared into the land."

"Are you sure?" said John.

"As eggs is eggs," said Roger.

WHAT SUSAN FOUND IN THE CAMP

"Who was in the boat?"

"I didn't see that," said Roger. "I just saw the stern of the boat disappear. We'd be seeing it now if it wasn't for the land being in the way."

"Come on," said John. "We've got to get *Wizard* down to the water."

In another minute he had coiled the muddy anchor rope in the bows, and Roger, barefooted, and Titty and he were hauling *Wizard* down along the edge of the little hard where the tops of the old piles showed above the mud and there was ground firm enough to let people move without getting stuck.

"Look here, John," said Susan. "Are you sure we ought?"

"We must," said John. "If it's just a native, it won't matter. But if it's savages, we've simply got to know where we are. That snake wasn't stuck in our camp for nothing."

"And we *must* find out what makes those marks," said Titty.

John stopped. "There may be more of them about," he said. "Look here, Susan. Will you and Bridget guard the camp. . . . ?"

"Susan," said Bridget. "We've left Sinbad all alone there."

"And do look at the shadow on the meal-dial," said Roger. "I bet it's short enough for dinner time. Put a stick to mark the place. We'll be extra hungry after hunting mastodons."

John and Titty were already in the boat.

"Sit on the bows, Roger," said John, "and wash your hoofs over the side. We've got enough mud in already."

The *Wizard* slid off into deep water. John spun her round, and with quick strong strokes of his oars and no splashes, rowed up the creek. Roger splashed first with one foot and then with the other, and his legs showed white again, as if he had been tearing black stockings off them.

"Quiet, Roger," said Titty. "What's the good of John being quiet if you make such a row."

"Keep a good look out," said John. "Don't talk. Titty, you make a compass of your hand, pointing which way the boat's nose ought to go. They may be close round the corner. If they hear somebody shouting 'Pull right' and 'Pull left' they'll know we're after them and get away altogether."

CHAPTER VIII

THE MASTODON'S LAIR

TITTY sat in the stern of *Wizard*, holding one hand just above her knees, pointing, now a little to the right, now a little to the left, so that John, watching it, need not look over his shoulder to see where he was going, and could give his whole mind to driving the boat along and getting his oars in and out of the water without a splash. The tide had still a long way to rise, and they could see nothing on either side but brown mud and the green line of grass and weeds against the sky.

The small island was still joined to their own by mud. The creek bent round it on its way to the Red Sea. Nothing seemed to be moving on the water.

"Over there. Over there," whispered Roger. "That's where it must have gone."

Titty's hand pointed suddenly sharp to the right. John backwatered with his left oar and the boat spun half round. Now, for the first time, he looked over his shoulder.

In the bend of the creek, opposite the little island, was an opening. John rowed straight for it and they shot into a narrow gully far below the level of the marshes.

"There's hardly room to row," whispered Roger. "Look out, Titty, I'll have to scull over the stern."

Titty and John changed places, and John with quick twisting strokes, drove the boat on into the

gully. There was mud close on either side of them,
and beyond the mud, steep banks with great holes
where lumps had fallen away.

"It's pretty shallow," whispered John. "I was
on the bottom just then. There it is again."

They turned another corner.

"There's the boat," whispered Roger. "But
there's nobody in it."

John gave up sculling and poled the *Wizard*
forward as well as he could, though the oar
stuck in the mud when he pushed at it. The
Wizard touched the mud, and stopped, only a few
feet from a small brown rowing boat. Beyond the
rowing boat was mud only. A rope ran from the
boat to the side of the gully, and at the end of it
they could see a small anchor, high on the bank.
Whoever or whatever had been in that boat had
made it fast before leaving it. But he or it had
not landed, at least, not here. Again they saw
those huge prints, a plain trail of them, two lines
of enormous round hoofmarks leading from the
water towards the anchor, and then away from
the bank and on round another corner, along the
muddy bottom of the gully.

"We'd better get ashore," said Roger.

John prodded downwards with his oar, and
brought it up black and dripping. "We can't land
here," he said. "We'd only sink. We've got to get
back. I saw a place where I think we could, just
after we left our creek."

Titty with an oar at the bows, John with an
oar at the stern, drove the *Wizard* back along
the gully, till the water was wide enough to turn
in. Near the mouth of the gully they came to the

place John had seen, where some of the bank had
fallen down. They prodded the fallen earth. It was
a good deal harder than the mud. One by one they
scrambled ashore. John took the anchor with him
and planted it in the top of the bank. They found
themselves on a dyke like the one that ran all
round their own island.

"She'll be all right here," said John looking
down at the *Wizard*. "The tide's coming in the
whole time. It won't be so hard getting back into
her."

"We haven't got any weapons," said Titty.

"Shan't want any," said John. "We're not attack-
ing. Only scouting. We've just got to find out."

From the top of the high bank he looked back
across Goblin Creek to the island they had left.
There were the tents and smoke from the fire.
Everything looked peaceful. He could even see
that Bridget was walking backwards, probably
pulling something along the ground for Sinbad.
War, even awkwardness with strangers, was the
last thing he wanted. But that carved snake in
the camp meant something. Strangers had been
there. And there was that boat and those enormous hoofmarks. There was nothing for it but to
go on.

"It'll get away if we're not quick," said Titty.

"Come on," said John, and they hurried along
the top of the dyke looking down into the gully.
They passed the anchored rowing boat, and hurried on, their eyes on the trail of huge hoofmarks,
in the mud below them.

"I say," said Titty. "Look at that. It's the
wreck of a ship."

The gully was bending round, and ahead of them a lot of gaunt black timbers were sticking up above the mud.

"An old barge," said John.

"She must have been here hundreds of years," said Titty. "Just bones of her left."

Then, as they came nearer, they saw that though the stern part of the barge and the middle had all been broken or rotted away, the bows, close under the bank, still looked like the bows of a seagoing ship. The forepart was still decked. There was a rusty windlass, and a hatch, and the heavy tabernacle that once had held the mast. A rusty chain ran through a hawsehole in the bulwarks, over the dyke, to a rusty anchor bedded in the meadow. The sides of the old barge had fallen away aft, but forward they had been newly tarred. There was a small square window below the bulwarks. And someone had put new paint, blue, and yellow, on the scrollwork round the barge's name, the bright red letters of which looked as if they were hardly dry.

"*Speedy*," said Roger. "She won't go very fast now."

"Never again," said Titty, thinking of water foaming under those old black bows now wedged into the mud.

"They must have just shoved her out of the way here, and left her to rot," said John.

"But why have they bothered to put new paint on her name?"

"Both sides," said Titty, who had walked on till she could see the other side of the barge's stem. "I say, John. There are no more hoofmarks on this side." She lowered her voice. "Perhaps it's lurking in the wreck."

"There's a regular path on the marshes over there," said John. "He's probably got away ... What's that? Listen."

There was a noise of splitting wood.

"It's inside," said Roger.

"Keep quiet," said John.

"If it's natives," said Titty, "we could just ask if they've seen it."

"Seen what?"

"A mastodon," said Titty, "Or whatever it is that makes those hoofmarks."

"Hullo," said Roger. "Somebody must be living here. Look at that."

A thick cloud of yellow smoke had poured suddenly out from the top of a rusty iron pipe that stuck up through the deck close by the ancient windlass. Knee deep in the rank grass of the dyke, they stood and stared and sniffed the pungent smell. There could be no doubt about it. One end of the wreck was derelict, but the other was still in use. That new tar on the bows, the new paint on the name, and now this smoke from the chimney, showed that, even if the *Speedy* would never sail again, even if it was only a matter of time before most of her would fall apart and disappear in the mud, someone still had a use for part of her. One end of her was wholly dead, but the other was very much alive. It was as if they had come across a skeleton and on looking at the skull had been greeted with a wink.

They stood there, looking up and down the

SPEEDY

narrow winding gully, across it to the marshes of
the mainland, to distant fields, trees, and farms,
back towards the Secret Water, and Goblin Creek,
and their own camp on the other side of it. They
could see flashes of white, the tops of their tents
along the dyke. But near by everything was wild
and desolate, marshes, the creek that was more
like a ditch than a creek, mud, and the derelict
old barge. And here, with not a human being in
sight except themselves, there was smoke pouring from that rusty chimney, and the noise of
splitting wood had changed to the crackle of a
new lit fire.

"Someone's looking at us," whispered Roger.
"I saw a face ... it's gone now ... someone was
looking at us through that window."

"We'd better clear out," said John. "It isn't
our island."

"Couldn't we just ask?" said Roger.

But John had turned and was walking back
along the top of the dyke. "It'd be all right if we
were afloat," he said to Titty. "We could row up
here at high water, and try to get out the other
side, to see if it's really an island. Whoever it is
may be on deck then, swabbing down or something. . . ."

"I say!"

A boy had come through the *Speedy*'s fore (and
only) hatch. Bigger than Roger though not as tall
as John, he was dressed in a rather ragged grey
jersey and his muddy grey trousers were tucked
into socks. He had a mop of stiff sandy hair. His
eyes shone bright blue in a face burnt brick red
by the sun.

"Where are his boots?" said Roger. "Has he got stuck too?"

"Hullo," said John.

"I say," said the boy. "Is that your camp over there? Sorry I barged in. I thought you were somebody else. As soon as I saw you coming I tried to clear out. I thought you hadn't seen me."

"We didn't," said Roger. "But we saw your boat."

"We wanted to know what made those hoof-marks on the mud," said Titty. "Do you keep it in the barge?"

The boy laughed and then was serious again.

"I left something behind in your camp," he said.

"I know," said John.

"I meant to come and take it away again after dark."

"Oh! He mustn't do that," exclaimed Titty. "He'd only frighten Bridget."

"We'll give it back," said John.

"We wondered what it was," said Titty.

The boy opened his mouth to speak and shut it again. "Just a game," he said after a pause.

For some moments nobody said anything. Then the boy spoke again.

"Look here," he said. "Do you know the Lapwings?"

"I saw lots this morning," said Roger, "when we were walking round the island."

"Not those," said the boy. "*Lapwing*'s a yacht. Look here. How did you get here? I never saw you come. I wasn't here yesterday."

"We came in a boat," said John.

"You didn't know about the Lapwings?"

"No. We've never been here before."

"I thought it was rum," said the boy. "Because they said they were going to camp on Flint Island as usual. But when I saw your camp I was sure they'd changed their minds. I didn't think anybody else knew about this place."

"We didn't," said Titty. "We're exploring. We aren't exactly shipwrecked. But we can't get away till our ship comes back. We're marooned."

"Marooned," said the boy, considering. "Do they know at the farm?" He looked far away across Goblin Creek, to the island beyond it.

"In the Native Kraal?" said Titty. "They know. One of them brought us some milk this morning, but that was just to see what we were like. We've got our own milk, in tins."

"Kraal's a good word," said the boy. "My father's got a Kraal, too. Over there." He pointed south over the marshes. "You can't see it. Hidden by the trees. So it's just as good as if it wasn't there. There's nobody here except just them . . . " Again he looked away towards the distant farm, a bit of tiled roof showing above the little trees. "Only the Lapwings and me . . . until you came."

John said, "Look here, I'll go and bring that thing if you put it up in our camp by mistake."

"Never mind," said the boy. "I'll come across and fetch it."

"Do you live here?" asked Roger.

The boy considered.

"Like to come and see?" he said at last.

"Very much," said John.

"It's too far to jump," said Roger.

But the boy stooped and from below the bulwarks lifted a broad plank and stood it on end,
and then let it fall forward so that it made a
bridge between the wreck and the dyke.

"Make sure that end's firm," he said.

Roger was first on the plank. Titty had taken
a step or two after him when he stopped dead.

"Look out, Titty," he said. "If two of us are on
it, it'll jump and Susan'll be in an awful stew if I
go in the mud again."

"It'd be a job to get you out," said the boy.

One by one they crossed the plank and stepped
down on the wreck. It was like standing on the
deck on a ship of which nothing was left but the
bows. Looking aft, there were gaunt ribs sticking
up out of the mud, and the remains of the stern.
But where they were standing, everything was
solid. The deck was scrubbed and clean and there
was new paint on the bulwarks that ended in mid
air.

"I began looking after her just in time," said
the boy. "Look here. I'd better go first, just to
clear things out of the way down below."

He slid out of sight, backwards, down the steep
ladder in the hatchway. The others followed him,
one by one, and, for a moment stood blinking at
the foot of the ladder. A lot of light came down
through the hatch, and a little from each of the
two small square windows that had been cut high
up in the sides. But all the woodwork was black
with age, and it was a minute or two before they
could see what sort of living place this was that
the boy had made for himself in the bows of the old
wreck. There was a rusty little stove, into which

the boy was pushing some scraps of wood. There
was a sort of bunk, built into the side with rugs
in it. There was a table made of thick black wood,
roughly nailed together. "Made that out of some of
the old planking," said the boy proudly, and John
thought, though he did not say, that it might very
well have been rather better made. There was a
good solid seat that had clearly once been the
thwart of a boat. There were shelves, very rough,
along the walls. An old hurricane lantern, not lit,
hung from a beam. There were nails driven into
the beams, and into the walls, and from these
nails hung all kinds of things, fishing lines on
wooden winders, a net of some kind, begun but
not finished, with a big wooden needle, half full
of string, stuck in among the meshes. In one
corner were some fishing rods, and beside them,
leaning against the wall of the cabin, were three
more carved sticks, like the one they had found
stuck in the ground by Susan's fireplace. Roger
saw them first.

"More snakes?" he said.

"Eels really," said the boy. "Snakes don't have
a fin down their backs."

"I thought there was something funny about
it for a snake," said Titty.

"What are they for?" asked John.

"They're . . . " and then the boy pulled himself
up. He had just been going to say something, but
changed his mind.

"Don't tell us if it's a secret," said Titty. "Is the
thing that makes those hoofmarks secret too?"

The boy threw back his head and laughed.
"Don't you know splatchers?" he said.

"Splatchers?" said Roger.

"Splatchers," said the boy. "For walking on the mud."

"Gosh!" said Roger. "Like snowshoes?"

"I'll show you," said the boy. "I always leave them outside so as not to get mud all over old *Speedy*. It's only at high tide the water comes up here, and I couldn't get home without them, or get to my boat, or anything."

"They make marks just like a mastodon," said Titty.

"I've never seen one," said the boy.

"Neither have I," said Titty. "But like an elephant anyway."

The boy busied himself with his fire, took a saucepan from its hook on the wall, and opened a parcel with bacon in it. They watched him. "Susan's cooking our dinner," Roger said absently.

Titty looked at John.

"I say," said John. "Why not come back with us now to get your eel and have dinner. Unless you *want* to cook. We've got an enormous lot of grub."

"I don't mind," said the boy. "And if you want to see those splatchers. . . . "

They climbed on deck once more. The boy went to the edge of the deck furthest from the bank. A rope ladder hung there, and beside it, on hooks, were the splatchers, two large oval boards, with rope grips in the middle of them for heel and toe, and stout leather straps for fasteners. The boy unhooked them and dropped them neatly so that they fell flat on the mud with their fastenings uppermost. He hauled on a pair of seaboots and went down the rope ladder.

"Mud's very soft here," he said. "If I didn't drop them first I wouldn't be able to stand to get them on."

With his weight on one of the splatchers, he put his foot in the right place on the other and made it fast. Then with his weight on that splatcher he strapped the other on the other foot.

"Now," he said, and was off, swinging each leg in a wide circle so as not to trip himself with the big oval boards on his feet. Off he went, with a loud sucking noise, as he lifted the splatchers from the mud, one two, one two, one two, one two, leaving behind him the mastodon track of enormous hoofmarks. Off he went, swinging his legs, running easily along the muddy bottom of the creek where they knew the mud was so soft that in ordinary seaboots he could not have taken a step without being bogged.

He turned and came running back, left his splatchers on the mud, climbed up his rope ladder and, a little out of breath was once more beside them on the deck of the old barge.

"Gosh!" said Roger. "Can anybody do it?"

"It needs a bit of practice," said the boy. "I'll get the plank in, if you'll go ashore. I never leave it up when I'm not here."

"Are there other savages?" said Titty.

"I say. Did he tell you?"

"Who?"

"The man from the farm . . . the Kraal."

"He said there was one of them about," said Titty. "Is it you?"

"Oh well," said the boy. "If you know that. . . . He oughtn't to have told you really."

SPLATCHERS

"Sorry," said Titty. "We didn't know the savages were a secret. We'll pretend we don't know. We'll just call you the Mastodon."

"My name's Don," said the boy.

"Short for Mastodon," said Titty.

The boy laughed. "It doesn't matter your knowing about savages," he said. "At least I don't think so. If you've been marooned, it's really right for you to know."

A shrill whistle sounded in the distance.

"Grub," said Roger, hurrying across the plank. "That's the mate's whistle."

"I'll catch you up," said the boy. "Where's your boat?"

"Close to yours."

Titty and John followed Roger ashore and along the high bank above the gully. The boy pulled in the plank, slipped down the other side of the wreck, and, hardly a moment later, they saw him running below them on the mud with that queer swinging run, leaving behind him a beautiful trail of mastodon hoofmarks. By the time they reached their boat, he was already in his, and they pulled out into Goblin Creek close together.

Roger was first ashore on the other side, and ran up to the camp.

"Extra plate, Susan," he shouted. "Extra plate. The Mastodon's coming to dinner."

CHAPTER IX

MAKING A FRIEND OF A SAVAGE

"OH bother!" said Susan, but not very loud.

"What's it like?" said Bridget.

But Susan had darted to the stores tent and was digging out another soup plate. The trouble was that she had already poured out the soup into five plates and there was none left in the saucepan. Roger had said enough to let her know that whatever the Mastodon might be, it ate like ordinary people, and she had to spoon a little soup from each of the five full plates into the sixth before the guest arrived. To see this being done would make any guest wish he had not come.

She was just in time. Six plates, each practically full of soup, lay in a row by the fire when John, Titty and the Mastodon followed Roger across the saltings and came to the dyke and the camp.

"Titty," said Bridget, "it isn't true."

"What isn't?"

The Mastodon was shaking hands with Susan and did not hear her answer: "You said he had a trunk."

But the next minute she had decided that he had a nice grin, and was shaking hands with him herself, though, looking closely at him, she saw that he was not very hairy either.

"Do sit down," said Susan.

The Mastodon looked uneasily at the carved

101

stick which was still in the ground where he had stuck it.

"I say," he said. "You know I'm awfully sorry for butting into your camp. I thought it was somebody else's. I'll take the totem away."

"Is that what it is?" said Titty. "Is it the totem of a whole tribe?"

"Four of us, really," said the Mastodon. "We count their grown-ups missionaries."

"He can run over the mud like a duck," said Roger, and after taking his first mouthful of soup, put his plate down and jumped to his feet. "I say, Susan, you forgot," he said. The sun was high overhead, and the stick in the middle of the meal-dial cast a very short shadow. In that short shadow Roger planted the cleft stick that had already been made for the purpose, wrote "DINNER" on a bit of paper and wedged it in the cleft.

"We haven't got a clock with us," said John.

"It's so that we get regular meals," said Roger.

"It's a fine idea," said the Mastodon.

"Why is your totem an eel?" said Titty.

"Mud everywhere," said the Mastodon. "Eels like it, and so do we. And we catch eels and eat them and get eelier and eelier. There's nothing much else you can catch except flatfish and they're dull. But eels can wriggle through anything and out of anything. An eel's a jolly good totem to have when you don't want to get into trouble with the missionaries. . . . Not that they're half bad," he added.

"To eat?" asked Roger.

"Not the missionaries," grinned the Mastodon.

"We've never tried. No. I meant the missionaries aren't bad. They come round from Colnsea in a yacht and anchor by Flint Island and they put the rest of the tribe ashore in tents. And the Eels have each got a boat."

"Sailing boats?" said Titty.

"Little ones," said the Mastodon. "Dinghies."

"We've seen them," said Roger.

"What rot," said John. "Of course we haven't."

"Yes we have. Pudding faces," he added half under his breath.

"What's their yacht like?" asked John.

"Square sterned cutter. Painted yellow. White sails. *Lapwing*'s her name. They've taken her to Pin Mill to have something done to her deck."

"We *have* seen them," said John. "They were at Pin Mill yesterday and the day before. We saw the three dinghies go alongside."

"What did you call them?" the Mastodon asked Roger.

"Well," said Roger. "I called them pudding faces. But that was only because they had boats and we hadn't. Not then. I wasn't near enough to see what their faces were like."

"Good names for savages," said the Mastodon, "but they're Eels really. I thought they were still at Pin Mill, and then, when I saw your camp, I thought they must have come in yesterday while I was away."

"Why do you say they're eels?" said Roger.

The Mastodon hesitated. Then the words came with a rush.

"Oh look here," he said. "If you're marooned it won't matter a bit your knowing. Your being

explorers makes it right too. They always shove
a bit in their books about savage rites and so on.
That's how we got the idea. The others won't
mind. I'll explain to them. You see the eel is the
totem of the Children of the Eel. That's the name
of the tribe. But it's an awful secret. Even the
missionaries don't know. You see if they did they
might feel they ought to stop us having human
sacrifices."

"What?" Even Susan was startled at this.

"We do it every summer holidays," said the Mastodon. "You know, a good big fire, and necklaces
dangling from the totems, and tomtoms going, and
a corroboree and everyone dancing like mad and
the victim waiting to be sacrificed."

"Who's the victim?" said Roger.

"Daisy," said the Mastodon. "She's a bit skinny,"
he added, "to make a really good victim. But she's
the best we've got. . . . "

He was looking almost enviously at the plump
Bridget as he spoke. Everybody noticed it. His
words faded off into silence.

"Bridget's not going to be a sacrifice," said
Susan hurriedly.

"She'd make a perfect beauty," said the boy.
"She's much smaller than Daisy and much . . .
well, you know what I mean. Some people can't
help being thin. It doesn't matter generally but
savages stuff their victims like anything. And of
course if we were a different tribe it wouldn't
matter. . . . With Herons for instance, scragginess
would be all right . . . but the Eels' victim ought to
be fat. Of course I should have to ask the others,
but I don't believe Daisy would mind. The savages

would come charging down on the explorers' camp, pick the plumpest. . . . "

"Oh no, you can't have Bridget," said Roger.

"If you did want one of us for a victim," said Susan, "you'd better take me or John."

"I wouldn't mind," said Roger.

"Anybody but Bridget," said Titty. "All right, Bridget. Don't go and cry. Nobody's going to make you a human sacrifice."

"I think you're beasts," said Bridget. "You always make out I'm too young for everything. And now Daddy and Mummy have let me come. They think I'm old enough. And you won't let me be a human sacrifice when somebody wants me. . . . "

"Do you really want to?" asked Susan.

"Oh do let her," said Titty. "She'll be all right."

"Why shouldn't she if she wants to?" said Roger.

"All right, Bridget," said John. "If you're jolly good, and always do what the mate tells you. . . . "

"And never forget to say 'Aye, aye, sir'," put in Roger.

Bridget cheered up and looked hopefully at the Mastodon.

"I think it'll be all right," he said. "But I'll have to ask the others first."

"Chops in the same plates," said Susan. "We always do if we can to save washing up," she added, remembering that the Mastodon was a visitor and not one of the crew.

By the time bananas had followed the chops the explorers and the savage knew a good deal about each other. He had heard something, not much, about their North Sea adventure. He was very pleased. "That makes it much better," he said. "They can't object when they know you've come from Holland quite lately. Coming across the sea makes you properly explorers." He was thinking all the time of the other savages. "You see," he said. "We've all promised to keep it secret. They're awfully keen not to have crowds of people coming in and spoiling everything."

"That's just what we felt when we thought strangers had been camping on Wild Cat," said Titty.

"Wild Cat?" said the Mastodon, and they told him of the lake in the north, and the camp on that rocky, wooded little island, and the alliance with the Amazon Pirates.

"Do you do signalling too?" asked Roger.

"Rockets," said the Mastodon.

"Morse?" said Roger. "And semaphore, with flags?"

"Savages don't."

"We do," said Roger.

"It's all right for explorers," said the Mastodon. "Not for savages. We've got our own way."

"Awfully useful for secret messages," said Titty. She dived into her tent, and brought out Nancy's message, with the skull and crossbones in one corner, and the row of dancing figures. She showed it to the boy, keeping her finger over the letters that John had written under each of the dancing figures.

"Looks like a corroboree," said the boy.

"It's a message," said Titty. She took her finger away, and showed the letters. "It says 'Three million cheers'."

"What does it mean?" said the boy.

"Well," said Titty. "We don't know. Something they've done, probably. Nancy couldn't have known what was going to happen here."

"She couldn't have guessed we were going to have a Mastodon to dinner," said Roger. "We didn't know it ourselves."

John showed the boy Daddy's rough pencilled map of the islands and the Secret Water.

The Mastodon looked at it with care.

"But it's wrong," he said pointing with a finger. "There's a way through there at high water. That's an island, not just a cape. And you can get miles inland if you go on past the mouth of this creek. And there are two islands there, not one. . . . And . . . "

"That's just it," said John. "We're going to get it all properly mapped before they come back to take us away."

"It'll take a long time," said the Mastodon. "With only one boat."

John showed him the work done that morning, the rough map of the island they were on, with bearings laid down from point to point all round the sea wall.

The Mastodon considered. "Jolly good," he said. "But what about the channel between the island and the mainland?"

"We were going to sail round," said John. "You couldn't see it properly from the dyke."

"You'd have a job to find it anyway," said the Mastodon. "And you ought to put in two channels not one. Three really. Look here. Let me help. Tide's up now. Let's go. We ought just

to be able to get round and back over the Wade
before the tide drops again."

"What's the Wade?" asked Roger.

"Road to the mainland," said the Mastodon.
"Under water when the tide's up."

"How long will it take?" said Susan.

"Ought to do it in an hour," said the Mastodon.
"If we go north about. That'll mean we're going
against the tide to the point, and we ought to
have it with us nearly to the Wade and then we'll
have the ebb this side of the watershed to bring
us home." He pointed on the map to the place
where they had seen the road over the mud, and
explained that the tide came up from both sides
to meet there, and poured back both ways when
the ebb began.

Titty and Roger were already on their feet.

"What about Sinbad?" said Bridget, and a
moment later, "Where *is* Sinbad?"

" 'Sh," said Titty at the door of her tent. "He's
gone to sleep."

Sinbad, his stomach round and full after his
dinner, had gone into Titty's tent and curled himself on her sleeping bag. His round fat stomach
rose and fell. Titty crawled in and without waking
him, lifted the blankets and pulled them together
to make a sheltering wall about the sleeping
kitten.

"He'll be all right for an hour or two," said
Susan.

"Tired, probably," said Titty. "He's done enough
exploring for one day."

They crossed the saltings and went down to
the boats. Already much of the old piling that

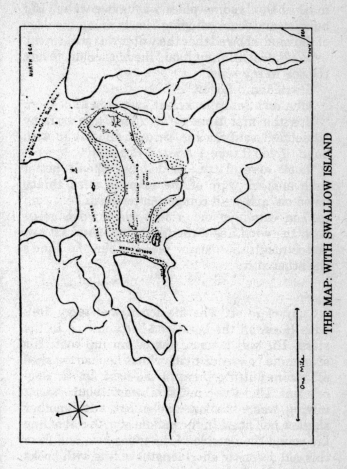

THE MAP: WITH SWALLOW ISLAND

marked the landing place was under water. But bubbles and foam, slipping slowly along the edge of the mud, showed that the water was still rising.

"We'll do it all right," said the Mastodon. "Who's coming in my boat?"

"I will," said Roger.

John and Susan looked at each other.

"It's the first time we've sailed this boat by ourselves," said Susan. "Bridget and I'll go with John, if you'll take Titty and Roger."

"Look here, Titty," said John. "You'd better take another copy of the map, to stick things down on, and we'll compare afterwards."

"You can give me a tow when we're going with the wind," said the Mastodon. "And I'll tow you through the narrow places when the wind's the other way."

*

They were off. The Mastodon was away first, with Roger in the bows and Titty sitting in the stern. His was a small, tarred rowing boat. His splatchers, clear of mud which he had washed off before putting them in the boat, lay at Roger's feet. Under the middle thwart, where he sat rowing, was a shallow wooden box, with another shallow box fitted in the middle of it. A coil of line lay round the outside of the inner box, and from this coil dozens of short lengths of line with hooks on them lay in notches in the sides of the inner box, so that all the hooks were in the middle, not touching each other and safe from getting tangled up with the main coil.

"What's that?" asked Titty.

"Eel line," said the Mastodon.

"Do you fish with minnows?" asked Titty, remembering fishing for perch on the lake.

"No," said the Mastodon. "Lugworms. If you lift that bit of sacking, you'll see them. Just behind your feet."

Titty stooped down. Under the seat in the stern was another shallow box, and her heel was just touching a piece of wet coarse canvas, that lay in the box like a blanket in a bed. She lifted a corner of it. Underneath it, on another layer of wet canvas, lay a squirming mass of the most horrible looking worms she had ever seen. Each worm seemed to be in two parts, one thin, tapering and shining, the other bloated and hairy.

Titty held the canvas for a moment, staring at them, and then, hurriedly closed it down again.

"Do eels like them?" she said.

"Don't they just? Flatfish, too, and whiting when they come up. It's harder work getting worms than catching fish when you've got them. I was digging two hours this morning to get that lot."

"Oh ... I see." Titty saw once more those mastodon tracks across the mud and the little heaps that had looked as if someone was making mud castles.

"We've got fishing things," said Roger.

"There's a good place at the mouth of the creek," said the Mastodon. "Specially at low tide."

Meanwhile John was getting up the *Wizard*'s sail, not too easily. They could see from the Mastodon's boat that things were not going quite right. Susan was lifting the boom clear and holding it up while John was pulling at something. They had made the ship's baby sit in the bottom of the boat.

"He's never set it before," said Titty, thinking that the Mastodon might be getting a poor idea of the explorer's seamanship. "Daddy set it for us yesterday. He's got it now." The sail was up, John was tidying ropes at the foot of the mast, Susan was steering, the *Wizard* was moving through the water and the head of the ship's baby showed above the gunwale. "That's all right."

The Mastodon laid to his oars, and they were soon out of the creek, and rowing along close to the northern shore of the island.

"Less tide close in," he said.

A narrow opening showed in the saltings. Titty with a pencil marked it on her map.

"Only a drain," said the Mastodon. "But you can't tell unless you go in and have a look. Even at high water you can't get more than a few yards up there. But the other place I told you about, on the other side of the island, doesn't look any bigger, and we've gone right through with the whole fleet, the Eels, I mean, and come out in the main channel on the other side."

"Do let's do it," said Titty.

"John's gone aground," said Roger.

The *Wizard*, following close behind them, was also dodging the tide, but John had forgotten that with her centreboard down she needed more water than the Mastodon's rowing boat. They saw him hauling the centreboard up a little way, and sheering out into the channel.

"Good enough wind," said the Mastodon. "She'll beat the tide easily."

"I say," said Roger. "Are we going right out to sea? It's out of bounds."

It did look like it. At the mouth of the Secret Water there was nothing to be seen but rippled blue water. The sands were covered, and far away on the horizon, they could see the tall brown sails of barges, and the smoke of a steamship.

"Only round the corner," said the Mastodon between strokes of his oars.

"Can't we pull for a bit?" said Titty.

"I'll stick to it till we get round into the other channel. Then we'll have the tide with us. Want to save every minute here."

Titty marked down the opening of another tiny creek or ditch running up into the saltings.

They came at last to the end of the island and cut across inside the crossroads buoy. Ahead of them was the island of shingle and bright yellow sand and the two or three yachts at anchor they had seen the day before. They were turning into the channel to the town.

"There are the dhows we saw yesterday," said Titty.

The Mastodon looked over his shoulder. "Traders," he said. "Probably slavers. But they haven't caught any of us yet. *Lapwing*'s not there. She usually anchors just in there and they make a camp close by. The sand dunes give them good shelter. The real reason they camp there," he added, "is because there's no chance of setting anything on fire. Good bathing too. It's the only sandy bit of beach for miles."

"We never set things on fire," said Roger. "We nearly got burnt once," he went on, but caught

Titty's eye and stopped. Oh well, perhaps she was right. The Mastodon might think it was showing off.

The *Wizard* turned the corner and came after them, rapidly catching them up.

"Can you throw them our painter?" asked the Mastodon.

Roger coiled the painter and threw it. Susan grabbed it, the panting Mastodon rested on his oars, and the *Wizard* took on the extra load.

"Did you see those two creeks?" called John.

"I marked them," called Titty. "But they don't go anywhere."

"They couldn't go far anyway," said John. "Because of the seawall. There isn't a gap in it. I say, is that the place you call Flint Island?"

"Yes," said the Mastodon.

"Why Flint?" asked Roger.

"Because if you land and go along the shore when the tide's out you've got a good chance of finding flint arrowheads and things. The missionaries collect them."

"Gosh!" said Titty. "Prehistoric?"

"Yes. We swop most of the ones we find for stores."

They passed the anchored yachts. The dyke on their right curved suddenly away and a creek opened into low weedy marshland.

"Is this the channel?" shouted John turning towards it.

"Not the main one," shouted the savage guide. "Look here. We'll do them both at once. You go straight on, and you'll find another opening, with a few more traders moored in it. Not the next one.

The first one you come to with boats in it. Go in there and keep in the middle. We'll go through this one and meet you. Tide's still flowing. We'll just be able to do it."

"Right. Cast off the top rope Mister Mate."

"Goodbye," shouted the ship's baby.

"Goodbye," shouted the able-seamen.

The Mastodon was already rowing. They shot in between marshy banks and weeds, and a moment later could see nothing of the *Wizard* but the top of her sail. Presently that too disappeared. The able-seamen were alone in his boat with the savage.

Roger looked a little anxiously at Titty, but remembered that after all, they were two to one, even if the Mastodon did look as if he would be pretty tough to fight if he happened to turn hostile to explorers. But the Mastodon seemed to have no such thoughts in his head. He was rowing as hard as he could between banks that were growing narrower and narrower.

"This tide isn't as high as it might be," he said. "We're going to have a job getting through."

CHAPTER X

THE STRAITS OF MAGELLAN

JUST for a moment, in the sudden loneliness that came when she realized that she could not see *Wizard*'s sail any more, Titty almost felt like saying that she thought it would be better if they all kept together. Suppose the savage were to live up to his totem. Eels. Slippery eels. You never knew where you had them. Supposing it was all a trick and the Mastodon, rowing as hard as he could along this narrow winding ditch where you could see nothing but reeds and mud, had planned an ambush. . . . Supposing round one of these corners they came upon a whole tribe. . . . Suppose others were lurking in these sodden patches of mud and reeds.

But the Mastodon, rowing fit to bust, did not look as if he were thinking of plots. Titty remembered that she was an explorer. She marked on her map the place where they had left the main channel and begun this queer voyage through the marshes. She could not measure the distances, and she had no compass to take bearings, so she turned the map over and, as the ditch twisted and turned, she drew a single line, now bending one way now the other, with every curve and wriggle of the ditch. It would be easy to fit it in afterwards.

"Which way do we go?" said Roger. "It divides in two."

The Mastodon stopped rowing, and his boat ran instantly aground. Just ahead of them the ditch turned into two ditches, one twisting to the right, the other to the left. Both seemed about the same size.

"Right I think," said the Mastodon. "But it's a long time since I've been through."

He pushed off from one side of the ditch with an oar, ran on the mud on the opposite side, pushed off from that, and rowed on. Titty marked on the back of the map the place where the ditch forked. Her line began to look as if she were making a drawing of zigzag lightning.

The ditch bent round to the right, and forked.

"Right again," said the Mastodon.

His oars almost touched the sides of the ditch as they passed through a narrow place.

A heron got up from close in front of them. Three wing flaps took it out of sight.

"I say," said Roger. "Isn't that the dyke?"

Ahead of them, above the reeds, was the straight line of a high grass-covered bank.

"Must have gone wrong at the last divide," said the Mastodon.

There was hardly room to turn, and Roger hopped out on a tussock of mud and weeds to pull the bows of the boat round.

The Mastodon rowed back to the last place where the ditch forked and this time took the turn to the left.

"Got to hurry," he said grimly. "Tide's stopped rising. We may be too late to get through."

"Hadn't we better go back to the main channel?" said Titty.

"Oh no," said the Mastodon. "We'll do it yet. We're all right this time."

"Hullo," said Roger a few minutes later. "It's come to an end."

The boat slid into a little pool and stopped. There was nothing ahead of them but mud and weeds, and no way out but the way by which they had come.

"Sorry," said the Mastodon, worked the boat round and started back. "We'll have to go right back to that first place where we ought to have gone left."

This time worry showed clearly on the face of the savage guide. Titty knew he was badly bothered.

"It's the tide," he said at last. "Going down. We don't want to get stuck."

"Hullo," said Titty. "Isn't there water through there?"

They had just passed a narrow drain, and Titty looking through the gap had seen something very like open water.

The Mastodon backed with both oars.

"It's worth trying," he said. "We could do it yet, if only we were in the right channel now."

He edged up to the muddy bank and scrambled out.

"Come on," he shouted. "It's the other channel. Quite near, if only we can get her through."

He jumped back, all muddy, into the boat, and tried to pole her into the gap. She moved in a few yards and stuck.

"She's aground," he said. "Look here. Could

you get out, both of you, and I'll try to lug her through?"

Roger, for the second time that day, got mud over his knees. Titty was luckier. They found themselves on a bit of soft boggy ground, and for the first time, were able to look round them and see what sort of place this was. Away to the right of them they could see the long dyke, curving round the island. Behind them, to the left of them and in front of them were saltings, reedy marshland, cut up into islands by narrow channels now, soon after high tide, full of water. Twenty yards away was a wider channel, and they could see that it wound its way towards water that was really open.

"Quick, quick," said Roger, jumping from one tussock of rank grass to another.

Titty followed him, and waited where the narrow drain widened into a bay at the side of the channel they had missed by taking the wrong turn.

"Here's a good place for getting in again," she said, "if only he can get the boat through."

"She's moving all right," said Roger.

They could not see her, but they could see the Mastodon, poling her along.

"Stuck again," said Roger. "Gosh! He's gone in."

The Mastodon had stepped out over the stern, and was pushing the boat before him.

"Why doesn't he sink?" said Roger. "He's got his splatchers on. Good old Mastodon. He's done it. Here she comes."

The boat slipped suddenly forward, and the Mastodon nearly fell. In a moment, he had his

splatchers off and was in his boat again, poling
with an oar. A moment after that she slid out
from the drain, and the explorers were getting
aboard once more.

"Never mind the mud," said the Mastodon. "I
can wash her out afterwards. If only we manage
to get through."

"Let me take an oar," said Titty.

"I can row," said Roger.

"I know her ways," said the Mastodon. "Better
let me. There isn't a minute to lose."

The weedy banks flew past them on either
side, but presently flew not so fast, though the
Mastodon was rowing just as hard, and the water
was foaming under the bows of his little boat.

"Tide's going out," he said between his teeth.

"There's *Wizard*," shouted Roger.

"That's mud," said the Mastodon. "There it
is again. We've got jolly little water under us."

"What would we do if we got properly stuck?"
asked Roger.

"Have to wait till the tide's gone out and
come up again enough to float us."

"After dark?" said Roger.

"Long after," said the Mastodon. "About three
o'clock in the morning. Good, good. Deeper water
already. But the others oughtn't to have waited
for us. They've got to get across the Wade. And
your boat's deeper than mine."

The *Wizard* was sailing slowly towards them in
the main channel, a wide stretch of water between
the reeds. Bridget was waving.

The Mastodon waved them on. John understood, and swung round. The wind had dropped

and the *Wizard* was sailing no faster than the Mastodon could row. Titty was hurriedly marking on the back of her map the channel through which they had come. "I'll just have to guess that bit where we went wrong," she said.

"Make it clear we ought to have turned left when I turned right," said the Mastodon. "Well," he said more cheerfully. "You see there are two ways through. Three really. The main channel's the way they went, but there's this other way inside it."

"Like Cape Horn and the Straits of Magellan," said Titty. "*Wizard*'s gone round the Horn, and we've come through the Straits."

"What happened?" asked John, as the two boats came nearer together.

"We got mixed up with Terra del Fuego," said Titty.

"We had a beautifully narrow squeak getting through," said Roger.

"Took a wrong turn," said the savage guide. "Look here, you oughtn't to have waited. It's going to be a squeak getting home across the Wade. You see it's a watershed, and the tide's going down."

"Had we better go back the way we came?" suggested Susan.

"Oh let's go right round," said Roger.

The Mastodon showed what he thought by laying to his oars and rowing on. The shores were widening on either side, and they were coming out into a broad lake of shimmering water which covered the sea of mud that they had seen in the morning. Here and there, ahead of them, a withy waved gently in the tide.

"Leave all those withies to starboard," called the Mastodon. "They mark the edge of the shallows on this side. Keep fairly near them."

The weed banks were further and further away and it was hard to believe that there was only a narrow channel of water deep enough for sailing. It looked as though they could sail for as far as they wanted in any direction.

"What are those other withies?" called John, pointing to some far away towards the mainland.

"They mark the road over the Wade," said the Mastodon. "There you are, right ahead. Those four posts that you can see above the water. That's the shallowest place. Deeper water either side of them. Hard bottom. Causeway right across."

They came nearer to the four posts, black posts, with a high water mark showing near the top of them. They came level with the posts. They passed them.

"That's that," said the Mastodon. "We'll have the tide with us now. . . . " His voice changed. "He's gone between the posts. . . . He's touched!"

They saw the *Wizard* stop dead. They saw John's face suddenly worried. They saw Susan jump to pull up the centreboard, as the *Wizard* swung round broadside and began to heel. Then the *Wizard* began to move again, came back on her course, and was presently gliding beside them.

"Narrow thing," said the Mastodon. "He oughtn't to have gone between the posts."

"I ought to have pulled the centreboard up before we got there," said John. "But she doesn't sail well without it unless the wind's dead aft."

They had no more trouble, but slipped slowly

homewards, watching the shore from which in the morning they had seen the hoofmarks of the Mastodon on the mud over which they were now sailing. There was the landing place belonging to the native kraal, there the cart track from the kraal coming over the seawall and down to the causeway the end of which was already beginning to show above water. Far away on the other side the Mastodon pointed out other withies marking a channel that at high water would let them reach the mainland.

They slipped slowly on. The weedbeds were coming nearer again. They were passing the little Bridget Island that at low water was part of their own. They were passing the opening of the channel that led to the old barge hulk, the Mastodon's private lair. They came round into Goblin Creek and back to the landing place below the camp from which they had started.

"Well," said John. "We've circumnavigated it. I've got an awful lot to put on the map. I say, there are several bits I want to ask you about."

"I've got a rough sketch of Magellan Straits," said Titty.

John looked at her.

"You went round Cape Horn," she said. "You'll see when we put it all in."

"I wonder if Sinbad'll be pleased to see us," said Bridget. "Coming back from a voyage."

They went up to the camp. Bridget peeped into Titty's tent.

" 'Sh!" she said. "He's still asleep."

"Not much good as a watch cat," said Roger.

But just then the kitten stirred, got up, and

walked slowly out, stretching its hind legs and the whole of its body as it came out of the tent.

"Are you a good watch cat?" said Titty.

The kitten rubbed against her leg, opened its mouth and mewed. "He wants some milk," said Bridget.

"All right, Sinbad," said Susan. "You shall have some. But you haven't really earned it."

John, Titty and the Mastodon flung themselves on the ground to compare maps, fitting the wriggling line of the Magellan Straits into the space east of the dyke that John had marked in the morning. An enormous lot of the big blob that in Daddy's rough map had seemed to be all one island had turned out to be marshes. "That's quite right," said the native guide. "That's where we ran up against the dyke and had to turn back. And that bit's another island. And so's that. And there's another way in between the two of them."

"Don't put it in," said Titty. "Not till we've sailed through it."

"I'll leave it just dotted," said John. "Between Magellan Straits and the Horn."

"What are we going to explore tomorrow?" asked Roger, who liked exploration better than mapping its results.

"Is that an island where we landed when we came to *Speedy*?" asked Titty. "You can't tell from Daddy's map whether it is or not."

"Yes," said the Mastodon. "And there are more further up. And islands on the northern shore. You can see the way in if you walk along the dyke."

"Let's go and look," said John. "Just half a

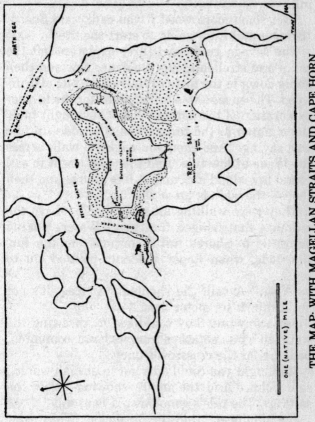

ONE (NATIVE) MILE

THE MAP: WITH MAGELLAN STRAITS AND CAPE HORN

minute while I copy this bit from my map into Daddy's. There'll be a good lot ready for Titty to ink."

"Get some more wood if you can," said Susan. "Bridget and I are going to start the fire."

The savage guide and three explorers left the camp and strolled along the dyke, now and then going down to the foot of it to pick up bits of drift-wood. The savage was full of plans for the further exploration of his native wilds. "You ought to do the channel to the town when the tide's up," he was saying. "And then you ought to walk across the Wade at low tide. And then you ought to sail round my island and map it like yours. And then there's the islands up at the top."

They were walking along the dyke, above the marshes that fringed the Secret Water, looking across it to shores full of promise on the fur-ther side, when Roger suddenly pointed out to sea.

"A sail! A sail!" he shouted. "At least it's not got a sail. It's a motor boat."

Far away out they could see it, throwing the water in white splashes from its bows, coming in, heading for the crossroads buoy.

"I thought you could only get in at high water," said John. "And the mud's showing below the saltings. The tide's gone down a long way."

"Fishing boat," said the Mastodon. "They draw nothing. Get in and out any time. She'll be turning into the channel by Flint Island. They never come up here."

He turned away and pointed up the Secret Water. "You ought to go right up as far as ever you can go," he said. "We go up there sometimes to visit a trading post."

"Trading post?" said Roger, his eyes still on the distant motor boat.

"Ginger beer and chocolate," said the Mastodon. "But that other place I showed you was better."

"I say. They're coming straight on," said Roger. "They haven't turned."

"That's rum," said the Mastodon. "Not a local boat either. Strangers. They've mistaken the channel."

"Towing a sailing boat," said John.

"They're stopping," said Roger.

Foam was no longer flying from the bows of the motor boat that was now well inside the Secret Water. She was slowing down.

"Green," said Titty. "Like the one at Pin Mill."

"Hullo," said the Mastodon. "Somebody's getting into the sailing boat. Girl. Or is it a boy? There's another. I say, I do believe it's the Eels. Something's happened to *Lapwing* and they've come along to say so."

Titty remembered that the Mastodon was a savage, and that he said he would have to explain to the others about them. It would never do, before he had explained, for the rest of the tribe to find him hob-nobbing with a lot of explorers.

"Won't they be going straight to the *Speedy*?" she said.

But the Mastodon did not answer.

"I don't know who else it can be," he said. "And yet . . ."

"They're dumping stuff into the boat," said Roger.

The green motor boat was slipping slowly through the water with the sailing boat pulled up alongside, so that the explorers could see only the mast of it nodding beyond the green gunwale. People seemed to be in a hurry about something.

"There goes another bag," said Roger. "And what's that long bundle?"

"How many of them are there in the sailing boat?" said the Mastodon. "I only saw two. Red caps."

"Two," said Roger, "and two men in the big boat. Hullo. They're letting them go astern. We'll see better in a minute."

One of the men in the motor boat was walking to the stern with the painter of the sailing boat. The little nodding mast slipped back. A little brown sailing boat slid into sight. The people in it were struggling with a white sail.

"He's cast off," said Roger.

"They're turning round," said John.

The motor boat began to move ahead. The men in it pointed towards Goblin Creek. Someone waved from the sailing boat. The motor boat swung slowly round, and then, suddenly picking up speed, shot away towards the mouth of Secret Water and the open sea.

A white sail was being hoisted in the little boat. Up it went, stopped fluttering and filled with wind. Someone in a red stocking cap was steering. Someone else in a red stocking cap was busy by the mast.

"Hoisting a flag," said Roger. "Do their flags have eels on them?"

But there were no eels on the flag that suddenly

fluttered from the mast head. The flag was black, with something white on it.

"Skull and crossbones," said the Mastodon. "Well I'm blowed. Whoever can it be?"

"Hey!" Titty was shouting at the top of her voice. "Hey!"

"Ahoy!" shouted John.

"Ahoy!" yelled Roger.

"Do you know them?" said the Mastodon.

"It's Nancy and Peggy," said Titty. "It's the Amazon pirates. Hey! Hey! Ahoy!"

"Three million cheers!" said John.

"Gosh!" exclaimed Titty. "That's what Nancy meant. She knew they were coming. And Daddy and Mother never said a word."

"Swallows ahoy! Swallows ahoy!" A hail came over the water.

They saw Peggy standing up and waving. They saw Nancy pull her firmly down, as the little boat heeled to a sudden puff and came sailing in towards the mouth of Goblin Creek.

CHAPTER XI

WAR OR EXPLORATION?

"Ahoy!" shouted John, as he saw the Amazons turning towards the shore. "You can't land there. All swamp. Further in. Land where you see our boat."

"Aye, aye," shouted Nancy.

John, Titty and Roger set off at a run, and the Mastodon followed them, doubtfully, lagging a little behind.

"Susan," shouted John. "It's the Amazons!"

"They're here," yelled Roger.

"They're only ragging," said Susan. And then, looking over the saltings, she saw the sail of a boat, and then the red caps of the Amazons. "No, they really are. Come on, Bridget."

"Sinbad, too," said Bridget, and grabbed the startled kitten and ran after Susan to the landing place.

"This side. Close along the piling. Step out between the piles. Soft mud everywhere else."

"All right, Peggy. Let the sail flap till we get unloaded. We'll never get the tent and things out if we have the sail down on the top of the lot."

"Keep that bag out of the mud, Roger."

"Hullo, Ship's baby! Hullo, kitten!"

"We just couldn't believe it was you," said Titty.

"Well it jolly well is. Didn't you get our message? Look out, John. I've stuffed our compass into that."

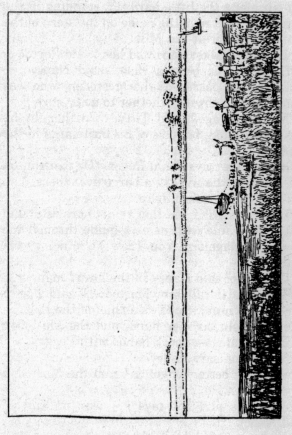

ARRIVAL OF THE AMAZONS

"Good," said John. "We've only got one. Another'll make all the difference."

"It's *Firefly*," said Roger, who had worked himself out along the little hard till, standing in the water, he could read the name on the stern of the boat. "I saw her at Pin Mill."

"Captain Walker borrowed her," said Peggy.

"Gosh, it has been a rush," said Nancy ... and stopped, looking at the Mastodon, who was waiting, not knowing whether to go or stay.

"He's a savage," said Titty. "We thought he was a Mastodon, because of his hoofmarks in the mud."

"Big as tea-trays," said Roger. "He can run on the mud, and he lives in a barge over there. You can't quite see it from here."

"He's got a tribe, but they're not here yet," said Titty. "He came with us as a guide through the Straits of Magellan. You know we're doing real exploring."

"Greeting," said Nancy in the grand manner.

"Titty and I call him Mastodon," said Roger. "He doesn't mind. But he's a chief of the Eels."

Nancy held out her hand, and the Mastodon shook it, and then shook hands with Peggy.

"My Mate," said Nancy.

"Well, I'd better be going," said the Mastodon shyly.

"Jibbooms and bobstays ... why on earth?" said Nancy.

"Oh I say," said John. "There's no need. Aren't you going to help with the map? There's lots more to do."

"What map?" asked Nancy.

"You'll see," said John.

"Come on, noble savage," said Nancy firmly. "You take the other end of the tent and go first." And the Mastodon, carrying one end of the long roll of the Amazon's big tent, followed by Nancy with the other end on her shoulder, found himself leading the way up to the camp.

Everybody carried something. Roger lowered the black flag with the skull and crossbones on it, ran, splashing, across the saltings, fastened it to a surveying pole, and planted it beside the Swallow flag in the middle of the camp. Even Bridget, with Sinbad in her arms, managed to carry a pair of Peggy's shoes, that she had taken off in the boat in order to get into seaboots for landing.

"Plenty of room for another tent," said Susan. "There's a good flat place just this side of that willow bush."

"Gosh," said Roger. "Things'll happen now."

"Looks to me as if they've begun," said Nancy. "The one thing we hadn't got at home was savages. Hi, Mastodon, just lug at that end of the bag and the tent'll come out poles and all."

"Dump the bags on the groundsheet," said Peggy. "I say, this is a gorgeous place."

"You don't know how gorgeous," said Titty. "It's real exploring this time. Miles of it. Islands and straits and everything changing all the time because of the tide. There's a Red Sea with a track across it at low water and at high water you can sail. We saw the tracks of Pharaoh's chariots this morning, and we sailed over it this afternoon."

"When did you leave Beckfoot?" asked Susan when the Amazons' tent was pitched, and Nancy and Peggy were tightening their guy ropes.

"Yesterday morning," said Peggy.

"It was one long stupendous rush," said Nancy. "Where's my knapsack?" She rummaged in it and brought out a sheaf of telegrams. "We didn't know for certain till the day before yesterday. The D's had gone, and Captain Flint and Timothy couldn't talk about anything but copper, and then Mother got a letter from your Mother asking us to come and Mother wrote and asked which day, and after that we were all of a dither. We didn't think there'd be an answer for at least two days. Then came the first telegram and our spirits shot up like rockets. Your Mother couldn't have sent a lovelier telegram."

"What did she say?" asked Titty.

Nancy showed the first telegram:

> MRS BLACKETT BECKFOOT
> EXPECT NO COMFORTS BUZZ THEM ALONG
>   MARY WALKER

"Doesn't sound a bit like Mother," said John.

"Daddy said he'd sent a telegram for her," said Titty.

"Good one anyway," said Nancy. "Well, we began getting ready at once, and then Captain Flint and Timothy came in, and the telephone rang again and there was another.

> BLACKETT BECKFOOT
>   BRING TENTS
>   WALKER

We thought that couldn't be your mother because she knows we've only got one. And we were packing the tent up in the garden when the next telegram came.

BLACKETT BECKFOOT
        BRING COMPASS
                WALKER

By that time we knew something was really up, and Captain Flint and Timothy got interested too, and said it must be some more prospecting. But Timothy said there were no minerals in these parts. Captain Flint said you must have found something or other.

"And they lent a hand with the tent and I was packing the compass and Mother was scurrying round with clothes and then another telegram came.

BLACKETT BECKFOOT
GUMBOOTS AND OILIES PUT THEM IN FIRST POSSIBLE TRAIN
                WALKER

"After that everybody was fairly whirling, and nobody really slept, and Captain Flint and Timothy rushed us round to the station in Rattletrap first thing in the morning, and we spent the night in London with Aunt Helen. . . . "

"Not the Great Aunt?" said Roger.

"No. A good one," said Nancy. "And then your friendly natives met us at Ipswich and rushed us to Pin Mill. We just saw Miss Powell's and had one look at the *Goblin* and then we were dumped into that motor boat and your natives said Good luck and were off for London and we were off for here. Buzz was the right word from the beginning."

"I knew Daddy was up to something," said Titty.

"They never said a single word," said Roger.

"I know now why Mother put in too many mugs and plates," said Susan.

At that moment, Peggy, admiring the flags, tripped over the supper peg of the meal-dial and kicked it out of the ground.

Roger darted to put it back. "Look out," he said, "or there won't be any supper."

"What's that?" said Nancy.

"Meal-dial," said Roger.

"I say, have you got a watch?" exclaimed Susan. "Thank goodness you have. I went and forgot my alarm clock in *Goblin*."

"Here you are," said Nancy. "But a meal-dial's even better. Wouldn't Dick have liked it?"

"Oh good," said John. "We'll be all right about tides now. A meal-dial's only good for meals."

"It's no good even for meals," said Roger, "unless the sun's shining. No sun no shadow and we'd all starve."

"Bet *you* wouldn't," said Nancy.

Roger disappeared into his tent. A moment later everybody was startled by the noise of a penny whistle.

"It's only Roger," said Bridget.

"Come out of that," said Nancy, "and let's see the horrid instrument."

"Can't," said Roger. "The wind sends all the notes wrong. I'm playing welcoming music in spite

of Nancy being so beastly rude. What tune would
you like?"

Suddenly the Mastodon, who had been listening
in silence, spoke to John. "I say," he said. "I really
have got to go. I forgot those worms. I've a night
line to set."

The music ended in the middle of a bar.

"Can I come too?" asked Roger.

"You can lend a hand with the oars," said
the Mastodon. "It's much easier with two."

"Come back to supper," said Susan.

"Oh I say," said the Mastodon. "I was here
to dinner."

"There's lots of grub," said Susan.

"Of course you'll come back," said Nancy.

"We've got an enormous cake," said Peggy.

The Mastodon hesitated. "I'd love to come," he
said. "Look here, will all of you come to supper in
Speedy tomorrow?"

"I should think we jolly well will," said Roger.

"In your lair?" said Nancy. "Of course we'll
come."

The fishermen went off to the landing place.

"What about inking some of it in?" said John,
and Titty went into her tent and came out with the
map on a drawing-board and her case of drawing
things.

"What on earth are you doing?" asked Nancy.

"Mapping?" said Peggy.

"You show them what we've done," said John,
watching the Amazons anxiously.

"It was Daddy's idea first," said Titty. "He was
coming, too, and Mother, and we were going to
make a proper map of this place. This is what he

did for us to start with. All unexplored. And this
bit in the middle is the bit we've done. I'll put it
on the ground so that you can see better. That's
this island. This is where the Mastodon lives in a
wreck. The idea is to get the whole map explored
before the relief ship comes to take us away
again."

"We'll get on faster now you've come," said John.

Nancy went down on her knees beside the
map. "Let's have a look," she said. The true lines
of the island had been drawn. A thick pencil line
marked the dyke, and outside it, not so thick, a
wavering line showed the edge of the marshes.
The straight lines of the compass bearings, going
from point to point, looked like a net holding the
island to the paper.

"All those straight lines'll be rubbed out when
Titty's done the inking," said John.

"I've only got black ink here," said Titty.
"But when we get home we'll put each journey in
with dotted lines, different sorts of dots. Explorers
always do."

She filled her pen with ink, and began her
work, while Nancy and Peggy looked over her
shoulders.

"It's a grand place for a war," said Nancy.
"Better than Wild Cat and our river. Surprise
attacks from all sides. And savages too."

John and Titty looked at each other in horror.

"We've sailed all round this island," said Titty.
"We had to begin with that. We're going to do a
new bit every day. And gradually the explored
part, properly mapped, will come spreading out
till the whole thing's done."

"What a place for war," said Nancy again. "Specially with savages. Think of an attack ... war canoes coming through there ... and savages creeping through the reeds. ... "

"But there won't be time for any war," said John.

"And the Mastodon's a friend," said Titty.

For some time the Amazons watched in silence.

"You'll get a medal from the Royal Geographical Society," said Nancy at last. ... "The Walker Expedition."

Both John and Titty noticed that she said "you" instead of "we".

"You're in it too," said John.

"It isn't Walkers anyway," said Titty, taking her pen from the paper and holding it well away from the side of the drawing-board for fear of a blot. "It's Swallows and Amazons as usual. The Swallows and Amazons Expedition."

"But we haven't got *Swallow* or *Amazon*," said Peggy.

There was silence while Titty dipped her pen and drew another careful line. Then she spoke again. "Archipelago Expedition ... Secret Archipelago Expedition ... S.A.E. ... The S. and the A. will do for Swallows and Amazons as well. We've got their flags. And we've called this island Swallow Island ... unless you'd rather not. ... "

"No, that's all right," said Nancy. "Secret Archipelago Expedition it is. At least I vote for that."

"So do I," said John.

"Can I ink in the kraal?" said Titty.

"It's in the right place," said John. "I got a bearing of it from three different posts."

Titty inked it in and in small capital letters wrote "NATIVE KRAAL" and away towards the eastern end of the island she wrote "HERE ARE BUFFALOES". Then, drawing tiny clumps of reeds, just three short thin strokes in a bunch, she began putting in the marshes outside the dyke.

"Giminy," said Nancy. "If it's going to be all like that it's going to be jolly fine. We'll discover an Amazon Island too."

"Wait till we've rubbed out the pencil marks," said Titty much relieved. It would have been too awful if the Amazons had set their hearts on war.

The inking went steadily on.

"How many savages are there?" said Nancy suddenly.

"He's the only one so far," said John. "But he says three more are coming."

"You can't have much of a war," said Nancy regretfully, "with only one savage against six of us."

"Seven," interrupted Bridget, "and eight counting Sinbad."

"Sorry, Ship's baby," said Nancy. "Well, seven to one's no good. It ought to be a handful of explorers holding a stockade against a howling horde. Look here. Peggy and I are sick of being pirates."

"Oh I say," burst out John. "There simply isn't time. We've cut two notches already. Two days gone. If we go and start a war now we'll have 'unexplored' sprawling all over the map. And the Mastodon won't be much good as a guide if he's got to think of ambushes. He's going to be jolly useful as it is, and anyway we've promised him Bridget for a human sacrifice when the others come. It's no good having battles and massacres as well."

"They thought I wasn't old enough but I am," said Bridget.

Nancy considered, looking round from the camp over Goblin Creek and the marshes and island beyond them, and the wide Secret Water with the low-lying coast beyond it. It certainly did seem waste, but you couldn't have much of a war with a solitary savage and all the Swallows set on peace. She glanced down at Titty, who was crouched over the drawing-board working away with her pen. Of course it was different from the lake in the north where, even when in bed with mumps, she had always set the tune for everybody.

"Exploring's going to be jolly good fun," said Peggy.

"Galoot," said Nancy. "Of course it is. I'm only thinking. When's Bridget going to be a human sacrifice?"

"When we've done the map," said John.

"If the other savages agree," said Susan. "He said he'd have to ask them, so you mustn't count on it, Bridgie."

"He said their sacrifice was too skinny," said Bridget.

"Right," said Nancy. "Exploration first."

"Good," said John.

"And it's all right being friends with the Mastodon?" asked Titty, looking up from the map before taking another dip of ink.

"Why not?" said Nancy. "Explorers meet savage chief. They make him presents. I only wish I'd thought of bringing some beads."

"Can't do any more tonight," said Titty at last, wiping her pen and putting it away.

"Let's rub out the pencil marks and have a look," said John.

"Ink's not dry," said Titty, and put the drawing-board in her tent, safe from explorers' wandering feet.

"Supper's ready," said Susan, who had for some time been busy at the fire. "Scrambled eggs."

"Good," said Nancy, jumping up. "Shall I go and yell to Roger and the savage?"

"I'll whistle," said Susan, but before the first blast of her whistle had died away they saw the fishermen coming up from the landing place.

"I say," called Roger. "We've put out a line with twenty hooks. He's going to bring us some of the fish when he takes it up in the morning."

Seven explorers and a savage shared their scrambled eggs, after which Peggy dealt out huge slices from the cake they had brought from Beckfoot.

Towards the end of the meal, Nancy fell oddly silent. It was Peggy who was telling the others about what had happened at High Topps after the Swallows had gone south, and how the D's, also, had been called away to join their parents. Nancy did not interrupt, even to say "Galoot". Titty could see from her face that she was turning something over in her mind. John, looking at her anxiously, began to fear that she was relapsing into thoughts of war. More than once the others laughed at things in Peggy's story of what had in the end been done to Timothy, and Nancy did not laugh with them. More than once she laughed to herself when the others were perfectly serious. She did her share of washing up without a word.

"What's the matter?" said John at last when Nancy suddenly broke into a cheerful chuckle.

"Nothing's the matter," said Nancy. "Jibbooms and bobstays! Everything's just right. I'm only thinking about the savage chief. We ought to do things properly. Look here, Mastodon."

The Mastodon looked at her gravely.

"Look here," she said again. "We're explorers. You're a savage chief. We ought to load you with presents, but we haven't got a single bead."

"I've promised him some of our fish-hooks," said Roger.

"Good," said Nancy. "Why not?"

"I say," said the Mastodon. "I don't want to take any unless you've got plenty."

"We've got a whole packet," said John.

"Barbecued billygoats!" said Nancy. "Bother the fish-hooks. Do let me talk. Look here. We're explorers and we've met you amd made friends . . . Haven't we?"

The Mastodon stared at her. "Yes," he said.

"Then the next thing to do is to prick our fingers all of us, and rub the blood in each other's wounds, so that we're blood brothers. . . . "

The Mastodon grinned. "That's what we did, when we first made our tribe, and the others got in a row with their missionaries about it. Daisy went and had a sore finger for about a week."

"We won't get into a row," said Nancy. "There's nobody to make one. And then, if we're blood brothers it'll be all right for you to help in the exploring. And if there was your blood in us, you could borrow one or two of us if you happened to be short of savages. Let's do it at once. Who's got any needles? Come on, Susan. You'd better prick Bridget's finger for her and I'll do Peggy's. She'll never prick herself."

"I don't want to have my finger pricked," said Bridget.

"You shan't," said Susan.

"I'll prick my own," said Peggy. "If you don't go and hurry me."

"Good," said Nancy. "Where's a needle? It won't really matter about Bridget if she doesn't want to. . . ."

"But then I'll be left out," said Bridget. "All because I'm too young."

"It isn't because you're too young," said Nancy. "It's only because you don't want to have your finger pricked."

"Well, I don't," said Bridget.

"Come on, Bridget," said Roger.

Bridget's lip quivered, and for the second time that day, Susan, who was an expert in Bridget, knew that something had to be done about it at once.

"No one's going to prick your finger," she said. "And there's no need for anyone else to prick theirs. We can make an alliance with the savages without any blood at all."

"It's all right," said Titty. "There was bread at supper, and lots of salt in the scrambled eggs. He's eaten our bread and salt and we're going to eat his tomorrow. That's all that really matters."

"I don't mind doing it," said the Mastodon, choosing a finger to be pricked.

"No need," said Susan, and then, privately to Nancy, "Look out. It's after Bridget's bed time."

"All right," said Nancy. "Bread and salt counts. Pity about the blood all the same. What time are you coming in the morning, Mastodon?"

"I'll come over as soon as I take up the night line," said the Mastodon. "But it's low tide about ten. We shan't be able to do much till the afternoon. Not in boats anyway. And I've simply got to go now. I left old *Speedy* in an awful mess."

"Come on, Bridgie," said Susan. "Bed, and quick too, if we're going to be up early enough to go blackberrying before we start exploring."

*

The Mastodon rowed away in the dusk. The explorers watched his boat until it disappeared.

"Mastodon Island?" said Titty, looking across the creek.

"All right," said John. "If he doesn't mind."

"He's a first rate savage," said Nancy. "I wonder what the others are like."

Back at the camp, Susan met them with a finger to her lips.

"Human sacrifice asleep," whispered Roger.

"So's Sinbad," said Titty, looking into her tent and bringing drawing-board and indiarubber to the light of the fire. She looked sideways across the map. "Ink's dry now," she said. For a moment she used the indiarubber, and then, blowing at the map, and dusting it lightly with her fingers, she handed it over to Nancy, to take her mind off savages and war.

"You've done a jolly good lot already," said

Nancy, looking at the island, its seawall, its landing place, the native kraal, the camp, the Straits of Magellan and Cape Horn, all neatly inked in the middle of the map with Commander Walker's blobs and wide blank spaces lying unexplored all round it.

"But just look what a lot there is to do," said John.

"Don't let's put any more on the fire," said Susan. "It isn't like Wild Cat where we always had plenty of wood."

"It's a pity about that blood business," said Nancy, handing the map to John. "It would make things a lot better."

"Bridget does get so upset if she thinks she's being left out," said Susan. "And it doesn't really make any difference."

There was an odd smile on Nancy's face, lit by a flame as she stirred the dying fire.

"You never know," she said. "It might make quite a lot."

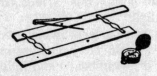

CHAPTER XII

BLOOD AND IODINE

NANCY woke the camp with a war cry long before the shadow on the meal-dial was anywhere near the breakfast peg. Susan, who had Nancy's watch in her tent, saw that it was terribly early, but knew that there was no hope of getting anybody to sleep again with the sunshine pouring through the walls of the tents. Everybody but Bridget went down to the landing place and had a morning wallow, getting so muddy on their way up again that it took another wallow in the pond to get them clean. Bridget, who could not swim, did the next best thing in standing by the pond and letting the others empty bucketfuls of water over her head. John cut the day's notch in the flagstaff. There was no sign of the Mastodon. They had breakfast. They wrote the first Report of the Secret Archipelago Expedition. Everybody signed it, and Susan put it in a stamped envelope, meaning to ask the farmer to post it next time he went to the mainland. Roger went twice to his look-out post to see if the Mastodon had come out to take up his night-line. John and Nancy were looking at the map considering what to explore next. "He said we couldn't do much boatwork until the afternoon," said John, looking at his tide-table. "High tide's not till 3.36."

"Don't let's decide till he comes," said Titty, wiping the last of the breakfast mugs.

Secret Archipelago Expedition

Report to Geographical Society's
Headquarters:— Pin Mill

All well Reinforcements arrived (Thats
what the three million were cheering about)
Swallow Island circumnavigated, via
Magellan Straits and via Cape Horn
Savage Chief tracked to his Lair by hoof—
—marks as big as teatrays. He is our
native guide and faithful friend. More
of his tribe coming

Signed:—   Wizard   Firefly
        Captains   John   Nancy
        Mates   Susan   Peggy
        Able Seamen Titty + Roger
        Ships Baby   BRIDGET
        Ships Kitten X sinbad
                        his mark

(Beckfoot Papers Please Copy)

THE REPORT[1]

[1] See page 287 for Semaphore Alphabet.

"He's going to bring us some fish," said Roger.

"He probably won't turn up at all," said Nancy. "Now, if only we'd done the blood business he'd have had to."

Bridget changed the subject. "Aren't we going to get some blackberries?" she said. "Susan promised."

"All right, Bridgie," said Susan. "Foraging party. We're going blackberrying while you make up your minds. We can't live off the land altogether, but that hedge is black with blackberries."

"Good against scurvy," said Titty.

"Give a yell when you're ready," said Susan. "Come on, Bridgie. There's your basket."

"I'll come too," said Peggy.

"More hands the better," said Susan.

"So'll I," said Roger.

"Not your hands," said Susan. "We only want hands that know their way to the baskets. Yours always go somewhere else by mistake."

"Oh look here," said Roger. "That was when I was as young as Bridget. I promise I won't eat a single one."

"Come on then," said Susan. "You can eat every tenth blackberry. But all the others go into the basket. It's no good picking them if there isn't enough to go round."

The blackberrying party, of Susan, Peggy, Roger and Bridget, went off along the dyke and inland towards the hedge that Susan had noticed when she had been too busy surveying to do more than taste the ripeness of a blackberry or two. John, Nancy and Titty crouched more closely round the map.

"The trouble is," said John, "that it isn't only boatwork that's no good except when the tide's up. The mud runs so far out that there are jolly few places where we can land."

"We could get ashore on Mastodon Island, like we did yesterday," said Titty.

"Bother that Mastodon," said Nancy. "We ought to have told him to turn up early."

"We don't really know him well enough," said Titty. "It isn't as if he was one of us."

"That's just what I mean," said Nancy. "We ought to have grabbed our chance last night. A drop of blood would have done it."

"We couldn't," said John. "There'd have been awful trouble with Bridgie. Whether we pricked her finger, or didn't and left her out."

"There's another thing," said Titty. "We don't know what the rest of the Eels are like."

"They must be all right," said Nancy. "Or they wouldn't be Eels. It's as good as anything we've thought of ourselves."

"But perhaps he wouldn't have wanted to," said Titty. "He took his totem away."

"Galoot!" said Nancy. "Oh. Sorry. I was forgetting you weren't my mate. But don't you see he had to? How could he leave it in a camp of white explorers? It's a totem of the Eels, and we're not Eels. One drop of Eel blood in our veins and it would have been all right."

"What about rowing across now and digging him out?" said John. "You haven't seen his lair yet."

"Let's," said Nancy.

The three of them walked down to the landing

place, but went no further, for out on the creek was the Mastodon himself hauling in his night line and coiling it in the bottom of his boat.

"Coming in a minute," he shouted.

They watched the dripping line coming in, the Mastodon stopping at each hook, putting it in its place and then hauling in afresh.

"There's a fish," said Titty. Something white and splashing came up out of the water, and the Mastodon held it up for them to see.

"Flatfish," said John, "by the look of it."

"There's another," said Titty.

But after that they saw no more. The line came in hand over hand, and the boat moved slowly across the creek, but hook after hook came in bare, and presently the Mastodon was hauling up the weight to which the end of his line was made fast. He stowed that with the rest of his tackle, and then, bending his oars pulled hurriedly towards them.

"Karabad . . . " he said cheerfully as he landed, and cut himself short. "I was forgetting you weren't Eels," he said. "Good morning."

"Good morning . . . I say, was that Eel language?" said Titty.

The Mastodon turned rather red. "It was a mistake," he said.

"Secret password?" said Nancy.

"It just began to slip out," said the Mastodon.

"If only we'd bloodied each other," said Nancy.

"Come along to the camp," said John. "We're just deciding where to explore next."

"Well just for a minute," said the Mastodon. "But I can't stop this morning. You're coming

to supper in *Speedy*, and I've got to go to the
main first. I say, will you bring your own mugs?
I've only got four, just enough for the Eels." He
looked at two flounders in a bucket in the stern of
his boat. "Look here, it's no good giving you these.
Little miseries. Not worth eating. And every bait
gone. I bet the others were eels. There's nothing
like them for not getting hooked." He emptied the
bucket into the creek, and the two little flounders
flapped away, like pancakes come to life.

"Mastodon," said Nancy suddenly. "Did you
mean it last night? Would you have blooded
with the rest of us?"

"It was you people who didn't want to," said
the Mastodon.

"If only Bridget was a little older," said Titty.

"It'll be low water pretty soon," said the Mastodon. "You can't do much in the boats. But what
about this afternoon? Tide won't be high till half
past three. I've got to go home to get some things,
and I want some more netting string from the
town. Run right out. And there may be a letter
from the tribe. . . . "

"Do they use native post?" asked Titty.

"Have to when there's no other way," said
the Mastodon. "They're almost sure to send a
letter before they leave Pin Mill. . . . I've got a
pretty good plan for today," he went on. "I'm
going straight over the marshes from *Speedy*, easy
enough with nothing to carry. But I'll be loaded up
when I come back. You know when we passed the
Wade on the way home yesterday I showed you
where the withies mark a channel going right in
to a landing place on the mainland. You ought to

have that in the map. Couldn't you explore that
while the tide's coming up? Start from here about
half past two. There's a channel all the way in.
We've marked a lot of it. It twists about a bit, and
we've put marks at the bends, secret ones. You'll
see them when you're close to them, but not from
the shore. If you work your way up there, there's
a fine landing place. It's an old barge quay really.
I'll get all my stuff there by high water and meet
you there. And then we'll load it into your boats
and dump it in *Speedy*, and there might be just
time to sail round my island before you come to
supper."

"Good idea," said John. "And this morning
we could be mapping it. We could get ashore at
the corner even at low water and do all the land
part without a guide. Then we'll have both sides
of the creek done. And the Amazons have never
seen *Speedy*."

"Shall I leave the plank up?" said the Mastodon
doubtfully.

"Oh no," said Nancy. "We won't go aboard if
you're not there. We'll be seeing *Speedy* when we
come to supper."

They came up to the camp and explained that
the others had gone to get blackberries. They gave
him the Report in its stamped envelope, to be sent
off, by native post, in the town. They showed him
the map with the work of the day before all neatly
inked and the pencil markings rubbed out. He
pointed out on it the place on the mainland where
he wanted them to meet him.

"Your island'll be done next," said Titty. "Do
you mind if we call it Mastodon Island?"

"Not a bit," said the Mastodon. "But, look here, I mustn't stop another minute. It's a fearful trek overland, and if I'm not at the landing place at high water you'll have to start back without me, or you'll get stuck. And I may be held up at home . . . at the kraal. . . . "

"We know," said Nancy. "Native business."

"There's nearly always something," said the Mastodon. "If it isn't clean shirts it's something else."

He turned to go back to his boat.

The quiet side of the island was broken by a sudden loud wail.

"Bridget," said John. "She's hurt herself."

They stood still and listened. There was another wail, as if Bridget had taken a long breath and was using it.

Then came Susan's voice, very angry, "Roger!" a gasping howl cut off short from Bridget, and a very cheerful shout from Roger, "Hurry up, Susan. Hurry up!"

A moment later Roger and Bridget appeared on the top of the dyke. Roger had Bridget by the elbow and was running her along. Bridget, perhaps because she had no breath to howl with, had stopped wailing. Roger was waving frantically with his free hand, and at the same time stooping to encourage Bridget.

"Hi!" he shouted. "Hi!"

"Roger!" shouted Susan again, and presently her bobbing head showed behind the dyke and then they saw her running in pursuit.

John and Titty ran to meet them.

"Hi," shouted Roger, again. "Somebody must

fetch the Mastodon. Oh good," he shouted. "Come on, Susan. He's here."

"What's happened?" called Titty.

"Quick. Quick," shouted Roger. "Bridget's scratched herself. She's bleeding beautifully. All right Bridget, it's stopped hurting. Don't suck it. Don't waste it. Come on. Where's a bucket?"

"Jibbooms and bobstays!" cried Nancy. "We're saved. Well done Bridget! Good for you Roger!"

She grabbed the Mastodon by the hand and hurried him towards the others.

Susan came panting up. "Roger," she cried. "What did you make her run like that for? Poor old Bridgie. Everybody gets scratched blackberrying. Wait a minute and I'll put a drop of iodine on it and a bit of sticky plaster."

Peggy came up. "Poor old Bridget!" she said.

Nancy took charge. "Good old Bridget!" she said. "Here's a clean plate. Let it drop. Titty, get hold of a needle for the rest of us."

Bridget, looking from one to another, had stopped crying, though a tear was still wet on her cheek. She looked at her finger and, at the sight of the blood on it, opened her mouth to wail again.

"Well done, Bridget," said Nancy. "You've saved the whole show. Don't suck it. Save that drop."

Susan came out from the tent with her First Aid Box already open and the iodine bottle in her hand.

"Let's see it, Bridget," she said. "It'll be all right in a minute."

"It's all the better for it to bleed," said Nancy, carefully catching a drop that was just falling from

the tip of Bridget's finger. "Don't put the iodine on
it yet. Good for you, Titty. Take a needle, Mastodon. What's the colour of Eel's blood?"

Titty was handing round a packet of needles.

"What are you doing, Nancy," said Susan.
"Turn round Bridget. I can't get at it if you
stand like that."

Roger, who had already taken a needle, was
standing with his back to the others. He turned
suddenly round. "I've done mine," he said, squeezing the first finger of his left hand. "Where's the
plate?"

"Oh, Roger!" said Susan. "Put some iodine
on it at once. How do you know the needle was
clean?"

"New one," said Roger. "It didn't hurt. At
least only for a moment. Here's another drop."

"Titty!" exclaimed Susan. "Don't be such a
donkey. John!"

"Oh look here, Susan," said Nancy. "We can't
miss a chance like this. Bridget may never scratch
herself again."

Susan hesitated. "You ought to dip the needle
in iodine," she said. "And you'll all get blood poi-
soning anyway. What are you going to do next?"

"Mix all the blood together and rub it in. Come
on Susan. Perhaps you're right about the iodine.
Dip your needle, Titty. You too, Peggy."

"Ouch!" said Titty.

"You haven't got as much as I did," said Roger.
"You'll have to pinch it pretty hard. Gosh! The
Mastodon's fairly jabbed himself. But nobody's
got as much as Bridgie. Wasn't it a good thing I
thought of it?"

THE BLOODING

"Now then, Susan," said Nancy. "Come on, ship's doctor. You ought to do it better than anybody."

Susan chose a spot on her finger with great care. "All right," she said . . . "I've done it. But I'm not sure we ought to mix some iodine with it before rubbing it in, and I'm going to."

"Good idea," said Nancy. "It'll make the blood go further anyway. Who hasn't done it? Oh well done, John. Let me have the plate. Here's another drop. Peggy!"

"I can't."

"Barbecued billygoats! You can."

"It won't go in."

"Give me your hand," said Nancy. "I'll do it. No don't go and pull like that. Hold your hand still. Turn the other way. Talk to her, Roger!"

"PEGGY!" shouted Roger at the top of his voice. She looked round.

"All over," said Nancy. "It went in all right. That finger's as soft as butter. No, don't suck it. We want every drop."

There was now a small, a very small puddle of mixed blood in the middle of the plate, which Roger was greedily offering to anyone who seemed to have a drop ready to add to the rest. Susan poured a little iodine from the bottle and stirred it with the tip of her finger.

"What do we say?" asked Titty.

"Swallows and Amazons and Eels for ever!"

"Nothing about blood brothers?" said Titty.

"Blood brothers . . . and sisters till death do us part. That ought to do."

"Hurry up," said Susan. "I must put something on Bridget's finger to keep the dirt out."

"Say it all together," said Nancy. "Can you say it, Bridgie? You're the most important. We couldn't have done it if it hadn't been for you. Swallows and Amazons and Eels for ever. Blood brothers and sisters till death do us part. Now then."

"Swallows and Amazons and Eels for ever. Blood brothers and sisters till death do us part."

Even Bridget got it right first time.

"Now everybody rubs her wound in the blood . . . or his," said Nancy.

"Gosh!" said Roger. "It stung worse than the needle."

"Ow," said Bridget.

"Good," said Nancy. "That shows it's really got in. Vaccination's never any good unless it hurts. You only have to be done twice over. Come on, Mastodon, don't hang back."

The Mastodon obediently rubbed his finger in the now drying puddle. "It's a pity the tribe isn't here," he said. "But I don't believe Daisy would have done it again."

"I did," said Bridget, and everybody laughed.

"Well, didn't I?"

"You gave more than anybody else," said Roger.

"Everybody's going to put some more iodine on now whether they like it or not," said Susan.

Everybody did, and Susan put a neat bandage round Bridget's scratched finger.

"I've simply got to bolt," said the Mastodon, "or I'll never be back at the quay by high water." He

started for the landing place, followed by his new
brothers and sisters.

"Well, it's all right now," said Nancy. "We've
all got Eel blood in us, and you've got some of
all of ours."

"I say," said Titty. "Is it all right now for
us to know that word you were going to say?"

"Oh yes," said the Mastodon. "It's the word
to say when you meet another Eel or are
saying Goodbye. It's Karabadangbaraka. And
the answer's the same word backwards. Akarabgnadabarak."

"Half a minute while I write it down," said
Titty. "Say it again."

The Mastodon said it slowly. "The countersign's
the difficult one. Daisy always gets it wrong with
the gnad. She keeps on saying 'gand' instead."

"Akarabgnadabarak," said Titty, writing it as
she spoke.

"Don't let anyone else see that," said the
Mastodon.

"I'll burn it as soon as we know it by heart,"
said Titty.

"And what about the totem?" said Nancy.
"Now we've all got Eel blood in us."

"All right," said the Mastodon. "I've got to
nip across to *Speedy* before starting home. If
you come across right away I'll give it you now."

"Let's all go," said Bridget, who was looking
proudly at her bandaged finger.

"Are there any blackberries on your island?"
asked Susan.

"Lots."

"We'll catch you up," said John. "Just half a

second while we get our compasses and things."

The Mastodon pushed off his boat.

"Karabadangbaraka!" Titty called after him.

"Akarabgnadabarak," he shouted back.

"Great Congers!" said Nancy gleefully to herself.

"What?" said John.

"Oh nothing," said Nancy. "It's only the Eel's blood beginning to work."

CHAPTER XIII

MASTODON ISLAND

THERE was a hurried rush to the camp and back, for baskets, surveying poles, compasses and blank copies of the map. The ship's kitten, who was having a nap after his breakfast, was left in charge. The explorers were on their way only a few minutes after the Mastodon. They found his boat at the mouth of the small creek that ran in behind Mastodon Island, and they went ashore close beside it, carrying their anchors to the top of the bank. The little creek was dry almost to the mouth.

"It won't be high water till half past three," said John. "He says we ought to start about half past two to meet him at that place."

"Lots of time to do the island first," said Susan. "And then we'll have dinner, and while you're meeting him, Peggy and I and Bridget are going to make a blackberry and banana mash. I bet the Eels don't know it. We'll take it to *Speedy* to add to the feast."

When they came along the dyke to the old barge, they were just in time to see the Mastodon drop down her side and get his feet fixed on his splatchers.

The totem in its blue, red and green paint gleamed in the sunshine on the top of the dyke where the Mastodon had planted it.

"Thank you very much," they called down

to him.

"I'm awfully late," shouted the Mastodon. "Can't stop another minute. You'll find the best blackberries close to the heronry."

"Where's the heronry?" called John.

"Those high trees," shouted the Mastodon. "The tops are full of nests. We very nearly decided to be herons instead of eels. But Daisy decided eels were best. I say, I've thought of a whole lot of things we can do when the rest of the Eels come. Four's nothing. But with seven of you as well."

"Eels for ever!" shouted Nancy, and added, to John, "I told you it would make all the difference."

"There may be news from the others at home," shouted the Mastodon. "Anyhow . . . No time now. We'll talk tonight."

"Grand Council," called Nancy. "Eels for ever!"

"Karabadangbaraka!" shouted the Mastodon joyfully.

"Akarabgnadabarak," shouted seven explorers from the top of the dyke, as they watched the Mastodon, with a flapping empty knapsack in one hand, run, with that queer swinging gait of his, so that his splatchers should not catch each other, across the soft mud at the bottom of the creek. They watched him struggle up the bank on the further side, hang his splatchers on a bush, and race off over the marshes.

"I don't wonder you thought he was a mastodon," said Nancy, looking down from the dyke at those huge round hoofmarks on the mud of the creek. "And what a place he's got to live in."

"Wait till you've seen the inside," said Roger. "Susan and Bridget haven't seen it either."

"How do you get into it?" asked Bridget, looking at the wide gap that separated the bows of *Speedy* from the bank.

"He's got a drawbridge," said Roger. "Jolly springy too. You and Sinbad'll both have to cross it on all fours. There'll be water all round it. It'll be as good as the houseboat, only we won't be making the Mastodon walk the plank."

"Why not?" said Bridget.

"Because you scratched your finger," said Roger.

"Oh," said Bridget. "Because he's a blood brother and sister. I said it right first time."

"Look here," said John. "Let's begin. This island looks just like ours and we'll do it the same way. It looks as if there's a dyke all round, with marshes outside it and dry ground inside. That heronry'll be jolly useful, too. We'll be able to see the tallest of the trees from anywhere."

"Why do you want to see it?" asked Peggy.

"Not to get lost," said Nancy. "But I don't see how you could on an island."

"It's like this. . . . " said John.

Nancy and Peggy, for once, had something to learn. The others, now experienced surveyors after their work on Swallow Island, showed them how to take bearings from that bamboo to another on another corner, and to the tallest tree on the heronry which served as a bamboo pole without having to be planted. Bit by bit, they worked all round the island, and though, perhaps, the resulting map was not up to the standard of the ordnance survey, it gave a much better idea of the island than the mere blob that Daddy had roughed out in pencil.

Their map showed all the really important things. There was the line of the dyke, with its fringe of saltings. There was the heronry shown by drawings of trees. Though it was not the nesting season they had been lucky enough to see a heron alight on the top of a tree, "backwatering" (Titty's word) with its wings, as it brought its feet forward to take hold. Most important of all, there was the old barge, *Speedy*, resting in the mud of the narrow channel that divided Mastodon Island from the mainland.

They had done a good morning's work when, at last, they worked round to *Speedy* again. John and Titty were very much relieved. They had been rather bothered by all that talk of war. They had been a little afraid that the Amazons would not see how important it was, when exploring, to explore, and to make a map as nearly as possible as good as the one they would have made if Daddy had been there to help them. But, though Nancy had all the time been trying new eelish swear words on her tongue, she had worked as hard as any of them. The Secret Archipelago Expedition was going to be the most successful they had ever made.

From the far side of Mastodon Island, they had seen other islands, far more than Daddy's map had promised. And now with two boats of their own, and Nancy no longer hankering after war, and the Mastodon an ally, a friend and a blood brother, and more friendly savages to come, they felt there really was a chance of carrying their explorations, north, south, east and west to every bay and island of these inland seas.

It had been a successful morning in another

way. They had found a lot of dead wood and
sticks under the heronry, and every stick was
worth having in this place where good fuel was
so rare. It was lucky, as Roger pointed out, that
the herons had not wanted them all for their nests.
Everybody but Bridget was carrying something
for the fire. Bridget, because she was going to be
a human sacrifice, was allowed to carry the totem
in the hand that was not bandaged. She sat in the
bows of *Wizard*, holding the totem as a figurehead,
when they left Mastodon Island and rowed across
to the landing place below the camp.

Back in the camp, the totem was planted
in its old place by the meal-dial.

"He's taken away the four shells," said Roger.

"Of course," said Titty. "Those were meant
for the four savages of the tribe."

"We'll give it something better," said Susan.
"Let's give it Nancy's watch. You don't mind, do
you?"

"Good idea," said Nancy, and unstrapped her
wrist watch and then, fastening the buckle,
slipped it over the eel's head of the totem,
and let it hang there.

"Totem and clock-tower," said Roger. "One
o'clock, too. Look at the dinner stick. We'd got
it in just the right place. The shadow's going to
touch it in a minute."

"Dinner in half an hour," said Susan. "No
chops left. We'll hot up a steak and kidney
pudding. And what about tinned pears?"

"I'll be opening them," said Peggy.

"Wriggling Elvers!" said Nancy. "My throat's
as rough as the inside of a seaboot."

"I'm jolly thirsty, too," said Roger.

"Ration of grog," said John. "We've earned it."

"Splice the mainbrace," said Nancy.

Bottles of ginger beer were dealt out, with a warning not to gollop them and have nothing to drink at dinner. The explorers wetted their throats while the survey of Mastodon Island was added to the map. Nancy and John compared the rough maps they had made and pencilled in darkly the outline on which they finally agreed. John, working carefully with the parallel rulers to check the important bearings, copied the result. Daddy's map began to look more and more like a real map instead of like a lot of lines that might be water or earth or anything else. The beginning, with Swallow Island, Cape Horn, the southern part of the Secret Water and the northern part of the Red Sea, by taking in Mastodon Island had made a notable push into the west.

"I do believe we're going to get it all done," said John. "If the rest of the Eels are half as good as the Mastodon, we'll have six boats for doing all the rest."

It was a very cheerful dinner, though John was in rather a hurry to get it over, and kept looking at the totem clocktower.

"We've got to meet him at high water," he said. "He says you can't get to the place except then, and we've got to find the way ourselves. The sooner we start the better."

"We mustn't miss him," said Roger. "I expect he's bringing grub for tonight."

"Peggy and I've been thinking about that," said Susan. "He's all by himself and there's such

an awful lot of us. There'll be the banana and
blackberry mash to take. We'll want a few more
blackberries, and we've thought of something else
to help in case of need. We're not coming with
you. Bridget's done enough exploring for one day.
We're going hunting for the pot."

"Hunting what?" said Roger.

"Mushrooms," said Susan. "I spotted some yesterday on the buffalo grazing grounds."

"We thought we'd take some stewed mushrooms with us," said Peggy. "Ready done, so he
won't have to cook them."

"And a tin of pemmican," said Susan. "Living
alone, he probably doesn't know what a lot seven
explorers can eat. It'd be awful if at the last
minute he hadn't got enough to go round."

"We needn't say anything about the pemmican,"
said Titty. "We could just keep it hidden in the
boat and remember it was there if it was wanted."

"Let's get started anyway," said John.

THE NATIVE KRAAL

CHAPTER XIV

WITCH'S QUAY

THERE was little more than enough wind to fill the sails as the two boats of the explorers drifted up Goblin Creek and round the island into the Red Sea. John and Roger were in *Wizard*. Titty had joined Nancy in *Firefly*.

With one of the rough copies of Commander Walker's map in each boat, they were off to chart the winding channel to the old quay of which the Mastodon had told them, and, if possible, to get there at high water and to meet the Mastodon on his return from civilization. Civilization, houses, railways, motor cars, and all the rest of it, seemed very far away as the two boats drifted along with the tide. Only, in the distance a thin tower, like the stump of a pencil, and a few white houses and the top sail of a barge moving beyond them out at sea, reminded them that there was anything outside this secret world of mud and weeds and gently moving water.

The narrow channel widened and the Red Sea lay before them.

"If only it was always like this," said Nancy. "So that we could sail anywhere, any time. I don't see the good of tides. What's the good of a sea if it's all going to be mud in a few hours."

"It's like breathing," said Titty. "Up and down. Up and down. It makes everything alive."

"Um," said Nancy. "When the tide's out everything goes dead. Hullo. We touched then. I'll get the centreboard half up."

The two boats sailed slowly on, side by side.

Wider and wider the Red Sea opened before them. To port was the long low dyke of the island, and shimmering water over the mudflats where Titty and Bridget had seen the long trail of the Mastodon's hoofmarks. To starboard all was new. The bank on that side was further and further away. Little clumps of weeds standing in the water hinted of shallows, but beyond them water stretched into a misty distance. Somewhere over there they were to meet the Mastodon. An old barge quay, he had said, but there was no sign of anything but sunlit water and small islands of weeds.

John was sitting on the middle thwart of *Wizard* searching for signs of a marked channel. Nancy in *Firefly* was doing the same. Roger and Titty were steering.

"Starboard a bit," said John, and Roger altered course.

Titty, catching Nancy's eye, did the same.

"There's one of those little trees, sticking up out of the water on the port bow," said Roger.

"We can't go wrong if we head for that," said John. "It's a withy. We passed that on the way home when we sailed round the island. We'll go to it, and then we may be able to see something else."

"We haven't really begun the unexplored part yet," said Titty.

"How do you know there really is a channel over there?" said Nancy.

"There's a good wide opening shown on Daddy's map," said John. "And the Mastodon said we'd find the marks in it as we went along."

"More withies ahead," said Nancy.

Far ahead of them was a line of withies, bending in the tide, perhaps a hundred yards or two hundred yards one from another.

"That's where the road goes," said John. "We saw them yesterday, and you see those posts, just showing? That's the place we bumped on coming home . . . the high bit half way across the Wade. We've got to turn south before coming to them or we'll miss the way altogether."

"What's that away to starboard?" said Titty.

"It's a stick, it's a stick," cried Roger.

"Steer for it," said John. "Pretty well south from here. That's all right. It'll mark the beginning of the channel."

Both little boats swung round. Roger and Titty hauled in their main sheets, and steered for the little branch of leafless twigs far away over the water. John and Nancy were busy with their compasses.

"It can't be anything else," said Nancy.

"Better have the centreboards nearly up," said John. "The wind's free, and anything's better than getting stuck in the mud with the boards down."

Titty, just nipping the end of her tongue between her teeth, kept a straight wake as she steered.

"That clump of weeds is pretty close," she said. "Is it all right?"

Nancy watched the weeds coming nearer and nearer. There was clear water all round them.

She took an oar and prodded over the side.

"Keep as you're going," she said.

"Aye, aye, sir," said Titty.

The weeds slid by and were left astern.

"What about the other withy?" asked John. "It looks a long way to port." He pointed to another thin sapling with twigs on the top of it, far to the left of the one they were now coming near.

"Can't be anything to do with us," said Nancy. "Everything looks clear ahead."

"Keep her as she goes," said John.

"Aye, aye, sir," said Roger.

"Get bearings from this withy to the posts on the Wade and to the native's landing-place."

"Moving too fast," said Nancy. "You do the one to the Wade and I'll do the other."

"She's steering funnily," said Titty.

"What's happening?" said Roger. "I say, John! I thought it looked a bit shallow."

Side by side, *Wizard* and *Firefly* lost speed and came to rest. They were aground, yet clear water stretched far away on every side of them.

"Suffering Lampreys!" cried Nancy. "Let go your sheet."

Roger had already let go of his, and for a minute or two both skippers wrestled with the oars, making their able-seamen move now forwards now aft as they worked to get their ships afloat again. The mud was so soft that prodding at it was very little good.

"I say," said Roger. "What'll happen if we can't get off, and the tide goes down and leaves us here? We can't walk over it like the Mastodon. And we haven't even a bit of chocolate."

"Even he couldn't walk over mud as soft as this," said John. "She's coming. Nancy's off too. We ought to have gone for that other withy after all. He did say the channel twisted a lot, but I never thought it'd turn right across like that."

Again the little boats were sailing, this time in a new direction, almost at right angles to their old course. John took a bearing from one withy to the other. Nancy tried the depth and washed the mud off the blade of an oar at the same time.

"We're in the channel now all right," she said.

"This is much worse than the Magellan Straits," said Titty. "There we only had to find the right ditch and keep to it, and here there are no banks to show where the ditch is and where it isn't."

When they came to the next stick, John lowered *Wizard*'s sail.

"Don't want to get stuck again," he said. "I can't see another mark anywhere."

Nancy brought down the sail in *Firefly*. "Sit in the bottom of the boat, just for a minute," she said. "I'm going to stand on the thwart to have a look round."

"Don't have her over," said John.

"I won't," said Nancy.

"He said some of the marks were secret ones," said John.

"Well there just aren't any," said Nancy. "And it looks pretty shallow everywhere. Weeds showing all over the place. Hullo!"

"Seen anything?"

"There's something floating over there. Not moving. Must be anchored whatever it is."

"I can't see anything," said John.

Nancy hopped down and took the oars.

"Plenty of water," she said. "I'll paddle gently in case of it getting too shallow."

"There *is* something," cried Titty. "It looks like a necklace."

"Galoot . . . " said Nancy. "It can't be."

"It is," said Titty.

"Sorry," said Nancy. "So it is."

Nancy stopped rowing, and *Firefly* slid slowly through the water towards a floating ring of old corks threaded on a string. Titty reached over the side as they drifted by.

"It's tethered to something," she said. "Shall I lift it up?"

"No. No," shouted Nancy. "We don't want to move it if it's a mark. Come on John. We're all right so far."

"Where do we go next?" asked Roger.

"Let's get this put down first," said John, and then, standing up in the boat, looked anxiously round over a waste of water. Some ducks swimming along the edge of a clump of weeds began to swim faster, and suddenly splashed up into the air and flew away.

"One of them's left behind," said Roger.

"Perhaps it's hurt," said Titty, and looked at it through the telescope. "Oh, it's only a bottle . . . floating."

"Why doesn't it move?" said Roger. "It must be swimming against the tide. Or is it high tide already?"

Titty looked at it again. "It's the wrong way up," she said.

"Come on," said Nancy. "Good for you, Titty.

I ought to have spotted it. Bottles always float neck upwards when they're just bobbing about. That one's anchored. Come on, John. We've found the next mark."

From near the bottle, an old lemonade bottle, anchored to something on the bottom, they saw a withy, a stick with a bunch of twigs, like those that marked the channel outside, though not so big. John saw it first, rowed straight for it and, a moment later, stuck fast. Nancy backwatered in *Firefly* just in time to save herself from joining John on the mud.

"There must be another mark to go for first," said John. "You know if we go on getting stuck like this we won't be there before the tide turns, and then we may not get there at all."

"Let's go back at once," said Roger. "I say, will we ever find the way?"

"I've got it all down all right so far," said John.

"Look there," said Nancy. "There's another lot of corks. Probably we ought to go round them before going for the stick."

She pulled away, went back to the floating bottle, and from there rowed to the ring of floating corks.

"Come on," she said. "It's all right. Deep water all the way. Now for the stick."

"We can't go straight for the stick from here. There's a tuft of reeds right ahead. She's touching. Look out, John. We're stuck again."

"There's another bottle over there," said John, who had got *Wizard* free of the mud and had just arrived at the second ring of corks. "Gosh!" he cried. "I've got it. Port and starboard buoys.

We've got to leave all bottles to starboard and all corks to port. Why on earth didn't he tell us?"

"Then what does the stick mean?" said Roger.

When they came to the stick, they knew. From beside it they could see another anchored bottle away to the south, and to the west two more sticks, the further of them close to the shore.

"There must be a landing place in there. There's a fishing boat pulled up there. The stick just marks where the channels divide. Half a minute while I jam that down."

"Is that where we're going?" said Titty.

"Can't be," said Nancy, who was down in the bottom of *Firefly* with compass and map. "Almost due west, and we ought to be going almost south."

"There's nothing like a quay in there," said John. "Come on. Next bottle."

This way and that the channel wound, each turn of it marked by a ring of corks or an old bottle, corked and anchored by its neck.

"It doesn't look as if we're going anywhere," said Roger.

"It's getting narrower anyway," said Titty. "We must be getting to the end."

Ahead of them long low banks of weeds pushed out into the water, and were closing in on either side. Nobody who did not know could have guessed that there was a way through. Even John began to feel doubtful, watching his compass, and noting the course from secret mark to secret mark.

And then, suddenly, they saw it. Paddling carefully, *Firefly* close astern of *Wizard*, they were making for a ring of corks close to a bank of mud

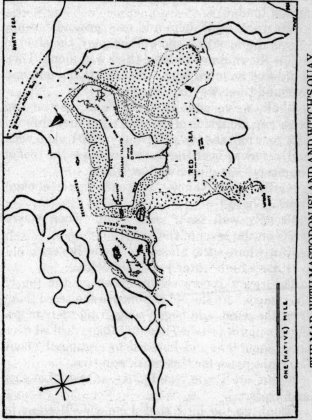

THE MAP: WITH MASTODON ISLAND AND WITCH'S QUAY

and weeds. As they reached the corks they could
see round the bank, and ahead of them, only a
few hundred yards away was an old wooden quay,
with a house on it, and a couple of boats pulled up
on dry land.

"Hurrah!" cried John and ran aground again.

Even here, within sight of the quay, they had to
follow the channel and feel their way along. They
could find no more marks to guide them, and had
to sound their way in with an oar.

"Well, we've done it," said John, as the two
boats ran alongside of the quay, and they climbed
ashore. From the top of the quay they looked back
and, far away over the water, could see the roof of
the native kraal on Swallow Island.

"Gosh!" said Nancy. "It looks simple enough
from up here."

"It jolly well isn't," said John, "when you're
down on the level of the water."

"But where's the Mastodon?" said Roger.

"It isn't high water yet," said John.

The two skippers settled down on the top of
the quay where the old storehouse sheltered them
from the wind, and began comparing their maps.
For a minute or two Titty and Roger looked over
their shoulders and listened to argument about
the right place for this mark and that.

"Come on, Rogie," said Titty at last. "Let's go
and explore."

"Don't go too far," said John. "We'll want to
start the moment he turns up."

"Perhaps we'll meet him," said Titty.

Long years ago there must have been busy
barge traffic in and out from this old quay when

there were no railways and poor roads and everything that could be was carried by water. They could see that the quay had once been bigger. They found the remains of an old crane, and heavy rings, now almost rusted through, to which in old times the barges had made fast. But now the wood of the quay was rotting, and water was working in and out through gaps in the piling. The storehouse was empty. Beside the quay was an open space, big enough for a wagon to turn round in. But there were no cart tracks, and grass and thistles were growing through the sand.

There were footmarks in the sandy ground.

"Natives," said Titty. "We'd better go carefully."

"What are these squiggles?" said Roger. "Somebody's been drawing snakes."

"Eels!" cried Titty. "You can tell by the head and the fins. Hey! John! The Mastodon's been and gone."

John and Nancy came running along the quay and looked at the squiggles in the sand.

"Eels all right," said John.

"Why on earth couldn't he wait?" said Nancy. "The tide's still coming in."

"They're all pointing the same way," said John.

"Patterans," said Titty. "I bet he drew them to show us which way he's gone."

"Here's another," said Roger, who had already left the edge of the quay and was moving in the way the eels were pointing, stooping and looking at the ground.

"And another," said John.

"He must think us galoots, to draw such a lot," said Nancy.

Eel after eel drawn in the sand and all wriggling
in the same direction led them across the open
space towards the mouth of a green lane. Titty
ran ahead into the lane, and searched the ground.
The others followed her.

"He couldn't draw eels in the grass," said Nancy.

John went back to the last of the eels they
had seen. It was not as straight as the others. All
were wriggly lines, but it was easy to see which
way they were going. This last one had a decided
kink to the left.

"He's turned off here. Or hasn't he?"

Away to the left was a broken down wooden
fence, with a wicket gate in it, and beyond
it a thatched cottage, a very small cottage of
tarred black wood standing in a small potato
patch.

John went to the wicket gate, which stood
half open, and there, on the ground between the
gateposts, was a wriggly line. There was another
on the path across the potato patch.

"He went in here," said Titty.

"Come on," said Nancy. "I'm going in too."

One of the windows of the cottage was broken,
but there was a bit of paper stuck over it, and a
geranium on the sill inside.

"Somebody's living here," said John doubting
whether to go or not.

Somebody tapped at the window. The door of
the cottage opened and a bent old woman stood
on the threshold, leaning on a stick.

"Looking for young Don?" she whispered, and
coughed. "Lost me voice, I have. He've put his
bag in the shed."

She pointed to a lean-to shed at the end of the cottage.

"Thank you very much," said John.

The old woman stood there, watching them.

"New friends for him," she cackled. "Not seen you before."

"May we go to the shed?" asked John.

The old woman did not answer. She began to cough, and her cough turned into a laugh and then into a cough again. She went back into her cottage.

John led the way to the shed. Just inside it was a sack, with a bit of rope round the mouth of it. A bit of paper lay on it, skewered to the sack with a splinter of wood. They read it together.

"Please take this lot in your boat. Bringing the rest. Don't wait for me after the tide turns or you won't get back. If I don't get back in time I'll go overland." There was no signature except a drawing of a wriggling eel.

"What are those words crossed out?" said Nancy.

"Bad something," said John. "Bad news."

They looked at each other. What bad news could there be?

"Oh well," said Nancy. "He's crossed them out anyway. You get hold of one end, John, and I'll take the other."

They hove up the sack, which was very heavy, and carried it past the cottage and out by the wicket gate. The cottage door was closed, but they could see the face of the old woman, coughing and laughing, looking at them through the broken pane by the geranium.

"I bet she's a witch," said Titty, remembering

her mother's story of the Obeah Woman. "Wrinkles deep as ditches on her brown face. A native witch. I wonder if she's got eel blood in her too."

They took the sack to the quay, and lowered it down into *Wizard*.

"Tide's still rising," said John. "But it must be nearly high water."

Roger worked his way down by the side of the quay, and stuck a bit of wood into the mud, and crouched on the bank to watch it. John looked out over the Red Sea, at the distant line of their island.

"Sing out the moment it stops rising," he said. "Come on, Nancy. Let's get on with the chart. It's that bit where the other channel starts that looks wrong."

Titty crouched on the bank by Roger.

"Something must have happened to make him write 'Bad news'," she said. "And then something else must have made him cross it out."

CHAPTER XV

THE MASTODON WISHES HE HADN'T

"It's begun to go down." Roger's shout disturbed the map-makers on the quay. Titty had joined them, to see the two maps which now more or less agreed with each other, though it was hard to tell which of the pencilled lines were meant to count and which would have been rubbed out if only the surveyors had not forgotten to bring an indiarubber from the camp.

"Come on then," said John.

"What about the Mastodon?" said Nancy.

"He said we weren't to wait for him. There's jolly little water anyway, and you know how it runs out once it starts. We can't wait. If we don't get out before the water goes, it means not getting home till tomorrow morning."

"And we haven't even iron rations," said Roger, coming up and untying *Wizard*'s painter.

"He said he was going to do his best to get here," said Nancy.

"I'll run to the lane and see if he's in sight," said Titty.

"Go on, Able-seaman," said Nancy.

"But buck up," said John, dropping down the side of the quay and reaching with a foot for *Wizard*'s middle thwart. "All aboard!"

"Aye, aye, sir," said Roger.

The *Wizard* drifted slowly from the quayside.

Nancy, standing up in *Firefly*, hung on to the piling.

Titty came running back. "Not a sign of him. I say, hadn't one of us better wait? I will. I'll come back with him overland."

"We can't leave you," said John. "Susan would only get worried."

"Half a minute then," said Titty, and went to the place where they had found the first eel drawn in the sand, scratched it out and drew another heading out towards the creek. "Just to show him we've been and gone."

"Look here, we must start," said John. "It's dropped inches already." He began to row. "Come on Nancy. With the wind like this we'll be able to sail, once we're clear of those weeds."

"Buck up, Able-seaman," said Nancy. But, even after Titty had dropped into the boat, and she was rowing after *Wizard*, Nancy did not row as hard as she could. Her eyes were still on the quay and the open space behind it. The thought of getting stuck on the mud bothered Nancy a good deal less than it did John and, while he was thinking mainly of Susan and the camp, she was still hoping against hope that the Mastodon would come running out of the green lane before it was too late.

"Oh well," she said at last. "It's no good waiting any longer," and bent seriously to her oars. She gave one hard pull and then backwatered so suddenly that Titty nearly shot forward off her seat in the stern.

"Coming!" she shouted. "Coming!" spun the boat round and headed for the quay. John stopped rowing and waited for them. The Mastodon with an

enormous knapsack on his back, a parcel in one
hand and a big milk can in the other was stag-
gering to the quayside.

"Karabadangbaraka," said Nancy as she
brought *Firefly* back to the quay.

"Akarabgnadabarak," panted the Mastodon,
but Titty had a queer feeling that he had not
wanted to say it. She looked round, wondering
if some native was within earshot, someone who
ought not to be allowed to hear password and
countersign. There was nobody. Perhaps it was
not that he had not wanted to say it, but only
that he was out of breath.

"Sorry I was late," said the Mastodon. "I had
to wait in the town till the last possible minute."

"Lucky we hadn't started," said Nancy. "If
we'd got round the corner of those weed banks
we shouldn't have seen you."

"Jolly glad you waited," said the Mastodon. "It
would have been an awful job humping this lot
overland. I say, you did get the sack, didn't you,
from the hut?"

"We got it all right," said Nancy.

"Did you have much trouble in getting in?"
asked the Mastodon.

"Show him our sketch map, Titty," said Nancy.
"We went aground once or twice at the bends."

The Mastodon stared at the map, which looked
like a tangled spider's web to anyone who did not
know that the little circles meant rings of corks
and the black spots bottles and the letters noted
down at the side of each one of the maze of straight
lines was a compass bearing.

"I say, Nancy, John's putting up his sail."

"We'll do the same," said Nancy. "And the Mastodon'll steer. Do you think you'll be able to read the map?"

"I'll manage better without," said the Mastodon, and grinned, for the first time since he had come aboard. "But you'd better do the steering."

"All right," said Nancy. "Titty, you steer, and the Mastodon'll be pilot, and I'll check the marks as we go past them. Hi! John! Wait for us. The Mastodon's going to pilot, so that we shan't waste time running aground."

"All right," shouted John, with relief in his voice. "I'll follow you close astern." He kept *Wizard*'s sail flapping loose in the wind till *Firefly*, with Titty at the helm, the Mastodon sitting on the middle thwart, and Nancy, map in hand, sitting on the bottom boards, sailed past with the water bubbling under her bows. Titty, glancing over her shoulder, saw him haul in his sheet. The sail filled, and *Wizard* came foaming after *Firefly* a couple of boat's length astern.

"Sorry we started," called John. "But I got in a bit of a stew about not being able to get out. The water's going down like anything."

"Quite all right," said the Mastodon. "You wouldn't have had any time to spare if you'd made any mistakes, and if you did go aground you might be high and dry before you could get off again. Starboard a bit. . . . " He pointed with his right hand. "There's a shallow patch here. . . . That's right. . . . Port again. . . . . Now starboard. . . . Straight for those corks. . . . "

John gave Roger the tiller and settled himself in the bottom of the boat with the compass, checking the courses from mark to mark, and now and then making small corrections on his map. Nancy was doing the same. The Mastodon just waved the map away when she wanted to point something out to him. He was a pilot on his own ground, and had no need for maps. Also the tide was pouring out, and the boats were sailing fast and he had no time to spare to look at anything but the marks he knew. First one hand lifted, then the other. "Port. . . . Starboard again. . . . Straight for the withy. . . . Not too close . . . Now for that bottle. . . . " This was very different from the slow careful way in which John and Nancy had felt their way up the winding channel. The Mastodon never even bothered to test the depth with an oar. He knew. As they came to one mark he had already got his eyes on the next. He never had to look for it.

"Giminy," said Nancy, when, at last, they reached the open water of the Red Sea, and could see the withies marking the road that still lay under water, and the four posts just showing in the middle. "You must know it pretty well."

"I was born here," said the Mastodon.

"What about the Eels?" asked Titty, and it was as if a shadow crossed his face.

"Oh yes. They know it too."

"Really well?"

"Daisy did it in the dark once."

"Great Congers!" said Nancy, looking back at that puzzling maze of water and weed patches.

"What?" said the Mastodon.

"Jolly good work," said Nancy.

"But what was it you said? Something about congers?"

"She's been getting eelier and eelier," said Titty. "Ever since last night."

"What's the matter?" exclaimed Nancy, looking at him.

"Keep her as she's going," said the Mastodon. "Don't turn yet. It looks deep there but it isn't."

"The map's pretty well right," called John. "There was just that one place where I'd got muddled. Did you tick off all the marks?"

"Yes. But it's going to be an awful job getting it clear for the final copy."

"We'll do it in *Speedy* after supper," said John.

"He's got a grand lantern," said Roger.

Again Titty saw that odd unhappy look on the Mastodon's face.

"What do you call that place where we met you?" she asked.

"Witch ... " The Mastodon stopped short. ... "It's got two names, really."

"What's its Eel name?" asked Titty. "Never mind about the other one."

"Witch's Quay," said the Mastodon, and then, "I don't see how it can matter your knowing that."

"Of course it doesn't now we're Eels," said Nancy, and again that queer shadow crossed the Mastodon's face. Titty saw it but Nancy was busy writing "Witch's Quay" on her map.

It was not until they were already in the narrows coming round the island into Goblin Creek that anybody mentioned the Eels again.

"No news of the rest of the tribe?" asked Nancy.

"Well there is, really," said the Mastodon. "They may be here any time. They may be here now. That's why I was so long. I thought they might be coming to the town for stores at high water. But they hadn't got there when I left."

"Three cheers," said Nancy. "An extra three savages'll make a lot of difference. Specially as each of them's got a boat."

The Mastodon did not answer.

"I say," said Titty. "There isn't really any bad news, is there?"

The Mastodon looked at her, and even the cheerful Nancy saw that he was worried.

"It's my fault if there is," said the Mastodon.

"Native trouble?" said Nancy consolingly. "We know. It's often practically impossible to keep clear of it."

John hailed from the other boat. "What about landing?" he called. "Will there be enough water for us to bring the boats round to *Speedy*, or shall we have to put the things ashore at the mouth of your creek?"

"We'll get to *Speedy* all right," shouted the Mastodon, "if you're sure you don't mind?"

"Eels for ever!" said Nancy. "Don't be so polite."

Sails were lowered, and John and the Mastodon rowed *Wizard* and *Firefly* up the narrow winding little creek that led behind Mastodon Island to the old barge. The tide had gone down a long way, but there was still water for them to come alongside.

"Too late to get right round," said John, seeing mud ahead further up the creek.

"Never mind," said Nancy. "We've got a fearful lot for the map already."

The Mastodon climbed up his ladder, and they hoisted up his knapsack and the big bag and, more carefully, his parcel and the milk can.

"Coming aboard!" said Nancy, without waiting to be asked. She swung herself up and over the rail to the deck. Roger was beside her in a moment, then John.

"Come on Titty," Nancy called down. "I've made fast. I say, Mastodon, what a lovely place you have."

"You haven't seen what it's like down below," said Roger. "It's as good as a real ship."

"Shall I go down first?" said Nancy, lifting the knapsack. "Or will you go and we'll pass the things down?"

The Mastodon dropped his parcel down the hatch, and then went backwards down the ladder, holding on with one hand, and carrying the milk can in the other. Nancy lowered the knapsack after him. Roger lugged the sack across the deck. John and Nancy lowered it between them.

"Got it?" called Nancy.

"Got it," said the Mastodon.

"All clear?" said Nancy, and came down the steps, followed by the others.

"Pretty good, isn't it?" said Roger.

"Giminy," said Nancy. "I don't wonder you don't bother about a tent."

The Mastodon stood there silent, looking oddly bothered and unhappy.

"Aren't you going to unpack?" said Nancy.

"Only provisions," said the Mastodon glumly.

"Do let's see," said Roger.

"Never mind if you don't want to," said Nancy. "And don't you worry about native trouble whatever it is. You've only got to give them time. We've got a Great Aunt who makes things fairly awful but we always bounce up again somehow, and we manage to do things right under her very nose. . . . "

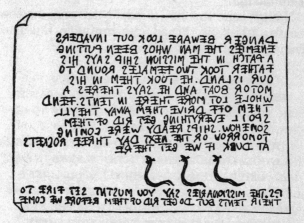

THE EELS' LETTER

"It isn't that sort of trouble," said the Mastodon. "Look here, you'll have to know. I ought never to have let out about the Eels. I got a letter from the rest of them this morning. And it's about you."

"But we don't know them yet," exclaimed Titty.

The Mastodon was fumbling in his pocket. He pulled out an envelope.

"Hullo," said Nancy. "Are those eels in the corner? We always put a skull and crossbones."

The Mastodon did not answer. He took a folded sheet of paper from the envelope. "You'd better read it," he said.

"But I can't," said Nancy, staring at meaningless letters and words in an unknown language. "I say, have the Eels got a language of their own?"

"It takes a bit of practice," said the Mastodon. "It's easy really when you're accustomed to it. There's a looking glass on that wall. You hold it up to that."

Nancy held the bit of paper up and, in the looking glass, it turned into ordinary English. They could all read it.

"DANGER BEWARE LOOK OUT INVADERS ENE-
MIES THE MAN WHOS BEEN PUTTING A PATCH
IN THE MISSION SHIP SAYS HIS FATHER TOOK
TWO FEMALES ROUND TO OUR ISLAND. HE TOOK
THEM IN HIS MOTOR BOAT AND HE SAYS THERES
A WHOLE LOT MORE THERE IN TENTS. FEND THEM
OFF DRIVE THEM AWAY THEYLL SPOIL EVERY-
THING GET RID OF THEM SOMEHOW. SHIPS
READY WERE COMING TOMORROW OR THE NEXT
DAY THREE ROCKETS AT DUSK IF WE GET THERE."

There was no signature, except a lively drawing of three eels. Underneath the eels there were another two lines of writing:

"PS. THE MISSIONARIES SAY YOU MUSTN'T
SET FIRE TO THEIR TENTS BUT DO GET RID OF
THEM BEFORE WE COME."

They read it and read it again with lengthening faces.

"But who are the two females?" said Nancy. "We haven't seen any grown-ups about at all."

"They mean you and Peggy," said Titty.

Nancy turned suddenly red. She was just going

to burst out with something, but stopped herself and swallowed indignantly.

"Two females indeed!" she said at last, under her breath.

The Mastodon was looking at them miserably.

"It's going to be awful," he said. "They'll never understand. If only they'd been here it might have been all right. But now they'll come and I've gone and spoilt everything. Nothing's secret any longer. I've gone and told you everything . . . even the passwords. And I've been helping instead of driving you away. I don't know how it all happened. They'll think it was simply treachery."

"Oh look here," said Nancy. "It doesn't matter. When they come you can just try to turn us out. We'll put up a stockade and defend ourselves. It'll be as good a war as anybody could want. If there aren't enough of you, some of us'll help on your side."

"It's not that," said the Mastodon. "Daisy won't want anybody here at all. I ought to have kept right away. I would have done if I hadn't gone and thought you were them, and then coming to your camp, and letting out one thing after another, and what can I tell her about the blood brotherhood business?"

"Great Congers and Lampreys," burst out Nancy. "We can't deblood ourselves now."

"I can't either," said the Mastodon. "That's just it."

John had listened, in silence.

"Look here," he said at last. "If you think they wouldn't like it, you'd better not let us come here for supper."

The Mastodon looked at him gratefully.

"If I could only have explained to them," he said.

"Let's put it off," said John. "We'd better go and tell Susan now."

"I'm most awfully sorry," said the Mastodon. "I'd got everything ready. Mother gave me a ham when I told her how many you were. And she's put in an extra lot of stores."

"I thought that sack was pretty heavy," said Roger.

"It'll keep," said Nancy.

"It's all my fault," said the Mastodon. "I don't know how it all happened. Everything just slipped out. . . . Of course, Daisy doesn't know you were marooned," he added hopefully.

"Cheer up, Mastodon," said Nancy. "We won't come. But I don't see why you shouldn't come to supper with us instead. Savage spy in paleface camp. Nobody could object to that."

"Better not," said the Mastodon. "Look here. You take the ham. . . ."

"Oh we can't do that," said Titty.

Silently they climbed up through the hatch and came on deck. Silently they went down into their boats.

"You'll explain to the others," said the Mastodon, looking down from *Speedy*'s deck.

"Come on, Mastodon," said John suddenly. "You come to supper with us, even if it's the last time."

"I'd really better not," said the Mastodon. "I say, you know I am most awfully sorry."

"It's not your fault at all," said Titty.

"Anyway, thank you very much for all you've

done," said John. "Showing us channels and things."

"I oughtn't to have done it," said the Mastodon.

They rowed silently away. The Mastodon stood for a moment watching them from the deck of the old barge. The bright colours of her name, *Speedy*, in the painted scroll-work on her rail, seemed almost to mock them. The gaudy bit of painting looked so much more cheerful than they felt.

Nancy stopped rowing to give the Mastodon a parting wave. The others waved too. The Mastodon waved back and then turned sharply round and went below. For a few minutes they could see the old barge, a wreck, with nothing to show that it was the lair of a savage. Then, as the creek twisted, it was hidden by the high banks.

*

Not a word was said by anybody as they rowed down Goblin Creek to the landing place.

Bridget came running to meet them as they walked up the path across the saltings. "Hullo!" she said. "We're all ready."

Peggy was close behind her. "Is it time to start?" she said. "We've made a huge lot of blackberry and banana mash. My wrist's nearly bust with mashing them. And Susan's got a saucepan full of mushroom stewing now. We went to the kraal and she got a jug of cream."

"I'm going to carry my own mug," said Bridget.

"We're not going," said Roger.

"I wish we could fry every eel in the world

except him," said Nancy. "It isn't only your wrist that's bust."

"Not going?" said Bridget.

"What on earth's happened?" said Susan the moment she saw them.

"It's the rest of the Eels," said John. "They're coming, and they've got to know about our being here, and they've sent him a letter telling him to clear us out. And he doesn't know what to do because he's made friends with us first."

"He wishes he hadn't blooded," said Titty.

"He showed us the letter," said Nancy. "Jolly clever. All the letters inside out and the words the wrong way round. They knew about me and Peggy coming in the motor boat. . . . "

"Two females," said Roger with a grin.

Nancy scowled at him. "They knew about the camp. They told him to chivvy us out. They told him to do anything short of setting our tents on fire. So he couldn't very well have us to supper. Those beasts may be here already. And he thinks they'll think he's a traitor. He'll never come with us again."

"They're going to send up rockets at dusk," said Roger.

"Why didn't you bring him along here?" said Susan.

"Wouldn't come," said John.

"Oh, I say!" said Bridget. "Does it mean they won't let me be a human sacrifice? I think they're horrid. And I bled more than anybody."

"He blooded with them before he did it with us," said Titty.

"They want the whole place to themselves," said Nancy.

"Cheer up, Bridgie," said John. "We'll sacrifice you ourselves."

"But I've never even seen *Speedy*," said Bridget.

"We've done a huge lot of blackberry mash," said Susan, "and the mushrooms are just ready to take across."

"They won't be altogether wasted," said Roger. "We can eat them here."

"We'd better have supper right away," said Susan. "I'll open a tin of pemmican."

"He had a ham," said Roger. "And simply tons of grub."

"Well we've got tons too," said Susan. "Bother those Eels."

What with pemmican and stewed mushrooms, a mash of blackberries and bananas, and a bottle of grog to each explorer, it was too good a supper to allow much talking. It was so good a supper that even Nancy, though still fierce at being called a female and having her most private plans upset, cheered up a little.

"Well," she said, "if it's going to be war...."

"But it isn't," said John. "They won't have anything to do with us. And the worst of it is, we shan't have a guide any longer. But we didn't count on having one. And anyway we've done a tremendous lot before we've lost him. Come on Nancy, let's get at those maps. I'll just fetch the parallel rulers."

No inking was done that evening. There was the survey of Mastodon Island to work out, in which everybody had taken a hand, besides the mapping of that corkscrew channel going in to Witch's Quay. The explored part of the map had spread that day both east and south, and they were hard at it with pencils and rulers until Bridget had long gone to bed and it was too dark to see. Dusk fell, and dark.

"Where's Roger?" said Susan suddenly. "And Titty?"

There was the flicker of a torch along the dyke. Roger and Titty came back into the camp.

"Well, they aren't here yet," said Titty.

"How do you know?" said Nancy.

"No rockets," said Roger. "We've been watching for them."

CHAPTER XVI

ENEMY'S COUNTRY

"Not a sign of the Mastodon," said Roger.

"He won't be coming here anyway," said Titty.

They had gone down to the landing place after breakfast and, barefooted, black to the knees with mud, were working *Wizard* down towards the water.

Peggy came down to join them, left her boots on the saltings, and began pulling at *Firefly*.

"You push at *Wizard*'s nose," said Roger, "and then we'll come and help to get *Firefly* out. The mud's most beastly sticky."

"Have they decided yet?" asked Titty.

"Still at it," said Peggy. "But one thing's settled. We're all coming. John says the Mastodon won't do anything to our tents. He knows we're marooned and can't get away. Besides, he's a blood brother even if he wishes he wasn't. But once the others come we'll have to leave a guard all the time. Today'll be the last chance of exploring with the whole expedition. Susan's packing the grub now."

"Bother the beastly Eels," said Titty. "Roger, don't splash!"

"Eels," said Roger. "I felt one wriggling round my toes."

"Well, you needn't send the mud flying all over the place."

"Where are we going?" said Roger.

"Don't know," said Peggy. "Nancy wanted an

attack on the Mastodon. She said that if we captured him and held him prisoner we could tell the other Eels that if they weren't decent we'd never let him go."

"Good idea," said Roger. "We could take his worms too, and do some fishing. I say, we could make him fish and be a prisoner at the same time . . . a sort of tame cormorant."

"John and Susan said 'No'. Susan said we can't have him a prisoner in our camp because there isn't a spare tent. Nancy said it was quite warm at nights and we could tether him like a goat. John said it wasn't as if he was an enemy. It's not the Mastodon's fault that the other Eels want the whole place to themselves. And somebody'd have to guard him all day, and he's too strong for anybody except John, and that would mean that the map would never get done. So we're just going exploring without him."

"He was fine as a native guide," said Titty.

"But if he doesn't want to be one any longer," said Peggy.

They worked first *Wizard* and then *Firefly* down to the edge of the water. They had just got *Firefly* afloat when they saw the rest of the expedition coming down the path across the saltings, everybody carrying something. Bridget carrying Sinbad, John with the compass and a knapsack, Nancy with a compass and a bundle of surveying poles, and Susan with a kettle of drinking water.

"Where are we going?" asked Roger.

Nancy answered. "We're going to explore Flint Island while we can. We shan't be able to do it when they're camped there so if we don't get it done now there'll be all that lump left unexplored."

"I say," said Roger. "What if they come while we're on their island?"

"We'll see their ship in plenty of time to clear off," said John.

"It'll be six to three anyway," said Nancy.

"Four with the Mastodon," said Titty.

"They'll be six too," said Roger.

"They won't make their missionaries fight," said Nancy. "And who cares if they do?"

"You always leave me out," said Bridget.

"We'll be seven," said Nancy.

"And Sinbad."

"Jibbooms and bobstays. Eight if you like," said Nancy. "Who's coming in our boat? Hop in Bridget. You and Sinbad'll fit in fine before the mast. We've got room for one more, or a lot of baggage. All right, Roger."

Titty looked at Nancy but said nothing. She knew very well why Nancy had stopped swearing like an Eel.

"We don't want a row if we can help it," said John.

"I suppose it's no good even trying to collect the Mastodon?" said Peggy.

"Bob-tailed galoot," said Nancy. "Can't you understand he's wishing he'd never met us?"

The two little boats were loaded up. The explorers, sitting on the gunwales, washed their feet or their boots over the side so as not to fill the boat with mud. Sails were hoisted and a good south-west wind soon blew them out of the creek into the Secret Water. Everybody just glanced up the creek as they left it, but there was no sign of the

Mastodon. They had only known the Mastodon a
couple of days, but, after all, they had made a
blood brother of him and it was as if they had
lost an old friend, besides having pricked their
fingers for nothing.

But out in the sunshine on the Secret Water,
with the sails pulling, and the cheerful lap-lap
under the forefoot, nobody could feel grim for
long. Just to look at the other boat, foaming
along, made each crew feel how fast they were
going.

"Ahoy, Admiral," said Captain Nancy. "Race
you to the point."

"All right. Whoever's first to the buoy with a
cross on it. We've got to go round that to get into
the other channel."

"Shift your weight up a bit, Peggy," said Nancy.
"Giminy, they're gaining on us already. Is anything wrong with our sail?"

"I could get the boom down a little by the
mast," said Roger.

"Go ahead. That's better. Cock the peak up
all you can."

First one and then the other boat shot ahead
as their crews tried different dodges to get the
most out of their sails. The shores of their island,
already mapped, slipped by. Before them the
Secret Water opened to the sea. Far away, brown
sailed barges were coming out of harbour with the
last of the ebb to get the whole six hours of the
flood tide to help them on their way to London.

"Bother the sun," said John. "I say Susan.
Is that the crossroads buoy?"

"Sun's in my eyes too," said Susan, "but I

think it is. Yes, there's the cross on the top of it."

"Roger's spotted it," said Titty, looking across at *Firefly*. "They're going to win."

"They're too near the shore," said John. "Nancy doesn't know about tides. More tide here. We're going faster than they are because we're out in the stream."

But, out in the middle, while the shore was still hiding it from *Firefly*'s crew, the explorers in *Wizard* were the first to catch a glimpse of the golden hummocks of Flint Island. It lost them the race.

"Gosh," said John. "Look at those masts. Is that *Lapwing* there or not?"

"It's only the dhows," said Titty. "Three of them. They've been there all the time."

"John," cried Susan. "Look out for your steering."

Wizard had swung right round into the wind. Her sail was flapping, and though John got her going again in a moment and back on her course, he passed the buoy a boat's length astern of *Firefly*.

"We won," cried Bridget.

"Nothing much in it," said Nancy. "It's as good as old *Amazon* and *Swallow*. Where now?"

"Starboard," called John. "Look here. You follow us. We've been through here with the Mastodon and I've got it on my map. Leave those black buoys to port, and keep clear of the withies on this side."

The channel suddenly narrowed. There was a sandy bank between it and the open sea. Ahead it stretched inland, a shining lane of water.

"What is there up there?" called Nancy.

"Town," said John.

"Native Settlement," said Titty. "And Cape Horn and Magellan Straits where we nearly got stuck with the Mastodon."

"Bother the Mastodon," said Nancy. "Where are we going to land?"

"There's a sort of bay just before we come to those yachts," said John. "That looks good enough. Up with the centreboard, Mister Mate. We don't want to bust it. Good. Stand by to lower sail. . . . Now. . . . "

There was a gentle scrunch and then another, as the two ships of the explorers touched the steep, sandy beach.

*

For some minutes after landing, the explorers kept together. They felt a little as if they had broken into someone else's house. The *Lapwing* was not in the anchorage; there were no tents among those sandy hillocks; the island was deserted; but they felt as if they might at any moment come face to face with the rightful owners.

Susan was the first to find the savage camping place. Close behind the steep rise of the beach there was a hollow in the sand. A small circle of charred stones was in the middle of it. "Here's where they camp," said Susan. "Lucky beasts. They've found stones to make a proper fireplace. And look at these logs. Much better than we get."

"Open sea on the other side of the island," said John. "They'll get real driftwood."

"Let's bag some," said Roger.

"No," said Susan.

"We'll get lots of our own," said Titty.

They looked round the hollow and found the marks of tent pegs.

"Pretty good place they've got," said Nancy.

"Wouldn't it be awful if they came while we were here," said Titty.

"They won't," said John. "We'd see them coming across from Harwich long before they were anywhere near. And anyway they won't come till high water. Come on, Nancy. Let's start. Skip along to the point, Roger, and plant a pole. And we'll have one at the other side of the bay, and then one in the middle."

"Have you been right up the channel?" asked Nancy, standing on the edge of the hollow and looking at the ribbon of water winding inland. "Ow! I say, Bridget, look out for this sea-holly. It's as prickly as the land kind. You'll be losing some more blood for nothing."

"Not as far as the town," said John. "We turned off round Cape Horn."

Nancy was looking at her copy of the map. "Hadn't we better get that done too while we can? And what's this gap between Magellan Straits and Cape Horn?"

"We've got to keep a look out to sea," said John. "So as to spot them coming."

"Peggy and I'll do it on our own," said Nancy. "Or we'll toss you for it. One lot works up to the town and the other does the island and keeps a look out."

John hesitated. "Go ahead," he said. "Work

up with the tide. It's just turning. It won't be high water till about half past four. "That's when they'll be coming if they do come. But we'll have to clear out as soon as we see them."

"That's all right," said Nancy. "If we see your boat's gone we'll know what's happened and nip back home through the Red Sea."

"Look here," said Susan. "If you do get to the town, could you telephone to Miss Powell's to say we're all right? Mother'll have got that Report this morning, but I promised we'd ring up if we got a chance. Woolverstone 30."

Nancy scribbled the number on the back of her map. "Right," she said. "Lots of things have happened since we sent the Report. I'll tell her. Enemies on every side. Hostile savages threatening massacre. All well and love from Everybody."

"All well's what matters," said Susan.

"Don't go off without your share of grub," said Roger.

"Jolly good idea of Nancy's," said John, as the *Firefly* sailed away. "Once the savages are here it'll never be safe to go out of sight of the camp. We've got to get every scrap done that we can do before they come."

"And then just write 'Cannibal Tribes' over all the rest," said Titty.

*

Steady work with the compass and surveying poles went on through the rest of the morning. They mapped the channel which, dry at low water, made Flint Island really an island when the tide came up and not just the nose of a promontory as it was shown on Daddy's rough sketch. Before the tide came up and filled it, they made a hurried expedition along the sands beyond it, where Bridget found shells and Sinbad played with them, and they picked up good bits of driftwood for a midday fire on which to boil their kettle. There was a moment's horror at the thought that the two explorers in *Firefly* would get none of the tea, but it was remembered that if they did indeed get to the town, they would be able to have something else instead. "Lapping up grog like anything," said Roger. "I bet Nancy thought of that before she started."

Susan made a new fireplace of her own, down on the seashore, well away from the fireplace of the Eels. And all the time, no matter what they were doing, surveying, exploring, marking things down on the map, or eating their well earned meal on the single beach, their eyes kept turning seawards watching for the *Lapwing* with her fleet of little boats and the savages who had sent orders that they were to be driven away at all costs. After dinner, when the tide had cut off Flint Island from the main and was pouring in through the channel, they saw that they were not the only watchers.

Out near the mouth of the Secret Water the Mastodon was fishing from his anchored boat. He too was watching for a cutter, with three dinghies astern, coming in from the sea, ready to meet them when they arrived and, no doubt, to confess that instead of driving the explorers away, he had made friends with them, swopped blood with them, and given away to them the secrets of the Eels.

"Gosh!" said Roger. "I wish he'd come in for me. I bet he's got a spare line in the boat. I wonder if he's seen us."

"Of course he has," said Titty.

"Shall I wave?"

"No good," said John. "Much better leave him alone."

An hour before high water, mapping came to an end. They had done as much as they could do and, for the time, turned into coastguards, looking out to sea for an enemy vessel and keeping an eye also on that other watcher who still lay out there alone in his boat. The tide turned. The ebb began, and they saw that the Mastodon was getting up his anchor. Nothing was moving out at sea, except the big mainsail and tiny mizen of a barge so far away that they could not see her hull. The Mastodon stowed his anchor, took to his oars, and presently disappeared.

"Going home," said John. "Well, they won't be coming in now."

"He'll be alone again tonight," said Titty. "Isn't it beastly not being able to talk to him?"

"It isn't our fault," said John.

The Mastodon was hardly out of sight before, looking the other way, up the channel leading to the town, they saw *Firefly* coming back. The wind had dropped, and though the sail was set, somebody was using oars, and rowing as hard as she could.

"Ahoy!" shouted Nancy as soon as she was near enough. "Ahoy! Buck up. Get afloat!"

"It's all right," shouted Roger. "They aren't even in sight."

"They won't be coming now. It's after high water," called John. "There's no hurry."

Peggy, steering, brought *Firefly* in to the beach.

"Barbecued billygoats!" cried Nancy, jumping out. "No hurry! Get afloat as quick as you can. They're not coming from the sea. They're coming the other way. We've seen them. They're anchored up there close to the town. They'll be here any minute. They must have got in at high water yesterday. If the Mastodon had waited a bit longer instead of meeting us at that quay he'd have seen them."

In two minutes the explorers were all afloat, and Flint Island, deserted once more, was ready for its savage owners.

"Did you get right up to the town?" asked John, as the boats moved out into the creek.

"Of course we did," said Nancy. "We worked slowly up with the tide like you said. We've mapped the whole channel. . . . Amazon Creek it's going to be. . . . You've got Swallow Island. . . . And we had a good look at the gap between Magellan Straits and Cape Horn. It runs straight in towards the dyke and joins the Straits."

"The Mastodon said it did," said John.

"We landed twice," said Peggy. "Two good places. We had our grub on a sort of landing stage, and we got lemonade from a shop."

"I told you they would," said Roger.

"Did you telephone?" asked Susan.

"Rather," said Nancy. "Your mother was there. She'd just got back from London, but she's going up there again tomorrow. She said the Report was a beauty, and she sent her love, and she said you were to be sure not to starve Roger."

"Oh look here," said Roger. "You made that up."

"Are you sure it was the Eels?" said John, looking back up the channel towards the town.

"Couldn't be anybody else. We passed a yellow cutter at anchor on our way in, and then we saw three dinghies close to the town and when we were coming back just now the dinghies were by the cutter, and we read *Lapwing* on her stern, and we heard one of the missionaries tell them to hurry up and help make sail."

"We shan't be able to do much exploring once they've come," said John. "There won't be a hope of getting the map properly finished."

"The Mastodon did say I could be a human sacrifice," said Bridget.

"They don't want one," said Titty.

With the ebb running out and the wind light and ahead, sailing was useless, and the two boats rowed side by side up Secret Water and into Goblin Creek. For all that they could see, nothing had changed. Yet everything had.

"Better fill our water-cans tonight," said Susan. "We don't want to run into them at the kraal."

John and Susan, Nancy and Peggy, carried the two water-cans to the farm, each water-can slung from an oar. Even at the kraal they were not allowed to forget that things had changed. "Seen anything of them savages yet?" laughed the man as he filled their cans for them. "Only one? The other'll be all over the place tomorrow. I met their dad when I was across in the town. He bring the yacht in yesterday, and they'll be camping down at the mouth tonight."

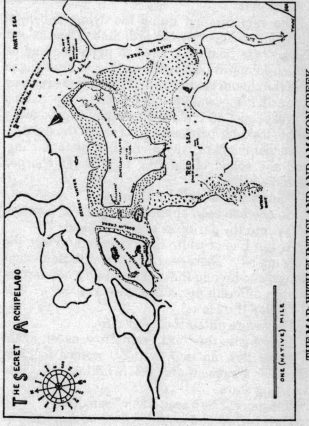

THE MAP: WITH FLINT ISLAND AND AMAZON CREEK

Back at the camp they had a rather silent
supper.

*

Dusk fell.

The explorers sat round the dying embers of
their fire. Bridget was in bed. Sinbad was asleep.
Nancy was holding a torch to light the map on
which John was tracing the outlines of Flint Island
and the channel to the town. Titty was sharpening
a pencil. Peggy was yawning. Susan was polishing
a grease spot off a plate. Roger had slipped away
to his look-out point at the corner of the dyke.

Suddenly there was a shout, a distant bang,
and the sound of running feet. Roger charged
into the camp.

"Didn't you see it?" he shouted.

No one had seen anything. Roger was pointing
away into the darkness over the island.

A thin line of white light streaked up into the
evening sky. There was another of those distant
bangs, and high in the darkness half a dozen stars
shot in different directions. A rocket.

"That's the second."

They were all on their feet now.

"There goes the third," said Titty, as yet again
a spark flew up into the sky, seemed to hang
there for a moment and, before falling, burst into
shooting stars.

"I wonder if he's seen them," said Titty.

They turned and looked across the dim creek at
the dark line of Mastodon Island on the other side.

"He won't have seen them if he wasn't watching," said Roger.

THE SECOND ROCKET

But a minute later they saw a glimmer of light. There was a bang at the other side of the creek. A rocket hissed up into the sky and burst. Three red stars curved from it, fell slowly and died as they fell. All was dark once more.

"Fireworks?" said Bridget, who had crawled to the mouth of her tent on hearing the stir outside.

"You ought to be asleep," said Susan.

"They've come," said Nancy.

"I wonder if I ought to stay awake," said John.

"Shouldn't think they'd try to do anything till tomorrow," said Nancy. "But I bet it's war now whether you like it or not."

That night not one of the explorers slept without waking. First one, then another, stirred in sleep, woke, and listened, now to the stir of wind in the reeds, now to an owl hawking over the marshes, now to the noise of a train on the mainland far away, now to the distant hooting of a ship coming into harbour. First one of the explorers and then another stirred, listened wide-eyed, and slept again.

CHAPTER XVII

A STATE OF WAR

THE explorers woke in a new, unfriendly world.
Everything about the camp was the same as
usual. The boats (John and Nancy ran down to
see before breakfast) were just as they had left
them. The same curlew was whistling over the
marshes. The same gulls and oxbirds were busy
on the edges of the mud. The same sun had risen
in the east and the same shadow was darkening
the breakfast peg of the meal-dial. But the whole
feeling of the place was different. Last night they
had seen the rockets that announced the coming
of the savages. And the savages, even before they
had arrived, had made the Mastodon ashamed of
his blood brotherhood, and sorry for his friendli-
ness.

John and Nancy, after looking at the boats,
separated and went north and south along the
dyke, eyes and ears alert.

"Nothing moving on Secret Water," said John
as they met again at the camp, to find the others
half way through breakfast and Sinbad licking an
already empty saucer.

"Red Sea's nearly dry," said Nancy. "And tide
still going out. They won't come that way for a
bit."

"What about the Mastodon?" asked Titty.

"No signs of him."

215

"Do you think they'll come at all?" said Susan. "Won't they just pretend we aren't here?"

"The letter the Mastodon got said 'Drive them out. Fend them off'," said Titty. "And then it said he wasn't to set fire to our tents. I should think they'll probably try something."

"Of course they will," said Nancy. "And we'll jolly well smash them if they do."

"Let's burn their beastly totem," said Roger.

"Jibbooms and bobstays! Why on earth?" said Nancy. "We've bought it with our blood."

"I bled more than anybody," said Bridget.

"Won't it make them mad to see it there?" said Titty.

"Who cares?" said Nancy. "It's ours now. We're Eels just as much as they are."

"Somebody'll have to stay in the camp," said John.

"I've got to anyway," said Titty, "to catch up with the map. There's simply masses to ink in."

"There won't be much more," said John sadly. "We'll have to keep within signalling distance all the time. We'll have to go back with half the map unexplored."

"You'll want a sentinel," said Nancy. "You know what it's like when you're drawing. They could come and take the tents away and you wouldn't notice."

"I'll be sentinel," said Roger.

"You'll be wanted for surveying," said John. "Specially if Titty's staying in camp."

"Can't I be sentinel?" said Bridget.

Nancy laughed.

"I'm old enough," said Bridget.

"I don't see why not," said John. "We'll be within sight all the time. Got to be. All they've got to guard against is a surprise. If they keep watch on the dyke they'll see the enemy coming even if we don't. If they see anybody they lower the flags. We'll keep on looking, and the moment the flags go down we'll come racing back. It isn't as if there was a real horde of savages so that they could attack from all sides."

*

An hour later the exploring party with the two boats sailed out from the creek. Bridget, Sinbad and Titty were at the landing place to see them go.

"Down the flags at the least sign of danger," said John as he pushed off. "And get as much of the map done as you can."

"Aye, aye, sir," said Titty.

"Aye, aye, sir," said Bridget, and then a moment later, "Couldn't you hear him? Sinbad said it too."

"Good for him," said John.

*

"I suppose they will be all right," said Susan, as the *Wizard*, close behind the *Firefly*, slipped across the Secret Water.

John looked back. The tents were already hard to see, but the flags were fluttering in the sunlight, and on the skyline a small bright blue figure was walking solemnly along the top of the dyke.

"Bridget on sentry go," said Roger.

"They'll be all right," said John.

*

*

"What am I to steer for?" asked Peggy.

Nancy, who was sitting scowling in the bottom of *Firefly*, looked over her shoulder.

"Straight for the creek on the other side," she said.

For a time neither of them spoke.

"If it was only us," said Nancy at last. "We'd go straight for their camp, bang an arrow into the middle of their fire and see what happened."

"We haven't got a bow with us," said Peggy.

"It's not that, you blessed gummock. It's John and Susan. Titty too. They don't want a war if they can help it. They want to do their map. And the savages are just as bad. If only they'd been decent we'd have had six boats to work with, and four native guides, and we'd have got the whole thing done and had time for a bit of war as well. And tomorrow it'll be our turn to stick in the camp all day with nothing to do and nothing happening. It was all waste jabbing our fingers."

"I wish we hadn't," said Peggy.

"Too late now," said Nancy. "If I could I'd suck the Eel blood out and spit it away."

*

The other boat was closing in on them as they came to the wide mouth of the inlet for which they were making. There was mud on either side, and green topped muddy banks. The water, narrowing between the mud flats, stretched far ahead.

"We're going to have a job to get ashore," said John. "The Mastodon said there's a landing on

each side. But it may be only when the tide's up.
Gosh, I wish he was here."

"There he is," said Nancy.

Far away on the other side of Secret Water
a little rowing boat was coming out of Goblin
Creek. A spot of bright blue on the dyke showed
where the sentinel, Bridget, was keeping an eye
on it.

"He isn't coming this way," said Roger.

"He's going to see his horrid little friends,"
said Nancy.

The Mastodon, shaving close round the mud
spit at the mouth of Goblin Creek, turned east,
and they watched him for a long time steadily
rowing away.

"Well, it's no good watching him," said Nancy.
"Let's get ashore."

*

With the Mastodon rowing away down the
Secret Water to meet the Eels, it did not seem
likely that anything much was going to happen.
He, no doubt, was going to get into trouble for
having been too friendly with the explorers, but
they could do nothing about it. They settled down
to their work. Nancy and Peggy, black to the
knees, struggled ashore on the eastern side of
the inlet. John, Susan and Roger landed fairly
dry at the remains of an old hard on the western
side, like the one by their camp in Goblin Creek.
Poles were set up as landmarks, and both parties
did the best they could, taking bearings from one
pole to another and to the promontories, the kraal
and the other landmarks on the islands they had

already surveyed. Every now and then they kept looking for the sails of the savages or glancing across the Secret Water to see the flags still fluttering above the camp, a sign that all was well.

But, though the flags flew above the camp, the savages, without even showing themselves, had made the work of the explorers very difficult. They could not do things properly when they had to stay within sight of those flags and within reach of their boats, ready to row across if Titty and Bridget signalled a warning. They did their best with the coastline but were not able to settle the most important question of all. Were they on islands or just on odd-shaped promontories? They could not go far enough away from their landing places to make sure. Neither of the exploring parties were pleased with their work. At last Roger complained that the sun could not get any higher, that the shadows of the surveying poles were growing longer again, and that if they were in the camp the meal-dial would be showing that it was after dinner-time. Nancy and Peggy came rowing across to join the others, scraped the mud off their legs with handfuls of grass and agreed with Roger that it was time for grub.

"What's your bit like?" asked John. "Is it an island or not?"

"I don't know," said Nancy. "There's a sort of creek that looks as if it might join this but we couldn't go far enough to see. Dry at low water. We wallowed across it. Mud to our ears. One little bit's an island. We've put it on our map. What are those birds that keep on fluttering and diving ... white with black hoods. ... ?"

"Terns," said Roger.

"Tern Island. ... They're diving all round it." She scribbled in the name and gave John her map, on which was a spider's web of lines and bearings. "Poor old Titty," she said, looking at the work of John, Susan and Roger.

"It won't look as bad as this when we've worked it out with the rulers, and copied it ready for her to ink it in."

"What about Peewitland for the rest of it?" said Peggy.

"Ours is the Blackberry Coast," said Roger. "Susan's found a better lot here than anywhere."

"We won't put 'Coast' in till we're sure it isn't an island," said John. "Just look over there. All that mud and water. Nearly as big as the Red Sea. Either it's a lake or it comes into this creek. And if there's a way through further up Secret Water, a North West Passage, that'll be a sort of Arctic Sea and Blackberry's an island not a coast. We found two ditches, but they don't go right across. But there may jolly easily be a passage further along."

Half an hour later, when they had drunk their pop and eaten their sandwiches and a few of the fruits of the Blackberry Coast, John and Nancy stood looking across Secret Water to the distant fluttering specks above the camp.

"They're all right over there," said John, "and the tide's rising fast. Let's go a little way up and see what it looks like."

"I'm coming, too," said Roger, who was heartily sick of surveying poles.

"Peggy and Susan'll keep a look-out," said Nancy. "Come on."

They paddled down the mud of the old hard and got afloat in *Firefly*, but they had not gone very far before they heard behind them a bad imitation of an owl.

"Owl at midday," said John, grinning, remembering something that had happened long ago. "Something's up."

There was Peggy on the dyke near the mouth of the creek, earnestly signalling.

"What's she saying?" asked Roger. "Gosh, she does go at a lick." Peggy's arms had hardly shown one letter before they were in a new position showing another. "M . . . A . . . S . . . T . . ."

"Mastodon," said Nancy, without waiting for any more. She pulled back as hard as she could.

"He's coming back," called Peggy.

"Alone?"

"Yes."

They hurried ashore, and joined Susan, who was lying on a dry patch of ground, watching the little rowing boat coming fast up Secret Water with the tide. The Mastodon stopped rowing just before turning into Goblin Creek. Suddenly he turned his boat and rowed across towards the watchers.

"Good," said Nancy. "He's talked them over. He's coming to say it's all right."

But, as the Mastodon stopped rowing and turned round within shouting distance of the Blackberry Coast, they could see that he was not looking very cheerful.

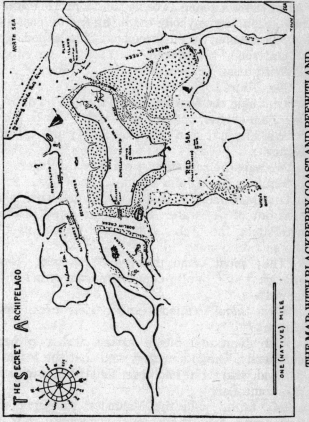

THE MAP: WITH BLACKBERRY COAST AND PEEWITLAND

"Shall I give the password?" said Roger. "Kara-badang and the rest of it."

"Shut up," said John. "Wait till he does it himself."

But the Mastodon gave no password. He might have been just anybody inquiring from a passer-by. "You haven't seen three boats?" he called.

"Only one," said Roger.

"With a sail?"

"No. Yours."

"Oh," said the Mastodon, and then, "You didn't see them earlier, before I started?"

"We haven't seen anybody but you," called Nancy.

"We saw the rockets last night," said Roger.

"Shut up," said John again.

The Mastodon waited a moment, with his oars out of the water, looking far away to the west along the Secret Water, and then away to the east once more.

"They must come this way," he said. "Not enough water yet to come through behind the island."

"Lost them?" called Nancy. "Eels *are* a bit slippery."

Both John and Susan looked at her rather doubtfully. They knew very well that the Mastodon was wishing he had never told them anything about the Eels.

"My fault," said the Mastodon. "I ought to have gone first thing in the morning, but I thought they'd be coming to *Speedy*."

"Poor beast, he'd awfully like to be friendly," said Nancy under her breath. "We haven't seen them. Not today," she called aloud. "And we've been on the look-out."

"May as well let him know we've got our eyes open," she added quietly.

"I've been to their camp and there's nobody in it," called the Mastodon, "*Lapwing*'s there. And they've put up their tents. Perhaps I ought to have asked the missionaries. I'd better go back. They must have been sent to the town for something."

He spun his boat round and pulled away, back once more towards the mouth of the Secret Water.

The explorers watched him out of sight. Suddenly Peggy said, "Supposing he's wrong and they didn't go to the town. . . . "

"Not the whole way," said Peggy. "But suppose they got across and landed early, before the tide went down too far."

"Barbecued billygoats," said Nancy, who seemed to have shaken off the effects of the Eel's blood. "They may be on the island now."

"But they aren't," said John. "They couldn't have kept hidden all the time. Titty and Bridget would have seen them and signalled."

"You've got to remember they're Eels," said Nancy.

"They aren't invisible," said John. "Look here, the water's coming up well. We ought to be able to take a boat and find out if there is a way round behind all this. I'm pretty sure there must be. It ought to be all right if we go full tilt. They'll be a long time if they've gone to the town."

But Peggy's idea was bothering Susan now.

"It's no good taking the boats away," she said. "What if Titty signals and we want to get back? If you go up the creek you may be right out of reach. And look here John, we ought to be on our own island long before high tide."

"She's right," said Nancy. "No good our being here keeping a look out on the Secret Water when they can bring their whole fleet sailing up the Red Sea."

"They can't yet," said John.

"They'll be able to soon," said Nancy.

"I'm going back," said Susan.

*

It was almost a calm, and it was not worth while to hoist the sails. They rowed grimly home. Today's surveying had amounted to next to nothing compared with the big areas explored on other days.

For a moment the flags at the camp were hidden from them as they rowed across, but they saw them again as they came to the mouth of Goblin Creek.

"That's all right," said Susan. "Just for one awful moment I thought they'd gone."

"John," said Nancy. "I've been thinking. I was wrong about the totem. What about yanking it up and taking it across and leaving it on *Speedy*. If they don't want us, we don't want them or their beastly totems. Let them find it there."

"Perhaps we'd better," said John. "He probably wishes he'd never given it to us."

"Of course we could burn it," said Nancy.

"Better just take it back," said John.

"I'd like to fry the lot of them," said Nancy.

"And eat them," said Roger.

*

No one met them at the landing place.

"Rotten sentries," said Roger.

"Don't pull our boat up, Peggy," said Nancy. "We'll want it in a minute to take that totem back."

She led the way up the track to the camp.

"Hullo," she said. "Titty's thought of it too. She's taken the totem down."

Titty, hard at work, did not hear them coming.

"What have you done with the totem?" asked Nancy.

Titty, pen in hand, started violently.

"Gosh!" she said. "Lucky I didn't blot. I've nearly done."

"Where's the totem?" said Nancy. "We're going to hurl it back."

Titty stretched her cramped arms and rolled over.

"Isn't it there?" she said.

"No it isn't," said Nancy. "There's the hole where it was and there's my watch."

"Where's Bridget?" said Susan.

"Sentry-go on the dyke," said Titty.

"Oh look here, Titty, you must have pulled it up. It was here when we left."

"But I haven't touched it," said Titty. "Perhaps Bridget . . . "

"Bridget!" called Susan. "Run along the dyke and fetch her, Roger."

"She was here not long ago," said Titty. "Then she went off with Sinbad."

"She'd never have taken the totem," said Nancy.

"Well, I haven't touched it," said Titty.

"Gosh," said John. "You've made a lovely job of the map."

"Bridget! Ship's brat! Bridget!" They heard Roger calling along the dyke.

Susan, packing away the knapsack and the empty bottles, heard a sudden doubt in his voice. She started up. Roger was coming back along the dyke, calling now and again, and looking far away over the meadows.

"I can't see her anywhere," he said, as he came back into the camp. "She's been at the corner by the little island. I found her hair ribbon on the path."

"Blow your whistle for her," said John.

Susan blew the mate's whistle that was usually enough to bring Bridget on the run. There was no answer.

"All shout together," said Roger.

"Bridget! BRIDGET!" Six explorers shouted at the top of their voices, standing on the dyke by the tents and looking in all directions over the island.

There was no answer.

"She can't have gone far," said Titty. "She had Sinbad with her. She was just walking up and down on the dyke."

"She's gone down to the water and tumbled in," said Susan.

"Oh no . . . no . . . no . . ." said Titty.

"It's nothing like that," said Nancy, and they

turned to see a surprising glitter in her eyes. "Can't you see? The totem's gone too."

They stared at her.

"She's a prisoner. She's been taken by the Eels. They've grabbed Bridget and they've grabbed the totem too. Come on Roger. Where did you find that ribbon?"

"It's my fault," said Titty, "trying to get the map done. I ought never to have let her go out of sight."

Nancy, with Roger trying to keep up with her, was already racing along the top of the dyke.

CHAPTER XVIII

EAGER PRISONER

It had been a dull morning for Bridget after the others had sailed away leaving her and Titty to look after the camp. Titty was so far behind with the map-making that she could think of nothing else. There were the separate maps and charts of the channel to Witch's Quay to compare and to transfer in pencil to Daddy's map, together with the work done on Mastodon Island, and Nancy's map of the channel to the town, besides the map of Flint Island, and the marshes between Magellan Straits and Cape Horn. And the pencilled outline was only the beginning. All had to be done in ink. The marshes had to be shown by dozens of tiny tufts of reeds, a boat or two or a fish had to be put in to distinguish the water from the land, and if there was room without making things too much of a muddle, she meant to mark with dotted lines the actual journeys of the explorers. Titty had been much too busy to talk. Bridget had begun by being an active sentinel marching up and down the dyke. She had seen the Mastodon row away. Then, needing company, she had helped for a time by keeping the separate maps from blowing away, but stones made better paperweights than Bridget's fingers. For a time she had held the little bottle of Indian ink, but from the point of view of the person who had to dip a pen in it the bottle was really much better on the ground where it was not so likely to move about. Then, as sentinel again, she had walked to and fro, looking far away at the explorers on the other side of the Secret Water and watching for signs of the savages. She had seen the shadow of the meal-dial creep slowly round, shortening as it crept, until at last it had darkened the paper label marked "Dinner". She had waited to disturb Titty till the shadow touched the paper. Then she had brought out the sandwiches, the oranges, the two bottles of ginger beer that Susan had left for their dinner. Titty was still drawing, lying on her stomach with her nose in the map. "Dinner's ready," said Bridget. "All but Sinbad's."

Titty put down her pen, corked the ink bottle and rolled stiffly over, stretching her cramped arms.

"Not half done," she said. "All right, Ship's baby. I'll open Sinbad's tin."

"He's been squeaking for it like anything," said Bridget.

Even dinner had been rather melancholy after the first cheerful moments when Sinbad had been lapping up his milk and Titty and Bridget had been biting into their sandwiches, three explorers feeding together in their camp. They were at the orange stage when Bridget asked, "I say, Titty, tell me about human sacrifices. Have you ever been one?"

"No," said Titty, "but don't you go thinking about that. It isn't going to happen. They aren't going to have anything to do with us and the Mastodon isn't either any more."

"But what about all the blood?"

"They don't know about that," said Titty, "but it wouldn't make any difference if they did. They've made him wish he'd never even talked to us."

"I think it's beastly," said Bridget.

"It jolly well is," said Titty, "but the map's the main thing. We're going to get it done even without the Mastodon."

*

After dinner when Titty settled down to work again, Bridget and Sinbad wandered off along the top of the dyke. Just at the corner where the dyke turned east was a good place for a sentinel. From that point you could see all along the dyke to the camp and beyond it. You could look the other way and see the patch of marsh at the corner that turned into a tiny island at high tide. You could see the creek curling towards the Red Sea. You could look out eastwards over the whole island to the distant prairie and its grazing buffaloes.

Bridget sat down. Yes, this was a very good place for a sentinel. You could see without being seen, because of the tall grass on either side of the trodden path along the top of the dyke. She looked at the camp, the row of white tents, where Titty, hard at work again, was deaf and blind to everything except the following of pencilled lines with a careful pen. Bridget felt sleepy. She played with Sinbad for a minute or two, but Sinbad also had just had dinner and was inclined to sleep.

The sentinel lay down and tickled Sinbad behind his ears.

It was very hot.

The sentinel rested her head on her arm and looked at Sinbad on Sinbad's own level.

The sentinel dozed.

*

Titty, Able-seaman and draughtsman to the expedition, scratched in tuft after tuft of reeds, three little upward strokes with a fine mapping pen for each tuft. The blank map, that might have been anything, was coming alive, inch by inch. The explored part was slowly spreading over it. Water, dykes, marshland, channels were beginning to look like what they were, very different from Daddy's rough pencilled scrawls and the plain white spaces of the unknown. One, two, three strokes to a tuft, and each tuft the same distance from the next one, made marshland really look like marshland. That cow in the buffalo country really was not bad. Better perhaps if its horns were a wee bit longer. Anyhow anybody would know that was a ship marking the Secret Water. But never mind that. More tufts. She must get all this lot done before John and Nancy and the others came back with a new lot of explored country to put in. One, two, three. One, two, three. Ow, that tuft was a bit too near the one before. What was that noise by the tents? Bridget of course. Poor old Bridgie, not going to be a human sacrifice after all. One, two, three. One, two, three. Titty never turned her head.

*

From the further side of the dyke a savage watched her. He lay on the slope of the dyke

between the row of the tents and the little pond.
Between two tents he could see her. He looked
along the dyke to the north. A black hand and
arm waved in the grass. All clear. Inch by inch
he crawled up over the edge of the dyke, and
between two of those white tents. Yes. There it
was, only half a dozen yards from that girl. What
had those palefaces hung round its sacred neck? A
watch? Eel-like he wriggled forward. Titty moved
and he lay still. She dipped her pen and went on
working. Flat to the ground he wriggled on. His
hand was on the thing he had come to take when
she moved again, but it was only to stretch her
fingers cramped from holding the pen. She never
turned. A moment later the watch lay on the
ground where the totem had been and the savage,
clutching his prize, was slipping back into hiding
on the further side of the dyke.

*

Bridget woke slowly. It was as if a scarlet
curtain hung before her eyes, the sun through
her closed eyelids. She opened them and blinked,
still more than half asleep. She had a queer feeling
that she was not alone. She rolled over and saw
Sinbad. Of course it was Sinbad. He had been
there all the time. How long had she been asleep?
He must have been very lonely to have started
playing by himself. She saw the kitten crouching
to the ground, his tail switching slowly from side to
side. The kitten pounced. He had pounced on the
tufted end of a weed that was lying on the path.
Sleepily, Bridget watched him. He was crouching
again, and that same weed seemed to be a little

A SAVAGE WATCHED HER

further from him. He pounced and as he pounced
the flowery tuft slipped out of reach. The kitten
waited, puzzled, close to Bridget's head. The weed
began to twist as if someone were twiddling the
other end of it. Bridget's eyes followed it into the
grass. The grass parted and Bridget found herself
looking straight into another pair of eyes, dark,
sparkling, smiling at her through the stalks.

"Sh!" said a voice, just as Bridget was going
to jump up.

The grasses opened wider, and Bridget saw
that she was looking into the face of a girl who
was lying on the sloping side of the dyke, just
high enough to bring her head to the level of the
footpath on the top.

"Who are you?" said Bridget, whispering,
though there was no one else to hear, and
then, suddenly, she guessed.

"Kara ... kara ... karabadangbaraka," she
stuttered.

"Akarabgandabarak," said the girl instantly.

"Gnad," said Bridget. "Gnad ... You're Daisy.
He said you always said 'Gand' by mistake."

"He's said lots too much," said Daisy. "Who
are you?"

"I'm Bridget, and ... "

"Sh!" said Daisy. "Just a minute ... All right.
What?" She was talking to someone else, whom
Bridget could not see.

"Stuck in the middle of their camp," said
a boy's voice. "Beastly cheek. They must have
swiped it from Don. They'd even hung a watch
on it. So Dee kept *cave* and I eeled it out. One
of them was there too, but she didn't spot me."

"Where's Dee?"

"Coming."

There was a stir in the grass on the island side of the dyke and someone shot over the dyke and into hiding again.

"Good," said the voice of Daisy.

"Dum did a lovely bit of eeling," said a third voice. "The paleface never stirred. How do you think they got it?"

"They've got the password too." That was Daisy's voice.

Her face showed again through the grasses.

"Hi, you!" she said.

"Yes," said Bridget.

"Don't get up. . . . Wriggle down on this side."

Bridget did as she was told, and crawled through the grass down the steep side of the dyke.

Two boys and a girl, crouching below the dyke where they could not be seen by anybody on the island, watched her arrive. For one moment even Bridget was a little startled. Except for their faces all three were shiny and black. All three were in bathing things, but it was hard to see where bathing things ended and mud began. The savages. There was no doubt about it. Bridget had her chance and knew it.

"Karabadangbaraka," she said.

"I told you so," said Daisy.

"Akarabgnadabarak," said the two boys together.

"Has he asked you yet?" said Bridget.

"Asked us what?" said Daisy.

"He said he'd have to ask you. But I really

am old enough. Even John and Susan said so. So it all depends on you."

"What does?"

"Well, I'm quite old enough to be a human sacrifice, and not a bit skinny. . . . " She looked at Daisy whose mouth had fallen open. . . . "And he said I'd do very well, only he'd have to ask you first. . . . "

"Tide's high enough to get through to *Speedy*," said one of the boys. "Better go and see what he's been up to."

The girl seemed to think for a minute. "No," she said at last. "Let him come and find us." She whispered to the boys, and then turned to Bridget.

"You'll have to be captured first," she said.

"Then you will let me," said Bridget.

"Come along," said Daisy.

"Can I bring Sinbad?"

"Who?"

"Our kitten. They rescued him at sea. . . . "

"Really at sea?" said the boy called Dee.

"On the way to Holland," said Bridget.

"Can you catch him?" said Daisy. "He can be a prisoner too."

"But not a sacrifice," said Bridget. "They all promised I could. Come on, Sinbad. Quick."

Sinbad himself seemed anxious to join them. He pushed through the grass. Bridget picked him up.

Daisy, the female savage, was talking earnestly to the other two. "Well, if we can't, we can't," she said. "But we're going to try." She turned to Bridget. "Now then. You keep close to me. Pity your dress is so clean. That blue can be seen for miles."

"It was much cleaner before I slipped," said Bridget.

"You could roll in the mud," said Daisy.

"Susan wouldn't like it."

"Who's Susan? Missionary?"

"Mate," said Bridget.

"All right," said Daisy. "So long as you don't get seen. We shan't because of the mud. That's why we do it. But a dress as bright as that. Well, if anybody does see you we'll just have to bolt for it and leave you behind."

"Oh no," begged Bridget. "They said I could if you'd let me."

"On the trail," said Daisy, who seemed to be in command, though the boys were bigger in size. "Dum leads, Dee at the rear. Nobody shows a head above the dyke. If we see anybody we'll all go down in the mud, Susan or no Susan. . . . "

"I mustn't really," said Bridget.

"Let's hope you won't have to. Come on, prisoner!"

"And you'll let me be the human sacrifice?"

Already the savages were on the move. The one whom Daisy called Dum galloped ahead, keeping well below the top of the dyke, looking keenly about him, a stooping, running figure the colour of the mud. Daisy followed him with Bridget, who was carrying the kitten. The other savage, whose name seemed to be Dee, came after them, looking behind him every now and then as if to see that they were not pursued.

Bridget in her blue shirt trotted cheerfully along with the mud-coated savages. John and Susan and Titty had been wrong after all. Even

Nancy had been wrong. They had all said that the savages would have nothing to do with them, and that even the Mastodon would not be able to keep his promise. Well, they were wrong. Bridget was extremely happy. She was going to be a human sacrifice after all.

They hurried along the foot of the curving dyke close to the mud of the Red Sea. Bridget wanted an answer to her question, but was soon too short of breath to speak, and anyhow the answer must be Yes or they would never be taking her with them. How wrong the others had been.

"I'll carry the kitten for a bit," said the female savage.

Bridget handed Sinbad over and they ran on.

Suddenly the foremost savage stopped dead, took three or four quick steps to one side, stooping low, and threw himself full length in the mud. Bridget suddenly found herself flat in the grass. The female savage had pulled her down, put the kitten into her hands, and rolled sideways off the dyke. Bridget looked round. The third savage had disappeared. If she had not known exactly where to look for Daisy, Bridget could have thought she was alone.

"Flat as you can," came a whisper from Daisy lying in the mud. "It's the farmer. Bother your dress being so bright."

"I've got a lot more mud on it now," said Bridget breathlessly.

"Good."

Some distance ahead of them a man was standing on the top of the dyke, watching the rising tide spread over the mud of the inland sea. He had not seen them. Bridget lay still. For a moment the man seemed to be looking directly towards them.

"It's the man from the kraal," whispered Bridget. "He's a friend."

"Don't move. He's a paleface." The answering whisper came from the mud.

The man seemed to look right round the horizon. He turned, strode off the dyke and was gone.

The savages gave him a minute or two.

Then, glistening with fresh mud, they were up and on the move once more. Just before they came to the place where the road from the farm came over the dyke they stopped, and the foremost savage signalled to them to wait while he scouted. Bridget lost sight of him again and again while he wormed himself through the grass.

Then she saw a black arm flung in the air.

"Coast clear," whispered the female savage, and they ran on, crossed the road, and, still keeping well below the top of the dyke, turned a corner. Here the water ran close in to the land. Three small sailing dinghies lay some distance away among the weeds. The foremost savage was already plucking at an anchor hidden in a tussock. A long painter slapped and dripped as he tugged, and a dinghy left the weeds and shot in towards the shore. Daisy and the other savage did the same and three little boats were dragged in and grounded at their feet.

"Hop in," said Daisy.

"My boots are awfully muddy," said Bridget.

"Not as muddy as we are. We'll wash the boats out afterwards."

Bridget scrambled in, Daisy after her. The other two savages pushed off in their boats. All three rowed out and away into the channel. Presently mud banks and weedy marshes hid the island.

They stopped rowing and let the boats drift.

Bridget wondered what was going to happen next. There was a splash, and then another. Two savages had gone overboard, bobbed up again and were hanging to their boats with one arm while they washed the mud off with the other.

"Won't be a minute," said Daisy. "We've got to think of the missionaries." The next moment she too was over the side, and rapidly changing colour.

Presently the three savages climbed in again over the sterns of their boats, not exactly white, for they were very sunburnt, but looking almost as if they were explorers and not savages at all.

"No wind," said Daisy. "Tide coming in. We'll have to row like smoke."

The three savages bent to their oars. The three little boats foamed through the water. The marshes closed in on either side as the channel narrowed, and presently opened again.

"We've done it all right," said Daisy.

"Where are we going?" asked Bridget.

"Our camp," said Daisy.

"I knew I was old enough," said Bridget.

CHAPTER XIX

HOT ON THE TRAIL

"Here's where I found it," said Roger.

"Here's where they got her," said Nancy. "Look at the way the grass is all broken. Someone's been lying here on the side of the dyke."

"But look at all the mud on the grass."

"She's fallen in the mud," said Susan. "Anything may have happened."

"Well if she's been in the mud she's got out again," said John. "She couldn't have got all that mud on the grass before she went in."

"I say, look here," said Roger. "Someone's been fairly wallowing." He had gone down the side of the dyke and was looking at the muddy ditch that at high water cut off the marshy point and made an island of it. "Looks as if it was a young hippo. It couldn't be the Mastodon?"

"He's been away all day. We've seen him," said John.

"Those aren't Bridget's footmarks," said Peggy, who had also gone down to the edge of the ditch. "They're longer. Besides, if she'd taken her boots off we'd have found them. Whoever made these had bare feet."

"Somebody's been lying down here," said Roger. "And here's another lot of mud."

Nancy, stooping low, was moving along the foot of the dyke. Suddenly she straightened herself. "Susan," she said, "have a look at this."

In the soft ground at the edge of the mud was a group of clear footprints. Some showed toes, but there were a few smaller ones without.

"Those are Bridget's," said Susan. "I'd know them anywhere."

"She stood here," said Nancy, "and somebody else with no shoes on was talking to her. Two other people. That bare foot's bigger than the other one. Eels, I bet you anything."

"But why didn't she yell?" said Titty. "I'd have heard her."

"Not if you were drawing," said Roger. "When you're drawing you have to be prodded."

"Perhaps she didn't yell," said Nancy. "Perhaps she couldn't. Gagged. Bound hand and foot." She pulled up short on seeing Susan's face.

"Come on," shouted Peggy. "This is the way they went." She had gone on along the foot of the dyke, and was pointing to a trail of broken and bent grass, and to another lot of footprints on a soft patch of ground.

"They couldn't have got ashore here," said John, looking out over the marshes, "or got afloat again. They may be still on the island."

"Come on. A rescue. A rescue," cried Nancy. "Catch them before they get to their boats."

The explorers, like a pack of hounds, nose to the scent, hurried along the foot of the dyke. Bent and trodden grass showed the way the savages and their prisoner had made off.

"Hullo," Roger, who was galloping ahead, suddenly stopped. "Here are footprints going the other way."

"Well," said Nancy. "They had to get here first. The Red Sea's been dry most of the day." She hurried on.

"Cheer up, Susan," said John. "We'll get her again."

"She'll have been awfully frightened," said Susan. "I ought never to have left her. It isn't Titty's fault. You know what it's like when she's doing something."

"Can't think how they managed it," said John.

"Good Eels," said Nancy.

"Beasts," said Titty.

They hurried on below the dyke towards the place where the cart track from the farm came over it and down to the Red Sea, where, already, the waters had met over the Wade and the mudflats were narrowing as the tide crept over them.

Roger, who was again running ahead, stopped once more.

"Someone fell down," he said. "You can see where they lay on the grass."

"But look here," said Nancy. "This is mad. More wallowing. Look at this. What on earth were they doing, going off the bank and rolling in the mud?"

"Don't wait," said Susan. She hurried on, following the track clearly marked in the grass. "It doesn't matter what they did. We've got to find her. I do wish I'd stayed in the camp with her."

Where the cart track came down to the Red Sea there was damp ground for a few yards and no grass on it.

"It *is* Eels," said Roger. "Two running barefoot, and Bridget."

"Three of them," said John. "That pair's different from this, and these are smaller than either. Three barefoot and Bridget."

"Oh don't wait to look at them," said Susan.

They ran on, and suddenly found they were running through grass that had never been trodden. The trackers spread out up and over the dyke, like hounds that have lost the scent. Away to the right were the marshy islands of the Magellan Straits. Away to the left were quiet fields with grazing cattle. The sun shone warm on the red brick of the native kraal in the middle of the island. Far ahead of them was the line of the open sea, and the golden sand dunes of Flint Island. But there was never a sign of savages or prisoner.

Peggy was the first to turn back, and within a minute she was calling to them.

"Got something, Peggy?" called Nancy, and added, "She's a galoot on some things but pretty good on tracks."

Peggy was pointing at the ground. The tide was lapping near the bank, and by a tuft of grass she had found heavy footprints, and three deep holes with torn edges. From this tuft it was as if lines had been lightly scratched on the mud. People had been trampling there. People had jumped from one soft tussock to another.

"Boats," said John. "They had their anchors here. They've gone."

Titty was already on the top of the dyke, racing back as fast as she could run.

"That's it," cried Nancy. "Come on. They've taken her with them to their camp. We can't get after them without boats. Come on. Back to our landing place." John, Susan, Peggy and Roger pelted after her, with Titty already far ahead of them.

Breathlessly they reached the camp. Breathlessly they splashed down the marshy path to the landing place. Nobody bothered to wash the mud off, as they tumbled into the boats and pushed off, six of them, three to a boat.

"You steer, Roger," said Susan. "John and I'll take an oar each."

"I'll manage all right," said John.

"No," said Susan, who felt that every moment counted, and could not bear the thought of sitting there doing nothing while someone else rowed.

"I'll keep time with you," said John.

Nancy saw what they were doing, and for different reasons did the same. "Titty'll keep us straight," she said. "Can't let them beat us. Go it, Peggy. One. Two. One. Two. Lift her along."

The two boats shot out of Goblin Creek and began the long pull down the Secret Water.

*

"What are we going to do?" asked Roger.

"Get her back," panted John.

*

"What are we going to do?" asked Titty.

"Bust those Eels," jerked Nancy, as she swung forward with her oar.

*

It was hard rowing against the tide, but they came at last to the buoy with a cross on it and the channel leading between their island and the sandy dunes of Flint Island. Both boats swung round to the right as if going up to the town. There were the yachts they had seen at anchor, three of them . . . no . . . four. Another had come in since yesterday and was lying in the bay nearer the mouth of the channel than the other three. The fourth was the yellow cutter.

"There's their ship," said Roger.

"Better go straight to it and ask for her," said Susan.

John wiped his forehead. "We can't do that," he said. "We don't want to get them in a row with their missionaries."

"But if they've got her aboard," said Susan. "They ought never to have taken her."

"There's only a little punt lying astern," said John. "They won't have taken her there. Hullo. Nancy's seen something."

Nancy and Peggy had stopped rowing. Their boat was a little way ahead and Nancy was pointing in towards the shore.

John and Susan pulled on, Susan watching the yacht all the time, looking for any sign of a prisoner.

"Their boats," said Roger.

Three small sailing dinghies lay in a row, pulled well up on the bright golden beach of Flint Island. There were no tents to be seen, but plenty of footmarks going up from the shore.

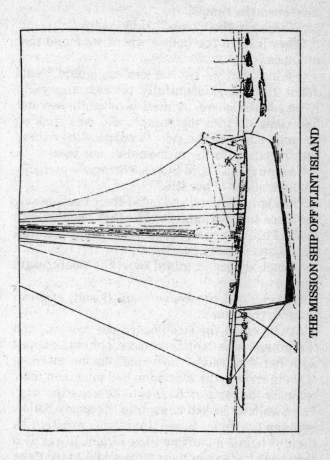

THE MISSION SHIP OFF FLINT ISLAND

"They've landed," said Nancy quietly. "What do we do? Go in quietly, grab their boats and then rush the camp?"

"Where are their tents?" said Peggy.

"They'll be in the hollow where we found that fireplace."

"Funny they've left no one on guard," said John. He looked doubtfully towards the yacht lying off the shore. A man in a white sweater had come up into the cockpit and was shaking his pipe out over the side. "I suppose they think they're safe with the missionaries out there."

"Do hurry up," said Susan. "Bridget's probably frightened out of her life."

They rowed in and grounded their boats beside the three small sailing dinghies they had last seen at Pin Mill. Nancy and John took the anchors well up the steep sandy beach.

"Somebody stand guard over the boats," said Nancy.

"Never mind the boats," said Susan, and ran towards the dunes.

At the top of the steep beach she stopped, and the others, who had been close behind, stopped with her. No wonder now that, on the morning of their arrival, the Mastodon had mistaken their camp for the camp of the friends he was expecting. The Swallows looked down into the sandy hollow between the dunes to see three tents exactly like their own, and a fourth a little larger. It was as if somebody had taken their tents and planted them in a new place. But it did not seem that anybody was there. They had expected to come upon the Eels and their prisoner, not upon a deserted camp.

"They must have known we were after them," said Nancy.

"Bridget! Bridget!" Susan called again.

"No good shouting if they've got her gagged and bound," said Nancy.

But at that moment, Bridget herself, neither bound nor gagged, crawled out of the larger tent.

"Hullo, Susan," she called. "They've agreed. They say I'm quite old enough and I'm going to be a human sacrifice after all."

"Oh, Bridget," cried Susan. "Are you all right?"

"What happened?" said John.

But others were coming out of the tent. Two boys and a girl, all in black bathing things.

"Karabadangbaraka!" All three spoke together.

For a moment nobody answered.

"I remembered it," said Bridget. "And she did say 'gand' instead of 'gnad'."

"They didn't hurt you?" asked Roger fiercely.

"Of course not," said Bridget. "And they're going to tell him it's all right."

"Karabadangbaraka," said the girl earnestly, and then stamped her foot. "Aren't you Eels?"

"Look here," said John. "There's absolutely no need for you to be friends with us if you don't want to. But it's no good trying to make us clear out, because we can't. We're marooned. We can't go till the ship comes to take us. And anyway I don't see why we should. There's plenty of room."

"It was all a mistake," said the girl. "We didn't know what you were like till we caught Bridget. We had no idea you were blood brothers."

"You oughtn't to have taken Bridget," said Susan.

"It was too good a chance to miss," said the girl. "And here's something else of yours. We thought you'd bagged it." She darted back into the tent and came back with the painted totem pole.

"But how did you get it?" said Titty. "I never left the camp all day."

A slow grin spread over the face of the larger of the two boys.

The girl looked at Susan. "Are you Eels or are you not?" she said. "You've never given the countersign."

"Congers and Lampreys," said Nancy, and gave Susan a look as powerful as a battering ram. "Try us again."

"Karabadangbaraka," said the three savages.

"Akarabgnadabarak," burst from the seven explorers.

"That's all right," said the girl. "I'm Daisy. These are my brothers. We're all Eels. They're not twins, but everybody thinks they are. I call them Dum and Dee, you, know, Tweedledum and Tweedledee, and you can too as you're blood brothers. You must be John and you're Susan. And that's Roger. Which is the one with the funny name?"

"Oh no," said Bridget. "This is Susan. That's Peggy. This is Titty. And that's Captain Nancy. I told you. She and Peggy are pirates when they're at home."

"Not here," said Nancy quickly. "It's a much better place for savages than pirates. And with Eel blood in us. . . ."

"Oh but look here, Nancy," said John, who saw her turning savage before his eyes. "We've simply got to finish the map. The last two days we've done hardly anything."

"What about the map?" said Daisy. "What's it for? I couldn't make head or tail of what our prisoner was saying."

"Exploring," said Titty. "And the Mastodon was helping. That's why we did all the blooding. And then your letter upset everything and he wished he hadn't."

"We'll all help," said Daisy. "It's the best thing he ever did. And Mastodon's a lovely name for Don. I wish we'd thought of it ourselves."

"Where is he?" asked Nancy.

"He's been looking for you," said John.

"We haven't seen him," said Daisy.

"He's pretty miserable," said Nancy.

CHAPTER XX

ALL'S WELL

THE Mastodon, low in spirits, was rowing down the channel from the town. Twice already that day he had been to Flint Island and seen only the missionaries' ship, no savage boats at their usual landing place and empty tents in the camp of the Eels. He had seen the signals last night and they must have seen his answer. All morning he had been expecting them. They could not have sailed through the Red Sea, because until late in the afternoon there had been no water to let them. He had been sure they would come sailing up the Secret Water, three little boats, as they had come sailing many times before. But they had never come. Again and again he turned over in his mind what he was to say to them, to explain how and why instead of fending off the explorers he had made friends with them and even made them blood brothers of the Eels. Would they understand or would they not? Would Daisy ever forgive him for letting out the secrets they kept even from their own missionaries?

Almost he hated the explorers. Somehow they had swept him off his feet, and he had found himself eagerly telling them things he had no right to tell unless after a council of the tribe. Get rid of them? Why, they had made him welcome them instead. And then for the hundredth time he began to find excuses for them and for

himself. They were not just invaders. They had
been marooned. They could not get away until a
ship came to take them off. And it wasn't as if
they were just camping. They were explorers, and
what could be more natural than that they should
meet savages and that the savages, in return for
beads and things (Oh bother! He hadn't even got
the fishhooks to show Daisy what had happened)
should act as guides? And then that map business.
They'd never get it decently done without someone
who really did know something about mud. A poor
show they would make of it. And then he began
to feel a traitor to the explorers as well as to the
Eels. It had been pretty awful rowing past and
seeing them at work without him when he had
promised to help. And they had been jolly decent
about it. Not one of them had reproached him with
a single word. They had just watched him row by,
and today, when he had spoken to them from a
distance and asked if they had seen the Eels, they
had answered him just as if he had not let them
down.

And now the Eels would be thinking. . . . Well,
what would they be thinking? They must have
been expecting him to come to Flint Island? And
he had been expecting them to come to *Speedy*.
It had never happened before that they had not
got in touch with each other almost as soon as
they arrived. Perhaps they had thought he would
come rowing around in the dark last night. Perhaps they had wanted a council round the camp
fire. And he had just sat tight in *Speedy*, carving
a new totem to take the place of the old one he
had given to the explorers. Pretty good totem,

too, he could not help thinking, as he looked at it propped in the stern of his boat . . . though, of course, it was a pity that the paint wasn't dry. But what would Daisy say when he had to tell her that he had given another totem just as good to the strangers she had told him to drive into the sea?

And where were the Eels anyhow? He had been sure they had gone up to the town in the morning, been held there by the falling tide and had waited for the afternoon flood. And now he had rowed the whole way up to the Yacht Club Hard. And no one had seen them that day. He had just missed them the day before. He was rowing disconsolately back. He knew where *Lapwing* was anyhow, and there was only one thing to do, though it was rather humiliating to a savage. He would have to ask the missionaries. Daisy would have something to say about that too. If savages could not find out about each other without inquiring from paleface missionaries they were pretty poor savages.

He rowed steadily on, down the middle of the channel. He passed the first of the three anchored boats. What was it Titty called them? Arab dhows? Not bad. Even Daisy would like that. He passed the second, and the third. Now for *Lapwing*. He must be close to her. He lifted his oars and turned round. There she was and . . . No need to ask the missionaries after all. There were the three little boats of the Eels drawn up on the beach. And two other boats, most awfully like. . . . What on earth had happened? Had the explorers attacked them? Seven to three. And he had not been there to help. Every single thing in the world was going wrong. His oars bit the water with a splash.

"Hullo, Don!"

He looked up. This was no moment in which to talk to missionaries. But there was the he-missionary looking out from *Lapwing*'s forehatch.

"Hullo," said Don.

"We've got the kettle on here," said the he-missionary. "If you're going across to the camp, will you tell them to come when we ring the fog-bell? Tell them they can bring their friends. You too, of course."

"Thank you very much," said Don, dipped his oars again and rowed as if in a boat-race for the beach! Friends! FRIENDS! Why there might be no camp left. He had told the explorers that Daisy had ordered him to get rid of them and do anything short of burning their tents. The explorers might well have decided that attack was the best part of defence. Seven to three. What could the Eels have done against them? Don rowed as hard as he could, drove the bow of his boat up the shingle, jumped from it, threw the anchor out and charged to the rescue up the steep slope of the shore.

"Hullo, Mastodon!"

Dum, or was it Dee? greeted him before he had gone more than a couple of yards.

"What's happened?" panted Don, and gasped. "Mastodon" the Eel had called him. But that was the explorers' name for him. What, indeed, had happened? He ran up to the top of the slope and looked down into the sandy hollow of the camp.

A whole crowd of people were eagerly talking by
the tents.

"Karabadangbaraka!" called Daisy with a
laugh.

"Karabadangbaraka!" they all shouted together.

The Mastodon could hardly believe his ears. All
was peace. Eels and explorers were together, and
Daisy, Daisy herself, had been the first to give the
secret password in the presence of the people she
had said were to be driven off at all costs.

"Akarabgnadabarak," the Mastodon answered
at last in a very puzzled voice.

Then, stuck in the sand in the middle of
the camp of the Eels, he saw the totem that he
himself had planted in the camp of the explorers.

"It's a beauty," said Daisy. "We thought they'd
grabbed it so we took it away without their
knowing. We got a prisoner too. We'd no idea
that they were Eels, till Bridget told us. It's the
best thing you've ever done. And we're all going
to call you Mastodon. Don's as good a short for
Mastodon as it is for Donald. Just the name for
a savage. You'll have to make another totem for
us."

"It's in my boat, but the paint's still wet. . . . "
said the Mastodon. "You see I'd made this one for
you, and put it in their camp by mistake. . . . "

"They've told us all about it," said Daisy. "Best
mistake you've ever made. And now they're going
to let us help with the exploring, and four's not
many for a corroboree, but we can have as many
of them as we want. . . . "

"Daisy says it's all right about me," said Bridget. "I asked her."

"We're going to take them to the upper waters tomorrow. . . . All six boats. . . . "

The Mastodon looked from face to face, and saw not a hint of blame on any of them. Daisy must have forgotten the orders she had sent. The explorers must have forgotten that for two days their blood brother had held himself aloof. The same thing must have happened to Daisy that had happened to himself and everything was very much all right.

"But how did you get their totem?" he asked.

"Good eeling," said Daisy.

"They got it and got away again without my noticing anything," said Titty ruefully. "I was in the camp all the time and never knew."

"Not your fault," said Daisy. "Dum's our best Eel. He could scalp a whole camp full and the victims wouldn't know till they saw their own scalps hanging round his waist. . . . "

CLING, CLANG . . . CLING, CLANG . . . CLING, CLANG! . . .

"What's that?" said Nancy.

"It's the missionaries," said the Mastodon. "They said I was to tell you to come to *Lapwing* for tea. The others are to come too. . . . "

"Oh, we can't," said Susan.

"You must," said Daisy. "It'll be a bit sardiny in the cabin. I wonder if they know how many. Come on. They'll be awfully sick if you don't . . . COMING!" she yelled at the top of a shrill voice. . . . Then, almost whispering, she added, "No Eels. You've never heard of them. Nothing about prisoners. . . . Nothing. . . . Eels. What are eels? Fish, I think, or are they reptiles? Anyway, just part of natural history. . . . "

The Mastodon ran back to his boat and brought the new totem and set it up beside the other. "Look out for the wet paint," he said.

"You can collect yours when we come back after tea," said Daisy to the explorers. "Come on. Everybody ready? . . . Prunes and prisms. . . . Come on. . . . "

"Suffering Lampreys!" exclaimed Nancy. "However do you do it? You even look quite different."

" 'Sh!" said Daisy. "What a quaint expression. I wonder where you picked that up. . . . I think, perhaps, we had better come in your boats, so as not to have too many clustering round the *Lapwing*."

Wizard and *Firefly*, heavily laden, six in one, five and a kitten in the other, were ferried across to the *Lapwing*. Eels and explorers had somehow vanished. Anybody might have taken them for members of a picnic party.

The missionary and his wife, who looked just an ordinary pleasant couple of grown-ups, were waiting to receive them, with fenders handy, but unnecessary, as both John and Nancy showed that they could bring boats alongside a ship without damaging the paint.

"Well, this is delightful," said the she-missionary. "So you have found friends already."

"I am afraid there are an awful lot of us," said Susan.

"The more the merrier," said the he-missionary. "We've a big kettle, but not quite enough cups. But

I daresay some of you won't mind drinking out of
saucers."

"Sinbad'll like it," said Bridget.

"So'll I," said Titty hurriedly.

"And me," said Roger.

*

It was a very pleasant tea party of the sedater
sort. Polite questions were asked and answered.
The missionaries had heard at Pin Mill about the
adventures of the *Goblin* and how she had got to
Holland, and Susan earnestly explained that they
had not meant to go to sea. Nancy and Peggy
wondered whether the *Lapwing* was as big as
the *Goblin*, and learnt that she was bigger. The
explorers were shown all over her, and, with a
good deal of squeezing, it was found that only four
need have tea on deck if the he-missionary sat on
the companion steps to pass up cups of tea and
buns when wanted, and the she-missionary sat in
the doorway between the saloon and the forecabin,
which she said was the best arrangement as she
had to keep within reach of the kettle. "In *Goblin*,
the cooking place is aft," said Roger, and added,
"I think this way, with the galley forward, is
almost cosier." The he-missionary showed John
round the decks, and Roger bolted out to join
him, because, as he explained afterwards, it was
too much for him to hear Nancy solemnly talking
about gardening. Daisy was sitting in the cockpit, entertaining Susan and Titty with a few
words about School Certificates. He caught her
sparkling eye and nearly darted back again, but
blew his nose instead (lucky that time he had a

handkerchief) and hurried forward over the deck
to ask an intelligent question about the working
of the winch.

The missionaries seemed very pleased that
their children had found companions. "That will
be very pleasant," said the she-missionary, when
she heard that they were all going to spend next
day together. "Going to the upper waters is
always one of our favourite picnics. Of course
there is not much to do there, but it is a lovely
place. Only you'll have to be careful about your
tides. You have to get there as soon as the
tide will let you, and start back the moment
it begins to fall. But the boys know all about
that."

Susan, at the right moment, rose to go. Daisy
and her brothers asked if John and Nancy would
mind putting them ashore, and the whole party
left the *Lapwing* after thanking the missionaries
for letting them come aboard.

"They're the politest children I've ever met,"
they heard the she-missionary say as they were
rowing off.

"Too polite to be good," said the he-missionary.
"Daisy's up to one of her games. I know that look
in her eye." But fortunately this sentence was not
heard by the departing guests.

"You did awfully well," said Daisy, as she
landed.

"Jolly nice missionaries," said Roger.

"They are," said Daisy. "But missionaries are
missionaries. It's no good being Eels if you don't
remember that. What the eye doesn't see . . . You
know what I mean. Well, it's much better not to

give them things to grieve over. Aren't you coming
ashore?"

"We've simply got to get back," said John.
"We've got things to put on the map. And supper
to cook. And there's a speck of wind too."

"Quick," said Daisy. "Don, you get it. You
mustn't go without your totem. We'll come to
the mouth of the channel with you. . . . "

Bridget held the totem as she sat in the
bottom of *Wizard* with Sinbad on her lap. John
steered. Susan sat on the middle thwart, when
she had hoisted the sail. Close behind them Titty
was steering *Firefly*, and a convoy of four savage
boats rowed hard to keep up.

At the mouth of the Secret Water the wind
freshened, and the two boats of the explorers
drew away. The savages turned back.

"Tomorrow early," called Daisy.

"We'll be ready," John called back.

"Karabadangbaraka," called Nancy.

"Akarabgnadabarak," came from Dum, Dee,
and the Mastodon.

From Daisy came something slightly different.

"Gnad . . . gnad," shouted Bridget. "Did you
hear, Susan? She said 'Gand' again. That's how
I knew it was her when I met her in the grass."

"Well, I'm glad it's all right," said Susan. "But
you did give me an awful fright when I thought
you'd fallen in."

"Dum and Dee," said Roger. "The silent brothers. They both ought to be called Dumb."

"They're grand savages," said John. "And with
six boats we'll be able to explore a hundred miles
a day."

"We mustn't waste them," said Nancy. "Great Wriggling Congers, Titty! Look out how you're steering. We don't want to bump the other boat. Eels for ever! Suffering Lampreys! What a time we are going to have!"

*

Late that night, after dusk, when Bridget was already in bed and the others were turning in, Peggy heard the noise of oars in the creek. "What's that?" she said. "They aren't going to attack again?"

They listened.

The Mastodon's voice, extraordinarily happy, sounded across the water. "I say. I'll bring my splatchers across in the morning."

"Good," cried John.

"Karabadangbaraka," called Nancy.

"Akarabgnadabarak!" a joyful reply came out of the darkness, and the sound of oars drew rapidly away, as the Mastodon rowed up the creek to make his way to *Speedy* and his lair.

CHAPTER XXI

SIX BOATS EXPLORE

First thing in the morning, even before the breakfast things had been washed up and put away, the Mastodon arrived in the camp bringing his splatchers with him.

"Karabadangbaraka!" he greeted them joyfully, and, almost before they had time to give the countersign, went on. "Everybody's coming to supper in *Speedy* tonight. I've still got that ham and all the grub Mother gave me when I told her I'd asked you the other day."

"Three cheers!" said Roger.

"We'd love to come," said Susan. "But we've gone and eaten the mushrooms and the blackberry mash we'd meant to bring."

"There's simply tons of grub," said the Mastodon. "The only thing I'm short of is mugs and plates."

"We'll bring our own," said Susan.

"And could Roger bring his whistle?" said the Mastodon.

"I'll begin practising at once," said Roger.

"You jolly well won't," said John. "One go a day's enough for anybody."

"All right," said Roger. "I won't. But it'll be John's fault if I play false notes tonight."

"I say," said John. "Do just look at the map. Is there a way through round the place where we were yesterday?"

"I don't know," said the Mastodon. "There is a sort of gap, but it doesn't look as if it went right through. Anyway there's nothing but mud on the other side."

"It's awfully important," said John. "You see, if there's a North West Passage then where we were yesterday's an island. If there isn't it's only a promontory. You can't tell from Daddy's map. What about going to have a look?"

"No good with a falling tide," said the Mastodon. "It's gone down a long way. Didn't you say you wanted to try my splatchers? Now's the time. No good starting for the Upper Waters till the tide turns again."

"Can I have a shot, too?" said Nancy.

"And me?" said Roger. "Hullo! Here are the others."

"Karabadangbaraka!" Daisy and her brothers were rowing up Goblin Creek.

"Akarabgnadabarak!" The Mastodon and the explorers went down to the landing place to meet them.

"It's all fixed," cried Daisy as she splashed ashore. "Corroboree tomorrow night. And the missionaries are going to let us stay till after dark. And high water's pretty late. Everything's just right."

"But you'll come to supper in *Speedy* tonight," said the Mastodon. "I've got a feast all ready."

"That's all right too," said Daisy. "Only we'll have to clear off pretty early. We'll have to be up at dawn tomorrow." She whispered in the Mastodon's ear.

"We're just going splatchering," said Roger.

"Ever done it before?" asked Daisy.

"No," said Roger. "But we've seen him do it."

The two silent brothers, Dum and Dee, looked at each other.

"We'll watch," said Daisy. "Who's going first?"

"I am," said Nancy, and stood on the splatchers while the Mastodon fastened the straps over her insteps.

Slowly, inch by inch, she moved the splatchers along the mud, grabbing at the gunwale of a boat to keep her balance.

"That's not the way," said Roger. "You ought to swing them round and fairly gallop."

"Let him try," laughed Daisy.

Nancy looked oddly worried, let go of the boat and took a few steps. "Come on John. You have a go," she said. She sat on the gunwale of the boat while the Mastodon freed her feet.

John stood on the splatchers and made the straps fast. He moved slowly off. "It's not as easy as it looks," he said. One foot slid from under him on the sloping mud. He tried to balance on the other. That splatcher also began to move like a toboggan. The next moment John was sitting in the mud. He tried in vain to bring a splatcher under him. It was no good. He rolled over and struggled back to the hard on all fours.

"That's quite enough," said Susan. "You'll have to take everything off."

"He ought to have moved much faster," said Roger. "And he ought to have leant forward."

"Let's see you try it," said John.

"One all mud's quite enough," said Susan.

"Oh let him try," said Daisy.

The Mastodon fastened the splatchers for Roger.
"Now you watch," said Roger. "You ought to lean
forward and swing your legs . . . like this. . . . " He
stood for a moment. A queer look of uncertainty
came into his face. Then, remembering how he had
seen the Mastodon go running along the bottom of
his creek, he threw himself forward. The first step
was all right. So was the second. At the third he
caught one splatcher on the other and fell on his
nose.

Dum and Dee said not a word but looked
at each other and rocked with silent laughter.

"It takes practice to be a Mastodon," said Daisy.

After that, the Eels were taken up to the
camp, to visit it this time as friends not enemies.
John and Roger spread their clothes on bushes,
decided that for the rest of the day they would
wear bathing things, like the savages, and had a
wallow in the pond to get rid of the mud that they
had not taken off with their clothes. Susan and
Peggy set to work to make packets of sandwiches
for the expedition to the Upper Waters. John and
Titty made copies of the blank map showing just
the part west of Goblin Creek, so that there would
be one for each of the six boats. The Mastodon,
squatting beside them, was admiring the work
that had been done, and pointing out one or two
places where he thought the surveyors had gone
a little wrong. A little way along the dyke shouts
of laughter told where Nancy, Daisy and the
Eel brothers were holding a private conference.
Bridget, rather cross at having been shoo'd away
by them, was playing with Sinbad. Roger, chivvied
from the camp, was practising "The Keel Row" on

his whistle down by the boats, and watching for the turning of the tide. Slowly the water went down, and at last began to creep up again over the mud.

Roger came running with the news.

"It's started coming up," he said.

"Give it at least an hour," said the Mastodon. "No good going before there's water in the channels."

Final preparations were made. Bridget unwillingly agreed that Sinbad should stay in camp. "He'll be miserable in a little boat all day," said Susan, and promised that he should come on the next expedition by land. The Mastodon pointed out that the bigger boats would have to keep to the main channels.

"The little channels'll be the hardest to map," said John. "Look here. Titty and I'll have to go in the Eels' boats. They're shallower than ours."

"I'm going with Daisy," said Nancy.

"In some places we may have to get out and push," said the Mastodon cheerfully.

"Do let's start," said Titty at last.

"What about having dinner first?" said Susan.

"Better eat under way," said the Mastodon. "We might just as well be drifting up with the flood."

*

Half an hour later the camp was deserted. Goblin Creek was deserted, too, but, if anybody had been looking from an aeroplane they would have seen something like a floating island moving slowly with the tide in the middle of the Secret Water.

It was a smooth, oily calm, without a breath of wind. *Wizard* had tied alongside *Firefly*. Nancy and Daisy, John and Dee, Titty and Dum, each couple in one of the tiny dinghies of the Eels had thrown painters aboard one of the larger boats. The Mastodon with Roger had rowed round them all, and ended by coming up close under *Wizard*'s stern. All six boats were closed together. Food was being passed from boat to boat, and everybody was busy eating.

Slowly the tide carried the floating island of boats up the middle of the wide channel. On either side there were low green shores, and wide stretches of shining mud. Ahead the glassy water lost itself in the distance. There, too, were green shores. The roof of a house showed far away and low green islands fringed with mud.

"Oughtn't we to be rowing?" said John at last.

"No good hurrying till the tide's a bit higher," said the Mastodon.

"I've started filling in my map," said Roger.

"But there's nothing to put in yet," said John.

"We've put it in," said Roger. "That's just it. And jolly good, too. Specially the bananas."

"But what's that got to do with the map?" said John.

"It's all right," said Roger. "I've just put in 'Here the fleet hogged', and so we have."

A little patch of ripples showed on the glassy water, and then another.

"Cat's paws," said Daisy.

"Wind coming," said John.

"Cast off," said the Mastodon. "Come on Roger.

If they're going to be able to sail, we'd better start rowing."

In a moment the floating island began to break up into half a dozen little boats. Roger and the Mastodon shot out ahead. In all the other boats people were getting up sails.

"Eels' wind," said Daisy, hauling her little sail up while Nancy, for once an idle passenger, sat on the bottom of the boat with a pencil and her copy of the map.

"Why Eels'?" she asked.

"It's just the wind we want," panted Daisy swinging on her halyard. "It's just a perfect wind. We'll be able to sail both ways without tacking."

Susan, in command of *Wizard*, had fixed her rudder, and put Bridget, for once promoted to able-seaman, at the tiller while she hoisted sail.

Peggy, alone in *Firefly*, was having slight difficulties but when John offered to come and help she answered, as if she was Nancy, "Jibbooms and bobstays! Shiver my timbers! It's only stuck. Barbecued billygoats! Up she goes."

Dum and Dee, anxious to show their passengers what savages could do, had their sails set and drawing almost before their passengers knew what was happening.

"I say," said Titty. "That was jolly good."

"Dead heat," said Dum. "Sometimes Dee's quicker than me, and sometimes not."

"What do we do now, White Chief?" asked Dee, grabbing the tiller and stepping over John's legs.

"Let's all go on together to where the channels divide," said John, curling round in the bottom of the boat, so that he could keep his chart on the middle thwart. "But let's keep near the northern shore. I haven't been along this bit. You see when we were doing that part we thought you were enemies and we had to keep within sight of the camp."

Dee chuckled. "You didn't keep quite near enough."

"You wouldn't have done it if Titty hadn't been so busy with the map," said John. "Anyway, it's a good thing you did. But it's a pity that we haven't properly done that northern shore. I say, is that an island ahead?"

"One of them," said the savage guide.

"Look here," exclaimed John a few minutes later. "What's that gap? Is there a way through? If there is, all that part where we were exploring may be an island."

Dee looked where John was pointing. There was a break in the long line of the dyke to the north of them.

"There may be," he said.

"Hi! Mastodon!" shouted John.

The Mastodon stopped rowing, and looked back. In this light wind, he was ahead of the sailing boats. "What is it?" he shouted.

John pointed. "Is that the gap you were talking about?"

"Yes," shouted the Mastodon.

The tide was carrying them past.

"I say, let's try it," said John.

It was at that moment that Bridget saw the seal. Ahead of them where the Secret Water seemed to lose itself in low green shores, there

was a spit of mud or sand and on it something had
moved. "Look," said Bridget. "Somebody bathing
and wallowing. Just like Dum and Dee."

Everybody looked that way in a hurry, bristling
at the thought of a stranger.

"It's a seal!" cried Titty, looking through the
telescope.

"It's the seal," said Daisy.

"It's George," said the Mastodon, and swiftly
and quietly rowed towards it.

The seal, idly sunning itself after a bathe,
might have been a sort of magnet. The whole
fleet turned towards it. Even John for a moment
or two had eyes for nothing else. After all, islands
do not move and seals do. And anyhow, Dee had
the tiller, not John, and Dee altered course with
the rest.

"First time we've seen it this year," said Dee.
"Don says it's been here again and again. But
we've always been somewhere else."

"Why does he call it George?" asked John, and
the same question was being asked in every boat.

"Why not?" said Dee, and his answer was
as good as any.

It might have been a regatta, with George,
the seal, as the finishing mark. All six boats
drew nearer and nearer to each other. Even the
quietest talk could be heard from boat to boat.
"Don't splash so," hissed Daisy at the Mastodon.
"Don't talk," said the Mastodon to Roger. "What'll
we do when we catch him?" Bridget asked Susan.
"Peggy, you've taken our wind," said Titty. "Well,
don't come so near," said Peggy. "He's seen us,"
whispered Dee.

The seal, lying flat on the mud, suddenly lifted a round grey head. Slowly, with no sort of hurry, he raised himself on his flippers and waddled towards the water. In the water, he lay awash for a moment, and was gone.

The fleet sailed on towards the place where he had been.

"He'll come up again," said the Mastodon.

"But where?" said Roger.

"There he is," said Daisy, and the whole fleet altered course together. George had come up a hundred yards away and more. His head and shoulders were above water. He was as interested in the fleet as the fleet was interested in him.

"Do let's get near enough to draw him," said Titty. "We ought to put him in the map."

But George had had enough of them. He dived, and though they sailed over the place where he had been they did not see him again.

John turned round to look for the gap once more. "I say, Mastodon, I ought to go and try that gap," he called. "It may really be a North West Passage."

"Tomorrow," called the Mastodon. "You couldn't do it now, not if you're coming along with the rest of us. Even if it does go through you'd have to wait for water. And if you went right round you'd be too late for all this." He pointed at the low marshy islands ahead of them.

John marked the gap with a big question mark. If that was a way through to the Northern Sea, it was certainly worth an expedition for itself alone. The opening looked as if it ran in a long way. North West Passage. And there might be a North

East as well. He would do one and Nancy would do the other. But now, with the tide sweeping them on, they must follow the savage guides.

"Who'd better go which way?" shouted Daisy.

"Two main channels," shouted the Mastodon. "And there's a creek to the south, and channels through the saltings in the middle. I'll go up the creek with Roger, because my boat draws less than any, and I'll be able to get to the top and back before there's water for any of the others. Then we'll work through the saltings and join you."

"Right," called Daisy. "There you are, White Chief. You take that one." She pointed to the opening of a channel. "Take him through there, Dee. Wait for us at the other side, if you get through first."

"Better get the sail down," said Dee. "There won't be room for sailing."

John lowered the little sail, watching the five other boats moving in a bunch along the edge of the marshes.

"Better let me row," said Dee. "You'll be busy with the map."

"Good," said John. "Hullo. Somebody else lowering sail."

"That's my brother," said Dee. "He'll have a time of it, getting through there. It's only about four feet wide."

"Down go two more."

In another moment all the other boats were hidden by land, and John, watching his compass, had no time to look at them even if he could have seen them. This mapping on the move was no sort of joke, and he wondered what some of the others were making of it. Due east to that point on Mastodon Island. He jammed that down, and then every few minutes had to put down a new compass course, as Dee, rowing now in water, now with his oars scraping the mud, worked his way between the banks.

"It's a much better channel than some of them," said Dee, watching John feverishly at work.

"Good thing we're going through with the tide rising," said John, "and before the mud's all covered."

"There's one of them," said Dee when, at last, they sighted clear water ahead, and, almost at the same moment, saw the mast of a small boat apparently moving on dry land to the south of them.

"There's another," said John.

"And another. That's the lot. No. There's one missing. Who is it?"

Five small boats met where the channels between the islands joined. *Wizard*, *Firefly*, the Mastodon's rowing boat, and two of the savage sailing dinghies. One, with Nancy and Daisy aboard, had not arrived.

"They've got stuck," said the Mastodon, standing in his boat and looking back.

"We got stuck three times ourselves," said Roger. "And once the Mastodon had to put on his splatchers and get out and push."

"We got stuck at least twice," said Titty.

"We got stuck a hundred times," said Bridget. "Didn't we Susan?"

"Daisy ought to have got through all right," said the Mastodon.

Dee and Don both turned their boats round to go back to the rescue. But there was no need. The top of a mast showed, moving through the marshes, and a few minutes later they saw the boat itself, being poled along by the savage Daisy on one side and an explorer with a red cap on the other.

"Hullo! What happened?"

"Stuck really hard," said Daisy. "We just had to wait for the tide. It didn't matter. There was a lot to talk about."

Both of them were smiling. It seemed to John almost as if they had been glad of the delay.

"What now?" said Roger.

"Better swop channels and go through again," said John.

Back they went, each boat taking a different channel from the one through which it had come. Already the water was higher, and this time nobody got stuck for more than a minute or two. Then back again, explorers in each boat plotting their tracks as best they could.

"Mango Islands," said Titty. "All swamp. Nowhere to land."

"There were two good landings up the creek," said Roger.

"We could land over there," said Bridget.

"Let's," said Titty. "It's a settlement. People in native costumes."

They rowed on through a bit of open water, with patches of mud still showing here and there. On one side of it was an old quay, with some native boats pulled up beside it. Behind the quay were cottages, and a field in which horses were grazing, flicking at flies with their tails. Under the quay, some men in shirt sleeves and trousers (native costume) were painting a boat. The explorers landed on a bit of gravel beside the quay, and climbed up it to have a look round from above over the Mango Islands and the channels through which they had come.

"That's where we go next," said the Mastodon, pointing across the open water to a gap in the bank on the other side. "It's a canal. But the water's not quite high enough yet."

John and Titty hurried off along the high bank of a creek and found that this bit of Daddy's map needed little change, though it did not show the canal, and did not mark the native settlement. By the time they got back the water had risen another foot, and the others were already in their boats ready for the last stage.

"Come along," said the Mastodon. "Roger and I'll go first. There won't be room for two boats side by side."

Six boats, one after another, left the open water and pulled into the narrow mouth of the canal. This was the queerest bit of exploration they had yet done, but easy to put on their maps, for the canal was almost straight. They stopped when the water ended and they could go no farther, close under some old, tarred piling that had once been a staithe for barges. The water was so shallow that they had to pole the last few yards.

"We haven't been here for ages," said Daisy, as, each taking an arm, she and Nancy hoisted

Bridget to dry land. "Let's go and see if the cow-man's still here."

Close to the staithe were some houses with an inscription on them to say that they had been built with stones from old London Bridge. Savages and explorers wandered round them, as if in a foreign country, and came to a farmyard, where cows were being milked in a wooden cowshed.

"Come for some milk, have you?" said the cowman, and sent his son for some glasses. "I remember you ... and you ... " he said, "but you're a stranger and so are you. ... "

There were hurried whisperings among the savages, and Daisy said, "We haven't a penny among us. We don't really want any milk."

"We've got plenty," said John. "Susan's got the expedition's purse. We won't have any unless you will too."

"Of course you must have some," said Susan.

"Well, we are jolly thirsty," said Daisy. "Thank you very much."

"Drink up," said the cowman, and the seven of them took turns with the glasses, because there were only three of them among the lot.

"Loving cups," said Nancy. "Troll them round."

"I say," said Roger, as they turned to go back to their boats. "He only charged twopence a pint. That's a penny less than at home. I mean, in our own country."

"Come overseas, you have," said the cowman, laughing.

"Well, we have," said Roger.

The cowman laughed again, as if Roger had made a joke, and no one explained that Roger

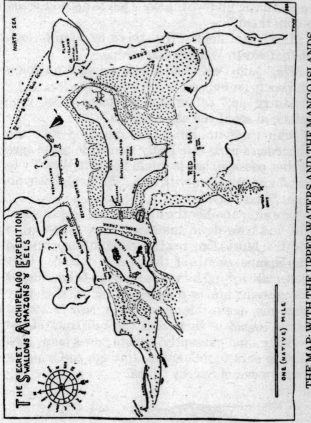

THE MAP: WITH THE UPPER WATERS AND THE MANGO ISLANDS

had been telling the exact truth. The water was still coming in when they went back to their boats.

"Hop in, Roger," said the Mastodon. "The wind's blowing straight down the canal. They'll be able to sail back, and we'll have a job to get to *Speedy* before them."

"Dee," said John. "Will there be time to look at that North West Passage?"

"No," said Dee. "Not unless we give up going to *Speedy* for supper."

"Hurry up," called the Mastodon. "Set your sails and see if you can catch us."

John gave in. First that seal and now the Mastodon's party. He badly wanted to make sure of that passage, but it would be pretty beastly to go off and take Dee with him. "We'll catch you all right," he shouted.

One after another the little sailing boats hoisted sail and blew down the canal. They shot out, to see the Mastodon, rowing hard, disappear into the channel south of the Mango Islands. They were close behind him, close enough to hear Roger encouraging him as if he were a horse, when they came out again into open water, saw Mastodon Island ahead of them and the tall trees of the heronry, and presently had to lower sails and take to oars to follow him through the winding western end of Speedy Creek.

CHAPTER XXII

THE MASTODON GIVES A PARTY

Round a bend in the channel, six boats swept in a bunch towards the ancient wreck in which the Mastodon had made his lair. Water was washing through the upright timbers, but the bows, newly tarred and painted by the Mastodon himself, looked, with the water lapping round them, as if they belonged to a barge still ready to put to sea. It was a close thing, but the Mastodon had got a fresh start while the other boats were downing sails, and he had just time to climb aboard with Roger before the rest of his visitors came alongside.

The Mastodon helped them over the rail when they had climbed the ladder much as if he was welcoming them aboard a private yacht. "Never mind about the mud," he said. "It'll wash off afterwards. No trouble at all. I always do wash down every morning. Oh well, if you do want to get it off, here's a bucket." He dropped it over the side and brought it up full of water. Those of his visitors whose feet were bare, washed the worst of the mud off. Those who had boots, followed the Mastodon's own example, got out of them, and stood them in a row in the scuppers. He was assisted as host by Roger, who showed Peggy, Susan and Bridget round the deck as if he owned the barge. "This is the windlass," said Roger. "You've seen the anchor up on the bank. This is where the mast used to be.

That's the chimney. . . . He's got a real stove. . . .
That's the way down to the cabin. . . . "

"Let's go down," said the Mastodon. "It'll take
a minute or two getting things ready. Thank you
for bringing those mugs and plates. I'll take them
down. You'll want two hands for the ladder."

Somehow or other eleven people crowded into
the Mastodon's cabin. For some moments people
could hardly move until the Mastodon begged
them to sit down, when they found places for
themselves on boxes, on his bunk, on his bench
and on the floor, while the Mastodon lit his stove,
put a kettle on and began to hack at a ham with
a carving knife.

Susan watched him for a minute or two with
increasing pain. "Do let me cut the ham," she
said, when she could bear the sight no longer.

"She's a dab at it," said Roger, and the Mastodon thankfully handed over and turned to other
things.

Roger was pointing out the fishing lines, the
nets that were being made, the cupboards, the
hooks for hanging clothes, when Nancy caught
sight of the looking-glass message that had caused
all the trouble, spiked on a nail on the wall.

"There it is," she cried. "There's their secret
message with the words all inside out. Jolly
clever. Have a look at it, Susan. It's as good as
any of ours."

The Mastodon's happy smile faded from his
face.

"Don," exclaimed Daisy. "It was all a mistake.
You oughtn't to have kept it." She jumped up,
grabbed the message, scrumpled it up and poked

it into the stove. "There you are. It's gone. Peace for ever!"

The Mastodon smiled again and went on digging tins of stewed peaches out of a sack.

"Until tomorrow night!" said Nancy.

"Of course," said Daisy. "And then corroboree and human sacrifice and peace for ever and ever. We're awfully glad you people came. The tribe's never been big enough for a proper war dance. . . . And, I say, you've seen ours. Do show us how you do your messages."

"You have to know semaphore," said Nancy. "It's like this." She took a piece of paper that had been wrapped round a loaf of bread. " 'Peace for ever', you said. Well look here. Those are the signals for it. Now put legs on them . . . like this. . . . "

"It looks like a war dance," said Daisy.

"That's just it," said Nancy. "Nobody who saw it would think it had anything to do with peace. Look here. I'll draw you the whole alphabet. It's the arms that matter. You can make the legs do anything you like."

Susan, cutting slices of ham, took up one end of the table. John, who had collected all the maps, spread them at the other end, comparing them side by side, and sometimes putting one on the top of another and holding them up against the light that came down through the hatch. It was going to be a tremendous job, making one map out of the lot of them and getting all those channels in their right places. He borrowed a sheet of paper from the Mastodon, who was busy with a tin-opener, and began to see what he could make

of it. A creek down there. Yes. Roger had done
that pretty well, and then the southern channel,
and the ways through the Mango Islands. . . . It
would pan out all right in the end, but it was
going to take time.

At first, while he worked, he hardly heard
the talk that was going on around him, but later,
when he came to rubbing out lines that had gone
wrong in his sketch and darkening others that
were there to stay, he heard sentence after
sentence that showed the other people were thinking of anything but mapping. "Barbecued Billygoats. . . . I mean Great Congers . . . It'll be the
best ever." That was Nancy's voice, urging something, and he knew that the explorer in Nancy
was only skin deep. That was the pirate coming
through. Or had the pirate got somehow mixed up
with the Eel? Oh well, it didn't matter, so long as
the map got done. Then he heard Bridget: "And
you have promised, haven't you? Even Susan says
I'm old enough." Then Roger, in consultation with
the brothers: "I don't see how we can make a really
good one. We've used nearly all the wood we could
find for boiling kettles." Then Daisy, breaking in:
"Don't you worry about that. You wait till tomorrow morning." "What about your whistle, Roger?"
said the Mastodon. "Oh Gosh!" said Roger. "I've
left it in your boat." Roger hurried up the ladder,
and presently "The Keel Row" sounded on deck,
and Daisy and Nancy and then Peggy and the Eel
brothers began stamping their feet in time with it.

Susan said, "Look here, John, put away those
maps. We'll want the table to lay out the feast. . . .
And there's no room to dance down here. Clear

SEMAPHORE ABC. "YOU CAN MAKE THE LEGS DO ANYTHING YOU LIKE"

out, everybody, if you can't keep still.

The final preparations were made by the Mastodon and Susan alone, hardly able to hear each other speak because of the thunder on the decks overhead. There was still plenty of light outside, but the Mastodon lit the hurricane lantern and hung it from a hook. Then, with a grin at Susan he unwrapped a big box of crackers. "Mother had got them for my birthday," he said. "But I told her it would be waste to keep them."

"Ready now," called the Mastodon, but no one heard him. "READY!" he shouted. The music of the whistle was cut off short, and musician and dancers came down to their supper.

Tea, ham, bread and butter, tinned peaches, cheese biscuits, chocolate biscuits, and cake went down well. There were paper caps in the crackers and Bridget looked well in a pink crown and the Mastodon even better in a pale blue bonnet.

"Jolly good feast," said Roger, when at last he could eat no more.

"Bridget and eel will be much better," said the Mastodon. "You wait till tomorrow night. . . . If only I catch a decent lot. . . . You won't want me for exploring tomorrow," he added. "You won't be able to do much anyway."

John looked at his map. "There isn't an awful lot left to do," he said. "The most important bit's that northern shore we didn't finish. We've got to settle whether there's a North West Passage or not round behind the Blackberry Coast. And we've got to find out if there's a North East Passage to make Peewitland an island. And then there's the road across the Red Sea."

The Mastodon looked up at the tide-table nailed to the wall. "High water before eight," he said. "That means low water about two. No good in boats with a falling tide. All through the middle of the day there won't be any water except in the main channels. Just right for doing the Wade."

"We'll do the road while the tide's out," said John. "And we might have a go at the Northern Coast while it's coming in again. The road won't take long. Couldn't you come then, to try that gap?"

"What about the ceremonial stew?" said the Mastodon. "Eels are awful to catch. I may have to keep at it all day as soon as I've got a good lot of worms."

"And we've got to get ready for the corroboree," said Daisy, looking at Nancy.

"We shan't want guides for mapping the road," said John. "And when that's done there'll be only that northern part left. But it's the most important bit of all."

"We'll get the whole thing done," said Nancy. "But don't you start thinking of going off on a voyage tomorrow afternoon. It's a waste of good savages not to be attacked by them. And if you're all away somewhere else, they'll have nobody to attack. And you can't have a decent war dance without a bit of war."

"We'll be ready for them," said John. "Four of them against seven. They won't have much of a chance."

Nancy grinned. "You wait and see. The Swallows'll be up against a horde."

The tide had begun to fall again when they

went up the ladder and looked round from the
deck. The explorers hurried down into their boats
to get away before the water left them. Daisy
and her brothers, with smaller, shallower boats,
waited for a last private word or two with *Speedy*'s
skipper.

"It was a grand feast," Roger called out.

"Thank you very much," shouted the others.

"Three cheers for the Mastodon," shouted Roger.

"Jolly good thing we didn't have it the other
night," said Nancy. "Much more fun with the
cabin busting full."

They rowed away.

"Race you home," said Nancy. "Starting now
with sails down."

There was frantic bustle in both boats. Yards
were yanked to mast heads, tacks hauled down,
rudders hurriedly shipped. Every second mattered
with only such a little way to go.

"Whoever gets a foot ashore first," cried Nancy,
as the two boats, almost touching, shot out into
Goblin Creek.

"Our rudder's a bit stiff," said Susan, who was
steering *Wizard*. "I say, Titty, are you sure you
got it properly shipped?"

"Let's have another shot," said Titty. "I jammed
it in in an awful hurry."

"It's sometimes wobbly and sometimes stiff,"
said Susan. "There's something awfully wrong
with it."

"Carry on as it is," said John. "You're steering
all right. We won't have a chance if we stop. Bring
your weight a wee bit forward Titty. Good. We're
gaining. Gosh, it's going to be pretty close."

"Wind's on our shore," said Susan. "Will you lower sail before we come in?"

"Lose if we do," said John. "Nancy won't. I've got the centreboard up. Steer for the mud just this side of the piles, and let your sheet go as you touch. Roger, are you ready to jump for it? She said 'First one ashore'."

"Aye, aye, sir," said Roger.

The two boats headed for the shore together. Peggy was scrambling forward in *Firefly*, ready to jump.

"Look out, Nancy," called John suddenly. "Give us room. Lots of piles under water. . . . "

He was too late.

"Bring her in the other side of the hard," he shouted to Susan. "Now . . . Let go your sheet. Jump, Roger. . . . Jump. . . . "

There was a simultaneous splash, as Roger and Peggy, from opposite sides, landed in the mud on the narrow pathway, and grabbed each other to save themselves from falling.

"Dead heat," said Peggy.

"Something's happened," said Susan. "We're stuck. It's the rudder. I can't move it at all."

Everybody in *Wizard*, except Roger who was in mid air at the time, had felt a sudden jar. *Firefly* had slid easily up the mud beside the hard and come to rest. *Wizard* had stopped as if she had hit a wall, her bows still afloat.

"She's on the piles," said John. "Everybody get ashore. I'll lower sail afterwards."

They scrambled out into the water. Bridget splashed up the pathway and ran to the camp to tell Sinbad he should have his supper in a minute.

John pulled gently at the boat. She moved a
little from one side to the other but not forward.
John waded to her stern and felt under water.

"Rudder's caught between two of those beastly
piles," he said. "I'll have it out in a minute."

"I say," said Nancy. "I'm awfully sorry. I thought
you were coming in on the other side."

"Well, so we have," said John. "But some of
those piles stick up a long way. . . . Look here.
You hang on to her."

John got hold of the slim wooden rudder with
both hands, reaching down under water. He gave
a tremendous tug and freed it.

"Fairly jammed between them," he said. "Oh
gosh! Look at this."

The rudder, in an ordinary way, swung on
two pintles which dropped into gudgeons. Titty,
hurriedly shipping it, had slipped the upper pintle
into place, but had missed the gudgeon with the
lower one, so that it was no wonder that Susan
had found steering difficult. And now, the upper
pintle itself had been bent sideways when the
rudder caught in the piles.

"We'll bend it straight again," said Nancy.
But John had already tried.

"No good," he said. "They've both got to be in
a dead straight line. And she's not our boat. I'll
have to take it to a boat builder."

"Karabadangbaraka!"

The three Eels were passing on their way home.

"Akarabgnadabarak!" replied the explorers.

"What's happened?" said Daisy.

"Bust a rudder," said Nancy.

"Where's the nearest boatbuilder?" called John.

"Up the town creek," shouted one of the Eels. "A good one close to the Yacht Club!"

The little boats were moving fast, they too racing on their homeward way.

"Palefaces!" Daisy's voice shrilled over the water. "Hi! White Chiefs!"

"Hullo!"

"You'd better wear hats tomorrow night."

"Why?"

"And stick them on with glue."

"What for?" shouted Roger.

"To save your scalps!"

With tide and wind to help them, the savages were already nearing the mouth of Goblin Creek, and out of shouting distance, before even Roger had thought of what to say to them.

The explorers went up to their camp. John carried the damaged rudder. The iron of the pintle was too strong to be bent by either of the captains. "It's a boatbuilder's job," said John. "We've got to have it put exactly right."

"Well, there's one thing about it," said Nancy. "You were going to do the road over the Red Sea tomorrow anyway. You could just as well go on into the town. It won't really be a waste of time, you haven't been there yet."

"And we can telephone," said Susan.

CHAPTER XXIII

RED SEA CROSSING: ISRAELITES

It was a broiling hot day. The hard sharp shadow of the meal-dial was moving towards the dinner peg. Nancy's watch, hanging on the totem, said that it was getting on for twelve o'clock, when the Wade would be dry, and the explorers would be able to cross the Red Sea, survey the road, and take the damaged rudder to the town. They were all going, except for Nancy and Peggy who had been to the town before and, full of plans for the evening, had almost turned into Eels already. Everybody wanted to see what the town was like, and it was the first chance they had had of talking to Mother on the telephone. Since breakfast they had been busy on the map. Yesterday's work with the six boats had given them a lot to do, John fitting six sketch maps into one, Titty copying and inking, and the others explaining what those squiggles meant which nobody but the one who had drawn them could understand.

The map was looking really like a map. Almost everywhere Daddy's broad pencil outlines had been rubbed out. Land and sea no longer looked the same. The huge unexplored areas had shrunk almost to nothing, except to the north of the Secret Water where, on the day that they had spent there, fear of hostile savages had made exploring almost impossible.

"It's getting on now," said Titty, lifting herself

on her elbows to look at her work from a distance.

"I do believe Daddy'll say 'Not bad'," said John.

"Meaning 'Jolly good'," said Roger.

"Just those two passages to make sure of," said John. "I say, Nancy. . . . Where is she?"

There was noise of singing. Nancy, who had wandered off to look out over the Secret Water, was coming back along the dyke and lifting up her voice in a tune that everybody knew. Everybody knew the tune, but something had happened to the words.

"The Congers are coming, Hurrah! Hurrah! . . .
With a tumty ti tiddley la la la . . . "

She broke off short and started again.

"She's making a song for tonight," said Peggy. "She began this morning as soon as she woke up."

John beckoned. Nancy looked over her shoulder, waved and tried another tune.

"The mud's all a-shiver
With fins all a-quiver.
    Big eels and little eels snaking along.

"Squirming and squiggling,
Worming and wriggling
    Answer the call of the savages' gong. . . .

"They're in sight," she said, as she came into the camp.

"It's about Peewitland," said John. "Couldn't you. . . . ?"

He got no further.

"There they are," cried Roger. "Why aren't they sailing?"

The three little boats of the savages were coming in at the mouth of Goblin Creek.

"Boats jolly low in the water," said Roger. "They've got a cargo." He set off at a run to the landing place, followed by the others.

"Karabadangbaraka!" Three joyful hails came over the water.

"Come on," said Nancy quietly. "Let them have it. All together!"

A combined roar of "Akarabgnadabarak!" came from the seven explorers.

"No wonder they aren't sailing," said Roger. "They've hardly got room for themselves. That's for the fire. I told them we hadn't got much wood."

Sticks and logs and bits of broken boxes stuck up above the gunwale of each boat. Each boat was loaded as full as she could be.

"Look at that," said Nancy. "Good old Eels."

"We've been up since five," said Daisy, as she pulled in to the landing place. "And just look at the result."

"It'll make a gorgeous fire," said Roger. "Enough to roast an ox."

"Just right to roast a sacrifice," said Daisy.

"Roast?" said Bridget rather doubtfully.

"All right, Bridgie," whispered Titty. "Human sacrifices always get rescued at the last minute."

"Has the Mastodon caught the stew?" asked Daisy.

"I saw him digging worms," said Roger. "He said low water's the time to start fishing. But

I'm not going to be able to help him. We're all going to the town."

"That's all right," said Daisy. "So long as you get back in time for the corroboree. And you'll have to because the Wade'll be covered again by four. I say, it's an awful pity about that rudder. . . . "

"The boatbuilder's close to the Yacht Club," said Dum.

"All hands to discharge cargo!" said John.

Daisy looked at Nancy, and got an answering wink.

"We'll do all that," she said. "The sooner you go the sooner you'll get back."

"The Wade must be pretty nearly dry," said Dee.

"You've all got boots," said Daisy.

It was clear that the Eels were anxious to see the explorers on their way.

"Well, I'm ready," said Susan. "Peggy's got one lot of sandwiches, and ours are in my knapsack. I haven't made a shopping list. But we'll do that on the way. Can anybody think of anything we want?"

"We ate the last bit of chocolate yesterday," said Roger.

"Can't you think of anything but chocolate?" said John.

"Of course I can," said Roger. "But chocolate's jolly important. All explorers have it. Scott and Nansen and Columbus. . . . "

"Not Columbus," said Titty. "It wasn't invented then."

"Well, I bet he'd have fairly hogged it if he'd had a chance."

"I've just got to catch Sinbad," said Bridget.

"Oh, look here, Bridget, we simply can't take him," said Susan.

"Not without seaboots," said Roger.

"With or without," said Susan.

"But you didn't let me take him yesterday," said Bridget. "You promised I could take him next time. And we're going to be on land, not in a boat."

"Why not leave him with us?" said Daisy.

"Great Congers!" said Nancy. "We can't have him. Just remember all we've got to do."

"He's coming with me," said Bridget. "He loves walking."

"In circles," said Roger.

And then, seeing danger signals in Bridget's face, Susan gave in and said Sinbad could come if he came in a basket.

"You'll have to carry him all the way," said John. "We've got to go like hares, and we can't have Sinbad holding us up while he's chasing his tail."

"Turning us into tortoises," said Roger.

"All right, Bridgie," said Titty. "Sinbad'll cross the Red Sea in a palanquin."

The Eels, leaving their laden vessels at the landing place, came up to the camp to see the explorers start.

"Get back as quick as you can," said Nancy. "And set out your sentinels. I bet you can't stop us. And don't go thinking the whites'll have it all their own way. Six full-blooded Eels, counting Peggy and me. One awful rush and the camp'll be full of a howling horde."

"We'll be ready for you," said John. "But look here, Nancy. Do get Peewitland mapped. No need to keep in sight of the camp now. If you get ashore there you could finish it up and find out if it's an island or not, even if you can't sail round it with the tide out. Then there'll only be the North West Passage left . . . if there is one."

"Aye, aye, White Chief," said Nancy.

"You can't have the sacrifice till I come back," said Bridget.

"Don't you worry," said Nancy.

"Give her lots of those cream buns in the town," said Daisy. "The ones grown-ups won't eat because of their figures."

*

They were off, hurrying in single file along the narrow pathway on the top of the dyke. Susan had an empty knapsack on her back. They had run short of cornflakes and sugar and with all the savages coming that night there were several other things that Susan meant to get. John was carrying the damaged rudder and a bulging pocket showed that he had not forgotten his compass. Titty had brought the telescope. Both she and John had brought copies of the map. Roger was carrying Sinbad's basket, and Bridget, close behind him, was putting a hand in now and then to tickle Sinbad and to make him feel he was part of the expedition and not a mere parcel.

Already the marshes below the dyke were clear of water. Where at high tide patches of weed showed above the surface, there were now lumps of weed-covered mud, with ditches running winding this way and that among them. And beyond the marshes was a wide smooth sheet of mud. The Red Sea was sea no longer, but mud with narrow rivers winding through the middle of it.

Titty had been looking forward to the crossing of the Red Sea ever since the first day when in the morning she had seen it a muddy desert with the strange tracks and diggings of the Mastodon straggling across it, and in the afternoon had been rowed over that same desert when circumnavigating the island. At low tide she had seen the road, with its cart track, and the withies here and there to mark where it lay. At high water she had crossed that line of withies in a boat, knowing that the road lay somewhere under her keel. But she had never walked along it. The Red Sea was the very name for that strange place. Israelites and Egyptians. A tidal wave, rolling in unexpectedly from the sea just when the Israelites were half way across, would turn them suddenly into Egyptians, drowning them and their camels and baggage trains and sacred cats. Titty just glanced back at the basket Roger was carrying. Sinbad. Some people might almost think it was an omen. The sacred cat in his palanquin. And then she remembered how very different was the sheltered life of a sacred cat from the short and far from sheltered life of Sinbad, who had already had all kinds of adventures and been rescued from a chicken coop floating in the North Sea. She laughed.

"What is it?" asked John.

"I was just thinking about sacred cats," said Titty.

"What?"

"And the Egyptians.... You know...." And she stopped. She remembered Bridget. No good talking to Bridget about the sea swallowing up the Egyptians, just when they were going to leave the island and walk out over the mud on that narrow road with salt water still in ruts, and the land on the further side still so very far away.

"Go on," said Roger. "Spit it out, Titty. What made you laugh?"

"Oh nothing," said Titty. "Just thinking about sacred cats and Sinbad. He's so very different," she finished lamely.

"Just as heavy," said Roger, and Titty snatched gratefully at the change of subject.

"I'll carry him for a bit," she said. "Of course, to make his basket a real palanquin we ought to sling it from a pole, but he'd probably be seasick, swinging about."

"It's a beastly awkward basket," said Roger. "And he will move about in it, so it's his own fault when it bumps against my knee."

At the point where the road from the farm lifted over the dyke and dropped down, a narrow strip of hard gravel, to the level of the sea, John stopped, put the rudder on the ground and had a look at his compass, squinting over it first at the farm, and then at the line of the road over the mud.

"We've got that all right," he said. "The kraal bears due north from here, and the road lies just about south by west. I'll take another couple of

bearings from the place with the four posts out in
the middle." He scribbled the bearings on his copy
of the map, and set out to follow Susan, who had
not waited but was already on the way out over
the mud.

"We'd better get there as soon as we can,"
she said as the others caught up with her.

"It doesn't take a moment just getting the
bearings," said John, "and we may be in even
more of a hurry on the way back."

"Before the tide comes in again," said Roger.
"It'd be a jolly long way to swim."

"There isn't going to be any swimming," said
Susan.

"We couldn't anyhow," said Roger. "Not with
Bridget and Sinbad."

"You weren't able to swim once," said Bridget.

"He used to swim with one foot on the bottom,"
laughed Susan.

"I can do that," said Bridget.

"Sinbad can't," said Roger.

The road was much better than they had
expected. There were deep puddles in it, left
by the tide. There was a layer of soft mud over
it, but never deep enough to cover their ankles.
Under the mud there was good hard gravel, and
it was easy walking, though they found it best not
to walk too near together, because nobody could
help splashing the mud about. There was nothing
but mud on each side of the road and Roger, just
trying whether it was hard or soft, very nearly
lost a boot in it.

"Gosh!" he said as he struggled back on the
hard track, with one boot muddy almost to his

knee. "It wouldn't be much fun crossing in the dark."

"Oh, look here," said Susan. "You can't go into the town with one boot as filthy as that."

"It'll be all right in a minute," said Roger. "There's still water across the road just ahead. We'll have to paddle and I'll wash it all off."

"We'd better wait till it's gone down a little more," said Susan, seeing a thin ribbon of water crossing the road and joining the channels on either side.

"It's only a few inches deep," said John. "I'll go first and try."

A minute later he was splashing through. "All right," he said. "Come on. Keep in the middle of the road. It isn't up to my ankles. There's another wet bit ahead. There must be two channels, not one. Here are the posts we sailed through. We'd have found deeper water on either side of them. Half a second, Roger. Make a desk of your back. I say, Titty. Hang on to the rudder a minute."

Roger set his legs apart and steadied himself, while John made pencil notes on the map which he put between Roger's shoulders.

"Don't wriggle," he said. "East by south to the point. North half east to the kraal."

"Don't tickle with the pencil," said Roger, trying to look upwards while still being a desk. "What is it? What is it, Titty? Hawk? I can't see anything."

Titty did not answer. She did not hear him. She was standing between the four posts, the tops of which had been awash when they had sailed through. She was looking straight above her and seeing not hawks or larks or infinite blue sky, but a few feet of swirling water over her head and the red painted bottom and centreboard of a little boat.

Bridget wriggled a hand into the basket to stroke Sinbad. Roger pulled at Titty's elbow. "I can't see anything," he said again.

"Neither can I," said Titty, "not really." She looked back towards the island and then forward toward the distant shore. When she had crossed the Wade in the Mastodon's boat, there had been water from shore to shore and the posts had been awash, with here and there just the top of a withy swaying in the current. And now, here they were, standing in the middle of what had been a sea, with drying mud everywhere, the tall posts standing up above their heads, and the withies sticking up out of the mud like sapling trees on land.

"In a few hours it'll all be water again," said Roger slowly.

"Hurry up, John," said Susan. "We've got to get to the town and back before that. And you don't know how long they'll take to mend the rudder."

They went on. The water was only an inch deep at the second place where it crossed the road. In a few more minutes there would have been none at all. But now, in all their minds except Bridget's there was that odd thought that presently the water would come back, meet over the road, widen and widen, till once more it stretched from the island to the main, a real sea, impassable unless in a boat. It would be hours yet before that could happen, but Bridget,

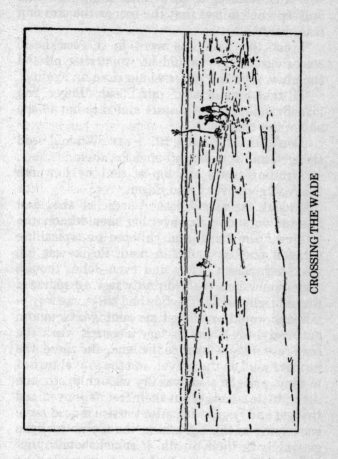

CROSSING THE WADE

who was thinking of quite other things, was the only one not to feel that the sooner the crossing was over the better.

"I bet the Israelites went at a good lick," said Roger. "They would be wondering all the time how soon the water would close up again."

"I'll take Sinbad now," said Susan. "Roger, you give Bridgie a bit of a start and race her to the end of the road."

"Don't let him start till I say 'When'," said Bridget, and splashed off ahead of them.

"Winning post's the top of that dyke where the road goes over," said Roger.

Bridget, far ahead, looked over her shoulder. She ran on and looked over her shoulder again.

"Now," she cried, and galloped on, splashing through puddles and thin mud. Roger was off, after her. Susan, Titty and even John, though they did not run, walked pretty fast. Of course it was all right really. The tide had still some way to fall, and would be a long time coming back again, but everybody found it very pleasant when the road rose steeply towards the land, and there was no more mud on the gravel, and the gravel turned to sand, and the sand was dry enough to stir and lift in little clouds about their feet as they joined Bridget and Roger who, after the usual dead heat, were lying in the hot sun on the top of the dyke getting back their breath. It somehow felt quite different to be on dry land again, instead of on a road that was under water for a good part of every day.

Again John took bearings, to make sure of getting the end of the road marked in the right place on his map. Susan dealt out sandwiches, and Sinbad was let out of his palanquin, to see what he thought of the new country and to get a bit of exercise.

"The mainland's quite different from any of the islands," said Titty. "More like a continent. You can see by the trees the salt water's been kept off it for ages."

Indeed, it was hard to believe that the country before them was not a thousand miles from the islands, creeks and marshes they had left behind. The bare cart track over the Red Sea turned beyond the dyke into a country lane, with high hawthorn hedges and here and there hollies, oaks and ashes meeting overhead. Away in the distance were woods and stubble fields, the thatched roofs of cottages and a line of tall telegraph posts marking the main road leading into the town. They could see motor cars flashing along it.

"Civilization," said Titty. "I don't suppose the people in the town ever dream they're so near the Secret Water and the Country of the Eels."

"What is civilization?" asked Bridget.

"Ices," said Roger, "and all that sort of thing." He looked hopefully at a cloud of thin blue smoke that, in the windless air, hung lazily above the town.

"Come on," said Susan. "We'll see if they've got any. Remember we've got to get back before the tide comes in again. Finish the sandwiches on the march. Catch that kitten. Puss! Puss! Come on Sinbad. We'll get you a lick of cream."

CHAPTER XXIV

CIVILIZATION

AFTER walking for half a mile along the lane without meeting even a cart, they came out into the busy traffic of a main road. They stopped at the corner just long enough for John to do a little compass work. The lane ran due north and south, the main road a little south of east. Daddy's map showed where the town was, down in the right hand corner, so John and Titty were able to pencil in both lane and road and to get them very nearly right. They went on, Bridget doing her best, and the others keeping pace with her. It was a longer walk than they had expected; sea-boots made hard work of it on the tarred road; and motor cars, roaring past, made them feel that even Bridget's best was very slow. Still, if you want to get anywhere you have only to keep moving, and presently fields and thatched cottages came to an end, there were houses on both sides of the road and they found themselves in the outskirts of a little seaside town.

Quite suddenly they felt that they were indeed explorers from the wilds visiting for a moment the haunts of the sedate and stay-at-home. The pavements were crowded with people dressed for a seaside holiday. Some of the younger ones carried spades and buckets. Others had model boats. Others had shrimping nets and fishing rods. Some were in bathing things, and were very sunburnt in the arms and legs, others were evidently new-comers, proper palefaces, with their skins a dismal white. But not one of them had a spot of mud. Sand? Yes. More than once they saw someone slip off a shoe and pour the sand out of it. But no mud, none at all. And the explorers, who had splashed across the Wade, were spotted with mud all over and were suddenly conscious of their muddy seaboots. They strode sturdily on. What did it matter if these people did stare, these people with their buckets and toy boats? What did these people know of the real thing, of islands unexplored, of savages who that very night would be dancing in corroboree?

John stopped a postman and asked him the way to the Yacht Club and was told to turn left in the middle of the town.

They hurried on, looking for the signboard the postman had said they would see.

"Keep a look-out for a shop where it says you can telephone," said Susan.

They were near the middle of the town before Roger pointed to a blue and white notice hung outside a grocer's shop. It said, "You may tele-phone from here."

"We'll telephone to Mother right away," said Susan. "And we can do our shopping at the same time."

John pointed to a clock hanging out over the street. "Gosh," he said. "Just look at that. Nearly two o'clock. The Mastodon said the Wade's dry for about four hours. The tide'll be up to it again by four, and I don't know how long the man'll take to mend the rudder. We've got to get him started first. We'll telephone while he's doing it."

They hurried on, saw at a street corner a sign-board pointing "To the Yacht Club," turned down that street, passed a pond where people were sailing toy-boats, found the Yacht Club, and two minutes later were talking to the boatbuilder.

"And when do you want it?" said the boat-builder, looking at the rudder and fingering the bent pintle and the twisted screws that held it to the wood. "Day after tomorrow do you?"

There was a moment of horror. "We wanted to take it back with us," said John. "And we've got to get across the Wade to the island."

The man looked at an enormous watch. "I've another job on hand," he said, "and my man's away. . . . "

"I'll help," said John. "If you think I'd be any good."

The man laughed and looked at his watch again. "We'll do the best we can," he said. "What time was it when you came across? You won't have much time to spare."

It was arranged that John should stay with the boatbuilder, while Susan and the others went to the telephone.

Things began to go wrong almost at once.

To begin with, when they came into the grocer's shop, he was busy serving a customer, wrapping up parcels and talking about the weather. "Beau-tiful and warm for the time of year," he told her. "Hotter than July. Good for the town now, weather like this. Brings the visitors and keeps them happy. A spell of rain would send them all away giving the town a bad name. Dependent on the weather we are here. As I always say, we ought to make the clerk of the weather a member of the town council. Then it would be up to him to do his best for us."

It was a long time before Susan caught his eye, and was able to ask the way to the telephone.

"Straight through that door, Miss," said the old grocer, and the whole four of them went through the door and found the telephone in the passage.

Then, as always happens when people are in a particular hurry, there was difficulty in getting the right number. And when at last she had got it, and Miss Powell came to the telephone and Susan asked if she could speak to Mother, the others saw her face change. "Not till three o'clock?" she said. "Don't let her go out again when she comes. We'll telephone again."

"What's happened?" said Titty.

"Daddy and Mummy aren't going to be at Miss Powell's till three o'clock. Oh dear. What time did John say we had to be back at the Wade?"

"Before four," said Roger. "And the boatbuilder said there wouldn't be much time to spare."

"Well, we'd better get the shopping done anyway," said Susan, "and then we'll go back to the boatbuilder's."

They left the telephone and went into the shop. Another customer was at the counter. They heard the old grocer talking. "Rain would send them all away giving the town a bad name. Dependent on the weather we are here. As I always say, we ought to make the clerk of the weather a member of the town council. . . . "

"I say," whispered Roger. "He's saying all the same things."

"But it's a different customer," whispered Titty.

Susan did her shopping, in a very worried manner. She had never made her list of the things she wanted and she was bothered at not finding Mother at the other end of the telephone. She bought a lot of cream buns of the kind Daisy had thought would do for fattening the human sacrifice. She bought a packet of cornflakes, a pound of lump sugar and a pound of soft sugar. She bought a tin of milk for Sinbad. She bought a tin of cocoa complete with milk ("It'll only want hot water and it'll be just the thing to have after the feast tonight"). She bought a fresh supply of chocolate and several other things, and the old grocer wrapped them up in separate parcels and began to talk.

"Beautiful and warm for the time of year, Miss . . . Dependent on the weather we are here. As I always say . . ."

Susan, out of the corner of her eye, saw Roger bolt out of the shop.

"What's the matter with Roger?" she said.

"I'll go and see," said Titty hurriedly and followed Roger.

It was very odd that once safely outside the shop they no longer felt that they must laugh out loud or die.

Susan, with all the parcels dumped in her knapsack, came out of the shop with Bridget. They went back to the boatbuilder's and found he had already taken all the metal work off the rudder.

"John," said Susan. "Daddy and Mother aren't

there. They won't be there till three o'clock. We'll have to telephone again. How much time are we going to have?"

"Not much," said John. "We'll probably have to run like hares. You know what telephoning is."

Susan looked at Bridget, who was carrying Sinbad's basket.

"We can't really do any running," she said. "You'll have to telephone and catch us up."

"There may not be time after the rudder's done," said John.

"Well, somebody must telephone," said Susan. "Mother'll be awfully disappointed if Miss Powell tells her we've been here and she doesn't have a word with any of us."

"Send the able-seamen and the ship's baby on ahead," said John. "Then they won't have to hurry, and we'll bolt after them and catch them up as soon as we can."

"Aren't we going to telephone too?" said Bridget.

"You can't," said Susan. "You know what it's like running. Joggling poor old Sinbad. John and I may really have to run for all we're worth. I'll tell Mother you couldn't help it."

"They'd better start now," said John. "Go ahead. Able-seaman Titty in charge. Just get along back. It's no good risking their having to run all the way at the last minute."

"All right," said Titty. "We'll take the knapsack too. It's no bother going slow, but awful if you're in a hurry."

"What about a bit of civilization before we start?" said Roger.

"Give them an ice apiece and get them going," said John.

They had their ices near the Yacht Club and then Susan walked back into the town with them, said "Goodbye" to them under the clock by the grocer's, and sent them on their way.

"Starting now, you've got lots of time," she said. "No need to hurry. We'll probably catch you up before you get across the Wade."

*

"I think they might have let us wait to telephone," said Bridget, as they left the shops behind them.

"They couldn't," said Titty. "By the time John's got the rudder and Susan's been able to telephone they might have to run like anything."

"I'm old enough to run too," said Bridget.

"Sinbad isn't," said Titty. "And you don't want him to be joggled to death."

"If they could have sent Sinbad on alone," said Roger, "they would. But somebody has to be with him. We're not sent on because we're too young. It's so that we don't have to hurry with the ship's kitten."

"It isn't only the ship's kitten who mustn't be hurried," said Titty. "Running makes people thin in no time."

"Like Daisy," said Bridget. "I never thought of that. What about those cream buns she said I ought to eat?"

"In the knapsack," said Titty. "We'll fatten you up a bit when we get near the Red Sea."

CHAPTER XXV

SINBAD'S CREEK

"No more motor cars and stink of exhaust," said Roger, as they left the main road and, no longer having to keep to the side for fear of the traffic, strolled comfortably down the middle of the green lane between high hedges that shut out the rest of the world.

There was a mew from Sinbad's basket, which, at the moment, Bridget was carrying herself.

"He wants to get out," said Bridget.

"We must get a bit further first," said Titty. "Then you can let him have a run."

"Good for him," said Bridget. "It isn't as if he had to be fattened up like me."

"Why good for him?" said Roger.

"I didn't say 'Good for him'," said Bridget. "I said 'Good *for* him.' Ship's kittens ought to have exercise."

"All right," said Titty. "He shall have a run in a minute."

They went on down the green lane, being lucky with blackberries here and there. All was well. No need to hurry now. Even if the others caught them up, they were already close to the Wade. Titty, in charge of the party, looked about for a good place to stop. She knew just what to look for . . . a place where people could properly make a halt when on the march, a place good to sit down in, a place with a bit of secrecy about it, a place where explorers resting tired limbs would not have suddenly to turn into children and get out of the way of some farm cart or other.

Roger found it. He had run on ahead to a likely looking bramble thicket. He had picked two really juicy ones for himself, good ones that dropped off as soon as he touched them, not the kind that have to be pulled and are sour even if black, and two more just as good for Bridget. He stopped short, with his mouth already open to call to her. Behind the brambles was the opening into a footpath, a footpath too narrow for carts, but with a hedge on each side of it.

"Roger's disappeared," said Bridget.

"Ahoy, Roger!" called Titty.

"Ahoy!" The voice came from behind the thicket.

"Ahoy! Come on. Here's a good place for a halt. Come on. There's even a tree to sit on."

"Don't go and get scratched, Bridgie," said Titty. "Do take care. We don't want any more blood, and Susan isn't here with the iodine."

"I've only torn my dress a little," said Bridget. "Come on, Titty. It's a lovely place."

Titty worked her way through the brambles, had one look, and went back into the lane. "It'll do all right," she said. "Half a minute while I lay a patteran, so that the others'll know where we are." She took a long stick and a short one, and laid them on the ground, one across the other in the middle of the lane, with the long stick pointing towards the blackberry bush. She went back into the footpath, twisted out of the straps of the knapsack and began burrowing into it. "Oh Gosh!"

she said. "The bag with those buns must be right at the bottom. They'll all be squashed."

"Better eat them," said Roger. "It's a good long time since we had dinner. And it was only sand-wiches."

"Anyway, here's a tin of milk for Sinbad."

"Can't I let him out now?" said Bridget.

"All right if you're sure you can catch him again."

"He always lets me catch him," said Bridget. "He likes to be caught. Come on Sinbad. You're going to have some milk. Where's his tin? Do spike it, Roger."

Sinbad, who had been mewing impatiently, put his head out of the basket the moment it was opened. Then a paw showed, then another. After that there seemed to be no more hurry. He stepped slowly out, and stretched first his front legs, then his hind legs, then his furry back, as if he had never been in a hurry at all.

Roger drove the spike of his scout knife twice, at opposite sides, into the top of the little tin. He looked round. "What about a saucer?" he said.

"Shove a bit of chocolate in your mouth," said Titty. "Here you are. Go and look for a dock leaf for him, and let him lick the milk off that. Bother those buns. I'll have to unpack everything."

Roger went off with a well-stuffed mouth. Titty emptied the knapsack out on the ground. It was as she had feared. Susan must have been very both-ered about the telephoning to forget that cream buns had gone in first when she dropped things like sugar, cornflakes, biscuits and chocolate on the top of them. The cream buns were in an awful

state. Roger was right. It would be just as well to
let him and Bridget eat what they could of them,
and see if Sinbad would lick up as much of the
cream as they had not been able to scrape off
the inside of the paper bag. Gosh! If she'd known
they were as badly squashed as this there would
have been no need to open that tin of milk. Titty
set aside the least damaged of the buns and let
Bridget do her worst with the others. "You'll jolly
well have to get the mess off your face before
Susan turns up."

Bridget set earnestly to work.

"Oh look here," said Titty. "You must keep
your hands off Sinbad while you're eating them.
Just look at the mess in his fur."

"Sorry, Sinbad," said Bridget.

"Hullo!" Roger came into sight.

"Where's the dock leaf?" said Bridget.

"Come along," said Roger. "There's a whole
lot just round the corner. And there's a creek.
It's dry, but there are two boats in it, and there's
an old fisherman with another boat upside down
on the bank. He's putting tar on it. I asked him
where the creek goes, and he says it goes into
the channel by the town. We ought to put it on
the map. Come along. You could have a look at
it while Sinbad's hogging."

It was the mention of the map that did it.
After all, Susan had said they needn't hurry,
and they had come pretty fast from the town,
and were quite close to the Red Sea. And if there
was a creek here, it was much more important to
put it on the map than just to get home early and
put the kettle on the fire. And anyway, she had

laid a patteran. The others would know where they were. Titty re-packed the knapsack, being careful to put the bag with the more fortunate of the buns on the top instead of at the bottom.

"Come on, Bridgie," said Roger. "You bring Sinbad. I'll take his milk."

"And you've got to carry those squashed buns somehow," said Titty.

"Inside or out?" said Roger.

"Anyhow you like," said Titty, "but leave enough for Bridgie."

"Daisy said I had to eat them," said Bridget.

"Open your mouth," said Roger, "and I'll push this one in. You'll want both hands for Sinbad."

"Mou . . . ffffff . . . " said Bridget.

"Don't choke her," said Titty. "That'll do. She can carry it like that." Bridget, gagged with a cream bun, and with Sinbad in her arms, twisted her head away from Roger who was afraid the bun was not far enough in, and started along the path.

"Don't go and bite it," said Roger, "or you'll lose more than half."

Titty, lugging the knapsack and Sinbad's empty basket, hurried after them. A pity she hadn't got John's compass. But of course John had never guessed she would find a new bit for the map on the way home. She stopped, dumped basket and knapsack, and pulled out of her pocket her rather crumpled copy of the map. She put a cross to mark the place where they had turned off the lane, and dotted in a bit of the footpath. Did it really lead to a creek? She picked the things up again and hurrried on.

An old man in a blue fisherman's jersey was working at a boat. Roger and Bridget were already talking to him. Sinbad was on the ground licking milk from a dock leaf that made a very good saucer. As Titty came up to them she saw a narrow ditch at her feet. A duck-punt and a small boat with a mast and a bit of rag at the masthead were lying on the mud. But there was not a drop of water to be seen.

"Oh well," said Titty to herself, "those boats didn't walk here."

The old fisherman swept his brush to and fro, spreading shining black tar on the bottom of his boat. The air was full of its pleasant smell. He dipped his brush in an old paint tin. Drops of tar fell on the ground.

"Don't put your feet in it, Sinbad," said Bridget, much as if she had been Susan talking to Roger. "Oh! He has. I was just too late to pick him up."

"Oh, Bridgie," said Titty. "He's smeared the front of your frock. And there's that tear as well."

"It would have been much worse if he'd rolled in it," said Bridget.

The old fisherman was talking to Roger, who had asked just the question that Titty was going to ask herself.

"Swim in it when the tide's up," he said.

"Where does it go to?" asked Titty.

"That join the main channel, that do," said the old man. He pointed. "If you walk along to that hedge end, you'll see the tide acoming in."

Titty considered a moment. "I'd better just go and make sure," she said. "I'll be back by the time you've finished giving Sinbad his milk."

"May I put some tar on?" asked Roger.

The old fisherman handed over his dripping brush, and began to fill his pipe. He winked at Titty. "Always glad to see someone doing a bit of work," he said. Titty smiled. Roger busy with the tar and Bridget stuffing cream buns and feeding Sinbad, were likely to stay where they were. She hurried off along the side of the ditch, to make sure of things before putting them down on her map. That hedge did not look a long way off, and it wouldn't take a minute to fill in the map if she could see the mouth of the creek from there.

Time slipped on. She could not walk fast along the slippery path above the ditch. She came to the hedge end. The ditch had widened. It really was a creek. Sinbad's Creek, it should be, because if Sinbad hadn't needed a dock leaf for a saucer it would never have been discovered. Lumpy tussocks stood up out of the mud, with belts of green weed showing how high the water would come. And there was water, creeping along the bottom of the creek, which stretched before her, widening and widening, till it came to the main channel where she could see boats lying at anchor. If only she had a compass to make sure of its direction. She looked for a bit of dry ground, sat down, and began to sketch it on her map. It was not a very good map, she thought, as she looked at it, but it was a beginning. Even the best of explorers cannot make perfect maps at first glance. Later, perhaps, she would be able to come with John and correct it. Anyhow, there it was, Sinbad's Creek, and, looking back past the hedge end and forward to where it opened into

deep water (deep, because otherwise those boats
would not be lying afloat), she was sure she had
got it pretty well right. And then she noticed two
things. First, that those anchored boats in the
distance were all pointing north. Second, that the
water at her feet was fast spreading out over the
mud. When she had sat down to make her map
the water had hardly come so far. Now, there
was quite a lot of it, and as she looked down at
it, she could see little white flakes moving with
it, working their way inland.

She jumped to her feet, put the map in her
pocket, and hurried back.

Roger, Bridget and the old fisherman were
admiring the tarred boat.

"We've finished it," said Roger.

"Find your way all right, Missie?" asked the
fisherman.

"Yes, thank you," said Titty. "Come on you
two. Where's Sinbad? I've been a lot longer than
I thought I would be."

"There's a short way back to the road over
that field," said the fisherman.

"We're not going back to the road," said Titty.
"We're going across to the island."

The old man glanced at the water creeping
up along the ditch.

"You'll have to jump to it, Missie," he said, "if
you're going to cross the Wade without getting
wet."

"Gosh!" said Roger.

"Where's Sinbad?" said Titty.

"He's somewhere close to," said Bridget. "He
was here a minute ago."

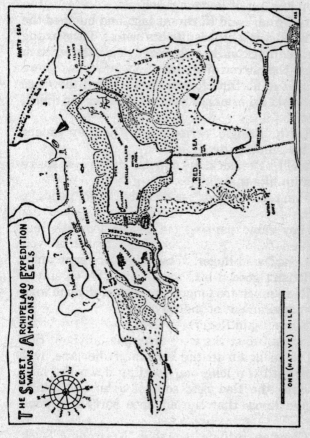

THE MAP: WITH THE ROAD TO THE TOWN AND SINBAD'S

CREEK

"There he is," said Roger. "Skip along, Bridgie. I'll get him."

But Sinbad had no idea of hurry, except to keep just out of Roger's reach.

"Got him," said Roger, at last, and bundled the mewing ship's kitten into his basket. Titty swung the knapsack on her shoulder, and started back along the narrow footpath.

"You've no time to lose," they heard the voice of the old fisherman. "That old tide come in quick, that do."

"Go it, Bridgie," cried Roger, as they caught up the ship's baby.

"He'll be seasick. I know he will if you shake him up like that."

"Can't be helped," said Titty. "Run, Bridgie, run."

They came panting out of the footpath into the lane.

"Good," said Roger. "They're not in sight yet."

"It isn't good a bit," said Titty. "We've stayed in there much too long. I say, Roger, did you kick my patteran out of the way?"

"Sorry," said Roger.

Titty's two sticks were lying just anyhow. She set them again in the middle of the lane, this time with the long one pointing down the lane towards the Red Sea, so that John and Susan should know that the advance party had gone on.

"Come on, Bridgie," she said. "Keep going. Stick to it. We may be only just in time. And if the others aren't quick they'll be too late."

"What for?" said Roger.

"Tide," said Titty. "We'll be Egyptians ourselves if we don't look out."

PATTERAN

CHAPTER XXVI

RED SEA CROSSING: EGYPTIANS

"Stop," said Bridget. "Stop. I can't run any more."

"Only a few more yards," said Titty. "Keep going. We'll stop as soon as we're in sight of the Wade."

They came out of the lane and ran up to the top of the dyke. Before them stretched the desert of brown mud with the road running across it to the island. The road looked clear, but on either side of it, almost meeting across, two wide tongues of water were spreading over the mud.

"The tide's come in a long way already," said Roger. "I bet the road's pretty wet where it dips in the middle. Shall I run on and make sure?"

"John knows about it," said Titty. "They're sure to be here before it's too late to cross."

Bridget sat down panting on the top of the dyke.

Titty stood beside her. Should she go on, or wait for the leaders of the expedition?

Roger went slowly down the dyke on the further side and a little way out on the road over the mud.

"What's Roger doing?" said Bridget.

"Looking for worms, probably," said Titty.

But at that moment, Roger, who was staring at something in the mud, suddenly turned. "Quick. Quick!" he shouted. "Titty! Bridget! Come on. They've crossed already."

"They can't have," said Titty, with a sudden

tightening of the chest. "They can't have," she said again, as she ran down the slope. But in her heart she knew they could. How long had she been off the road, getting that creek to put on the map? It had not seemed more than a few minutes. But minutes go fast when you are exploring. They, or at least Bridget and Roger, had never been very far from the place where the footpath turned out from the lane. They had heard nobody go by. But would there have been anything to hear? John and Susan, hurrying home, would not have been singing or even talking. They would have been just walking as fast as they could, expecting every moment to see the rest of the expedition somewhere in front of them. They must have passed the patteran without seeing it.

"Look," said Roger, pointing at the muddy road. "There are the tracks we made coming across . . . all our boots going the same way. And there are theirs going back. . . . Two pairs of boots. Two pairs. John's and Susan's. You can see the criss-cross pattern on the sole."

"Oh Gosh!" said Titty. "Bridget! Come on!"

Titty looked out ahead over the Red Sea of mud at those two arms of water creeping in, and the long low line of the island at the other side. The native kraal, red in the sunlight among its few green trees, looked very far away. There was no one on the island dyke. John and Susan must be already in the camp. Already they must know that Titty, Able-seaman, in command, had made a mess of things. Oh bother the ship's kitten. Oh bother Sinbad's Creek. If only they had never left the lane. If only there had been a dock leaf nearer at hand for Sinbad's milk. If only they had not come on the old fisherman. If only she had not tried to add that creek to the parts explored. If only. . . .

"They might have left us a patteran," said Roger. "Just to show they'd gone on."

"They thought we were ahead of them," said Titty. "They never saw ours."

They set out to cross once more that long road over the mud. Titty carried the knapsack, Roger the basket with the ship's kitten in it, and Bridget, the ship's baby, carried nothing at all and did not seem inclined to hurry.

Titty caught Roger's eye, looking at her doubtfully.

"We're in plenty of time," he said cheerfully, but she knew he meant it as a question.

"Lots," she said shortly, and Roger instantly slackened his pace.

"We've got to hurry just the same," she added quickly. "John and Susan must be in camp already and wondering where we are."

"They'll be jolly pleased when we show them we've got a new creek," said Roger.

"We oughtn't to have gone to look for it," said Titty. "It's my fault, but we ought to have kept to the road. Then they wouldn't have missed us."

"We wouldn't have found the creek if we had," said Roger.

"We had to stop somewhere," said Bridget. "I say, need we go so fast?"

"Remember the Eels are coming," said Titty. "And you mustn't be late, must you?"

"They'll wait for me," said Bridget. "They can sacrifice Daisy any time."

"You don't want them to have to wait?"

"No," said Bridget.

"Come on then," said Titty.

She glanced over her shoulder towards the mainland and then forward again to the low line of the island dyke at the other side of the Red Sea. The mainland already looked a long way behind them, but the island seemed hardly any nearer than it had seemed before they had started over the mud. It was going to be all right, so long as those two did not get frightened. But already there was water in those curling channels in the mud. And out in the middle of the Red Sea she could see that the water was close to the narrow brown line of the road. Away to the east where in the morning the mud had stretched almost to the opening of the Straits of Magellan there was water. Away to the west a wide river stretched to Goblin Creek. Gosh! If only they had not gone off along the footpath. If only they were more than half way across. She looked back again. Suppose they were too late and the waters met across the road, would they be able to get back to the mainland? If only she knew how fast the tide came in.

"Shall I go on ahead?" said Roger, "and signal if the water's beginning to meet?"

Titty looked at him. So the same ideas were in his mind too.

"We can easily go back if we have to," he said.

"We shan't have to," said Titty stoutly. "Go ahead if you like."

"Perhaps we'd better stick together," said Roger.

It was no good trying to go any faster. Bridget, a human sacrifice not wanting to be late for the ceremony, was doing her very best.

*

They were nearly half way across. The mainland behind them and the island before them looked equally far away. On either side of the cart track was water now instead of mud. The track was like a narrow bridge over the sea.

"The tide's a lot higher than it was when we came across," said Roger. "We'll be coming to the channel soon, where we had to splash through."

"It was only an inch or two deep," said Titty.

"Weren't there two channels?" said Roger. "We splashed through one and the other was nearly dry. Gosh! Look at it! . . . "

The road dipped before them, only a little, but even a little was enough to bring it below the level of the incoming tide. They had come to the first of the channels. For twenty or thirty yards the road was under water. It was not deep under water. Ripples over the ruts made the road still plain to see.

Titty looked back and forward and made up her mind.

"Keep along the middle where it's shallowest," she said cheerfully. "Don't splash more than you need."

"Come on, Bridget," said Roger. "We're more than half way."

He set out, with Bridget close behind him and Titty close behind Bridget. The water on the road was an inch deep round the soles of their boots.

After the first few yards it rose to their ankles.

"Which channel was the deepest?" said Roger over his shoulder.

"Both about the same, I expect," said Titty. "This one's all right."

"Look out, Bridgie," said Roger. "Don't put your foot in the rut. You'll have it over the top of your boot."

Close ahead of them now were the four stout posts between which *Wizard* had sailed. There the road was still dry. It rose inch by inch out of the water, firm honest cart-track. In another few moments they would be on it. The water was already not so deep. It was well below the tops of their boots. It was lapping round their ankles. It hardly covered the road, though of course it was deeper in the ruts. Roger broke into a run, sending mud and water flying.

"Roger!" exclaimed Bridget. "You've splashed me all over."

"Never mind," said Titty. "Come on. Once we get across the next channel we'll be all right. . . . "

"I say," said Roger. "I believe the next one's the deep one. Look at it."

Beyond the place with the four posts the road dipped again and disappeared and here there were no ripples marking the ruts. The road simply went down into the water as if it ended there. Only, nearly fifty yards away, they could see where it came up once more and ran straight over the mud to the island.

"It really *is* a Wade," said Roger.

Titty looked back. They were more than half way across. If only they could wade through this bit they would be all right. "Poor old Pharaoh," said Titty to herself. Well, they would have to try it. And if it was too deep they'd just have to splash back and run for the mainland, before it was too late.

"Careful where you step," she said. "Keep on the hard part."

They went on.

"It's all right," said Roger. "It's no worse than the other bit."

He was wading on with the water just above his ankles. Bridget was close behind him, and Titty ready to give a hand to Bridget.

"Ouch!" said Roger suddenly. "Look out for that hole."

"You haven't got it into your boots?" said Titty. "Keep in the middle. Look far ahead where the road comes up again. It's no good trying to see the road at your feet with all the mud in the water."

Roger stopped, standing on one foot and prodding at the bottom with the other.

"Deeper," he said. "I'm going to take my boots off."

"Don't waste time," said Titty. "Do remember the tide's coming in."

Roger took a step forward and one leg went over the knee.

"There," he said. "Now I've done it. Soft mud. I must be on the edge of the road."

"It's over my boots," said Bridget. She stood still and looked round at Titty.

"Never mind if it is," said Titty. "You've often got them wet before. Roger, you stay where you are. Let me feel for the way."

"I'm wet anyhow," said Roger. "And I know where the road is now." He plunged forward and found the water well above his knees. The next moment the basket with Sinbad swung up in the air and Roger floundered, tried to keep his balance, lost it, and fell with a tremendous splash.

"Come back," cried Titty.

"Lost a boot," said Roger struggling to his feet. "It's all right. Sinbad's basket never even dipped."

Titty waded towards him and took the basket. Roger, wet from head to foot, tugged at a boot that was stuck in the mud and wholly under water. It came free with a jerk and Roger took another step and all but fell again.

"It's jolly soft," he said.

"You must be off the edge of the road," said Titty.

"Am I to come on?" asked Bridget.

"No," said Titty. "Stand still. Look here, it's hard where I am."

Roger floundered a step or two and stood beside her. "On the road now," he said. "But the water's deeper than it was."

"Of course it is," said Titty almost crossly. "Tide's coming in. Stand here a moment. Take Sinbad. I'm going to try again."

She looked far ahead at the line of withies marking the invisible road, and waded on. Good. The road was still hard beneath her feet. Just a few inches of mud but hard gravel underneath it. It must begin to get shallower quite soon. If she could only be sure herself, sure enough to tell the others to follow her and splash right through. She took another step. Water trickled cold down the inside of first one boot and then the other. And Bridget's legs were much shorter than her own. She stopped, and almost before she knew it the water was tickling her knees. She made up her mind. They could not get through. The only thing to do was to turn round, get through the splash they had already passed and race back along the road to the mainland and safety.

"Turn round, Bridget. And you, Roger. Don't hurry. Get back. Get back to the dry place by the four posts. . . . All right, Roger. . . . I'll take Sinbad again."

"But what are we going to do?" said Bridget.

"Go back to the mainland," said Titty. "It'll be all right. We'll make a fire and get our things dry."

"But what about the feast?"

"John'll come for us as soon as he can bring the boat."

Titty glanced back towards the island. There was nobody in sight. One of the buffaloes lumbered up to the top of the dyke, stood there looking at her without interest and settled down to graze. Not a human being was about.

They waded carefully back to the bit of the road that was still dry between the shallow splash they had crossed and that other that was already too deep for them.

"Now then, run," said Titty, as soon as they were all three out of the water. "No time to lose. Tide's rising all the time, and that other place'll be deeper than it was."

"It jolly well is," said Roger a moment later. "It's over my knees already."

"You take Sinbad and the knapsack," said Titty. "And I'll carry Bridget." She handed over knapsack and basket, and stooped, soaking the edge of her skirt, while Bridget, beginning to be worried, climbed out of the water on her back. She staggered on.

"You're a good weight," she said, cheerfully.

"That's why they said I'd be better than Daisy," said Bridget.

"It's too deep," said Roger suddenly, and Titty lost her footing, and fell, with Bridget on her back.

"Gosh!" said Roger.

"I'm wet right up to my head," said Bridget.

"No good," said Titty, struggling up. "We can't get through. We've got to get back to the posts. Keep hold of my hand, Bridgie. You can't get any wetter."

"But how'll we get ashore?" said Roger, when the three of them had struggled back to the bit of dry road.

"John and Susan'll come back as soon as they find we aren't in the camp. They'll see us and bring a boat. We've only got to wait. Empty the water out of your boots."

The bit of road with the four posts on it, in the middle of the Wade, was shorter than it had been. At each end of it was a widening channel of water. On each side of it the water stretched as far as they could see, on one side to the Magellan Straits and the passage to Cape Horn, on the other side to Goblin Creek and the island of the Mastodon. And the water was rising, rising fast. Crossing the Wade in the morning Titty in imagination had been under water, looking up at the keels of

boats passing overhead. And now they were not
Israelites, crossing dryshod, but Egyptians. They
were trapped there in the middle of the sea. They
could go neither forward nor back and must wait
there, watching the narrow island of the road
shrink under their feet.

What would John do if he were in command?
Swim and fetch a boat? It would not be far to
swim to the place where the road climbed once
more out of the water. She was on the point of
flinging off her clothes when she remembered that
Roger and Bridget and Sinbad would be left there
waiting in the middle of the sea. Then she thought
of telling Roger to swim for it and bring help. But
supposing there was a current. Supposing he were
to be swept one way or other away from the road.
Everywhere else was soft mud. And if he were to
get stuck in it (and she had seen how easily that
might happen) she would have to leave Bridget
alone while she swam to help him. Bridget was
all right now, but it would never do to leave her
alone. . . .

"Do you think they'll see us soon?" said Bridget.

"Sure to," said Titty. "Give them time to get
to the camp and to find we're not there." She
spoke calmly, keeping the fear out of her voice
as she looked along the island shore. Never had

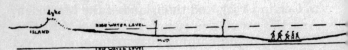

THE ROAD ACROSS THE RED

the island looked more utterly deserted. Even the buffalo had left the dyke.

"It's covered that pebble already," said Roger. "I'll put another one further back."

He scrabbled in the mud for pebbles, and laid a row of them, each one about a foot further than the last from the edge of the water. Before he had laid the last the first had disappeared.

"What are we going to do?" said Roger.

"Wait," said Titty. "We've only got to wait. And I'll serve out a ration of chocolate."

"Why not?" said Roger.

They went to the four posts, at the highest point of the road. That would be the last part to be covered. Roger hung Sinbad's basket from the top of one of the posts. Titty hung the knapsack from another, after burrowing into it for a slab of chocolate, which she broke into three equal pieces. Bridget and Roger nibbled chocolate. Titty took a bite of hers but found to her surprise she did not want it. Just for a moment she thought she was going to be sick. Why didn't somebody come up on the dyke and see them?

"It's like the Flood," said Roger. "It's a pity we haven't got an ark. I say, is it any good our yelling?"

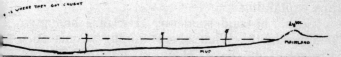

HIGH AND LOW TIDE

"Too far," said Titty. "They'd never hear. But we might as well try. We'll all yell 'Ahoy' together.".

Roger wasted a bit of chocolate by swallowing it.

"Now then," said Titty. "One ... two ... three ... "

"AHOY," they shouted.

"Again," said Titty. "One ... two ... three, AHOY ... OY ... OY!"

In spite of all three voices, well timed and doing their best, "Ahoy" sounded very thin when shouted from the middle of that great space of water and mud.

"Ahoy," shouted Roger.

"Shut up," said Titty. "Keep a look out and yell when you see anybody. No good just shouting at nothing." A little more shouting into emptiness and she knew the others would begin to be as worried as she was herself.

Roger went along the little bit of dry road. He came back looking grave.

"All my stones are under water," he said.

"Well, naturally," said Titty. She caught his eye, scowled at him and glanced over her shoulder at Bridget who was talking to Sinbad through his basket. If Roger knew things were pretty bad, it was no use pretending to him, but, whatever happened, they must keep Bridget cheerful.

Roger understood. There was no need to do any explaining.

"Gosh!" he said suddenly. "I wish I had my penny whistle. What about singing? Come on, Bridget. Let's have 'Hanging Johnny'. See if you've forgotten the words. ... "

Titty wished he had chosen a livelier tune, but "Hanging Johnny" was better than nothing.

"And then I hanged my granny," sang Bridget.

"That's not the first verse," said Roger.

"Haul away, boys, haul away," sang Titty, her eyes on the distant dyke.

"I hanged her up so canny," sang Bridget.

"So Hang, boys, Hang," sang all three.

Hanging Johnny worked through his relations in the wrong order and did not explain that people said he hanged for money till the last verse. But Roger made no more complaints and the choruses went with a will, though both Roger and Titty were thinking of something else. Surely someone would appear somewhere, and the sooner the better, before Bridget realized that their tiny island of road would shrink to nothing and that they would be left in the middle of the Red Sea, the waters of which would stretch from shore to shore.

"You sing one now," said Bridget.

"What shall we do with a drunken sailor?" sang Titty. Was that John's head moving above the dyke? "What shall we do with a drunken sailor?" No, whatever it was it was gone. "What shall we do with a drunken sailor?" And no one on the mainland either? "Early in the MORNING." Well, Bridget was all right so far. Keep going. "Way, hay, up she rises. Way, hay, up she rises." Has Roger spotted someone? "Way, hay, up she rises." No. He's only looking at the shore. Gosh, I wonder if we ought to have swum for it right away. "EARLY in the MORNING. " . . . Too late now.

"Go on, Titty," said Bridget. "Brasswork comes next. . . . "

"You sing it," said Titty. "We'll chorus."

"Set him polishing up the brasswork,
Set him polishing up the brasswork,
Set him polishing up the brasswork,
    EARLY IN THE MORNING"

"What about a fire?" said Roger. "A good column of smoke so that nobody could help seeing."

"No firewood," said Titty. "You can't burn mud. . . . I'll tell you what though. We can unwrap the parcels and burn all the paper. . . . "

"Lucky he wrapped everything up," said Roger. "He never guessed it'd be so useful. 'What I always say is they ought to make the clerk of the weather. . . . ' Good old grocer. . . . " Roger laughed again. "I bet he didn't know why I had to bolt."

"Let me light it," said Bridget.

"All right," said Titty.

"You must do it with one match," said Roger.

"If it doesn't blow out," said Bridget. "And it won't, unless you go and blow it. There's no wind really."

"There isn't much paper," said Titty, digging parcels out of the knapsack. "Look here, Bridgie. You and Roger eat the last of those cream buns. We can use their bag."

"The lump sugar's in a cardboard box," said Roger. "The sugar'll be all right without it till we get to the camp."

"The ginger biscuits are in a paper bag,"

said Bridget.

"Let's have it," said Titty. "And the corn-flakes have got a good burnable box. And he's put paper round the tins of milk and cocoa."

"I say," whispered Roger to Titty. "Ought we to burn Sinbad's basket? There's nothing else in the way of sticks."

"Can't," said Titty. "We can't have Sinbad loose if we have to swim."

Roger looked at the widening water between them and the shore.

"We'll manage, if we have to," said Titty quietly. "You and me with Bridget between us. Or I'll take Bridgie and you keep the basket as dry as you can."

"The ground's not very dry," said Bridget, who was busy arranging the fuel. "The paper gets wet as soon as it touches it."

"All the more smoke," said Titty.

Roger pulled out his knife and attacked one of the four posts on the high bit of the Wade. He got a shaving or two. "Jolly damp," he said. "I suppose they would be, going under water every time the tide comes in. . . . " His face changed as he spoke. Titty knew that he too was thinking how deep the waters would flow over the spot where they were standing. She scowled at him furiously. "Good for you, Bridget. Here's your match. Get the paper well lit and then the cardboard. . . . "

"There's some seaweed round that other post," said Roger. "That ought to make some smoke."

"Done it with one match," said Bridget. "I knew I could. I wish Susan had seen me."

"So do I," said Titty, and glanced again at the distant dyke.

The paper flamed up, burning much too fast, but the cardboard box, torn to narrow bits, caught fire, and a column of smoke drifted up and away. Roger put the seaweed on the top. The fire nearly went out, but heartened again, with a smell of burning kelp. Roger frantically cut a few more shavings, but nobody can make a big fire with nothing to burn, and presently the paper had burnt out, and they were simply wasting matches lighting and relighting small bits of charred cardboard and trying to light wet shavings that needed drying before they would kindle. The fire was over. The smoke signal had been made. There was not a sign that anybody had seen it.

"What'll Susan say when she finds sugar and ginger-breads and cornflakes all mixed up in the knapsack?" said Bridget.

"Tell us to separate them," said Roger.

The water was lapping over into the ruts on each side of the bit of road that was still uncovered in the middle of the Red Sea. The road was getting shorter and shorter. All was covered except that bit between the two pairs of wooden posts.

"Are we going to get wet?" asked Bridget suddenly.

"You can't get wetter than you are," said Titty. "You've been in once when I fell down. Look here. Don't let the ship's kitten get frightened. You tell him they'll be coming for us in a minute."

"All right," said Bridget and went to the post on which Sinbad's basket was hanging, to give the kitten words of comfort.

Titty and Roger went to the water's edge.

"Hadn't we better swim now?" said Roger.

Titty looked towards the island. "No," she said. "Not till we can't help it. Remember what that mud's like by the shore. We've got to wait till we can land on hard ground."

"It'll be jolly deep here by then."

"I know," said Titty. "And it's all my fault. We ought to have gone right on and not stopped till we were on the island."

"It was Sinbad's fault really," said Roger. "And mine a bit."

"No it wasn't," said Titty. "Why can't one of them look this way?" she added almost angrily. "Look here. We'd better take our clothes off for swimming, and make a bundle of them with Sinbad's basket on the top."

"Bridget knows how to float," said Roger. "And she'll keep still if you tell her to."

"Gosh!" said Titty. "It's the worst mess we've ever been in."

The water lapped about their feet, and they went back to the posts. The water crept over the road. The ruts were filled. The middle of the road was a thin line that disappeared. They were standing in water that stretched almost from the mainland to the island.

Roger suddenly began to struggle out of

his wet shirt.

"Not yet, Roger. Not yet," said Titty.

"Signal of distress," said Roger, wringing out the water.

"There's nothing to hoist it on."

"Give me a leg up," said Roger.

"It's worth trying," said Titty.

"Whistle for a wind," said Roger. "It's too wet to wave."

Bridget obediently tried but failed. The ship's baby was beginning to lose faith in the able-seamen.

"Go on, Bridgie," said Roger. " 'Spanish Ladies' is an easy one. Lick your lips first."

Some noise did come from Bridget's lips, and sure enough the light wind that had just rippled the water strengthened a little, as Titty took one of Roger's feet in both hands and hoisted him up, while Roger scrambled up the post, and sat on the top of it, taking a grip of it with both legs. Over his head one hand above the other, he held his shirt. A gust, that sent little waves lapping round the tops of Bridget's boots as she stood at the foot of the post, blew out the signal of distress and kept it flapping.

"Jolly good flag," said Roger. "It'd be better if it wasn't so beastly wet."

"Can you see anybody?" said Titty.

"The water's over my boots," said Bridget.

"Look here, Bridgie," said Titty. "You know how to float. Well, you're going to. You'll just have to lie on your back and keep still, and I'm going to swim you ashore. It's going to be as easy as easy."

SIGNAL OF DISTRESS

"But I can't," said Bridget. "Not for as long as all that. Isn't anybody coming? You said they were coming. And what about Sinbad?"

"Roger'll take Sinbad. It'll be all right. And then we'll run and get dry, and everybody'll be awfully proud of you."

"Would Susan let me?" said Bridget.

"Of course she would. And so would John. It isn't as if you were too young."

Bridget gulped.

"There's no other way," said Titty. "I'll keep tight hold of you all the time."

"When are we going to start?" said Bridget.

"Now," said Titty.

"And Sinbad'll get wet too."

"Roger'll keep him as dry as he can."

"And what about the things in the knapsack. The sugar and the biscuits for the feast?"

"Can't be helped," said Titty. "And I don't see how we can save our seaboots. Oh yes we can. We'll tie them to one of the posts and come and get them when the tide goes down again. There's some string in the knapsack. You stay here, and I'll go and get it from the post. We won't take Sinbad's basket off his post till we're ready to start. Better get out of your clothes. . . . "

"Will we lose them too? . . . "

"AHOY!" There was a sudden yell from the human flagstaff above their heads, and a frantic flapping of the signal of distress.

"What is it?" cried Titty, and at the same moment she saw.

"Saved," said Roger.

Far away, in the mouth of the channel leading to Goblin Creek a black speck of a boat was moving over the water.

Titty suddenly felt like laughing and crying at the same time.

"There you are, Bridgie," she said. "No swimming after all. He'll be here before the water's up to our middles."

CHAPTER XXVII

RESCUE AND AFTER

"THE water's a long way above my knees," said Bridget.

Titty judged the distance to that far away boat. The water would be a good deal higher before it could reach them, and already felt swirly and strong.

"Come on, Bridgie," she said. "We'll perch you on that other post."

"Shall I let go of this one?"

"Hang on to me."

She waded across the road, stumbling at one place where she suddenly found deeper water in a rut. The water certainly was coming in very fast. But nothing mattered now. The boat was coming. Only now she let herself know how she had feared the moment when, if there had been no boat, she and Roger would have had to get somehow across that wide water, with Bridget, who did not know how to swim, and Sinbad who would for the second time in his short life have been in danger of drowning.

"Up you go."

She hoisted Bridget up to the top of the post, left her there, perched like Roger, and herself stood, waiting at the foot of it.

"What about you?" said Bridget.

"I'm all right," said Titty. "We all are."

"It was my shirt that did it," said Roger. "Hullo,

it's not John. It's the Mastodon."

The water rose higher and higher, but Titty
cared no longer. The boat, with the Mastodon
rowing as if in a race, was coming fast towards
them. Wet? They were all wet. Roger had sprawled
in mud and water. Titty had fallen down. Bridget
had fallen with her. But wet clothes were nothing.
Much worse things had seemed like happening.
The Red Sea had closed over the road but, after
all, they had not had to swim for it.

Bridget, perched on the top of her post, watched
the boat and the quick flash of the Mastodon's
oars. Titty too had no eyes for anything else.
But Roger, now that his efforts as a flagstaff had
been successful, was thoroughly enjoying himself,
and was looking round to see if anyone else had
noticed his signals and seen the Egyptians out in
the middle of the Red Sea.

"Hullo," he shouted. "Titty! More boats!"

Three small boats were in sight coming from the
other entrance to the Red Sea, from the channel
between Cape Horn and the mainland. They had
no sails or masts. The people in them were rowing,
and rowing fast. Someone waved.

"Karabadangbaraka!" A breathless shout came
from the Mastodon's boat, now quite near.

"Akarabgnadabarak!" Titty, Roger and Bridget
turned round and shouted together.

In another minute the Mastodon, resting on his
oars, floated up to them. He could hardly speak,
he had been rowing so hard, and he looked much
more worried than any of the Swallows.

"You're pretty lucky," he panted. "The tide
comes in jolly fast. In another half hour you'd be

swimming. What are you doing here? You might have drowned yourselves."

"Did you see the signal of distress?" said Roger.

"Lucky I did," said the Mastodon almost crossly. "I say, you know there's deep water over here at high tide."

"We didn't mean to be Egyptians," said Roger.

"All jolly well," said the Mastodon. "John and Susan must be mad to let you."

"They didn't know," said Titty. "It was my fault . . . though I did put a patteran to show them." She took Sinbad's basket, and put it in the boat. "Come on, Bridget. Let yourself slip. I'll catch you." Standing nearly up to her waist in water, she helped Bridget down from the post and aboard.

"You get in now," said the Mastodon. "And then I'll go alongside Roger."

"Won't we be too many?" said Roger. "I'm all right. I can wait for one of the other boats. Hullo. What's happened to them?"

The people who had been doing the rowing in those far away boats had disappeared. Not a head, not a hand showed above the gunwales. The boats were drifting like derelicts with the tide.

The Mastodon had been rowing with his back to them, and, when he came to the posts, had had eyes only for the explorers he was rescuing. He now saw the other boats for the first time.

"Gone adrift," he said.

"There were people in them rowing a minute ago," said Titty.

"There aren't now," said the Mastodon.

And then the outline of one of the boats

changed. A lump, a head, showed above the gunwale. Someone was looking out.

The Mastodon laughed.

"It's all right," he said. "Come on down, Roger. Lots of room if we keep her steady."

"There's the knapsack on that other post," said Titty.

"We'll get it."

Heads and no more showed above the gunwales of the three drifting boats in the distance. The rescue of the Egyptians was being watched from afar, and the Mastodon had a broad grin on his face, as he pulled his laden boat across to the place where the road to the farm came up out of the water.

"What is it?" asked Roger.

"Are you laughing because we're so wet?" said Bridget.

"You might have been wetter," said the Mastodon, serious for a moment, and then, looking over his shoulder at those drifting boats he laughed again. Suddenly he stopped rowing, leant forward, gently prodded Bridget, and smacked his lips.

"Much plumper than Daisy," he said.

"We've been stuffing her with cream buns," said Roger.

"Good," said the Mastodon, and rowed on till the keel of the boat scrunched on hard gravel where the road came up again out of the water.

The rescued Egyptians stepped out.

"Thanks most awfully," said Titty.

"That's all right," said the Mastodon. "Better bolt to the camp as quick as you can. Your chiefs have been back ages."

"Aren't you coming?" said Roger.

"Not just yet," said the Mastodon, and rowed away towards the drifting boats.

*

"Come on," said Titty. "As fast as we can go. We'll have to change everything, and put our clothes to dry."

At a good jog trot, in soaked clothes, the water in their seaboots squelching at every step, they hurried in single file along the top of the dyke. Bridget, in front, set the pace, easing to a walk now and then, but never for long. Titty and perhaps Roger knew what a narrow escape they had had but for Bridget the adventure on the Wade was already no more than a wetting and a wetting already past. She was thinking of something else. Tonight it was to be, tonight she would be taking Daisy's place, a human sacrifice, the very centre of the ceremony.

*

"Gosh! Look what they've done!" Roger was the first to see the huge bonfire, ready for the lighting, that had been built while they had been away.

They came into the camp, and stared about them. There was Susan's fire, also ready for lighting, in Susan's neat fireplace, and there, below the dyke, was this colossal pile of driftwood, and old bits of boats and sticks, and broken up boxes and baskets, and bits of broken barrel.

"It's a beauty," said Roger.

"What's this post for?" asked Bridget, looking

at a stout post driven firm into the ground.

Titty looked at it and then at Bridget. "Probably for you," she said.

"Oh," said Bridget rather doubtfully.

"More totems," said Roger.

"They must have brought theirs," said Titty. "That's the Mastodon's. And look, they've hung a lot more shells on ours. But where are John and Susan?"

The camp was empty but for themselves.

"They've been here," said Roger, looking into John's tent. "Here's his map with the road to the town on it. They must be somewhere about."

"Quick," said Titty. "Let's get our wet things off before they come back. It won't be so bad if they find us all dry." She squeezed out Roger's shirt which had served as a signal of distress, wrung the last drops from it and spread it on a bush.

"Go on, Bridgie. Off with your things. Undies too. No. Don't go all wet into Susan's tent. I won't be a minute changing, and then I'll dig out a frock for you. You change too, Roger."

"I'm going to get into bathing things," said Roger, "and go down to the landing place and wash the mud off."

"Good idea," said Titty. "It's no good getting all muddy into clean things. I'll do the same. But Bridget mustn't bathe, and she isn't really very muddy, only wet. Here you are, Bridgie. Here's a towel. You just rub down for all you're worth."

Titty's wet things and Roger's joined Bridget's spread to dry on the bushes. Six seaboots were stood upside down to drain. Titty and Roger, in bathing clothes, raced down to the landing place, splashed into the water, got the mud off, and splashed out again.

"I've got another lot on my feet," said Roger, as they staggered up through the mud of the saltings.

"So've I," said Titty. "Hurry up. We'll sit on the bank and dabble our legs in the pond."

"Look at Bridget," said Roger. "Going to a party. . . ."

Bridget, dry and in a clean white frock, was earnestly tying her hair ribbon. "Am I all right?" she said.

"Quite," said Titty. "Haven't you seen the others?"

"No," said Bridget. "And Sinbad's gone straight to sleep."

"Let's give a yell," said Roger.

"Ahoy!" they shouted.

There was no answer.

"Come on, Roger, let's get clean anyway," said Titty.

They paddled their feet in the pond, sitting on the bank, and were already drying themselves, when, at last, they saw John and Susan coming along the dyke to the north of the camp.

"Here they are," shouted Roger. "Hullo!"

Neither John nor Susan answered him. They came on in grim silence.

"Something's happened," said Roger as soon as he could see their faces.

John and Susan walked into the camp.

"Titty," said Susan. "Where have you been?"

"Look here," said John. "It's really rather too

bad. We've been half round the island looking for you."

"We did leave a patteran," said Titty.

"Where?" said John, but did not wait for an answer. "We can't get the map finished, and it's your fault. Daddy's coming for us in the morning. Nine o'clock. I told him the map wasn't done and he said we'd have to leave it. He wants everything packed up and ready to put aboard at high tide, so as not to waste a single minute. He'd sent a message through the farmer. Didn't you see it stuck on the stick of the meal-dial?"

He held out a crumpled bit of paper, on which they read: "Your dad say he come for you at high water tomorrow. You was all away when I look for you."

"Tomorrow?" gasped Titty.

"Oh gosh!" said Roger.

"I'd got the rudder mended before three o'clock," said John, "and we got Daddy on the telephone first shot, and Susan and I raced home, and there'd have been just time for me to go and settle that North West Passage if only you'd waited in the camp instead of putting Susan in a stew and making us waste hours in looking for you. And now we can never do it. It's too late now, and the map's a failure without it."

"But we weren't in the camp," said Roger.

"Bridget!" said Susan. "Who told you to put on a clean frock?"

"The other one was wet," said Bridget, looking at the bushes, where clothes of all kinds were drying.

"Bridgie . . . Oh, I say Titty. You haven't let

her fall in. . . . And Roger too. And you. What on earth have you been doing?"

"We couldn't help it," said Roger. "It might have happened to anybody. It did happen to the Egyptians, only much worse."

"We got caught," said Titty. "You see. . . . "

*

A long shrill whistle sounded from somewhere behind the dyke. Susan started, dipped into a pocket, and brought out her hand empty.

"My whistle," she exclaimed. "Nancy must have got it, or Peggy. But what were you doing to get wet all three of you?"

"Sinbad discovered a creek," said Roger. "It wasn't Titty's fault."

A curious drumming noise sounded from somewhere north of the camp. It was answered by another, like that of two sticks being rapidly beaten together, somewhere to the south.

The explorers looked about them.

The drumming noise came again from close behind the camp.

It came again as if from the landing place, and again from somewhere else.

"What's that?" said John.

And then from all directions came the noise, not deep enough for a drum, a thin quick rattle, as if half a dozen corncrakes were calling to each other. There was nothing to be seen, but the noises were coming nearer and nearer, from all sides.

The story of the Egyptians was not told until much later, for suddenly wild yells sounded close at hand, "Kara . . . Kara . . . Kara badang . . .

Baraka . . . Baraka . . . Karabadangbaraka!"

Two seconds later the savages rushed the camp.

CHAPTER XXVIII

CORROBOREE

THE explorers, caught unprepared, had no time in which to make ready for defence. Nobody had expected anything quite like this. At one moment they had been standing rather miserable in the camp. Everything had gone wrong. Each one of them, except Bridget, was feeling somehow to blame and therefore ready to be cross with all the others.

And then, at that blast of Susan's whistle, blown by someone who had no right to have it, at that noise of drumming, now here, now there, now all about them, everything was changed. The savages were among them. Six of them, not four. And what savages! Feathers in their hair, bodies striped and splashed with mud for war-paint, faces patterned with mud, black bars on cheeks, rays of mud upwards from each eye, like the rays of the setting sun; Nancy had done her work well; even the Eels, who had helped her at it, had hardly known each other, when she had finished. And as for the explorers, when that howling mob rushed the camp from all sides, they stood there dithering.

But they had small time to dither. John, Captain John, the leader of the explorers, found himself hurled to the ground with two savages, striped like tigers, on top of him. A noose was slipped over his kicking ankles and pulled tight. The rope was taken twice round the middle of him and knotted,

PUTTING ON THE WAR-PAINT

and the two savages, leaving him trussed and
helpless, rushed on to help a small and rather
skinny savage who was struggling with Susan.
Roger found himself lifted off his feet by a savage
of enormous strength, who cried, "Eels for ever!
Don't wriggle like a lugworm. My war-paint's
hardly dry." Roger put his knees together, planted
them in the stomach of the savage and straightened out. The savage lost grip. Roger fell, was up
in a moment and away. The powerful savage dived
after him and caught him by the ankle. This time
there was no escape. The savage sat on the top of
him, roped his ankles and tied his wrists behind
his back. The small and skinny savage had been
having a difficult time with Susan who stood
firmly on her feet fending off attack after attack,
but three to one was too much, and while the two
savages who had made short work of John held the
struggling Susan, the small and skinny one wound
a rope about her, binding her elbows to her sides
and hobbling her legs. "Eels! Eels for ever!" they
shouted, and left her beside John and Roger, just
as two other savages, with black bodies and
striped arms and legs, brought along the captured
Titty, wound round and round with rope, one
carrying her feet, the other her shoulders.

"Don't frighten Bridget!" whispered Susan
urgently.

The savages laughed and ran back to join
the others.

Bridget, standing in the middle of the camp, had
watched the swift defeat of the explorers. Just for
one moment she had been startled by those leaping painted creatures. Then she had understood.

She had seen John, Susan, Titty, Roger brought to the ground and roped as prisoners.

"What about me?" she said. Susan need not have worried.

"Food . . . Food . . . Food. . . . "

The savages were closing in around her.

"Food . . . Food . . . Food . . . food for the Sacred Eel."

They were dancing in a circle, leaping and shouting. The moment had come, and Bridget, in her clean white frock, stood in the midst of a ring of jumping whirling figures. She stood there, smiling, wondering what was going to happen next. She began to recognize the savages. That large, long-legged one must be Nancy. She knew the tear in the back of Nancy's bathing dress. She knew the Mastodon by his stiff mop of sandy hair. Those two who had set upon John in the first attack must be Dum and Dee. She could not tell them apart anyway, and certainly not when they were all over stripes of mud. And that skinny one, who danced more fierily than any of the rest, must be Daisy who would have been the human sacrifice if they had not found a better.

Bridget waited eagerly. What exactly were they going to do?

The fiery, skinny savage left the ring for a moment, dived into the long grass and was back again, dancing nearer and nearer with something in her hands. She swung it to and fro, she waved it before Bridget's eyes, darted backwards, shot forward again and suddenly flung the thing over Bridget's head. Bridget clawed at it and was

relieved to find that it was only a necklace of
seashells.

"Marked for the Eels," sang the skinny savage,
her eyes sparkling through black rings of mud.

"Marked for the Eels," she sang and the others
took up the chorus.

> "Marked for the Eels,
> A juicy dish
> To feed the wrig-
> gliest of fish."

> "Marked for the Eels,
> So plump and fat
> They'll smack their lips
> To think of that."

There was a loud noise of smacking lips as
the savages came nearer. Bridget, in spite of
herself, drew back from them. First one finger
then another prodded her plump arms. They were
all round her. She moved again. Foot by foot she
moved as a savage finger touched her now here
now there. Suddenly she found that she was close
to that big post that had been driven into the
ground.

"Keep your arms down," said the skinny savage.

Another savage was busy at her feet.

They drew back. Bridget, standing against the
post, was roped to it, with a rope round her middle
and another round her ankles.

"Grab her and hold her," sang the Eels.

"Grab her and hold her,
Bind her tight.
The noble Eels
Feed well tonight."

The skinny savage darted away and came back with the lid of a tin. She was stirring something in it with a finger. She danced up to Bridget, one finger dripping red. Bridget felt something cold on her forehead, as the skinny savage drew a wriggling eel on it. The others danced before her, pointing at her.

*

The gloating of the Eels was violently interrupted.

Roger, from the moment he had been dumped beside the other captives, had been working to free himself. He had held his wrists as far apart as he could while that strong savage tied them. Now he was holding them close together and was working one against the other.

The rope was already a little slack. From where he lay he could see the savages closing round Bridget. He wanted to shout to her to hold out, but changed his mind in time. That would have served only to warn the savages.

He whispered to John, "I'll have this hand loose in a minute."

John, who had been better roped than anybody, tried to turn over and failed.

"What are they doing?" he whispered.

"They've got Bridgie," said Roger.

Susan struggled in her ropes.

"I'll go for them in another ten seconds," said Roger.

"Don't be a donk," said John. "What can you do against the lot? You must untie Susan and me first."

"And me," whispered Titty.

"All right," whispered Roger.

"What *are* they doing to her?" said Susan. "Singing . . . "

"They've put something round her neck," said Roger. "They're roping her to the post. They're going to sacrifice her right away. . . . I'm out. . . . at least one hand is. . . . And the other. Oh gosh! He's tied my legs with a granny and it's stuck. . . . "

"Cut it."

"It's one of our ropes."

"Never mind that," said Susan. "They'll frighten her."

Roger, in spite of the granny, got his hands free. Keeping as still as he could, for fear a savage should be looking, he freed his feet, worked himself inch by inch nearer to John, and in a moment had untied John's wrist. The savages had laid their captives side by side, and John, after he had got the stiffness out of his elbows, was busy with Susan's ropes before Roger had had time to free his feet.

"Now," said John.

"Oh look here," said Titty. "I've got one arm out."

"Keep still," said Susan. "I'll cut it. I don't care whose rope it is."

"Any of them looking?" whispered John.

"They've tied her to the post," said Roger.

"They're doing something to her face," said Titty.

"Come on," said John, leapt to his feet and charged at the savages.

"A rescue. . . . A rescue," shouted Roger, bowling a savage off his feet, stumbling himself, and going head first into the arms of the strong savage who had tied him up.

"Swallows for ever," shouted Titty, and threw her arms round the skinny savage with the red paint. The lid with the paint flew out of her hands and plastered itself on Bridget's white frock.

A huge splash of red paint on her white frock, and the red mark of the eel on her forehead made Bridget look indeed as if she were being slaughtered at the stake.

"All right, Bridget," cried Susan. "It's all right. We'll cut you free. You're going to be rescued."

"Oh go AWAY," shrieked Bridget. "Go AWAY. They're just in the middle of it. I don't WANT to be rescued."

*

Just for one moment the explorers wavered. But their rally, so far, had been successful. The very strong savage had had all the breath knocked out of him by Roger's head, which had hit him in the middle like a cannon ball. He was doubled up, gasping, unable to speak. The smaller savage was still on the ground. John was struggling with two savages, one of whom exclaimed, "Jibbooms and bobstays!" and hurriedly put it right, by shouting "Congers!" Susan, with two savages hanging on to her, was forcing her way towards the post to which the human sacrifice was tied.

The strong savage, recovering his breath, panted the word, "Karabadangbaraka!" The other savages echoed him.

"A rescue!" cried the explorers.

"Go AWAY," cried the human sacrifice.

"Karabadangbaraka!" shouted Nancy, and then, "you idiots, are you Eels or aren't you?"

"Akarabgnadabarak," said Titty, clinging firmly to the skinny savage who was doing her very best to get her arms free.

"Akarabgnadabarak," said John. "Go on, Susan, say it too."

"Akarabgnadabarak," said Susan.

"Akarabgnadabarak," said Roger. "I say, I'm awfully sorry I winded you."

The battle stopped. Explorers and savages, now all savages, stood breathless and panting, looking at each other.

*

"What about lighting the fire?" said Nancy. "The whole tribe's here. Eels and blood sisters . . . and brothers. Daisy lights it, of course. Go on, Mastodon, and bring the sacred stew. Roger'll give you a hand."

"It's close here," said the Mastodon. "I ferried it across before the attack. It ought to be still hot. And anyway it has to be finished in the bonfire . . . with the human bits. . . . "

"Gosh!" said Roger. "Does Bridget know?"

Daisy made a poor start at lighting the fire.

Match after match went out and nothing caught. Susan watched, and then could bear it no longer. She gathered a lot of dry grass, scrumpled it up into a wad and gave it to Daisy. "Try lighting this," she said, "and then push it well into the middle. Make a hole first."

The wad of dried grass made a good fire-lighter. Daisy, a skinny, but finely striped savage, pushed it well into the bottom of the huge pile of sticks and logs. There was a sudden heartening blaze. A noise of crackling came from the pile, and little flames could be seen, leaping and climbing in the middle of the pile. There was a roar as dry sticks in the heart of the pile caught fire, and flames shot up into the rising column of smoke.

"Eels. Eels for ever! Good. Here they are!"

Roger and the Mastodon came up from the saltings with a huge two handled cauldron. Daisy darted at them and lifted the lid. Inside the cauldron was a saucepan in water that was still steaming round it.

"It's been simmering for ages," said the Mastodon.

"Now for Bridget," said Daisy.

The cauldron, with its lid off, was put on the ground close to the human sacrifice.

Daisy, with a scout knife, danced up to Bridget.

"A bit from there," she said, and made to carve a slice from one of Bridget's plump arms. She danced away, lifted the lid of the stew, and dropped the invisible piece into the saucepan. With the lifting of the lid a smell of stewed eels rose into the air.

"Beauties!" said Daisy. "You've never had such a lot."

"They'll be better with some Bridget," said the
Mastodon, licking his lips. He too went up to the
post, carefully chose his bit, and carried it to the
pot, sniffing greedily at it on his way.

Nancy was particular about hers. "No bone,"
she said. "Fat and juicy. A good bit for sizzling.
Nice crackling to it, like pork." She picked her
spot, and carved out her bit so earnestly that
Bridget winced though the knife never touched
her.

"Don't frighten her," said Titty.

"I'm *not* frightened," snapped Bridget.

Everybody in turn carried tasty bits from
Bridget and dropped them in the stewpot. Then
the cauldron was pushed, not without risk of
singed eyebrows, into the edge of the bonfire,
and the exulting savages, clapping their hands in
time, and shouting the words of the tribe, danced
round the blaze.

Bridget, tied to the stake, a gory victim,
watched them for a time. The sacrifice had
been made. The best bits of her were cooking in
the pot with the Mastodon's eels, and she began
to feel they had forgotten her.

"What happens to me now?" she said, when
Titty danced near enough to her.

"Human sacrifices always get rescued at the
last minute," said Titty. "Half a minute and I'll
cut you free. You've got to dance the Eel dance
and take part in the feast."

A moment later the human sacrifice was caper-
ing with the rest.

"That's right," said Daisy. "As eely as you
can. Wriggle and leap."

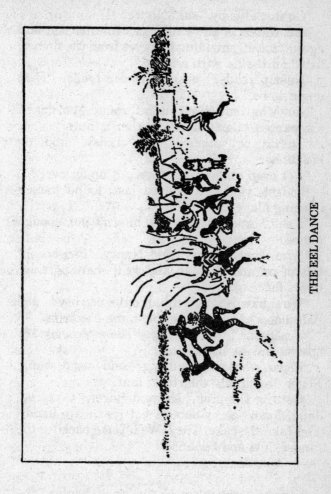

THE EEL DANCE

"Go it, Eel-baby," said Nancy.

The water in the cauldron came on the boil again. Susan, shielding her eyes from the flames, lifted off the lid with a towel.

"Nearly ready?" asked the Mastodon. "They ought to be."

Nancy hurled herself on the ground. "I'm done," she panted. "Can't dance another minute."

"They'll be satisfied," said Daisy, dropping beside her.

"Not even congers could keep it up for ever."

Bridget, who had started last, found herself dancing alone.

"I say," said Susan. "We haven't got enough plates."

"Who wants them?" said Nancy. "Fingers for bits of eel and Bridget, and we'll share porridge bowls for the juice."

"We'll have enough if half of us use bowls and half plates. And some people must use forks."

"Teaspoons," said Peggy. "There are six big spoons and six little ones."

"Roger, what are you doing?" said Susan, seeing Roger diving into the stores tent.

"Getting the grog," shouted Roger. "Come on, John. I can't carry enough bottles in two hands. You take the cake, Titty. We'll come back for the ginger nuts and bananas."

*

Sitting in the glow of the great bonfire, the blood brothers and sisters of the Eels feasted and drank. Two to a mug, for Mrs Walker had not provided for eleven to a meal, they toasted the sacred eel.

"Deep in the Atlantic he swims," said Daisy.

"Feasting on corpses," said Titty.

"Oh I say," said Peggy.

"Don't be a mudworm," said Nancy. "All the best eels feast on corpses. They like drowned sailors best."

Peggy pushed her plate away.

Nancy glared at her. "Like us feasting on Bridget."

"But I'm a human sacrifice," said Bridget. "Not a corpse."

"Just as good," said Daisy, licking her lips. "We've never had the eels tasting better."

"It's the bits of Bridget that make the difference," said the Mastodon.

"The Mastodon's got some of our blood in him, and you've got some of his," said Daisy. "And we're all Eels together, and these eels we're eating will make us eelier."

"And the Bridget we're eating'll make us plumper," said Roger. "Ha! I had a lovely taste of her just then. Very nutty. Go on, Peggy, have another try."

Bridget ate silently for some minutes, chewing carefully. "I can't really taste myself," she said at last. "But I haven't eaten eels before anyway, so I wouldn't know the difference."

"What are we going to do tomorrow?" said Daisy, and suddenly more than half the Children of the Eels turned back into being explorers.

"Oh Gosh!" said John. "You don't know what's happened. There isn't going to be a tomorrow. It's all over. The *Goblin*'s coming to take us off at high tide in the morning and we won't be able to get here again till next year. And I've never done the North West Passage. Thank goodness you did Peewitland today."

"But we didn't," said Nancy. "There simply wasn't time. There was such a lot to be got ready for the eel feast. The bonfire took ages to build. And then we had to go to Flint Island to get the war drums and things. And then it was time to come and meet the Mastodon. We were going to go round Peewit tomorrow. I say, I'm most awfully sorry."

"It can't be helped," said John. "I ought to have done the North West Passage and I haven't. And all that part of the map's silly if we don't know whether it's islands or not. I ought to have made sure long ago."

"It's all my fault," said Titty. "Going and looking at Sinbad's Creek."

"It wasn't," said Roger. "It was the Captain's fault and the Mate's. You made a good patteran and they never saw it."

"John told me to go home, and if we'd gone he'd have had time to go through the North West Passage, if there is one, instead of looking for us."

"Oh well, you'd have missed being Egyptians," said Nancy. "Barbecued Billygoats! I did wish it was me when we saw you perched on posts in the middle of the sea."

Susan stared with horror.

"What?" said John.

"Didn't you know we'd seen?" said Nancy. "We were sneaking round with the tide, so as to meet the Mastodon and paint him and get ashore where you wouldn't be looking for us, and surround the camp, and do a proper eely attack, and then we saw them. We rowed like fun, but the Mastodon got there first, and we were in full war-paint, so we just had to lie down in our war canoes. . . . "

"Was it you in those boats?" said Roger. "We saw people rowing, and then nothing but empty boats drifting along."

"But were you out in the middle of the water?" said Susan.

"Waving a signal of distress," said Roger. "If the Mastodon hadn't been jolly quick we'd have been swimming. Titty and I had everything planned."

"Oh Titty," said Susan.

"Jibbooms and bobstays," exclaimed Nancy. "Be an Eel, Susan. Nobody got drowned. They didn't even get wet. At least not very. And it was good exploring, too. We know now what the Red Sea can do."

"We knew without that," said Susan.

"We were only just too late," said Roger. "The waters had joined in front of us, and we tried to go through and it was a bit deep, and I went off the road by mistake. . . . And then we tried to go back, and it was too deep. And we lit a fire. And I got up on a post and waved."

"What did you say about Sinbad's Creek?" said Nancy.

"I'll show you," said Titty, and she went to her tent to get the sketch map made that day.

"Get the main map too," said John.

"Cheer up, Titty," said Nancy, as they were

coming back. "Nobody can really mind now it's safely over."

"It isn't that," said Titty. "But it was my fault, and now we've got to go back with the top of the map not done."

Dusk was falling, and some of the striped savages were piling more wood on the flames. Some of the wood was old planking from a broken up boat with copper nails in it, and the copper made green flames in the fire. By the flickering light, explorers and savages looked at the maps, and shared their mugs of steaming cocoa.

"That bit fits in there all right," said John. "And I say, where does that creek come out?"

The Mastodon looked at Titty's sketch. "It's all right," he said. "It comes out in the main channel, just here. . . . Can I mark it?" He felt for his pocket to get a pencil, forgetting that he was dressed in stripes of mud and a pair of bathing drawers. He took a bit of charred wood from the edge of the fire and marked the place.

"If only we hadn't got to leave the north all question marks," said John, looking away in the dusk beyond the mouth of Goblin Creek, over the Secret Water. "If we'd done that bit it wouldn't be so bad. All the rest's pretty good."

"Couldn't we do it in the morning?" said Nancy.

John groaned. "We've got to have every single thing ready to go aboard at high tide," he said.

"It's a splendid map anyway," said Daisy.

"Couldn't we finish it for you?" said the Mastodon.

Titty listened.

"No good," said John. "Savages are all right

as guides, and jolly useful, but we've got to do a thing like that ourselves. Explorers can't mark a passage unless they've been through to know it is one."

Titty prodded Roger secretly.

"Ow," said Roger.

"Sorry," said Titty, and prodded him again a moment later. This time Roger understood. Presently the two of them slipped away from the circle round the fire.

Titty talked earnestly for several minutes.

"I've got a bit of string that's long enough," said Roger when she had finished.

"Good," said Titty, "I'll get the other things."

They went back to the others, and worked their way in among savages and explorers and had another look at the map.

Dark was closing in when from far away sounded a long drawn hoot on a foghorn, followed by two others. Daisy and her brothers started up.

"Missionaries," said Daisy. "Watch."

A rocket soared into the dark sky behind the island, and burst into a shower of sparks.

"We've got to go," said Daisy. "We promised to bolt the moment they gave that signal. That was one of our rockets and we've brought one with us to show we've seen it."

She darted off and was back in a moment with a rocket on its long stick. She fitted it in the ground.

"Are you going to fire it off?" said Roger.

"Bridget is."

The human sacrifice fired the answering rocket. It hissed up into the darkness and scattered falling stars.

"Now we must bolt for it," said Daisy.

"But where are your boats?" said John.

The Mastodon was already running, surefooted even in the dark, down to the landing place.

"He's got them," said Daisy. "We landed and then he towed them round and anchored them out of sight behind the little islands."

"Our clothes are in one of them," said Peggy.

By the time the Eels and their blood relations had come down to the landing place, they could hear the sound of oars in the dark, and presently the Mastodon came pulling in, with the three small boats of the savages towing astern.

A minute or two later, four of the savages were rowing away, the Mastodon to his lair, the other three to the mouth of the creek.

"It's been just gorgeous," said Daisy. "And what we won't do next year. . . . "

Five explorers and two striped savages stood in the dark at the landing stage listening to the splash of oars.

"Karabadangbaraka!" the call came over the water.

"Akarabgnadabarak!" came the answer from the shore and from the Mastodon already near the mouth of his creek.

"Come on, Peggy. Wallow a bit and get the war-paint off," said Nancy. "I've got something to say to you," she whispered privately.

"Yes," said Susan. "You'll never get the mud out of your sleeping bags if you go into them like that. And look here, Bridget. You ought to be in bed already."

Nancy and Peggy, back from their wallow, dried

themselves by the embers of the bonfire. "Lucky it's too dark," said Nancy, "to see the blackness of the towels. But we won't want them again. Buck up with your drying. You've got to sleep while you can."

"What are you doing in the stores tent, Titty?" said Susan. "Putting things back? That's right. But we're not going to do any washing up till morning."

"Good," said Titty.

Bridget had gone unwillingly to bed, but slept as soon as her head was on her pillow. After all, she had been an Israelite in the morning, an Egyptian in the afternoon and a human sacrifice in the evening and that was about enough for one day.

"It just can't be helped about Peewitland and the North West Passage," said John. "Daddy'll understand. Hullo, Titty. Have you taken the maps into your tent?"

"I've got them all," said Titty. "Do you want them?"

"No," said John.

"Aren't you going to bed?" said Susan. "We've got to be up early. It'll take us all our time to get packed."

"I know," said John.

He stood for a minute or two watching the dying fire, looking into the darkness and thinking over the exploration of the week. The map was not finished. They had failed after all. Well, it couldn't be helped. The main thing now was to have everything packed and ready before the relief ship came in. He went to his tent, pulled his clothes off and settled down for the last night in camp.

*

In the tent of the Amazons, Nancy poked at Peggy. "Look here, Peg," she whispered, "If you squeak when I wake you, I'll never speak to you again."

*

There was a whisper in Roger's tent also.

"Titty." A hand reached out under the tent wall and felt about till it met another groping hand. "Have you got hold of it?"

"Yes."

"Don't go and pull too hard. I can't spare a toe."

"All right. I won't. And don't you pull too hard either."

"Is that you, Titty?" John had heard the whispering.

"Good night," said Titty.

"Good night," said John.

In the darkness of her tent Titty tied her end of Roger's bit of string tightly round her thumb. It was not too easy to tie it one-handed in the dark, and she knew before it was done why Roger had tied his end round a toe instead. But it was done at last. She gave a gentle tug. A tug, not quite so gentle, answered her. She lay down with the tied thumb outside the sleeping bag. With the other hand she reached out and felt a small pile of things beside her. Yes, she had forgotten nothing. She firmly sent herself to sleep.

CHAPTER XXIX

PACKING UP

JOHN stirred in his sleeping bag. There was sunlight on the walls of his tent. Time to get up? He pulled the bag closer round his chin. A spider at the end of an invisible thread was dangling in the doorway. It dropped a few inches. He watched it climbing again, spinning as it climbed. There was sunlight outside. Yet he woke with a queer feeling of gloom. It was like waking on the day after he had written *parvissimus* instead of *minimus* in an examination paper. Something had gone wrong. Suddenly he remembered what it was. The expedition had failed. They would be embarking that day and sailing home with the map unfinished, the North West Passage undiscovered and the North East Passage, that would make Peewitland an island, still no more than guessed at. Nancy had failed him ... even as he thought of it he could not help smiling at the thought of what she had done instead and at the memory of the savages ringed, streaked and spotted in their war-paint of mud. Titty had failed him ... no, that was not quite fair ... he ought to have seen her patteran. ... Still, the result of Titty's private exploration had been that he had not had time to do what he had planned ... and very nearly there had been a worse disaster. The skin on the back of his hands tickled with horror as he thought of those idiots letting themselves get caught by the rising tide. . . . If only they had done what they had been told to do, they would have been in the camp when he and Susan had got home and he would have been able to make a dart for the North West Passage to get that question settled before Nancy and her savages took charge. And now the map would have to be left unfinished till they came again, if ever they did come again. And it wasn't as if the unexplored bits were well away in the corners where they would be natural, almost right. There they were, bang in the middle, on the very shores of the Secret Water, spoiling everything. Islands, or mainland? . . . Who could tell? No one had had time to go and see.

Daddy would be disappointed . . . and then John remembered that Daddy, too, was under orders. He might be disappointed about the map but he would be still more disappointed if he were to come sailing in with the relief ship and find that he had been failed by John and that the explorers were not ready with tents packed, ready to go instantly aboard.

What time was it? He pushed his sleeping bag down to his knees, and kicking free from it, crawled out of his tent. John went to have a look at the meal-dial. The shadow had not reached the breakfast peg by several inches. He grabbed bucket, soap and towel, and had a hurried wash at the edge of the pond.

"Stuffy little beasts," he said to himself on seeing the door flaps of Roger's tent and of Titty's, hanging down instead of being tied back to let in air.

He dressed, rolled up his sleeping bag and

night things, slackened the guy ropes of his tent, jerked out the tent pegs, laid the posts aside and rolled up tent and groundsheet.

Susan put her head out. " 'Sh!" she said. "Bridget's still asleep."

"She'll jolly soon have to get up," said John. "*Goblin*'s coming and every single thing's got to be packed and ready. I'm just going to wake the others."

"Give them as long as you can," said Susan. "They'll only wake Bridgie. Let me get breakfast going first."

"What's the time?"

"Half past seven. Here's Nancy's watch. Hang it on the totem so it won't get forgotten."

"I'll be lighting the fire, while you're getting up. But buck up. I've left the bucket by the pond."

There was no trouble today in finding fuel. Charred sticks lying in the still warm ashes of the savages' bonfire were piled together over a handful of reeds in Susan's fireplace and burst instantly into a blaze.

Bridget put her head out. "Isn't it time to get up?" she said.

"Good," said John. "She's awake anyhow. Take your toothbrush and come along. There's only time to slosh two buckets over you. We've got to get everything packed. Go on, Susan. Blow your whistle. Gosh! I wish we had a ship's bell. Ahoy, everybody! Wake up, Captain Nancy! Kick your mate out! Roger! Titty! Heave out, you able-seamen! Show a leg!"

He stooped by the door of Titty's tent, reached in, got a good hold of the foot in her sleeping bag and hauled mightily, thinking to drag it out with Titty in it. He nearly fell, for the bag came very easily. There was nothing in it. Clinging to it with all its claws was a startled kitten, which, after one anxious moment, recovered its dignity, stood up, blinking in the sunlight, and began to stretch itself.

"Hullo!" said John. "Titty's up already. Out you come, Roger!"

There was no answer, and looking in he saw that Roger's tent was also empty.

John looked into the tent of the Amazons. Lumps in the sleeping bags showed where the explorers lay.

"Nancy!" he shouted. "Get up. We've the whole camp to pack."

There was no answer.

"Let me cold-sponge her," said Bridget, hopping round holding up her pyjamas with one hand and squeezing a sponge in the other.

"Go ahead," said John.

"But they aren't there," said Bridget a moment later.

"Of course they are," said John.

"They aren't," said Bridget. "Look. They've just stuffed things in their bags to look as if they were."

"Bother them," said John. "This isn't April Fool's Day. But it's a good thing everybody's up. They were jolly quiet about it."

"Where are they?" said Susan.

"They'll have gone down to have a last wallow," said John.

He emptied the bucket over Bridget twice and

a third time for luck and then set to work at the
stores tent, slacking the guy ropes and pulling up
the pegs. He saw Susan looking at a lot of bowls
and saucers still dirty from last night's eel stew.

"Oh gosh! I'd forgotten. All yesterday's washing
up to do. Don't worry about cornflakes. Give them
boiled eggs they can hold in their fingers. We're
only just going to have time."

"All right," said Susan. "Two eggs apiece. You
can eat two? Bridget? Done your teeth? Call that
face washed?"

"Yes," said Bridget, "and so it is."

"Mother won't say so. You come along here
and bring the bucket."

"Ow," said Bridget. "You're tearing the skin
off my forehead."

"What on earth did Daisy use last night,"
said Susan. "You're going to have that eel on
your forehead for the rest of your life."

"Oh leave it for now," said John. "We'll get it off
when we get home. But do let's have everything
waiting when the ship comes in. Look here. Can
I be taking down your tent? Skip to it Bridgie and
pack your knapsack."

"I say," said Susan, ferreting among the stores,
"who on earth mixed sugar and biscuits and cornflakes all together?" Titty had forgotten to tell her
how the Egyptians had found fuel for the fire in
the middle of the Red Sea. "And, what's happened
to the chocolate? I'm sure we had more than two
slabs left, even after the feast. And I didn't think
anybody ate bananas last night."

John looked round, puzzled. "What's become
of my compass?" he said.

"Oh dear," said Susan. "This is going to be as bad as packing to go to Holly Howe. Everybody always loses something at the last minute. The compass'll turn up when we get other things packed. Let's get breakfast over. Eggs are ready. . . . " She blew a long blast on her whistle.

She was answered only by a startled curlew and a sudden stir of gulls along the saltings.

"Blow again," said Bridget.

"Ahoy! Breakfast!" shouted John. "Look here, Susan. I'll go down and chivvy them up."

*

Five minutes later he was coming back from the landing place, feeling pretty cross with everybody in the expedition except Susan and Bridget, who, at least, were where they ought to be.

"Boats gone," he said gloomily, scraping the mud off his boots against a clump of grass.

"Both boats?" said Susan.

"Yes," said John. "I bet Nancy put them up to it. The whole lot must have gone off to say 'Goodbye' to the Mastodon."

"Well, their eggs are getting cold," said Susan.

"They won't care," said John. "The Mastodon'll make them stay to breakfast, and they'll take ages over it, and, oh gosh! do look at the time. And their tents still to do, and the *Goblin*'ll be in sight before they've begun to pack."

"I think they might have invited us," said Bridget.

"They jolly well knew we wouldn't go," said John. "They know we've got to have everything packed."

"Come and eat your breakfast, anyhow," said Susan.

Susan, John, Bridget and Sinbad breakfasted almost in silence. Bridget talked to Sinbad, but not much. John and Susan kept looking, now at the things to be packed, the tents still to be dismantled, the whole camp that had somehow to be turned into packages for quick and easy stowage, and now towards the landing place, expecting every moment to see the others hurrying home.

Three small white sails showed at the mouth of the creek.

"It's the Eels," said Bridget.

A few minutes later the three savages were splashing across the saltings.

"Karabadangbaraka," they shouted.

"Akarabgnadabarak!" said the explorers.

"Where's Nancy?" said Daisy. "Where's everybody? I say, White Chief, we're awfully sorry about yesterday. I mean about there being no time to go round Peewit. We'd have gone if we'd known it was the last day. But Nancy said she thought you were going to stay a lot longer. . . . "

"It's all right," said John as cheerfully as he could. "We'll fill that bit in next year. The bit I didn't do matters just as much. More, really."

"What about that eel on my forehead?" said Bridget. "Susan tried to scrape it off and it won't come."

Daisy looked critically at last night's work. "It's not a bad eel," she said.

"But what did you do it with?" said Susan. "Soap doesn't seem to touch it at all."

"Red paint," said Daisy. "It'll come off with a

spot of turpentine. And so'll all the gore on her
frock. It's only a small eel. I had an awful time last
summer, but that was when we tried tattooing,
and Dum and Dee painted eels all over me. You
should have heard the missionaries afterwards."

"But where are the others?" asked Dum and
Dee together, rather as if they wanted to change
the subject.

"Gone to say 'Goodbye' to the Mastodon," said
John. "And they jolly well ought not to have gone.
Daddy'll be here in another half hour."

"I'll go and tell them to come back," said Dum.

"Here's the Mastodon," said Dee.

"Karabadangbaraka!" said the Mastodon,
stamping his muddy boots.

"Akarab-gand-abarak," said Daisy.

"Gnad ... gnad ... " said Bridget. "I was
listening to see if you'd say it."

Daisy fiercely clamped her teeth. "We didn't eat
enough of you last night," she said. "Nothing but
chops and steaks. I never thought about taking a
nice bit of tongue. Wish I had."

"What are the others hanging about for?" said
John.

"Haven't seen them," said the Mastodon.

"WHAT? Then where are they? They've gone
off in both boats. Nancy really is a bit too thick,
and Titty and Roger ought to have more sense.
We've got the whole camp to pack and they know
it. And Daddy said there wouldn't be a minute to
lose, and he wanted us to have the stuff all ready
in the boats."

"I say," said Dum. "You know your relief ship.
What colour is her sail?"

"Dark red."

"I thought it was. There's a dark red Bermuda sail coming in from the sea now. We saw her in the distance."

There was a stampede along the dyke to the point from which, looking east, they could see the open sea. Far away out there, a triangle of red sail was moving in towards the outer buoys.

"I'm pretty sure it's the *Goblin*," said John.

He looked up and down the Secret Water. Not another sail was in sight. "Every single thing's gone wrong," he said bitterly. "We've failed with the map, and now Daddy's coming for us, and nothing's ready."

"Come on," said the Mastodon. "We'll help. All hands to stow the camp."

"Wriggle, you Eels," said Daisy. "We'll have the camp stowed in two flicks of a fin."

There was a general rush back to the camp. Four savages and three explorers hurled themselves upon tents, stores and bedding. Down came Roger's tent, Titty's, and the bigger tent of the Amazons. John and Susan, packing hard, hurried from group to group to explain just how the folding had to be done, when the tents were ready to be stuffed into their bags. Susan for once had no hand in washing up. Daisy and her brothers were not, perhaps, as thorough as Susan would have liked. But there the things were, washed, and one of the Eels was giving a final wipe to the last of the mugs with the camp dishcloth. "What about all these eggs?" said Daisy. "I don't know," said Susan. "Empty the water out of the saucepan, and put them back in it. It's their own fault if they aren't here for breakfast. Bridget, do go and see if you can see them."

The Mastodon shouldered the long heavy bundle of the Amazons' tent.

"No good taking things down to the landing place till they bring the boats back," said John. "They'll only get all over mud."

"We'll put them into our own boats," said the Mastodon.

"The relief ship comes for the explorers, and the savages ferry things off in their war canoes," said Daisy.

"It'll save a lot of time," said Susan. "But I do wish they'd turn up."

To and fro, to and fro, explorers and savages staggered to the landing place, dumped tents and bags and boxes and water cans into the boats of the savages, and splashed hurriedly back over the marshy saltings.

Bridget came running to the camp. "I can't see them anywhere," she said. "And it *is* the *Goblin*. Where's the telescope?"

"Where is it?" said John. "Has anybody seen it? And I haven't found my compass."

Nobody had seen the compass. Nobody had seen the telescope.

"Titty usually has it," said Bridget.

John and Susan looked round the place where the camp had been, at the pale places where the tents had stood, at the fireplace, where Susan's breakfast fire was smouldering out, at the big blackened ash-covered patch on which had blazed the ceremonial bonfire of the Eels. Nothing was left but the painted totem with a necklace of shells and Nancy's watch hung round the eel at the top of it and the meal-dial, the shadow of which had already left the breakfast stick behind. Everything else was packed in the boats of the savages ready to be ferried off. But what was the good of that with the explorers' boats missing and four explorers missing with them?

John was just going to pull up the long stick the shadow of which showed how time moved from meal to meal.

"Oh don't do that," said Daisy. "Do leave it for a relic."

"What about the totem?" said John.

"It's yours," said the Mastodon. "Isn't it, Daisy?"

"Of course," said Daisy. "Take it with you, and then, when you come again, you put it up and all the Eels of all the world will come wriggling to help."

John looked at Nancy's watch.

"Close on nine," he said. "Where can those idiots be?"

"Tide's slack already," said the Mastodon.

They went along the dyke to look out again.

Yes. There was the *Goblin*, the relief ship, sailing on to the Secret Water. Already she had left the open sea.

"Westerly wind," said John. "She'll have to tack. That may take a little longer."

"But where *are* they?" said Susan.

Bridget was the first to see them. "Look. Look," she pointed.

"What are they doing in there?" said the Mastodon.

Almost opposite the place where they were

standing, far up the wide creek that ran inland from the northern shore of the Secret Water a brown sail and a white were sailing together.

"Wave to them. Signal to them," said Susan.

John semaphored. B ... U ... C ... K ...... U . . . P . . . "I'm against the skyline all right," he said, "but they probably aren't looking."

"They're coming this way," said the Mastodon.

"Both of them," said Daisy.

"Starboard tack both of them," said Dee.

"They've simply gone off to have a last race," said Susan furiously.

"They'll never get back before the *Goblin* arrives," said John.

The relief ship was coming steadily nearer, beating to and fro across the Secret Water, now towards the north shore, now towards the island from which she was being watched by the explorers and the savages. The two small boats, sailing south down the creek had the wind on their beam, had no need to tack, and were coming at a great pace.

"They'll do it," said Daisy.

"They never will," said John, but in his heart began to hope they would.

"Which of them's ahead?" said the Mastodon. "White sail, I think."

"Brown," said Daisy.

"Jolly hard to see when they're coming straight at us," said Dum.

"Brown sail's to windward," said Dee.

"Go it, Titty," said Bridget.

"Go it, Nancy," said Daisy and then ... "Sorry ... Titty's all right but Nancy's more of an Eel."

"They're both jolly well all wrong," said John. "Going off racing on the last morning when they know they ought to be here. But, I say, I do believe they *are* going to do it."

"Go it. Go it everybody," shouted Bridget.

"What's Daddy doing?" said Susan.

Everybody looked from the two small boats racing towards them down the creek on the further side to the relief ship steadily beating her way up the Secret Water. Someone, Daddy, was by the mast.

"He's sending up a flag," said John.

A small bundle climbed to the crosstrees and suddenly blew out and fluttered in the wind, a dark blue flag with a white square in the middle of it.

"Gosh!" said John.

"What does it mean?" said the Mastodon.

"Blue Peter," said John. "Everybody repair on board. About to sail. He's in a frightful hurry. He's hoisted it before he's even got his anchor down."

"They're going to do it," said Daisy. "They'll be out of the creek in a moment, and we'll see who's ahead."

"If only they get here before the *Goblin*," said John.

"Pretty good race," said the Mastodon. "Look at that."

"Go it. Go it," shouted the Eels, as the two boats left the creek, bore slightly to starboard, and came racing side by side across the Secret Water. Almost it seemed that both boats were a little uncertain in their steering for a moment, as, coming out into the open, their helmsmen saw for the first time the red sail of the relief ship which up till then had been hidden from them by the land.

CHAPTER XXX

NORTH WEST PASSAGE

Tiitty put herself firmly to sleep, but, at the same
time, did her best to turn herself into an alarm
clock. Sleep she must, but oversleep she must not.
Roger, she knew, would sleep until she woke him.
Whatever happened she must not fail to wake
herself as soon as it was light. She slept for two
hours and woke suddenly in the dark. How long
had she been asleep? An hour, half an hour, four
hours? She did not know. Too early anyhow. She
tried to sleep again, but could not. Everything
depended on her waking at the right moment.
She lay there, fingering the string tied round
her thumb, and seeing in her mind's eye that
blank space at the top left-hand corner of the
map where John had drawn a question mark.
What was it like through that gap? Perhaps it
was only a creek leading nowhere. Well, the only
way to find out was to go and see, and tomorrow
morning early (or was it already today?) was the
only chance to put things right and make up for
the mistakes of yesterday. She began in her mind
to dot in the lines of a channel. . . . The dots were
like sheep. She counted them as she put them
in, lost count and, as the map was only in her
mind, had to begin again at the beginning. . . .
Dot . . . dot . . . dot. . . . She woke again, and found
the tent a little lighter. Almost she could see the
shape of it. Well, this time it was not worth while

393

to go to sleep. She would just lie there watching
the light grow, and at the right moment pull the
string for Roger. She heard gulls on the saltings
. . . far away.

She woke next time in a panic. Daylight was
in the tent. She could see everything, even the
little pile of things she had made ready the night
before. She pulled the string, and heard a startled
grunt from the next tent. Then there was silence.
It would never do if Roger were to start up with
a yell and wake the camp. She pulled again gently. Nothing happened. She pulled again, a long
steady pull. There was a sudden answering jerk
that nearly tore her thumb off. Then another. She
pulled back, three short pulls. Then the string
came loose. Roger had freed his toe. She hauled
it in, crawled to the mouth of her tent, and put
her head out into the cool morning air. Roger's
tousled mop was poking from his tent door.

"Are you really going?" he said.

Titty put her finger on her lips.

"Of course," she whispered. "Don't make a row."
She crawled out of her tent and shivered. Close
to Roger, she whispered in his ear. "Put on your
woolly. Bring an oilskin to sit on. It'll be warmer
when the sun comes up. And don't make a single
sound. Pretend you're one of the Eels."

"Boots?" whispered Roger.

"Wet inside," hissed Titty. "Better without.
Come on. Look out for treading on a stick by
the fire. . . . 'Sh."

For one awful moment she thought she heard
a sound in one of the other tents. Whatever it
had been she did not hear it again. Silent as

the very best of Eels, they crept out of the camp, down the dyke, and through the wet grass of the saltings. There was no fog, but a thin morning mist was rising. Silently Roger hauled in the *Wizard*. Silently Titty lowered into it the knapsack with the things she had thought necessary. All but silently Roger coiled the rope and put the anchor in the bows. The anchor just tapped the gunwale as he put it in, and, ankle deep in mud, the explorers looked at each other, and then back at the tops of the tents, just showing in the mist.

"Hop in," whispered Titty. "We'll clean the mud afterwards. Don't do any splashing now."

"Shall I row?"

"Not yet."

With Roger in the stern, Titty pushed *Wizard* afloat and sat down, gingerly getting the oars out, one at a time. A rowlock squeaked as she took the first stroke. She unshipped her oar, took out the rowlock, dipped it in the water and put it back. She tried another stroke. The leather of an oar, working in the rowlock, complained. She put the oar overboard, wetted the leather, and tried again. That was all right. With quiet strokes, dipping her oars without a splash, she rowed away, keeping near the bank, so that, even if anyone had been looking from the camp, there would have been nothing to see.

Slowly, for the tide was coming in, she rowed down the creek and out into the Secret Water. She turned west and stopped rowing. The banks slipped by. The tide, pouring up the Secret Water, was with them now and carried them along. The expedition was safely on its way.

"Roger," said Titty. "You'd better have breakfast."

"I think so, too," said Roger.

"Chocolate and bananas," said Titty, digging in her knapsack.

"It'll be warmer when the sun comes up," said Roger.

"It's warmer already," said Titty.

A low bank of cloud hid the horizon. Its upper edge was tinged with rose. Already the sun was climbing behind it. Ripples were crossing the water to meet them. A light wind was blowing from the west. For a minute or two they drifted with the tide. Titty got out the compass and put it at her feet. She laid the telescope, ready for use, on the thwart beside her. She unfolded a copy of the map, had a good look at it, and then looked up the Secret Water. She took a good big mouthful of chocolate and settled to her oars.

*

She stopped rowing only when they were close to the mouth of the gap that John had wanted to explore. There she shipped her oars and began desperate work with the compass.

"The point this side of Goblin Creek bears east by south," she said firmly. "Very near that anyhow. And the herons' trees on Mastodon Island are all in a row. Bearing south. We've got them marked all right. That fixes the gap." She put a cross to show where they then were, and lines with the compass bearings on them, one leading to the distant point, and one to the old heronry.

"Can't we sail now?" said Roger. "There's enough wind and we won't have to tack."

"We'd better," said Titty. "Then you can steer and I can have the map on the middle thwart. . . . We've done jolly well so far. It would have taken much longer if we'd tried to sail before."

She hoisted the brown sail. *Wizard* began to move through the water.

"Keep in the middle as well as you can, and let the sheet go if we touch. Whatever happens we mustn't sail hard on the mud and have to waste time getting off."

"Aye, aye, sir."

"Don't let her go too fast. Keep the sail flapping."

"Aye, aye, sir."

"Course is north-west," said Titty, looking at the compass and scribbling on her map.

"North-west it is," said Roger.

"You mustn't try to steer by compass though," said Titty. "Just try to keep in the middle, and I'll watch the compass and note down how she heads."

"Gosh," said Roger. "We're in for it now."

The banks on either side were closing in. They had left the Secret Water and were sailing with the tide up a narrow inlet. There was mud to right of them, mud to the left. Beyond the mud were low straight-topped dykes like the ones on which their camp was pitched. Ahead of them, the dykes seemed to draw together and meet.

"Don't believe it goes anywhere," said Roger.

"It must," said Titty. "Look at the way the water's moving along the edge of the mud."

"It's coming to an end. . . . Hadn't we better drop the sail and go slower?"

"We're all right so far. Gosh! What was that?"

There was a sudden soft bump. Titty dropped her pencil and hauled the centreboard more than half way up. Roger let the sheet fly. Titty stabbed over the side with an oar.

"Deep enough now," she said. "That must have been a shallow patch."

They slipped slowly on, but even Titty began to think that they were sailing up a blind alley.

The banks were now very near to them. In front of them a grass covered mound seemed to close the head of the creek.

"There's no way through," said Roger. "Hadn't we better turn before running aground?"

"If there isn't, there isn't," said Titty. "Anyway all that mattered was to find out. . . . Hullo. . . ." Her voice changed. "Look there. That lump doesn't join the dykes. . . . "

"Which way? . . . Quick," cried Roger. The channel, narrow as it was, divided into two.

"Right . . . Right," said Titty. "Starboard, I mean."

"The other looks bigger," said Roger, but already that grassy lump was to the left of them, and, cut off from the wind, they were moving up a narrow ditch. Titty poked with an oar at the muddy bank. The ditch bent to the right, as if to end under the dyke, then bent to the left, and suddenly the wind came again, they had lost the shelter of the grassy lump, and saw water stretching before them, a channel winding its way over enormous mudflats.

A duck with red beak and wide chestnut waistcoat watched them from the mound.

"Sheilduck," said Roger, "or drake," and then, "I

say, that other channel was all right too. It's an
island. Better make sure." Without another word
he swung the little boat round, and, sailing slowly
against the tide, drove back through a wider ditch
than the one they had come through. The grassy
mound was still on their left when they came back
to the place where the creek had divided.

"Good," said Titty. "Shelduck Island. . . . That's
one discovery anyway. Look out. She touched
then. . ."

But she touched only for a moment as she
turned, and then, with wind and tide to help
her, flew back up that western channel and out
into the inland sea of shining mud and rippled
water.

"What do we do now?" said Roger.

"She's heading north," said Titty. "Keep on.
Keep in the middle."

"In the middle of what?" said Roger, and
Titty had no answer for him. The water pouring
in through those two ditches, one each side of
Shelduck Island, was spreading over the mud.
On the right was a built up dyke. Below the
dyke was mud, then the channel in which they
were sailing, and then, to the left a wider stretch
of mud and beyond it, far away, another dyke,
guarding no doubt the meadows of the mainland,
for over there trees showed on the skyline.

Suddenly the dyke on their right ended. Mudflats stretched away as far as they could see. Their
channel, now as broad as a very wide river, curved
round over the mud.

"Heading east," said Titty. "We're behind the
land. Look. Look. There's a creek, and there's

another. But they don't go through, or we'd have
seen them on the other side."

There was some quick work with compass
and pencil.

"It's as big as the Red Sea," said Roger. "But
where's the way out?"

"There must be another way besides those
two ditches," said Titty.

She pulled out the inner tube of the telescope
and searched the distant shores.

"Look here," she said. "There's nothing along
this side, or John would have seen it that day
when you were over here, and Bridget got herself
captured."

"There isn't," said Roger. "I blackberried all
along."

"It must be somewhere right ahead."

"But the water's coming to an end. There's
nothing but mud."

"There's water beyond it."

"But the mud's in between. I told you so.
We're stuck."

Titty hauled up the centreboard. *Wizard* drove
on a few feet and stuck again. Titty hurriedly
lowered the sail, and Roger got a crack on the
head from the yard while trying to keep it from
going in the water.

"What now?" said Roger, rubbing his head.

For a moment Titty did not answer. She prodded
with an oar into the soft mud. The oar stuck.
Shaking it backwards and forwards she pulled
it free. She was just going to prod again. Then
she remembered that even if they could go no
further they were not trapped. The tide would

rise and float them again and they could get back
the way they had come. No. There was no need
for panic.

"What about more breakfast?" she said.

"I don't mind," said Roger.

"Two bananas left," said Titty.

The sun had risen clear of the clouds, there
was blue sky overhead, and the explorers ate
their last rations and looked about them.

"There's one thing," said Roger. "It's a jolly
lot better to be stuck in good old *Wizard* than
paddling about in the middle of the Red Sea. And
if there isn't a passage there isn't."

Titty looked at the low shores east and south,
and then back towards Shelduck Island. "We must
be half way across," she said. "And there's more
water ahead."

"Mud in between," said Roger.

Titty stepped up on the bow thwart, and stood
there with a foot each side of the mast, holding the
mast in one hand, and the telescope in the other. It
was true there was mud in front of them. It was as
if they had run aground in a sort of bay. The mud
stretched right and left to the low green line of the
land. But straight ahead, on the other side of the
mud, there was water again, another bay cutting
into the mud on the opposite side. Titty watched
it carefully.

"I say, Roger," she said. "Could you go up
the mast? The boat's sitting firm. She won't turn
over. And I'll sit in the bottom."

"Of course I can," said Roger.

"Go up then, and have a look at the water
the other side of the mud."

Roger was up the mast in a minute, and hung on there looking out.

"Just water," he said.

"Isn't it nearer than it was?"

Roger watched. "Of course it is," he said at last. "Tide's rising."

"Then there must be another way out," said Titty. "Or how does the tide get at it? Where does the water come from?"

There was no answer to that. From the mast-head it was easy to see that there were two sheets of water creeping towards each other over the mudflats. One was the water that had brought them so far. The other was coming to meet it.

"How soon'll they meet?" said Roger. "Look here, I can't hang on for ever, I'm coming down."

"We're going to get through," said Titty.

Inch by inch the waters came nearer to each other. The *Wizard* stirred, floated, moved on and stopped again. Titty, busy with her map, sketched in as well as she could as much of the coastline as she could see. Roger watched.

"I've been at that creek," he said. "But it doesn't go through. John hoped it did but it doesn't."

"Did he mark it on his map?"

"Yes."

"Good," said Titty. "That'll help," and she carefully took a compass bearing of the deep cleft in the coastline. "South-east," she said, drew a line and pencilled the bearing beside it.

Inch by inch the water, not deep enough to float the *Wizard*, crept on to meet the water that was spreading on the further side of the mud. The wide mudbank that had divided them shrank and shrank. It became a narrow isthmus, joining two sheets of mud. It was an isthmus no longer. The waters met across it.

"Roger," said Titty. "That's the way we'll have to go. Towards the place that other water's coming from. About north-east."

"She's moving. . . . No. Stuck again. . . . She's moving. Let's get the sail up, to blow her across as soon as she can float."

They hoisted the sail, and because the rudder was lower than the keel, they unshipped it, and made ready to steer with an oar.

"Whatever happens we mustn't smash the rudder again," said Roger.

Every few minutes the boat stopped, moved on and stopped again. Suddenly she was off, moving steadily, faster and faster.

"North-east," said Titty. "North-east. Keep her steady with an oar. I'm putting the rudder back. We're off."

"Deeper water," said Roger. "And we don't need the centreboard with the wind aft."

"We'll do it," cried Titty. "We'll do it."

Faster and faster the little boat slipped along over the smooth water. The entrance by Shelduck Island was very far away. But there was no sign yet of any other opening. On port bow and on starboard the land was coming nearer. Even Titty began to fear that the two lines of the land were all one and that they were simply running into a bay. And time was going on. If they had to turn back, would they ever be able to get home to the camp before the *Goblin* came

sailing in, when everything had to be packed and
ready? "Oh gosh!" said Titty to herself. "Have I
gone and made a mess of things again?" And then
she remembered that though now the water was
all one there had been two separate sheets of it,
and though one had come in past Shelduck Island,
the other must have come from somewhere else.

"Weeds ahead," cried Roger. "Lots of them."

"I know," said Titty.

"Dykes," cried Roger. "I say, Titty. . . . We'll
have to turn back."

"Keep her going as she is," said Titty.

"Aye, aye, sir. . . . As she is."

The little boat ran on. Clumps of weed were
sticking up out of the water to right, to left and
straight ahead. The usual dyke, built up to pro-
tect the land from flooding, was coming nearer.
It looked as if there could be no way through.

"There's a gap," said Titty. "Those two dykes
don't join."

"We'll be aground in another minute," said
Roger.

"Marshes right across," said Titty.

"Shall I turn round?"

"Yes. . . . No. . . . Wait a minute. . . . Keep her
as she is. . . . I can see water on the other side.

Nearer and nearer they came to the marshes,
lumps of mud edged with green slime, with narrow
trickles of water, and tall weeds. There were little
openings everywhere, but no proper channel. Not
one of the tiny creeks seemed to go more than a
few yards into the marsh.

Roger pointed. "That one's the biggest."

"Or that one," said Titty.

There was hardly time to choose. Hummocks of slimy mud were on either side of them. The narrow ditch, one of dozens, in which they found themselves, bent to the right, then left, then right again. They felt the *Wizard* graze the mud. She touched and touched again and stuck.

"Oh gosh!" said Roger, "and there isn't even room to turn her round."

"We've got to go on," said Titty. "There's open water the other side if we can only get her across."

They stepped out of the boat and, their feet slipping and sinking in the mud, tried to lift her on.

Roger staggered across one of the hummocks to look at another winding ditch. "I say, Titty," he called. "It's still pouring in. It must be ages before high water."

"Oh gosh!" said Titty. "I only hope it is. The camp's got to be packed by high water and if we're not back before they get up they'll be in an awful stew."

"Will Daddy wait for us?" said Roger.

"We've got to be back before he comes," said Titty. For one dreadful moment she saw the marooned explorers waiting on the shore, two able-seamen missing, the relief ship sailing in, and John doing his best to explain. But how could he, when he did not know where they were? And they could go neither back nor forward, but were stuck here, within sight of open water.

And then, suddenly, she saw that all these tall rank weeds growing on the marshes had rings stained on their stalks.

"Roger," she said. "All this is going to be under water. We've only got to wait."

"But have we got time?" said Roger. "Look here. Hadn't I better get to dry land, and go and signal to them for help?"

"Oh no. No," said Titty. "You'd only get stuck in the mud. And anyway, what could they do? We've just got to wait till the water rises."

"All right," said Roger. He took the telescope. "I say, there are terns over there. Diving. . . . Having their breakfasts."

"You've had yours," said Titty. "You're not hungry again!"

"Not exactly," said Roger, and pulled the end of his belt a little further through its buckle.

"We've only got to wait," said Titty again. "Some of those hummocks are already under water. Look here. She's in an awful mess. Let's get some of the mud off her inside."

Inch by inch the water rose. The marshes turned into a lot of tiny islands. Weeds were standing in water. Titty, looking ahead, tried to fix in her mind where the water had showed first. There it would be deepest.

The little boat stirred, stirred again, and, with the sail still set, began to slip forward.

"I'll steer just till we're through," said Titty. "You keep a look out."

The boat moved on, Titty steering to avoid the places where the weeds were thickest. It was like steering through a flooded field and trying not to hit the clumps of thistles.

Suddenly Roger shouted. "A sail! A sail! I

LIKE STEERING THROUGH A FLOODED FIELD

say Titty, they've spotted we've gone and John's come to look for us."

Titty groaned. That was the very worst thing that could have happened. If John had done that then the camp would not be packed in time, and the *Goblin* would come in to find nothing ready. Everything would have gone wrong, and once again good intentions would have come to a bad end.

"It's not John," said the look out. "It's the Amazons. He's sent them instead."

"Gosh! I wish I knew what the time was," said Titty.

The weeds were fewer in the water and lower. Twice the boat had touched but had not stopped.

"We're through," shouted Roger. "We've done it. I can see our island, and the native kraal."

"Come and steer," said Titty. She looked at the compass. "South. That's good enough. You steer and I'll get it down on the chart."

The other boat was beating to meet them. Peggy was steering, Nancy flourishing a paper.

"Ahoy!" she shouted. "We've done it. Circumnavigated Peewit. So that bit's all right. John'll get his map done after all."

Titty waved her own.

"We've discovered the North West Passage," she shouted. "What time is it?"

"Don't know. Susan's got my watch. I say, you haven't been right round?"

"Yes, we have," shouted Roger. "We had breakfast before sunrise."

"We didn't have any," said Peggy.

"We didn't want any," said Nancy firmly, and

then, "Look here. We'll race you home."

Roger looked at Titty. She was the better steersman and he knew it.

"Go on, Roger," said Titty. "Do the best you can. I've got to finish the map."

And so, neck and neck, the two expeditions raced down the creek towards the Secret Water.

"Did you pack your tents?" called Nancy.

"No."

"Neither did we."

"I say, Nancy," said Titty, "there's no tide. It must be high water."

"Barbecued Billygoats, don't I know?" said Nancy. "But we can't go any faster. They won't mind when they know what we've done. And anyway the *Goblin*'s not in sight. . . . "

But just then the two boats, side by side, shot out of the creek, and there was the *Goblin*, close at hand, beating up the Secret Water with the Blue Peter already fluttering from her crosstrees.

"Gosh! Oh gosh!" said Titty.

"Giminy!" said Nancy.

"There they are. All of them," said Roger. "The Eels and the Mastodon and everybody. . . . And the tents are gone. . . . "

"Stick to your steering," said Titty, and with fingers that would not keep steady, drew a line on her map that was meant to be straight but was not.

CHAPTER XXXI

FAREWELL TO THE EELS

THE two small boats crept into the creek together, *Firefly* half a boat's length ahead.

"We'd have won if you'd steered," said Roger.

"Couldn't," said Titty. "You did jolly well. And the map's done ... well, done enough to be added to the rest ... and we're not too late, and look, look, they've loaded the camp into Eels' boats." She crammed pencil and indiarubber in her pocket. "It's going to be all right after all." She looked back. The *Goblin* was already coming into the creek. Mother was steering, and Daddy was on the foredeck ready to drop the anchor. She looked ahead. All the four boats of the Eels were lying afloat, loaded to the gunwale, a savage at the oars in each boat. The tents had gone. John, Susan and Bridget were down at the landing place, the water lapping about their feet at the edge of the saltings. John was furiously beckoning. Bridget had Sinbad in her arms, and at the same time was trying to flap a handkerchief to welcome the relief ship. The saucepan must have been forgotten. Susan had it in her hand.

"Saved," said Nancy, who was by the mast of *Firefly*, all ready to lower sail. "Well done, the Eels!"

"Wait till he's anchored," they heard the Mastodon say, as the boats of the savages were moving out to meet the *Goblin*. "Give him room to round up."

"Titty," shouted John from the shore. "Get your sail down quickly."

"Turn her into the wind just a second, Rogie," said Titty, "and then go straight for the landing. . . . NOW."

Down came the sail. Titty hauled up the centreboard and the *Wizard* slipped on and grounded at the landing place.

"Look here, Titty," said John. "It's really rather too bad. You could have waited to go racing till we got back to Pin Mill. You knew Daddy was coming at High Tide. . . . "

"Pipe down, skipper. Pipe down." *Firefly* had slid in alongside and Nancy had hopped out. "She didn't go out to race. Neither did we. They've done the North West Passage. We've done the North East. The map's finished after all. Show him, Titty." She flourished her map in John's face. "We've only got to put them in. Peewit's an island all right. So's Blackberry. And who's late anyhow? Nobody. Barbecued Billygoats! Don't you see?"

Titty said nothing. She simply handed John her map, with all the bearings marked, the coastline sketched in, and a row of dots marking the course of the *Wizard* through the gap and across the Northern Sea.

John stared at it and then, as a long rattling noise showed that the *Goblin*'s anchor was down, he saw the boats of the savages, four of them, with all the gear of the camp aboard, shoot out from the shore. Everything was ready, just as Daddy said it should be. Not a minute was being lost. And, at the very last moment, failure had been turned into success. The whole map of the Secret Archipelago would be finished after all. There was nothing left to be done but to put the last bits in and to ink and colour it at home. He couldn't speak, but grabbed Titty's hand and shook it.

"What about us?" said Nancy. There was joyful handshaking all round.

"Did you have any breakfast?" asked Susan.

"Are those eggs?" said Roger, taking the lid off Susan's saucepan and looking to see what was inside.

"Hard and cold," said Susan.

"Who cares?" said Nancy. "Deal 'em out."

"Be quick," said Bridget. "We're waiting for your boats. Sinbad wants to go aboard."

*

The *Goblin*, rounding into the wind, had stopped moving.

SPLASH. . . . Grrrrrrrrr. . . . The anchor chain ran out. Commander Walker made fast, hauled on the topping lift, and had time to look about him.

"Well, Mary," he said. "They're a good lot. Tents struck and all ready. But how on earth have they managed to pick up such a lot of boats?"

Four boats, deeply laden, were rowing out towards the *Goblin*. Two others were at the landing place where people were busily rolling up their sails.

"But who are these?" said Mrs Walker. "I've counted all ours. Bridget, Susan, John, Titty,

Roger and the Blackett girls. All ashore. But these . . . ?"

"Friends, I suppose," said Commander Walker. "That's why our rapscallions were sailing instead of packing. I was thinking I'd have to court martial them. But it looks to me as if they'd done exactly what I told them."

The four heavily laden boats came nearer.

"Hullo!" said Commander Walker. "And who may you be?"

Daisy stopped rowing, grinned as widely as she could, and pointed first at the *Goblin*, then at the bundles that almost filled her little boat, then at the explorers ashore and then at the *Goblin* again.

She spoke.

"Eelalog orusagoon."

"Beg your pardon," said Commander Walker. "Say that again."

"Eelalog," said Daisy, pointing to herself, "Orus," pointing to the explorers at the landing place . . . "Agoon . . . "

The other three had also stopped rowing, and were looking first at Daisy, and then at Mrs Walker.

"Savages," said Mrs Walker.

"Of course," said Commander Walker. "Might have known." He hung a couple of fenders over the side, and pointed to them.

"Savee?" he said. "Makee fast alongside. Plenty quick."

Daisy pulled her boat nearer, and gave rapid orders in an unknown tongue.

"Catchee," called Commander Walker and threw her a rope. "Hey. You. Makee fast." He

threw a rope to the quietly smiling Dum, and put
over two more fenders on the other side. Presently
two of the savage boats were tied alongside. "Now
then," said the Commander. "Quick time topside
all that. Plenty quick. Bimeby chow chow." He
turned to Mrs Walker. "Lucky you thought of
bringing those bulls' eyes." And then, "You. Black
fellow. Strong man. Makee fast astern. Come topside. Help stowee."

It was extraordinary how well the savages
understood him.

In almost less than no time, *Goblin*'s cockpit was crammed with rolls of bedding, tents
in bags, and what not. Her decks were covered. Down below, Daisy and her brothers were
stowing things, and talking together in a language which really sounded very like English,
while Captain Walker and the Mastodon hove
package after package down the companion way,
and Mrs Walker was dumping things down the
fore hatch, and, at the same time, watching the
others at the landing place.

The boats of the explorers were coming off now,
sails stowed, masts lowered, and hard-boiled eggs
not wasted after all.

"Hullo, John," said Daddy. "Good man. I thought
you were running it a bit fine when I saw your
sails as we were coming in, but I was wrong.
Everything going like clockwork and not a minute
wasted. Let's have your painter."

John opened his mouth to speak and shut it
again. After all, everything was all right. Nothing
could have been smarter than the way in which
the savages had brought tents and bedding and

all the gear of the expedition alongside the *Goblin* the very moment her anchor had gone down.

"Hullo, Bridget," said her Mother. "I'll take the kitten. Now then. One pull and up you come. Hullo, Susan. All well? No accidents?"

"No need to ask," said Daddy. "Look at them. . . . Well, John, how did you get on with your map? I don't suppose you've had time to do much of it."

"Done it," said John.

"What? How much of it? I thought you said yesterday there was a lot to do."

"Only two bits," said John. "Titty and Roger did one. Nancy and Peggy did the other. We'll put them in on the way home."

He unwrapped the drawing-board with the map on it. Daddy looked at it.

"You've done the whole lot? . . . Well done, indeed. Why it's a blooming masterpiece. That's Titty's work, I know. That Walrus . . . seal . . . I beg your pardon . . . beats the band. And I like your buffaloes. . . . "

"It isn't inked, of course, said Titty. "I'll finish the inking tonight and put all our tracks in properly in different dots."

"It's pretty good as it is," said Daddy. "Just have a look, Mary. But what's all this up in the corner . . . 'Secret Archipelago Expedition . . . Swallows, Amazons and Eels. . . . ' Eels?"

"That's the tribe," said Titty.

"We couldn't have done it without them," said John. "Every single one of them's helped. We had six boats when we were doing the upper waters and the Mango Islands. . . . "

"Useful kind of savages," said Daddy looking round them. "What's become of that bag of bulls' eyes? Pass them round. Yes. That's the kind of savage to meet. Pity they don't know English. Hey, you. Chow, Chow. Suck 'em. Bulls' eyes. Plenty sweet . . . and a bit pepperminty too."

"How did you know they were savages?" asked Titty.

"Oh we knew all right," said Commander Walker. "They look it, don't they? There's a savage look in their eyes."

"You should have seen them yesterday," said Nancy, who had brought *Firefly* close to and was waiting till there was room to come alongside.

"Hullo the Pirates," said Commander Walker. "Your Mother's meeting you in London, to scrub and holystone you ready for school."

"We've had a lovely time," said Nancy and Peggy together.

"Hullo, Roger. Not down to starvation rations yet. Lucky we were able to pick you up before the grub ran out."

Just then the wind caught Bridget's hair.

"Bridget!" cried Mother. "What have you done to yourself? What's all that red on your forehead?"

"Blood," said Bridget. "Blood. I've been a human sacrifice. It's all right. Daisy says it'll come off easily with a drop of turpentine. And nobody's said 'Hullo, Sinbad'."

"Hullo, Sinbad," said Mother and Daddy together.

Presently the two boats of the explorers, *Wizard* and *Firefly*, lay astern, ready for the long tow to Pin Mill. Everybody was aboard. The *Goblin*

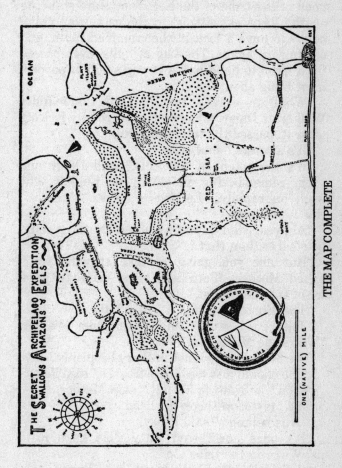

THE MAP COMPLETE

swarmed with thirteen people and a kitten, Daddy and Mother and the whole blood brotherhood of the tribe of the Eel. They were standing on the foredeck, sitting on the cabin-top, going below to have a look in the crammed cabin, and coming up again. The bag of bulls' eyes passed from hand to hand and a strong smell of peppermint hung about the ship.

"What on earth's that?" asked Commander Walker as Daisy, who had been carefully looking after it, passed the totem to John.

"It's a totem," said John.

"It's the totem of the Eels," said Daisy and then, remembering she knew no English, she went on rapidly, "Eelalog ... oris ... illa ... illa ... belango ... "

"Ah, yes," said Captain Walker. "Nothing could be clearer than that."

"But are you going to take it with you?" asked Mother. "Somebody must have taken a lot of trouble over it."

"The Mastodon made it," said Titty.

"Jolly good work," said Commander Walker. "Who's the Mastodon?"

The Mastodon grinned rather sheepishly.

"You should just see his hoofmarks," said Roger.

"Won't he want to keep it?" said Mother.

The Mastodon shook his head.

"Orus belango," said Daisy.

"It's ours now," said Titty. "He gave it to us. We're in the tribe too."

"We're all full of Eel's blood," said Roger.

"Properly vaccinated," said Nancy.

"I bled more than anybody," said Bridget.

"It's all right, Mother," said Susan. "We used a lot of iodine as well."

"Well, Mary," said Daddy to Mother. "We're going to hear some travellers' tales when we get home. We ought to carry that thing at the masthead. Give it Bridgie's hair-ribbon for a pennant. And where are your flags? We'll fly them from the crosstrees, as soon as we're off and I can take down the Blue Peter."

"Have we really got to start right away?" said Titty.

"We have. . . . I ought to have come for you yesterday, but I couldn't get down from London in time."

"Oh, I say," said Nancy. "It's a good thing you didn't."

"Why?"

There was a general silence. The rudder being mended in the town. . . . Half the expedition looking for the other half. . . . The Egyptians surrounded by water in the middle of the Red Sea. . . . The savage attack. . . . Corroboree and human sacrifice. . . . The dreadful blank spaces that would have been left on the map. . . . Everybody could think of plenty of reasons why.

"Susan," said Mother. "I don't know their language, but you can translate. . . . Will you tell them we're sorry we have to go off in such a hurry, and that we must try to meet again next holidays."

"They've got a boat," said John. "Bigger than *Goblin*."

"Well, if ever they come round to Shotley we'll be very glad to see them."

"Thank you very much indeed," said Daisy surprisingly.

"I thought you didn't know English."

"Oh well," said Daisy, and laughed.

"All for the shore," called Commander Walker and went to the foredeck. There were hurried goodbyes all round. John and Roger ran forward to help haul on the anchor chain.

The savages tumbled into their war-canoes, and cast off.

Commander Walker broke into song:

"Farewell and adieu to you noble natives,
Adieu and farewell to you bold savagees,
    For we're under orders
    For to steer for old England,
And we must be sailing across the wide seas."

"Karabadangbaraka!" shouted the explorers.

"It's all right. They won't tell anybody," called Titty, seeing an anxious look on the face of the Mastodon as he glanced at Daisy.

"Akarabgnadabarak!" shouted three of the savages.

"Akarab*ganda*barak!" shouted the fourth.

"Anchor's atrip," called Captain Walker. "You take the tiller, John."

John ran aft to the tiller. Captain Walker was hoisting the staysail. The *Goblin* gathered way. At her masthead was the totem of the Eels, a monstrous eel in red and blue and green, with a long white ribbon fluttering from it in the wind. Nancy and Titty had taken the flags from their staffs, and, when the Blue Peter came down, up

they went, the swallow flag to one crosstree and
the skull and crossbones to the other.

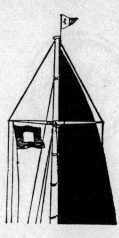

There was a cheer from the four boats of
the savages and an answering cheer from the
Goblin.

Then the savages' boats were hidden by the
land. The *Goblin*, with *Wizard* and *Firefly*, one
behind the other, towing astern, bore away down
Secret Water for the open sea. She passed the
cross-roads buoy. *Lapwing*, the mission ship, lay
at anchor. The explorers thought they saw the
missionaries waving, but they were not sure.
Then the mission ship was hidden by Flint
Island, and the *Goblin* was heading for her
home port. A fair wind and the ebbing tide
hurried her out across the sparkling bay. The
explorers, crowded aboard her, looked astern and

saw the islands of the Secret Archipelago merge once more into a long unbroken line on the horizon.

THE
ARTHUR RANSOME
SOCIETY

The Arthur Ransome Society was formed in June 1990 with the aim of celebrating his life and his books, and to encourage both children and adults to take part in adventurous pursuits – especially climbing, sailing and fishing. It also seeks to sponsor research, to spread his ideas in the wider community and to bring together all those who share the values and the spirit that he fostered in all his storytelling.

The Society is based at the Abbot Hall Museum of Lakeland Life and Industry in Kendal, where there is a special room set aside for Ransome: his desk, his favourite books and some of his personal possessions. There are also close links with the Windermere Steamboat Museum at Bowness, where the original *Amazon* has been restored and kept, together with the *Esperance*, thought to be the vessel on which Ransome based Captain Flint's houseboat. The Society keeps in touch with its members through a journal called *Mixed Moss*.

Regional branches of the Society have been formed by members in various parts of the country – Scotland, the Lake District, East Anglia, the Midlands, the South Coast among them – and contacts are maintained with overseas groups such as the Arthur Ransome Club of Japan. Membership fees are modest, and fall into three groups – for those under 18, for single adults, and for whole families. If you are interested in knowing more about the Society, or would like to join it, please write for a membership leaflet to The Secretary, The Arthur Ransome Society, The Abbot Hall Gallery, Kendal, Cumbria LA9 5AL.

SWALLOWS·AND·AMAZONS·FOR·EVER!

Join the RED FOX Reader's Club

The Red Fox Reader's Club is for readers of all ages. All you have to do is ask your local bookseller or librarian for a Red Fox Reader's Club card. As an official Red Fox Reader you only have to borrow or buy eight Red Fox books in order to qualify for your own Red Fox Reader's Clubpack – full of exciting surprises! If you have any difficulty obtaining a Red Fox Reader's Club card please write to: Random House Children's Books Marketing Department, 20 Vauxhall Bridge Road, London SW1V 2SA.

Other great reads ~~from~~ **Red Fox**

Further Red Fox titles that you might enjoy reading are listed on the following pages. They are available in bookshops or they can be ordered directly from us.

If you would like to order books, please send this form and the money due to:

ARROW BOOKS, BOOKSERVICE BY POST, PO BOX 29, DOUGLAS, ISLE OF MAN, BRITISH ISLES. Please enclose a cheque or postal order made out to Arrow Books Ltd for the amount due, plus 75p per book for postage and packing to a maximum of £7.50, both for orders within the UK. For customers outside the UK, please allow £1.00 per book.

NAME_____

ADDRESS_____

_____

Please print clearly.

Whilst every effort is made to keep prices low, it is sometimes necessary to increase cover prices at short notice. If you are ordering books by post, to save delay it is advisable to phone to confirm the correct price. The number to ring is THE SALES DEPARTMENT 071 (if outside London) 973 9700.

Other great reads from Red Fox

Dive into action with Willard Price!

Willard Price is one of the most popular children's authors, with his own style of fast-paced excitement and adventure. His fourteen stories about the two boys Hal and Roger Hunt in their zoo quests for wild animals all contain an enormous amount of fascinating detail, and take the reader all over the world, from one exciting location to the next!

Amazon Adventure
ISBN 0 09 918221 1 £3.50

Gorilla Adventure
ISBN 0 09 918351 X £3.50

Underwater Adventure
ISBN 0 09 918231 9 £3.50

Lion Adventure
ISBN 0 09 918361 7 £3.50

Volcano Adventure
ISBN 0 09 918241 6 £3.50

African Adventure
ISBN 0 09 918371 4 £3.50

South Sea Adventure
ISBN 0 09 918251 3 £3.50

Diving Adventure
ISBN 0 09 918461 3 £3.50

Arctic Adventure
ISBN 0 09 918321 8 £3.50

Whale Adventure
ISBN 0 09 918471 0 £3.50

Elephant Adventure
ISBN 0 09 918331 5 £3.50

Cannibal Adventure
ISBN 0 09 918481 8 £3.50

Safari Adventure
ISBN 0 09 918341 2 £3.50

Tiger Adventure
ISBN 0 09 918491 5 £3.50

Other great reads from **Red Fox**

Chocks Away with Biggles!

Squadron-Leader James Bigglesworth – better known to his fans as Biggles – has been thrilling millions of readers all over the world with all his amazing adventures for many years. Now Red Fox are proud to have reissued a collection of some of Captain W. E. Johns' most exciting and fast-paced stories about the flying Ace, in brand-new editions, guaranteed to entertain young and old readers alike.

BIGGLES LEARNS TO FLY
ISBN 0 09 999740 1   £3.50

BIGGLES FLIES EAST
ISBN 0 09 993780 8   £3.50

BIGGLES AND THE RESCUE FLIGHT
ISBN 0 09 993860 X   £3.50

BIGGLES OF THE FIGHTER SQUADRON
ISBN 0 09 993870 7   £3.50

BIGGLES & CO.
ISBN 0 09 993800 6   £3.50

BIGGLES IN SPAIN
ISBN 0 09 913441 1   £3.50

BIGGLES DEFIES THE SWASTIKA
ISBN 0 09 993790 5   £3.50

BIGGLES IN THE ORIENT
ISBN 0 09 913461 6   £3.50

BIGGLES DEFENDS THE DESERT
ISBN 0 09 993840 5   £3.50

BIGGLES FAILS TO RETURN
ISBN 0 09 993850 2   £3.50

Other great reads **from Red Fox**

Share the magic of The Magician's House by William Corlett

There is magic in the air from the first moment the three Constant children, William, Mary and Alice arrive at their uncle's house in the Golden Valley. But it's when they meet the Magician, William Tyler, and hear of the Great Task he has for them that the adventures really begin.

THE STEPS UP THE CHIMNEY

Evil threatens Golden House in its hour of need – and the Magician's animals come to the children's aid – but travelling with a fox brings its own dangers.

ISBN 0 09 985370 1   £2.99

THE DOOR IN THE TREE

William, Mary and Alice find a cruel and vicious sport threatening the peace of Golden Valley on their return to this magical place.

ISBN 0 09 997390 1   £2.99

THE TUNNEL BEHIND THE WATERFALL

Evil creatures mass against the children as they attempt to master time travel.

ISBN 0 09 997910 1   £2.99

THE BRIDGE IN THE CLOUDS

With the Magician seriously ill, it's up to the three children to complete the Great Task alone.

ISBN 0 09 918301 9   £2.99

Other great reads ✈ *from* **Red Fox**

Have a bundle of fun with the wonderful Pat Hutchins

Pat Hutchins' stories are full of wild adventure and packed with outrageous humour for younger readers to enjoy.

FOLLOW THAT BUS

A school party visit to a farm ends in chaotic comedy when two robbers steal the school bus.

ISBN 0 09 993220 2   £2.99

THE HOUSE THAT SAILED AWAY

An hilarious story of a family afloat, in their house, in the Pacific Ocean. No matter what adventures arrive, Gran always has a way to deal with them.

ISBN 0 09 993200 8   £2.99

RATS!

Sam's ploys to persuade his parents to let him have a pet rat eventually meet with success, and with Nibbles in the house, life is never the same again.

ISBN 0 09 993190 7   £2.50

Humour and Adventure in the Redwall Series

A bestselling series based around Redwall Abbey – the home of a community of mice and the adventures they find themselves in.

REDWALL

As the mice of Redwall Abbey prepare for a feast, unknown to them, Cluny, the evil one-eyed rat, is preparing for almighty battle . . .

ISBN 0 09 951200 9   £4.50

MOSSFLOWER

The gripping tale of how Redwall Abbey was established through the bravery of the legendary mouse, Martin.

ISBN 0 09 955400 3   £4.50

MATTIMEO

Slagar the Fox is intent on bringing destruction to Redwall Abbey and the fearless mouse warrior, Matthias. He'll stop at nothing – including Mattimeo, Matthias's son.

ISBN 0 09 967540 0   £4.50

MARIEL OF REDWALL

A young mousemaid is washed ashore on the fringes of Mossflower country. Battered and bruised, she makes her way to Redwall Abbey, where the story of her horrific ordeal unfolds.

ISBN 0 09 992960 0   £4.50

SALAMANDASTRON

Why did the sword fall from the Abbey roof? Who is the white badger? And can the good creatures triumph over Ferahgo the Assassin?

ISBN 0 09 91461 5   £4.50

MARTIN THE WARRIOR

Bedrang the Tyrant stoat holds many creatures prisoner in his fortress on the coast. But a young mouse, Martin, refuses to obey the Evil Lord, and plans a daring escape.

ISBN 0 09 928171 6   £4.50

Other great reads from **Red Fox**

Leap into humour and adventure with Joan Aiken

Joan Aiken writes wild adventure stories laced with comedy and melodrama that have made her one of the best-known writers today. Her James III series, which begins with *The Wolves of Willoughby Chase*, has been recognized as a modern classic. Packed with action from beginning to end, her books are a wild romp through a history that never happened.

THE WOLVES OF WILLOUGHBY CHASE
ISBN 0 09 997250 6   £2.99

BLACK HEARTS IN BATTERSEA
ISBN 0 09 988860 2   £3.50

THE CUCKOO TREE
ISBN 0 09 988870 X   £3.50

DIDO AND PA
ISBN 0 09 988850 5   £3.50

THE WHISPERING MOUNTAIN
ISBN 0 09 988830 0   £3.50

MIDNIGHT IS A PLACE
ISBN 0 09 979200 1   £3.50

THE SHADOW GUESTS
ISBN 0 09 988820 3   £2.99